The Little Library on Cherry Lane

KATIE GINGER

ONE PLACE. MANY STORIES

HQ
An imprint of HarperCollins*Publishers* Ltd
1 London Bridge Street
London SE1 9GF

www.harpercollins.co.uk

HarperCollins*Publishers*
1st Floor, Watermarque Building, Ringsend Road
Dublin 4, Ireland

This paperback edition 2022

1

First published in Great Britain by
HQ, an imprint of HarperCollins*Publishers* Ltd 2022

Copyright © Katie Ginger 2022

Katie Ginger asserts the moral right to be
identified as the author of this work.
A catalogue record for this book is
available from the British Library.

ISBN: 9780008422769

Everyone LOVES Katie Ginger

'So beautifully written. It made me want to move house
right now and set up by the sea!'
Tilly Tennant

'A delightful and delicious read for hopeful
romantics everywhere'
Sandy Barker

'Seaside, strawberries and a sexy hero – what's not to love?'
Mandy Baggot

'Simply delicious – summer escapes don't come
any more tasty!'
Jane Linfoot

'A hilarious romantic comedy that left me with a big smile on
my face'
Holly Martin

'A moving, festive, absolutely gorgeous read! Perfect for curling
up with this Christmas'
Samantha Tonge

'Does jumping up and down, cuddling my Kindle and
grinning from ear to ear count as a review?! … Katie writes
with such warmth and humour and I could feel every word'
NetGalley reviewer

'Loved it!'
NetGalley reviewer

'Sweet, heart-warming, and very enjoyable. This book is like
a warm chocolate chip cookie, you feel better for eating it,
get a bite of exciting chocolate now and again all while just

KATIE GINGER lives by the sea in the south-east of England, and apart from holidays to very hot places where you can sit by a pool and drink cocktails as big your head, she wouldn't really want to be anywhere else. *The Little Library on Cherry Lane* is Katie's ninth novel. She was also shortlisted for the Katie Fforde Debut Novel of the Year Award for her first novel *The Little Theatre on the Seafront*.

When she's not writing, Katie spends her time with her husband and two kids, and their dogs: Wotsit, the King Charles spaniel, and Skips, the three-legged Romanian rescue dog. (And yes, they are both named after crisps!)

For more about Katie, you can visit her website: www.keginger. com, find her on Facebook: www.facebook.com/KatieGAuthor, follow her on Twitter: @KatieGAuthor, or sign up to her newsletter here: http://bit.ly/3gbqMS0.

Also by Katie Ginger

The Little Theatre on the Seafront
Summer Season on the Seafront
Snowflakes at Mistletoe Cottage
Spring Tides at Swallowtail Bay
Summer Strawberries at Swallowtail Bay
Winter Wishes at Swallowtail Bay
The Secrets of Meadow Farmhouse
The Perfect Christmas Gift

To library lovers and workers everywhere!
Thank you!

Chapter 1

Five Years Previously

'So, Miss Martin, this is a bit of an unusual question, but—' The interviewer leaned forward over the desk. He hadn't stopped fiddling with the lid of his pen, using his thumb to flick it up so it came loose before pressing it back down again. 'Can you tell me, if you were a flavour of ice cream, which one would you be?'

What the sweet Jesus was this? Elsie plastered on a smile while inwardly cringing. *Ice cream flavour?* What in God's name was the man talking about?

She'd prepared for all sorts of different questions – read a thousand website posts about good interview technique, what to say and what not to say, how to dress and how to smile – but this was … odd. On long, sleepless nights when her insomnia had struck, she'd used the time wisely, even reading tales of some of the stupid things people had done in interviews, like bring their pets along or eat their lunch while talking. But even with all of that, she wasn't quite prepared for this. Luckily, the answer was easy for her.

'Vanilla,' she said as confidently as she could.

1

The man looked disappointed while Clara, the librarian who would be her boss if she got the job, seemed surprised, though at Elsie's answer or the stupid question, she wasn't sure. Hopefully the latter.

'And why's that?' the suited interviewer asked.

'Well, because …'

I'm the most boring person on the planet. I've never been anywhere or done anything interesting. I don't go out, I don't date. You certainly couldn't call the car-crash of a love life she'd experienced so far 'dating'. *I just … read*, she thought. But reading was the best pastime in the world. She couldn't say that of course and after a moment's hesitation found herself waffling on about how vanilla was the best thing to be in a customer-facing role like a librarian. 'It's important not to be judgemental about books because we all like different things and we want everyone to feel welcome in the library no matter what their age or taste.'

The corner of Clara's mouth quirked up and Elsie felt herself relax a little. More questions were fired at her and all the while she spoke, Elsie could feel her cheeks flaming as usual, growing redder and redder. God knows what colour she was now. Probably a shade of red that had only ever been seen on the sun. She tried to ignore it and focus on the questions.

The man scribbled something then sat back in his chair. 'And how would you deal with an untidy thatch?'

'I'm sorry?'

Clara giggled. She could be quite naughty when she wanted to be, and Elsie was sure she'd added that question just to make the man say it out loud.

'The thatched roof.' He pointed his pen up towards the ceiling, the loose lid wobbling where he'd flicked it up again. 'How would you deal with a problem with it, like some of it coming out or being disturbed by birds?'

'I'd probably call old Davy from down the lane – or a council-approved contractor,' she added quickly.

The suited man nodded and wrote something down.

'And finally,' said Clara in her usual kind, calming voice. 'Why do you want this job?'

Now *this* Elsie was prepared for, but how exactly to get started? 'I just love books,' she began with a slight tilt of her head. She pushed her curly hair back from her face. 'They're magical. They take you places you might never get the chance to see. They take you away from your troubles. They educate. They help you believe things can be different … better.' She paused as the suited interviewer raised his eyebrows. Carla gave a small nod to continue. 'The library has been like a second home to me ever since I was little. I've read every book in the children's section and since I've been old enough, I've been working my way through both fiction and non-fiction. And I love the way the library brings everyone together. Everyone comes here for one thing or another. I can't think of anywhere better to work. This would be a dream come true for me, to be surrounded by books all day and share that love with other people.'

She finally ran out of steam, hot and sweaty with the stress of it all, and placed her hands on top of one another in her lap, her fingers trembling.

Clara smiled and something in the flash of her eyes urged Elsie to relax. 'You certainly know everything there is to know about the library. You've been volunteering for years now. Even as a child you were always helping me to put books away after being curled up in the corner all day.'

'We do have other people to see,' the suited interviewer said, shooting a look at Clara like she was breaking some kind of rule by being nice to her. 'So thank you for your time and we'll let you know over the next couple of days.'

Elsie stood and offered her hand to shake. Should she have wiped it first? Was it sweaty? Too late now. She tried a confident smile. 'Thank you for seeing me.'

As she left, Clara gave her a wink when the man's back was

turned. She wanted to believe the wink was a good sign, but the chances were the other applicants were less socially awkward and far more confident. They probably didn't turn red as soon as a stranger spoke to them. There was nothing more she could do now. But it didn't stop her brain taunting her with the things she should have said. All the things she should have phrased differently zipped through her mind and a little voice deep inside accused her of ruining everything by blushing so fiercely. Why did her body have to react that way? She pushed the thoughts away, leaving the small back office and walking through the library to the front door.

Everywhere she looked she saw someone she knew. People smiled and waved or held up crossed fingers showing their support.

'Fingers crossed, Elsie,' Winston called.

'Good luck, Elsie,' Bernard shouted.

'I'm sure you've done well,' old Mrs Adams squeaked.

Elsie responded to their comments with grateful thanks and mirrored their gestures by crossing her fingers and squeezing them together as tightly as possible. She so desperately wanted this job. It wasn't an overstatement to say it was her dream role. She'd always thought being a librarian would suit her and she'd always wanted to work here at Meadowbank Library. It was the most perfect library in the world, situated on Cherry Lane in a small building near the grandly named Meadowbank River, though it was nothing more than a meandering stream that weaved through the centre of the village.

From the outside the library looked more like a village hall with its single storey and thatched roof but it was still picture-perfect to her. As was Meadowbank itself. A tiny, rural village deep in the Kent countryside miles from the racing modern world. They weren't without modern conveniences though. They had a little shop, a butcher's, a baker's, and even a deli that had recently opened. Yet, on all sides were rolling fields, woods, and pastures that slowed time and formed a bubble around them.

Out in the fresh air, Elsie took a moment to breath. Her skin still felt warm and clammy even without the heat of the sun, but the breeze cooled her a little. She paused by the benches in front of the library on the riverbank and watched the ducks paddle lazily about.

She'd done everything she could, she told herself again. She'd prepared as much as possible and she'd handled the quite frankly bizarre questions as well as anyone could, considering she had no idea what the right answer actually was. What if you preferred chocolate or pistachio-flavoured ice cream? What did they think that said about a person? And why did the man ask about disasters in the library? What sort of catastrophe was he expecting? The only thing that came close in Elsie's experience was ducks walking into the library and even then, as long as they didn't start pecking at the books, Clara tended to let them be. They always got bored and wandered off of their own accord when they were ready.

Elsie headed back to the cottage, taking a detour around the green and duck pond first. Her house was only a minute or two away and going the long way round didn't add much time, but she wanted to stay outside a bit more and cool down.

When she circled back to her house a moment later, the pristine front garden of the cottage bloomed in the sunshine. Small, evenly spaced flowers, and perfectly trimmed bushes that, up until now, had been looked after by her dad were a bright contrast to the plain white walls. The cottage was part of a pair that shared a large thatched roof. Most of the cottages in Meadowbank were thatched and had either flint stone walls or short fences around the small front gardens. No one had a high fence because how would you talk to your neighbours if you installed one of those?

She pushed open the front door, grateful that her cheeks had now cooled and returned to an almost normal colour. Keats, her tubby tortoiseshell cat, came to greet her. He wrapped himself around her legs, pushing his not-unsubstantial weight against her until she stopped and bent down to fuss his ears.

'Hello, my lovely boy. Want to know how it went? Okay, I think.' He purred in response.

The familiar scent of home – of lavender coming from the front garden and honeysuckle from the back – comforted her. Elsie stood up and walked around the sofa, flopping onto a seat. Keats followed. She picked up the property details of the cottage her parents had just bought and moved to in the Highlands. One day she'd go there to visit. One day, she'd visit all the places she'd read about that had piqued her interest. There were so many she'd lost count but maybe if she got this job, she'd take the plunge and travel. She'd overcome her shyness to get this far, and she could get to Scotland by train, after all. It might take a while, but she could do it. Possibly.

Gemma, her best friend who lived next door, was off travelling around Europe. She'd asked Elsie to go along too, but as usual, Elsie hadn't found the courage. And, of course, she had a pathological fear of flying. Flying meant getting in a tin box that zoomed through the air at a ridiculous speed with the highest chance of death imaginable. There was no point in telling her about all the safety checks planes went through, you couldn't wrap it up in a bow. It was a terrifying box of death. When she heard from Clara an actual job was coming up in the library, meaning she wouldn't have to volunteer anymore, it proved the perfect excuse not to leave. She couldn't risk losing the chance to live her dream.

When all the other children at school were playing cops and robbers, she'd played at being a librarian, talking about books, helping people choose them, checking them out with an imaginary stamp. It was all on computers now, but she smiled at the memory. Elsie tossed the estate agent's leaflet back onto the coffee table and crossed her fingers again, praying she'd done enough to win the suited man over. Clara had encouraged her to apply so she knew she had her support, but Elsie still had to tick the boxes and score more points than the other applicants. It was like a horrible game.

She let out a breath and allowed Keats onto her lap. He curled into a ball, and she stroked his silky soft fur. The cottage looked strangely empty without her parents' possessions in it. They'd left her most of the furniture but had taken all their academic tomes with them and the shelves in the alcoves were bare without the dense and dusty books. At least she could move all her novels down from her room now. It was hard to find her bed there were so many piles of them on the floor. Climbing back into bed in the middle of the night after she'd been to the bathroom could be particularly dangerous. She liked having the place to herself though. At 25, she thought it was time she lived on her own, but she hadn't ever wanted to move out of the village and nearer to her job in an office in Witchbury. She'd taken the day off to attend the interview today and crossed her fingers again.

'Please let me get this job,' Elsie begged again in the silence of the room. She raised her eyes, studying the ceiling, hoping that if any being controlled fate or destiny it was listening to her now. 'Please?'

Seeing her latest read on the arm of the sofa where she'd left it that morning, she picked it up. She'd do what she always did and disappear into its pages for a while. Hearing the comforting flex of the spine and feeling the paper beneath her fingers, she settled down, attempting to push all thoughts of the interview from her mind.

You never know, maybe the suited man liked vanilla ice cream over the more exciting flavours.

Chapter 2

Five Years Later

'They're at it again, Elsie,' Bernard said, tapping the computer screen with an aged finger. 'Following that poor girl around and taking pictures of her weekly shop.'

Elsie frowned in confusion while restacking the newspapers in the rack. She loved the smell of paper that perfumed the library air, though she preferred the scent of old paper that came from a well-worn book to the fresh newsprint in her hand. She couldn't imagine still working in a lifeless, stuffy office with air-conditioning and the recycled smell of Lynx body spray. Beyond depressing. 'Who, Bernard?'

'See this here.' Bernard's beard ruffled as pursed his lips and prodded the screen.

Elsie glanced at it. For once her eyes weren't puffy or burning with tiredness from another sleepless night and she was able to focus quickly, her mind working at a much faster speed than usual. The last few nights had been free from insomnia, and she'd slept like a baby, allowing her body to rest and recharge. The difference it made was incredible and the smile that had been growing wider with every good night, was now taking over her face.

'That poor Taylor Swift girl was spotted in a car park in Wigan last night. Off to Asda apparently, but she can't go anywhere without someone taking a photo of her. Poor love.'

Bernard was one of the older residents of Meadowbank and had been coming to the library for as long as Elsie had worked here, which was about five years now. His fascination with celebrity culture, and the apparent sightings of various movie stars and singers in the United Kingdom, had been a recent addition to his normal checking of the BBC News and Weather.

'How extraordinary,' Elsie replied. 'What do you think Taylor Swift was doing in Wigan? Popped over from LA, has she?'

Bernard sat back and considered. 'Maybe they don't have Asda in LA.' He shrugged. 'Maybe she can't get hold of Pringles.'

Elsie paused midway between folding *The Daily Mail* and slotting it into the rack. 'Pringles?'

'Yeah. Maybe you can only get those in England. I love the sour cream and onion ones. Not keen on that odd pizza flavour they do sometimes. Tastes like sick to me. Can you imagine though, Elsie? That poor girl can't go anywhere without the paparazzi following her. What a life.'

Elsie gave his shoulder a gentle squeeze as she went back to the desk. Though she had, on more than one occasion, hinted that it was unlikely for Taylor Swift to be spotted in Wigan, or Sharon Stone in a Halfords in Basingstoke, he'd never quite believed her. Bernard's voice carried the short distance between them.

'Look at this one, Elsie. That rapper Hissy Fit was spotted in Tooting.' He stroked his beard. 'I've always quite liked Tooting. It's got a funny name.'

Elsie bit back a laugh and rounded the desk to sort out the books poked through the drop box last night. She raked her fingers through her frizzy hair, then pushed her glasses up the bridge of her nose. The unseasonably warm weather was making her thick curls even more frazzled than usual and she had yet to find a product that could tame them. Karen, her supervisor, and the grumpiest librarian ever to walk the Earth, neither looked up nor smiled at Bernard's comment.

'He's going crazier by the day,' she muttered, scowling at the magazine in front of her.

Somehow, Karen managed to do all of the moaning and none of the work while Elsie did all of the work and very little moaning. At first, Elsie hadn't minded when Karen was appointed as her supervisor after Clara, the old librarian, had retired. She loved her job as it was and had to concede that she hadn't been brave enough to go for promotion. The idea of sitting in front of a panel answering questions and knowing she'd go as red as a beetroot had put her off. It had been all she could do to get through the interview for this job and she still hadn't quite recovered from being asked, 'What are your weaknesses?' to which she'd trailed off a list so long she'd been surprised they hadn't been deterred by her inability to face confrontation, speak in public, or dance with any discernible rhythm.

As a result of Elsie's inability to push herself, Karen had got the job even though she'd never particularly liked library work. In fact, Elsie knew full well she hated it. She hated the children coming in for story times, the older people who came in for Mingle and Mutter or just some company, and she had a particularly strong loathing for the book club because it meant finding all the special cups and saucers people had brought in from home. But Karen did like the extra money that came with the position and overseeing the rota, which meant she got first dibs on holidays and more than her fair share of weekends off.

Not for the first time Elsie wondered if she should stop being so afraid of actually doing things and take a chance once in a while. For a wallflower like her though, it was easier said than done. She'd had so many ideas for new sessions the library could run and local authors they could get in for book launches and talks, but when she'd tentatively raised them with Karen, they'd been pooh-poohed as too expensive or too highbrow.

'I can't bear any more of his looniness about random celebrities being seen in places they definitely wouldn't be unless their career had gone down the toilet quicker than a—'

'He's not a loony,' Elsie whispered. 'He's just eccentric.'

With a flick of the page, Karen tutted. 'Well, I am so bored of his eccentricities. It's all I hear every bloody morning.'

Stacking the books she needed to shelve into a manageable pile, Elsie said, 'He's like Winston; he likes his routine, that's all. Bernard loves coming in in the mornings and checking his websites. He's on his own too and it's more about company than anything else.'

'But Tooting?' Karen said. 'And Hissy Fit? I doubt he even knows who he is.'

Elsie had a mental image of Bernard listening to rap music while he made his morning tea and supressed a giggle. He didn't do anyone any harm and if it made him happy, who was she to judge? Glancing at the clock, she saw that it was nearly ten o'clock, which meant that any minute now, poor, lonely Winston would arrive to read the papers and chat to Bernard. Since his wife died nine months ago, Winston had needed the company the library and Meadowbank's community had to offer more than any of its residents. Elsie had a soft spot for him and made it her mission to check on him after his grief had been almost overpowering.

The Mingle and Mutter crew would be arriving too. It was the name they used for the specific time the older residents of the village were encouraged to stop by for a chat. Like most of their regular, community-focused events it was well attended, and Elsie always enjoyed listening to their stories of times gone by. Just as she'd finished checking her watch, Jocelyn Carmichael arrived with her friend, Mrs Picard.

'Morning, ladies,' Elsie called out.

'Morning, Elsie love,' Mrs Carmichael responded. 'Now, have you got any books put aside for me?'

'I do, actually.'

Elsie was always tasked with finding new reads for Mrs Carmichael because whenever she asked Karen, all she did was take a cursory glance at the new arrivals stand and point at something that was nothing like the books Mrs Carmichael actually liked. The old lady had rather specific, and somewhat X-rated tastes. She always bypassed local romance author Neve Chapstone (Elsie took a moment to admire the display of her books she'd made the day before) and had read all of the Fifty Shades books (and seen the movies). Elsie sometimes struggled to keep up with Mrs C's voracious reading habits. Luckily, she'd bulk-ordered some new books and couldn't wait to show her.

More of the village's older residents arrived and the library was soon buzzing with people. Elsie loved the library when it was quiet, but she loved it even more when it was full of discussions and people connecting over books.

'With all these oldies here I can feel myself ageing,' Karen groaned, running her fingers down her neck as if being near an octogenarian was making her jowly. 'It's like they're sucking the life right out of me.'

Elsie rolled her eyes, thankful that Karen didn't see as she eagerly read a feature on juice detoxes that didn't look a particularly healthy form of weight loss. Even though she could do with losing a few pounds, Elsie wasn't in favour of anything that meant you had to stop chewing.

As well as Winston, one of her other favourite customers was Patricia, the kind, middle-aged woman who led Baby and Toddler Toe Taps. Elsie was alerted to her arrival by a flash of purple passing one of the side windows.

'Morning, everyone,' Patricia trilled, her purple silk scarf trailing behind her as she marched in. 'How are we all today?'

Karen glanced up from her magazine and flipped another page. At this rate she'd run out of things to read by quarter past and might actually have to do some work.

'You look lovely today, Patricia,' Elsie said. 'I love your scarf.'

'Thank you, darling. Isn't it a glorious day? Have you seen that sky? It's the most brilliant blue. It's going to be a warm one, but I can't go out without one of my signature silk scarves.' She tossed it artistically over her shoulder.

'It is gorgeous today, isn't it? It's so warm already, I don't think it'll be long and we'll need to open the other door.'

Elsie much preferred the natural daylight that flowed in, to the harsher, functional strip-lighting in the ceiling. With the double doors pinned back, from her spot at the desk, she could see straight out to the riverbank and the cherry trees that dotted the way along it, under which several benches were nestled. The bright pink blossoms didn't last all that long, but as the weather was unseasonably warm with very little wind, they were still decorating the trees. Occasionally, the ducks would paddle down from the pond on the edge of the village green and hop up searching for crumbs. Elsie had to admit, if she ate her lunch out there, she'd sometimes leave titbits on purpose to attract them. She liked watching them plod around and they were as much a part of the village as the church, the tiny school everyone went to, and the fêtes and fairs that marked each passing season.

Sometimes, she'd take a walk around the large empty fields flowing out from the back of the library and to its side when she felt the need to stretch her legs. At this time of year, the grass grew high and the prettiest wildflowers dotted the wide expanse of green, puncturing the scene with vibrant dots of blues, yellows, and whites. Undoubtedly idyllic, it was the main reason she'd never left. Elsie glanced to her left where a couple of glass cases displayed the archaeological finds discovered nearby. There wasn't anything too exciting: certainly no Saxon hoard or hidden treasure, but Elsie loved their collection of Roman pot shards and Iron Age coins. It was amazing to think that the small village of Meadowbank had existed in one form or another from such an early age.

'I'm looking forward to today's Toe Taps,' Patricia said excitedly. 'I've got a lovely new set of toys for the kids to use.' She held up a carrier bag and Elsie could see bright pops of colour through the thin plastic.

'Oh, Patricia, you haven't gone and bought more toys, have you? You mustn't do that. We can get some out of the budget for you. You just need to let us know what to buy.'

'We can't reimburse you,' snapped Karen, finally closing the magazine and standing up. 'And we don't have enough in the budget to buy any either.' She turned to look at Elsie, annoyed with her for suggesting it, and Elsie's cheeks burned under the admonishment.

'Here's another one, Elsie,' shouted Bernard from the corner. 'Stroud this time. That judge from *World's Worst Chef*. What's her name? Alexandra Stump, that's it. She was seen in PoundLife.'

After peering into the bag Patricia had brought with her, Karen marched off. Elsie wasn't sure what she'd marched off to do. She'd probably gone to hide in her office, or the geography section: no one ever went in there. Elsie turned her attention back to Patricia, who shook her head and leaned in conspiratorially.

'I don't know how you put up with that woman. How she got the job, I'll never understand. She must be very good at interviews is all I can say. Right, I'd better go and get ready. We'll be starting in an hour.'

Tuesday mornings were one of the busiest in the library with Mingle and Mutter first thing and then Baby and Toddler Toe Taps. They'd tried spacing them out over the week, but the residents had made it clear that these were their preferred times and so Elsie had made sure that they catered for them.

Patricia headed off through the beautiful wooden archway that separated the main section of the library from a smaller one. The front area of it held children's books and behind it was the reference section. It wasn't an ideal layout because the kids' area could get a little noisy, but Karen had never agreed to a re-organisation, even though Elsie suspected she'd never even asked their boss.

Among the bright murals in the children's section was a hidden cupboard and Patricia kneeled down to take out the large blanket they used for story times and a bag full of random figures collected over the years that stood in as characters. What had begun as a few Barbie dolls and Action Man figures had, thanks to Patricia's skill with a crochet needle, grown to include a number of characters including ones of Patricia, Bernard, Winston, and Elsie with her glasses. She had made one of Karen too, but she only brought that out when Karen was off because she'd put her in a witch's hat and given her a giant wart on the end of her nose. The crochet figures were Elsie's favourites because they had the most personality, and it was wonderful to think a little piece of her and her friends was woven into the stories.

With another quick check of the large clock that hung over the door, worry mounted in Elsie's stomach. Winston was late. She'd become more and more concerned about him over the last month, sure he wasn't eating properly. His face had grown thinner and though he'd signed up to the Meadowbank equivalent of Meals on Wheels – Dinner in a Dish – she wasn't sure he was actually eating much. His grief since his wife had died had consumed him so fully, he had, for a while, lost the will to live. He'd perked up a bit at Christmas – a time Elsie was particularly worried about him – when as well as the gifts she'd given him, he'd received some from other residents thanks to the wishing tree that their local primary school teacher, Bella, had set up, but since then he'd been slowly going downhill, merely existing day to day.

As Elsie was about to go to the door to look for him, he ambled around the corner. It must have been a bad day for his arthritis as he limped whenever he put weight on his left leg. Elsie ran out from behind the desk and pulled out his chair for him.

'Thank you, poppet. Oh, you're a good girl,' he said as he flopped down. His thin grey hair had been slicked back and she noticed the dark shadows under his eyes.

Elsie took *The Times* from the newspaper rack next to the

15

computers. Everyone knew he read that paper first, so whenever it neared ten o'clock, the regulars who'd come for Mingle and Mutter would choose another, ensuring it was free for Winston. These were the things Elsie loved most about the quiet village she'd been born and raised in.

Bernard was still jabbing at the screen, moaning to Mrs Picard and some other ladies about celebrity sightings in places he'd never heard of, and after a final harrumph went in search of an atlas. He didn't trust Google Maps to show him where the little town of Upper Dicker actually was or if, in fact, it was real.

'No bike today, Winston?' Elsie asked as she handed the paper to him. Winston normally rode everywhere and to know that he hadn't meant his leg was particularly bad.

'Not today, poppet. My hip's playing up something horrible, even in this good weather. I must have slept funny. Do you know, even though I could spread out if I wanted to, I still find myself sleeping on my side of the bed?' The sadness that welled in his eyes tugged at her heart.

In an effort to cheer him up, Elsie said, 'Gemma should be here soon with our elevenses.'

'What cake do you think it is today?'

'I've heard it's lemon and pistachio Battenburg.'

Some of the sadness dissipated from Winston's face. 'Now that sounds just the thing on this lovely day. I don't think I've ever had that before. Have you?'

'Nope, definitely not, but it sounds delicious.' Elsie went back to the desk to retrieve the books for shelving.

Slowly, she ambled around the sections, tidying and ensuring the books were in order with the spines level, like soldiers lining up for parade. Though she wasn't normally one for singing her own praises, Elsie did have a remarkable knowledge of books. She couldn't claim to have read every book in the library, but she read widely and kept up to date with all the industry papers so she knew what was happening in the various genres. As Karen left the ordering to her, she liked to know what people were likely to ask for and to make sure they had it in stock. As far as she was concerned, reading wasn't just a hobby, it was part of her job and whenever she was alone, she couldn't help but open a book and slide into the world between the pages.

Pausing at the travel section as she returned a slightly outdated guide on Egypt to the shelf, she sighed. As much as she loved Meadowbank, lately, the world beyond the village had been pulling at her mind more than ever, leaving behind a wanderlust that had never touched her this way before. She'd always been more than satisfied with her sweet village life, but at odd moments, like the one today, she did wonder what it would be like to see the pyramids of Egypt that Elizabeth Peters described in her Amelia Peabody series, or glide down the Nile as Hercule Poirot had done. She shook the feeling away as she shelved the last few books and went to join Mingle and Mutter.

Before long, she was waving goodbye to the older generation as the new one arrived for Baby and Toddler Toe Taps. The chatter of Mingle and Mutter faded, and the air was filled with the gorgeous sounds of Patricia's singing and squeals of children's laughter as well as the off-beat banging of drums and some random clapping. Elsie couldn't help but join in as they sang 'The Wheels on the Bus' and had to tear herself away to shelve some books. Karen stayed in her office for the duration, which wasn't unusual and actually made life easier for everyone else. When they were nearly finished, Gemma arrived with cakes and treats from the bakery she ran with her partner, Orla.

'Here we are, kiddies. Mini blueberry muffins for you, and for my favourite librarian and her chums I've got a lemon and pistachio Battenburg, courtesy of Orla.'

The toddlers ran over to the desk while the mums gathered their babies. When Gemma deposited her tray, tiny hands grabbed greedily at the golden sponge studded with bursts of blue. Not many libraries had a cake delivery service, but the arrangement worked well for both the bakery and the library. The customers in the library received exquisite cakes every day (and it was probably one of the reasons the place was always so busy around this time) and Gemma and Orla could test out their new recipes without having to eat all the results themselves. Snaffling cake every day didn't sound like a bad thing, but the calories did, unfortunately, add up in the end.

'How busy are you this morning?' asked Elsie as Gemma swished her long, dark ponytail back over her shoulder.

'We've been manic and will be again soon when all the mums leave you and come to us for a restorative after all that singing. You do me a real favour,' she said to Patricia, who had left the mothers to chat while she had a sip from a water bottle and a slice of Battenburg.

Elsie took a couple of plates to Bernard and Winston and the few Mingle and Mutter customers who'd stayed around to choose new library books. Karen too magically reappeared and after grabbing a slice, ran off back to her office. 'And is Orla okay?'

'Yeah, she's great. She's holding the fort while Scarlett sits in a highchair at the end of the counter. When I get back, I'll take over with Scarlett while she serves, and we'll swap back again later.'

'You should have brought her along,' Patricia said. 'I'd be happy to look after her for you.'

Gemma tipped her head. 'You are a sweetie. I might do that next time. She can get quite stroppy if she hasn't burned off some energy.'

'It can't be easy running the bakery with just the two of you and raising a baby.'

'We are quite worn out at the end of the day. And speaking of the end of the day,' Gemma said, turning to Elsie, 'are you coming round for dinner tonight? Orla's making pierogies.'

Elsie's eyes widened. One of the best things about Orla's Polish heritage was that she made the most amazing food. Since Orla and Gemma had moved in together, pierogies had become one of

Elsie's favourite meals, though she wasn't gifted enough to make them herself. 'What time?' she asked, moving to the self-checkout opposite the desk and helping a customer take home some books.

'About seven? That gives us time to get Scarlett bathed and in her cot before you arrive. Not that she'll go to sleep but we're trying to let her fall asleep on her own with her mobile playing.'

'Sounds good. I'll bring a bottle.' Elsie noticed Patricia's face had suddenly darkened. 'Is everything all right, Patricia?'

'Oh, yes. I was just thinking of my grandson.'

They all knew there'd been a row in the Skinner family, but Patricia had only given them the barest details on the odd occasions she felt able to talk about it.

'My daughter's still not forgiven me for criticising Blake that day. It's been over a year now. And even though I keep texting and asking if we can meet up, I don't get any reply.'

Just as Elsie was about to speak, two shadows filled the small doorway, one tall and thin, the other short and round.

'Who're they?' asked Gemma, scowling as they blocked the exit, pointing and muttering together.

'I have no idea, but I have a horrible feeling that whatever they're here for, it isn't going to be good.'

Chapter 3

Karen appeared at Elsie's elbow and Gemma, who had an even lower opinion of her than Elsie did, backed away.

'Karen,' Elsie said quietly, watching the two men who had begrudgingly moved out of the way of a customer but had immediately filled the doorway again. 'Do you know who they are?'

'That's what I just came to tell you,' she whispered. 'You'll never guess what I've just seen.' If Karen was about to go off on a tangent with more scurrilous gossip, Elsie'd have to tell her to hold her tongue; Elsie wasn't the gossiping type and in a small village like Meadowbank idle tittle-tattle could ruin people's lives. But what Karen had to say was more than a little intriguing. 'Two posh cars just pulled up down the side and that's them.' She pointed at the door. 'Who do you think they are? When I saw the cars, I did think they might be better looking. Not like those trolls, but then, beggars can't be choosers and it's been a very long time since anyone visited my—'

'Maybe they're from the council,' Elsie said before Karen could go into another rant about her lack of love life.

Karen shook her head. 'If they are, they're pretty high up. I've never seen any of them here in Meadowbank before. Normally they can't be bothered with us.'

Which was why Karen got away with so much, Elsie thought but, as usual, bit her tongue. As she had to work with the woman it wasn't worth annoying her unnecessarily.

The squat and round gentleman had bright red cheeks and sweat gathering at his temples. His face had a doughy quality, like a child had modelled it out of playdough. So much so that his bulbous nose and wiry, trimmed moustache looked like they hadn't quite been attached to his face. The tall and thin man with him had receding hair and took from the inside pocket of his jacket a lanyard that he hung around his neck. From the vague outline on the badge, Elsie could tell he was from the council after all, but she couldn't see a department name. Perhaps he was new? Perhaps the other man was an architect hired to refurbish the library. He was certainly pointing at a lot of things and gazing around. There'd been other people poking about the place recently too. Though they hadn't all come inside, she'd spotted them through the window, gazing at the roof and mentally measuring the length of the walls. The few that had come in had been conspicuous by their lack of interest in any of the bookstands, weaving their way through and refusing any offers of help before scuttling away. A slight tingle of excitement welled in her stomach. If they refurbished the library, she might have the chance to put her ideas for a re-organisation forward after all, though she'd have to do it by email. She couldn't stand the thought of being face to face with these intimidating suits.

The council man said, 'Feel free to look around, Conrad', before walking towards them.

'Hide the cake, quick,' whispered Karen, grabbing the now-empty plate and slipping it under her magazine. Realising that too would land her in trouble, she slid the council Health and Safety Policy on top. They weren't supposed to have food and drink unless it was for a special event and supplied by the council canteen or an approved catering company. Patricia deftly grabbed

21

the last few mini-muffins and took them over to the children's section while Gemma tried to hide the tray behind her back.

'Ah, ladies, you must be …' He checked his clipboard. 'Karen and Elsie. Is that right?' They both silently nodded. 'Good. My name is Gareth Rees-Hale. I work for the council. Is it possible to have a word with you both?'

'At the same time?' asked Elsie. She nervously adjusted her glasses while Rees-Hale stared like she'd said something particularly stupid.

'Ideally. Yes.'

'It's just that …' She looked to Karen to take over, but she'd lost her tongue. 'You see, there are only the two of us, so if we both go at the same time, there'll be no one at the desk.'

'Don't you have any volunteers?' he asked sternly.

'Well, yes, but—'

'Then ask them. This is rather important.'

Again, Elsie looked to Karen. When Karen didn't move, she went to find Patricia, who had, on occasion, covered the desk in an emergency. Though she hoped that Rees-Hale was bringing exciting news, his dour expression indicated otherwise. A horrible feeling began to rise in her stomach, and it definitely wasn't due to the lemon and pistachio cake, which had, as usual, been delicious.

'Patricia—'

'Who's that?' she whispered, edging closer. 'I've had to hide the mini-muffins behind David Walliams. Don't let me forget them before I leave.'

'I won't. It's someone from high up. He wants to talk to me and Karen together.'

'Oh. Well, hopefully it's good news. Maybe they're going to rethatch the roof at last.'

'I hope so,' Elsie replied. 'Or maybe it's about the new appraisal policy. We got an email about it the other day. It was the most boring thing I've ever read, but, anyway, do you mind keeping an eye on the place while he speaks to us. I don't think it'll take long.'

'Of course. Good luck, sweetheart.'

Elsie headed back to Rees-Hale. 'Ready when you are.'

'My office is this way.' Karen suddenly perked up, leading them to her tiny hideaway at the back of the building. Once inside, she motioned for him to take her seat behind the desk with a deferential air. 'Would you prefer to sit here, Mr Rees-Hale?'

Clearly, she hadn't realised the latest copy of *Heat* magazine was out on the corner of the desk. When Karen spotted it, her eyes widened comically and she blushed as she said, 'Let me clear you some room.'

He took a seat, leaving Elsie and Karen to find ones for them-selves. Both ended up on spare tiny seats from the children's section that had been stacked at the end of the room. Elsie's knees were now only fractionally away from her chin, and she could see some of the hairs left from Keats, her tortoiseshell cat.

'Are they the only chairs you have?' Even seated, Rees-Hale towered over them. 'Can't you get some from out there?' He pointed to the main section of the library.

'These are fine,' said Karen, clearly eager to hear what the senior man had to say. 'Aren't they, Elsie?' Her eyes widened, a silent instruction to Elsie to shut up so he could get on with it.

'Yes. Yes, they're fine.' It didn't really matter to Elsie if she could smell her knees, she was more interested in the purpose of this visit than anything else.

'Right, well then, I'll proceed. I'm sure you've seen some men popping in lately.'

Elsie nodded.

'They've been assessing the building.'

The weight in her stomach lightened. They could do with getting rid of some of the old MDF bookshelves where the fake-wood veneer was peeling off, and as Patricia had pointed out, the building had needed re-roofing for ages. The next big storm could see them with buckets on the floor and the Health and Safety department certainly wouldn't like that. They could even change the lighting to something less eye-straining and more natural.

'I'm afraid I've come to notify you that we're selling the library for regeneration purposes.'

Elsie's stomach catapulted itself into her throat. All the breath was knocked from her lungs like she'd taken a physical blow to the chest. Though they didn't need pushing up, Elsie adjusted her glasses so she had something to do with her hands. 'Regeneration purposes? What does that mean exactly?'

'It means we'll be using this land for housing. In fact, the sale will be going through over the next couple of days. There'll be a formal meeting tomorrow at nine where you'll be placed at risk of redundancy, but we thought it best to speak to you first and let you know now. We've heard reports that the news has been leaked to the papers and we didn't want you to find out from there.'

'That's very kind of you,' Karen said, clearly eyeing up redeployment. Elsie couldn't bring herself to do the same. If she couldn't work in the little library in Meadowbank, she didn't want to work anywhere at all. Of course, she'd have to, the rational part of her brain told her. She had bills to pay. But this was the most wonderful library on the planet. Nowhere could compare to here. Except for maybe the Bodleian or the British Library, but she didn't want to move to a big city where she'd undoubtedly end up lonely and terrified. This was her home where everyone knew her.

'I'm terribly sorry to be the bearer of bad news,' Rees-Hale said, standing up. For him the meeting was over.

'But why?' Elsie asked, pushing herself out of the ridiculously small chair, which was no mean feat. 'We've got really good borrowing rates and … and everyone uses the library. Look how busy we are this morning, and this is just a normal Tuesday. Why do you have to build here? Surely there are other places.'

'Elsie,' Karen said through gritted teeth. 'I'm sure Mr Rees-Hale has to get going.'

'It's fine,' he said, holding out a hand in a conciliatory fashion.

24

'The area – this area in particular – needs affordable housing. We run lots of other libraries and we feel there'll be enough provision for the village.'

'But—'

'You'll have a chance tomorrow in our formal meeting to ask any questions and there'll be a public meeting in the evening, when we'll let the rest of the village know our plans.'

They won't like it, Elsie thought, but again bit her lip to stop the words coming out.

'I'd ask you both to keep this information confidential until I announce things tomorrow. I've been assured the Media team can stop it appearing in the local paper, but they've said things like that before so we're telling you just in case. Please put this notice on the door informing everyone that there'll be a public meeting here tomorrow night. They'll find out everything then. Do you have enough chairs out there?' He peered out of the small window in the fire-proof door. 'I doubt many people will come so you'll probably be fine if you just round up all the ones you've got.'

Without thinking Elsie let out an incredulous snort but then turned it into a cough under Rees-Hale's hard eyes. *You clearly don't know this village*, she thought. There was going to be uproar. And heartbreak.

'Obviously as council employees you're expected to be politically neutral and support the plans.'

'Of course,' Karen replied, eyeing Elsie. 'We understand.'

Neutral? How was she supposed to be neutral about their tearing the heart out of Meadowbank? About their tearing the heart out of her life. She thought of all the people out there right now, all the people who'd been there this morning. What about them? It was only now, as her legs almost gave way, that Elsie realised they were shaking.

For once, Elsie decided not to hold back, and racked her brains for another argument or evidence they were making the wrong decision, but her mind froze and her mouth opened and closed, no words coming out. Why when she wanted so desperately to scream and shout and make a fuss, summoning some courage and risking the worst of all possible things – a face-to-face confrontation – could she not think of anything to say?

Unfortunately, Rees-Hale didn't even see her attempt at an argument as he exited the office without so much as a backwards glance.

The door clicked shut behind him, and her heart sank at the same time her world came tumbling down around her. Despite the warmth of the day, a cold chill rippled through her body, and she shuddered.

What the hell was she going to do now?

Chapter 4

Elsie had finished her working day in a daze. Every action taken in the library, whether it be serving customers, dusting the display cases, or shelving books, had been completed on autopilot and the smile she'd fixed in place for the sake of her friends hadn't faded until she'd stepped inside her front garden.

The bright and blossoming flowers her dad had planted before they moved were still alive, though they weren't yet in full bloom. It was surprising really. Elsie watered them regularly and had replanted others but wasn't one to spend hours digging when each week brought new books to read. Some of the order her dad had liked was gone now, but she thought it looked better for it. In the summer the flowers tumbled into one another at the corners of the small front garden and in between she'd added small stone books. A perfect monument to her passion.

As soon as the cottage door opened, Keats weaved himself around her legs, meowing and causing her to stumble. 'Oh, Keats, stop it. Let me at least get inside.'

She hooked the keys onto the key rack attached to the wall. As with most things in her life, it was shaped like an open book, and had small hooks running along the bottom. Books – mostly novels – were everywhere in the small, sweet cottage. Where the shelves were full, stacks of books had been piled on the floor. Either side of the large fireplace, paperbacks came up to her knees, framing the fire, while other piles acted as coffee tables at each end of the well-worn, pale green sofa.

Some people mourned the advent of ebooks as the end of a good old-fashioned paperback, but Elsie had always been grateful for them. She didn't think her house could stand anymore books, though it never stopped her buying them. As much as she loved her e-reader, curling up with it of an evening, or taking it with her on those rare occasions she did leave Meadowbank, there were times when only a real book would do and the smell of paper fragranced the air of her cottage as it did in the library.

Despondency filled her and she threw herself into the armchair by the window, gazing out at the village. She pulled her legs up and hugged them, then straightened them out again. With no idea what to do with herself she fidgeted, adjusting the cushion behind her back. Keats jumped up onto her lap and she hugged him close, burying her head in his soft fur.

'Oh, Keats, it's been the worst day ever.' She was answered by his soft purr as he rubbed his face against hers. 'You're hungry, aren't you? Come on, I'll get you some food before I go next door.'

Though she felt guilty for leaving him on his own, she knew letting him onto her bed tonight would make up for popping out for the evening and she'd give him a little extra food so his food coma would keep him sleepy and happy. She was lucky that her best friend had always lived next door, there for her whenever she needed her. They'd clicked instantly at school and being neighbours all their lives had only strengthened their friendship.

Elsie moved through to the kitchen and took a pouch of cat food from the cupboard. As she gathered cutlery and his bowl, she also grabbed the wine to take next door. Luckily, she didn't need to change as she was already in her usual attire of trousers and a loose top. When she got another job, would she have to wear a uniform or buy a new outfit that was more suitable for a fancy office?

'Urgh,' she said out loud at the idea. Keats responded with a meow, and she laid his food bowl down, giving him a fuss before she stood up. 'I'll be back in a bit, Keats. Be good.'

Closing the door softly behind her, she took a breath of the blossom-scented air. It had been a wonderfully warm spring so far. The sun had shone brightly every day and though it was only April, the temperature had been climbing steadily since March. No one had expected it to last, but surprisingly it had, and with every pleasant morning, the weather had dominated the topic of conversation in the village.

In less than a minute, Elsie had walked down the path from her cottage, past Gemma and Orla's front garden, and was knocking on their front door.

Though Rees-Hale had told her to keep schtum, there was no way Elsie could hide the news from Gemma. As soon as the two gentlemen had left Karen's office and exited the building (still pointing at things as they went, which had annoyed Elsie greatly), Gemma and Patricia had asked her what was wrong. Whether it was shock at the news or Karen's sharp eyes, Elsie hadn't blurted out her true feelings and kept to the script: there was a meeting tomorrow and they were to set some chairs out. Patricia had bought the lie, but Gemma's gaze had lingered on Elsie, assessing her in that way only a best friend could. When their eyes met, Elsie had somehow managed to communicate that now wasn't the time to press for more details and Gemma had left knowing they'd catch up later.

Gemma opened the door and Elsie held out the bottle of wine.

'Tell me everything,' she said, swooping Elsie into a hug. Gemma's dark hair was loose from its ponytail and hung down past her shoulders, softening her face, which, given her outspoken nature, could sometimes appear harsh. After she released her, they stepped into the house and Gemma swiftly overtook her to get back to the kitchen and help Orla. 'I've been worried about you all day. I'd have called in again, but we've been manic, swapping backwards and forwards with Scarlett. So, tell me everything.'

'I'm being made redundant.'

Gemma's knuckles were so tense on the neck of the bottle, it was in danger of breaking under her grip.

'And worse than that,' Elsie replied, dropping her cardigan onto the back of the sofa and making her way to the kitchen, 'they're going to shut the library. Not just close it down, knock it down.'

'Are you sure?' asked Orla, bringing the pierogies to the small circular dining table at the end of the kitchen. The steam from the delicious dumplings fogged Elsie's glasses as she leaned forward to savour the smell.

Orla, who looked the complete opposite to Gemma with her white-blonde hair and pale skin, had this amazing habit of being clean and precise in the bakery, but incredibly messy when she cooked at home. After opening the wine to let it breathe, Gemma began tidying up, stacking dishes in the dishwasher and piling them in the stainless-steel sink. Every now and then one of them would stare at the video monitor on the worktop and check Scarlett was okay. She wasn't yet asleep and was happily rolling around in her cot, mumbling away to herself. Gemma and Orla worked like a well-oiled machine and Elsie longed to share something similar with someone special.

At 30, she hadn't yet found someone who made her heart sing and the chances of doing so in such a small village had been few and far between. A lot of the men she knew had been school friends and having known them for so long, she found it hard to think of them in any other way. They would forever be the small boys at school who used to tease her for blushing when her name was mentioned, or sniggered when she stumbled while reading out loud in class. Any relationship with someone from outside the village had lasted for a few disappointing dates that still made her cringe but nothing more. Gemma had met Orla when she'd been travelling around Europe. She'd gone to

Poland and been swept up in the beautiful city of Krakow. Elsie remembered receiving her postcards and emails. She'd stayed there longer than any other place because her connection with Orla had been instant, and Gemma had been unable to tear herself away. How Elsie longed to experience an instant connection like that.

'Rees-Hale told me the land's been sold and I don't think anyone would bother trying to convert the library,' Elsie said, removing one of Scarlett's bibs from the seat of her chair before sitting down. 'They're going to sell it off for affordable housing, which means they'll be knocking it down and building on the site.' She shook her head incredulously. 'How could they even think of such a thing?'

'I can't believe it,' said Gemma as they gathered around the table. She poured extra-large measures for them all and Elsie took a mouthful. The velvety red wine slid down her throat but did nothing to relieve the tension in her shoulders. 'Why would they choose our library? You're always so busy. I don't know anyone in the village who doesn't use the library. Apart from Kevin Hornsby whom we went to school with, but then since he was 15, he's preferred his reading material to come in magazine form with a half-naked woman attached.'

Elsie managed a small smile. 'They said it was because there was other provision elsewhere.'

'What they mean,' Orla said with a lyrical hint of her Polish accent, 'is that Meadowbank will give them the most profit. Most houses here are so expensive, even if they call it affordable, they'll be able to charge more money than if they built somewhere else.'

Gemma and Elsie nodded in agreement. As Elsie ate, she felt a slight easing for the few seconds the comforting food was in her mouth. 'I think you're right, Orla.'

'What will happen to you?'

'I'll either be made redundant or redeployed somewhere. I checked out the policy today and they'll move me to another department if there's a similar job available.' Gemma and Orla paused with their cutlery in mid-air, both knowing full well that if Elsie couldn't work in a library or possibly a bookshop, she had no interest in anywhere else. 'I know,' Elsie said. 'I don't want to be moved, but if they offer me a job and I don't take it, they can send me packing without any money at all.' She sighed. The only thing she knew for sure was that her job and the most wonderful little library in all the world were about to disappear.

Elsie outlined what she knew about the public meeting being held the next night, but as she spoke a fire started low in her belly and her fingers gripped her cutlery more tightly. It was all so wrong. While she couldn't deny the village needed some more housing – she'd only been able to stay here thanks to her parents – why did they have to knock down such a well-used and important place as the library? Everyone loved it and it provided not only books and learning but care and support. There must be other places in Meadowbank they could build. Farmers who wanted to sell some of their land or different plots owned by the council? It was all so they could make a quick buck. Everyone knew how bad the council's finances were. A warmth filled her cheeks as the flames inside her grew stronger.

'I bet they're doing it because it's not a fancy library,' she said, shoving more pierogies onto her plate as well as some of the gorgeous Polish sausage the deli stocked. As her anger built, she handled the spoon more violently and it clanged against the plate, echoing around the kitchen. Conversation paused for a second as Orla and Gemma watched her, surprised by her reaction, but Elsie carried on, unable to stem the words from her mouth. 'I bet if we were in a listed building or it was more than just a thatched box, they'd keep it and build somewhere else.'

'Probably,' agreed Gemma. 'Bunch of idiots.'

'That's putting it mildly. I know he says there's provision else-where, but our library is one of the most well used in the area. What they don't understand is that it might not be architecturally designed but it's important to the community.' She put her cutlery down as gently as she could manage with the frustration pulsing through her veins, but it still clattered onto the tabletop. 'It makes me so bloody angry! People – and by "people", I mean council bosses, so I use the term loosely – never value libraries. They never see how important they are to the community. I mean, look at us, we're always busy and it's not just about the books and borrowing rates. We get the older people in for some company, and they can't afford to buy lots of books on their pensions, plus they need large print, which you can't always get online or in shops. And then we have the kids' section, which is super busy during the school holidays, especially when it's wet. And you know how much the kids love Toddler Toe Taps and the weekend story time Patricia does.'

Orla topped up Elsie's glass, which had somehow gone down without her realising it. She was so calm and empathetic, she really was the perfect counterpoint to Gemma's fiery temper. 'Scarlett loves the Sunday afternoon stories. It's the only night of the week she settles well. Patricia wears them out and calms them down at the same time. She's a magician.'

'I could go on and on about who uses it and why knocking it down and building houses in its place is a bad idea. And I'm going to say all of this in my meeting tomorrow.'

'In the public one?' Gemma asked, clearly surprised.

'No, the one in the morning. I don't think I could speak in front of everyone. Not that anything I say will make a difference. They said the deal was going through already. This isn't one of those consultation-type things where they're obliged to get public opinion.'

'Do you know,' said Gemma, 'I don't think I've ever seen you this wound up. I mean, I can understand it, but ever since I've known you, you've had that live-and-let-live mentality or been too quiet to speak out. The last time you were anywhere near this mad was when the dreaded Karen got her promotion.'

'She hadn't even worked in a library before she got the job,' Elsie grumbled and shifted in her chair.

'You'd have walked that interview if you'd put yourself forward for it.' Sensing her discomfort, Gemma backed off. 'I'm just surprised you're so punchy. You're acting like me.' She flashed a mischievous grin.

Maybe acting more like Gemma, who had always been happy to say exactly what she thought, wasn't such a bad idea after all. An image of herself stood on the green marshalling the village with a rousing speech filled her brain before rapidly fading away. Just the idea of speaking in front of people sent an icy blast down her spine. Elsie dropped her head then adjusted her glasses. 'Maybe I'll write a strongly worded letter after my meeting. I've got to make my objections known somehow.'

A loud cry from the video monitor turned their heads. Scarlett was still rolling around in her cot but had decided the quiet gurgling wasn't getting enough attention and had resorted to wailing. 'I'll go,' said Orla, but Gemma stood up first.

'I'll go. You've been on your feet all day.'

'So have you,' she laughed.

'Yes, but you've done most of the feeds and somehow you've managed to get us ahead for tomorrow. I'll go. You drink your wine.'

Gemma climbed the stairs, calling out to Scarlett as she neared the top.

'Do you think Gemma will notice if I steal the last pierogi?' Elsie asked.

Orla glowed with pride that there was virtually nothing left of the feast she'd prepared. 'I'll tell her I forced you to eat it. You need looking after tonight. You've had such a shock.'

Elsie ate it quickly before her friend could return and nab some. As Orla chatted about the goings-on in the café today, they both watched the monitor as Gemma cuddled Scarlett then laid her down, tucking a thin sheet around her and turning her mobile on to play a lullaby. It was another warm evening and at least if

Elsie's insomnia kept her awake tonight, as she feared it would, it would be a nice night for a walk.

'Right, where were we?' said Gemma, coming back to the table. As she neared, she paused, her finger pointing at the now-empty plate. For the first time that night, Elsie felt a genuine smile pulling at her face. 'Did you eat the last pierogi?'

'No,' Orla replied, stretching out the word, clearly lying. 'I did.'

'I know you're lying, but I forgive you both.' She topped up their glasses, giving them a wry smile.

The warmth of their friendship enveloped her and Elsie forgot about the library and the fact she was going to lose her job. It lasted only a moment before it came crashing down on her again. She sighed and slumped down, resting her chin in her hand. 'Rees-Hale was clear I'm expected to be neutral about it all too. He said we have to publicly support the idea, but I can't bring myself to do that.'

'It's just such a shame,' Gemma said. 'If I wasn't so knackered, I'd be as angry as you. Like you said, look at all the people who use the library and most of them use it as a pretence to ask you advice on one thing or another. You're like a one-woman Citizens Advice Bureau because we all know Karen's about as useful as tits on a fish. Honestly, the only thing that woman's good for is as a bad example of how to be a librarian.' Elsie almost spat out her wine as she laughed while drinking. 'How many times have you found stuff out for people and dropped pages and pages of notes at their houses on your way home?'

It was true, a lot of people used Elsie as a sort of human search engine. It was one of the things she loved about her job. No matter if she was finding out when to sow seeds for someone taking up gardening (Mrs Thackeray's hobby hadn't lasted long even with the step-by-step guide Elsie had printed out) or finding out if you can be prosecuted for accidentally mowing the wrong lawn (young Dylan's part-time job hadn't taken off either), the feeling of helping people had always fulfilled her.

'And how do you feel about being redeployed?' Orla asked.

'At least I'll have a wage coming in.' The resigned tone in her voice was clear for all to hear but they all knew she wouldn't really be happy in any other job. Elsie questioned herself as to how long she'd be able to stand anything else. The answer was less than a second.

'Will it be to another library?'

'I doubt it very much.' She fiddled with her fingers. 'My conscience is telling me to scream and shout – well, not exactly shout – but fight as hard as I can for this, because I do believe the village will be lost without this … this hub of community spirit and love … but—' Elsie broke off as a whirl of movement distracted her. 'Gemma, what are you doing?'

Gemma had leapt up from the table and grabbed the notepad they used for the weekly shopping list. 'I'm writing that down because it's bloody brilliant. You might want to put it in your strongly worded letter.'

'But it's an impossible situation. If I do speak up, I risk not getting another job and I've got bills to pay. I know I don't have a mortgage thanks to Mum and Dad, but I still need to pay for the water and gas and all that sort of stuff, and working in a library doesn't pay a great deal.'

If only there was something she could do that didn't mean risking her livelihood.

'It completely sucks,' Gemma said. 'You know we'll get you through this, don't you?' She took Elsie's hand and Orla the other. Elsie gazed at her two best friends. Thankful for how lucky she was, she smiled at them, even though her heart felt heavy.

The rest of the meal was eaten with discussions about the new cake recipes Orla wanted to try this month and the latest thing Scarlett was doing. She was 6 months old now, though Elsie couldn't believe she was growing so fast, and she liked to babble away and giggle. She'd finally fallen asleep about an hour after they'd put her down and they were happy she'd settled on her own, even though she'd spent most of the time tiring herself out by rolling around her cot, chatting to herself.

'Are you in for a bad night?' asked Gemma, as Elsie gathered her cardigan and made her way to the door.

Stress always triggered her insomnia, and she didn't think she'd ever been through anything as stressful as this. 'I wouldn't be surprised.' She accepted the fact with a sort of coldness. It was inevitable. Horrid. But however much she hated it, it wouldn't change things. She knew full well what was coming. 'I'll follow my routine and hope for the best.'

'You can always call me if you start getting stressed or need to talk about it some more.'

'At 3 a.m.?' Though she teased, Elsie knew the answer. Of course her friend would be there for her in the early hours of the morning, when the night stretched out endlessly and tears of exhaustion threatened her tired and gritty eyes. Hopefully though, as up until today she'd had a few good nights in a row, it wouldn't come to that. That kind of reaction normally happened on night five or six.

'I'm there if you need me,' Gemma added, and Elsie gave her friend a hug.

'I know you are, but let's hope I nod off listening to my audiobook and don't wake up until seven. Besides, aren't you on morning baking duties tomorrow?'

Orla and Gemma swapped shifts in the bakery so one of them was there early while the other took the afternoon shift. It meant they shared the relative lie-ins and later finishes, and both got to look after Scarlett during the day. Gemma's family had relocated to Spain about the same time Elsie's parents had moved away, and with Orla's family still in Poland and none too thrilled at their daughter living in England, they were pretty much on their own. Elsie helped out where she could, but her job meant she couldn't look after Scarlett as much as she'd like. That might be about to change though, she thought sadly. She loved Scarlett but didn't have the same temperament teachers and nannies did for full-time childcare.

'Well,' Gemma said, 'if I'm getting up at five, I might as well get up at three.'

'Only someone who sleeps well all the time would say something like that. To an insomniac that makes no sense at all.'

With a hug, and a wave at Orla, who was making tea in the kitchen, Elsie left and headed next door to her cottage. She could already feel the anxiety washing through her veins and despite her hopes otherwise, the prospect of a long and sleepless night lay before her.

* * *

Most of Meadowbank's residents had never seen the village at two-thirty in the morning. They'd never experienced the quiet that stilled the air and pervaded every inch of the fields. Meadowbank was peaceful during the day, but there were always pockets of activity at the bakery, the butcher's, Annie's Tearoom, or the village shop. People gathered in little groups in the streets, chatting about the goings-on, the weather, and all manner of other things. But at this time of night – or morning if you wanted to be precise – there was a serenity to the land and a strange silence that not many people appreciated. A calmness held the village in a state of suspended animation that, to Elsie, brought with it the idea of how simple life could be if people didn't complicate it all the time. The belief that everything, including our lives, could be decluttered somehow, the same way the village was when night descended and left it bereft of all but the few nocturnal animals that scampered here and there.

As Elsie had thought earlier in the evening, it was a beautiful night with only a slight chill on the breeze. The sky was a deep, dusky black with hints of purple and the blanket of stars overhead glittered as far as the eye could see. Not a single cloud covered the expanse above her. For a time, she thought of Bernard and his celebrities, Winston and his papers, and Patricia and her stories. It had been awful not being able to tell them what was about to happen, and it felt deceitful somehow, but the truth would be out soon enough.

Regardless of her efforts, sleep hadn't come. Her usual bedtime routine had been followed: she'd eased herself into a hot bath, then sat in bed and read a book with a hot drink. Keats had snuggled into her, purring as he curled himself into a ball before she'd sprayed her pillow with lavender sleep spray. But though she felt tired listening to the gentle tones of her audiobook – an old favourite she didn't really listen to at all – she couldn't fall asleep.

After she lay in bed for hours, panic began to mount in her chest. Whenever she closed her eyes, thoughts raced at such a speed she couldn't identify one from another. Half formed and untouchable they merged into a nebula of worry and fear and loss. Before, her worries had been about her friends, the embarrassing things she'd said and done, the constant questioning of herself, but tonight she wondered how those small, petty things could have affected her so much.

As her body had been unable to reach the state of rest it required, she'd felt the adrenalin begin to pump and anxiety take over. It happened so often she could identify every stage of it, though nothing she'd tried had so far stopped it. Hot chocolates, warm milks, the soothing voice of the narrator reading her poetry, and counting sheep had never done anything to quiet her mind. She'd attempted to stay calm, but the time came when lying in bed was only making her more stressed, and she got up and dressed: a walk the best option.

The first time insomnia had gripped her she'd been at university: a lecturer had criticised something she'd said, causing the class to giggle at her embarrassment. Despite Gemma's attempts at making her feel better, by bedtime the humiliation had burrowed so deeply into her brain that she'd been unable to think of anything else and the long night stretched out before her, her mind constantly replaying the moment over and over again. She'd watched the clock tick to every half and full hour with a fear she'd never known before. It hadn't been until 5 a.m. that with shaking hands and unsteady breathing her body finally gave out. Elsie had hoped it had been a one-off, but since then, anytime she was stressed or upset the same thing would happen. Sometimes she'd be awake for only an hour, other times the whole night would go by without a hint of a snooze. It had taken a long time for her to accept that this was simply how she was, but it didn't make it any easier to deal with.

The waters of the duck pond rippled in the breeze as Elsie strolled around it. The ducks were all fast asleep, adding to the quiet. The streetlamps lit the green well, though there were patches of shadows down some of the smaller lanes where the lamps had been placed more randomly. But Elsie knew the land under her feet. Every tree root pushing up through the ground, every uneven paving stone. She followed the path of the stream to the benches that lined the banks by the library, taking a moment to sit and listen to the trickle of the water. She pulled her cardigan around her, enjoying the scent of cherry blossoms in the air, and a yawn overtook her: the first sign that her body might finally be preparing for sleep. Perhaps she should head back home and try again. She had work again tomorrow, and it was going to be tough. How could she watch everyone coming and going, knowing that the place they loved would soon be gone?

Elsie stole a glance behind her at the dark building. How would Bernard check his websites? He didn't have a computer at home and couldn't afford one. They didn't have any internet cafés like big cities had. What would Winston do if he didn't have people to talk to? She couldn't bear the thought of him relapsing into his desperate grief. Yes, the village would call in and look after him, but it was important he got out and about. She thought of his love of *The Times* and wondered if he could afford a newspaper subscription. Even if he could, who would he talk to about the things he read? Who would he do the crossword with? She'd have to call in after work, but where would work be? It was unlikely to be in Meadowbank or even one of the nearest villages. More than likely it would be in Witchbury, where the main council offices were.

And who would she be working with? Karen wasn't an ideal work colleague, but she could imagine a lot worse. At least Karen's love of magazines meant Elsie pottered around doing what she wanted all day. She didn't have anyone micromanaging her. Then there'd be office gossip and school-like cliques. While her colleagues in other council departments did worthwhile jobs, they weren't the types of things she wanted to do. Her natural habitat was to be surrounded by books of all sorts.

And what of all the other people who borrowed books every weekend, who used the reference section to find out about their ancestors, the parents who couldn't afford holidays so helped their children escape through books? So many people needed Meadowbank Library, not the 'alternative provision' elsewhere. But what difference could she make? She was just a shy, frizzy-haired, bespectacled woman who faded into the background. As a memory of the tittering in class came back to her, she knew again she could never speak out in front of everyone. All she could do was try to argue at her meeting tomorrow morning.

It seemed hopeless. It *was* hopeless.

But among the pain, the fire that had sparked earlier came to life again. She pictured herself in the meeting giving them what for. Listing unequivocally all the things that were wrong with the idea.

As another yawn overtook her and something rustled in the long grass of the riverbank, Elsie pushed her fingertips under the lenses of her glasses and rubbed her eyes. She had to at least try to get some sleep in what remained of the night. Those two yawns had been the closest she'd come so far this evening and it was going to be hard enough to control her emotions tomorrow without exhaustion heightening them further. With one last glance down Cherry Lane, at the library she adored, she trudged away.

Chapter 5

For Jacob Yardley, there was nothing exciting about his trip to Meadowbank, though he tried to gather some enthusiasm from the pretty scenery passing him by. After all, Meadowbank Affordable Housing was going to be his first solo development, or so his father said.

Conrad desperately wanted him to take over the construction firm he'd spent his entire adult life building up, but no matter how much Jacob tried to enthuse about the upcoming developments, it wasn't as fulfilling as he'd hoped. In the six years he'd been working with his father, this project had been the closest he'd come to feeling part of something worthwhile. Building top-of-the-range, luxury housing developments didn't interest him at all.

As the pressure his father exerted on Jacob to get involved and learn the business increased year on year, and the well-respected firm grew in reputation (it had to be said, in profit too), Jacob found himself backed into a corner with no choice but to smile and do his father's bidding. He didn't want to let the old man down, which his father had made quite clear would be the case if he didn't at least pretend to enjoy working for Conrad Yardley Construction.

Conrad was still heavily involved in the Meadowbank project

– as he was with everything – but this time Jacob had identified the location and the plot, and worked with the architects to design the housing. He'd hoped that extra level of responsibility would spark some sort of excitement for the trade, but it hadn't. The only thing he did fervently believe in was that every city, town, or village should have affordable housing. So many people had to leave their hometowns – the places they'd been born and raised; where their families and loved ones were – because they couldn't afford to buy there. Of all the projects he'd worked on recently, this one felt the most in-line with his values. Why should house prices rise so that only those from the cities could afford to buy them? People with money. Admittedly, these days that was someone like him. It was ironic: now that he could afford to buy a house in his own small hometown, he had to live in the city as that's where the firm's headquarters were. Jacob steered his sports car through the country lanes, relaxing a little as the warm air glided over him and admiring the idyllic scenes surrounding him. He'd been instructed to drive down to Meadowbank in time for the public meeting tonight, where along with the local council representatives, they'd announce their plans to the village. He'd then be staying to see the whole development through. Jacob couldn't deny getting some distance from his father would be a very nice thing.

Conrad had 'popped down' yesterday to make sure everything was in order with the senior council leaders. He liked doing the schmoozing and last night had confirmed Jacob was to run this one to the end. It had been a big boost to Jacob's confidence, though Conrad's idea of encouragement was to sternly tell him not to fuck it up or he'd never trust him again, but Jacob had learned from a young age to take what he could get from his father.

All thoughts of developments and architects' plans flew from his head as he enjoyed the scenery passing by and the smooth purr of the motor. It was a bit of a cliché for a single man to own a red sports car, but he'd fallen for the cherry-coloured Porsche and as he didn't have anything or anyone else to spend his money on, had treated himself. With the top down, the cool air flowing over him, and the sun on his face, he couldn't help but smile at the beauty of the moment.

He found Meadowbank as captivating as he had the first time. Fields surrounded on all sides. The different shades of grass made a patchwork of green and the afternoon sun bathed everything in a strong golden light. He'd have more than enough time to find his rental cottage and freshen up before the meeting this evening. Though he wouldn't change out of his suit. His father always said a well-cut three-piece suit made a man look powerful and authoritative. Jacob's mood dampened. He wasn't looking forward to it. Either people hated change or loved it. When big building projects were announced views were often extreme, at least in the first instance. After a time, most people got used to it and accepted what was to happen, but he had to get through the first shock of their finding out and rely on the public speaking and body-language training he'd been given over the last few weeks.

Slowing to round a bend, he spotted a few horses cantering across a field on the brow of a hill. Other animals were lazily grazing, and the pace of life relaxed as if time worked differently here. He'd felt it the first time he'd whizzed through the area on his research trip. Jacob's foot eased off the pedal.

As he hit the outskirts of the village, a bright ornamental sign stated the name Meadowbank, and underneath was a pretty picture of a horse and cart loaded with hay. Ahead of it, a farmer in a billowing shirt held the horse's bridle. An immediate sense of calm overcame him and seeing the sign firmed his resolve that everyone should be able to live in the place they grew up because who wouldn't want to live here?

The thatched cottages that lined either side of the road with small picket fences or low flint walls looked homely and sweet. The large green in the centre of the village provided an instant sense of community, just as the duck pond added charm. The warm weather had brought with it an abundance of flowers, including on the cherry trees that lined the riverbank and were in full, beautiful bloom. Even the quaint front gardens blossomed, the aroma perfuming the air.

The only trouble with the tiny lanes that ran off the central village green was that it was difficult to read the road signs. He had the satnav on, but more than once it had led him astray when it came to the countryside. The voice told him to turn left but he wasn't sure whether to follow it, and now he'd missed his turning. With a sigh, he began to drive around the green again but when he looked back up, a duck had waddled directly into his path.

'Shit!'

Jacob turned the wheel, swerving away from the creature and slamming on the brakes. The car veered towards the green, which thankfully was empty, but as he steered back towards the road, someone had appeared in the lane up ahead and was now in his path. He stepped harder on the brake, gripping the steering wheel with white knuckles. The car slowed and he thanked the bright blue sky and whatever being lived beyond it that he'd got the vehicle under control.

Though he'd regained command of his beloved Porsche, the woman in the road had been forced to step backwards, and as she did, she lurched to the side before tumbling to the ground. 'Shit,' he said again, before stopping the car and stepping out, hurrying around to help her. He found her crumpled on the pavement and immediately offered his hand to help her up. 'I'm so sorry. Are you all right?'

Now standing, the woman adjusted her glasses and brushed her hair back from her face. 'Yes, yes. I'm fine.'

The pretty eyes caught his attention as well as the unassuming demeanour. She appeared to be doing her best to be invisible, not meeting his gaze, but something about her struck him.

'The ducks here are very stubborn, aren't they?' he added, hoping to lighten the mood.

'Yes,' she replied with a small laugh. After a shy glance at him, she said, 'They're a law unto themselves in Meadowbank.' A gentle, very delicate flush appeared on the apples of her cheeks.

'I really do apologise.' His hand went to his chest, showing, he hoped, how genuine he was. He'd had some training on how to deal with difficult situations and the body-language consultant had told him to do this when he wanted to emphasise that he truly meant what he said. 'I was trying to find my way and when I looked back from glancing down the lane, a duck had waddled into my path.'

She peeked at him again before dropping her eyes. 'It's okay. Really. I'm absolutely fine. I just turned my ankle on a pothole when I stepped back.' She rubbed her elbow and twisted her arm to look at it. A tear had appeared in the fabric of her shirt.

'I'm afraid I've caused you some damage.' He brightened his tone, and a small smile lifted the corner of her mouth. There was something classical about her face as if she were the paragon of an English rose. He found it incredibly attractive.

'Nothing lasting.'

'I'm happy to replace your shirt. It's really the least I can do.' For some reason, this brought even more of a blush to her cheeks.

'Don't worry, please. It wasn't my favourite, anyway.'

'Can I give you a lift anywhere? Or help you back to your house if you're hurt?'

She looked up at him again and the deep brown of her eyes contained a warmth he'd never experienced before. 'I'm fine. Really. And I don't live far. It's actually easier if I walk.'

'Then, I wonder if I could I ask for your help,' Jacob replied, unable to keep the smile from his face. 'I'm trying to find Pond Cottage. Apparently, it's on Elm Lane but my satnav keeps lying to me about exactly where that is.'

She chuckled. 'It's not this turning, but the next one on and Pond Cottage is about halfway down on the right.'

'Thanks.' He suddenly found himself wanting to stay in her

company and know more about her. She really was very pretty, and her shyness rather endearing. 'I take it you live round here?'

The woman seemed to take a second to answer and he wondered if she was enjoying speaking with him or eyeing up an escape route. After another quick glance up at him she said, 'Yes, I've lived here all my life. It's a beautiful place.'

'It is. That's what drew me here too.'

'Are you on holiday?'

'I wish I was, but no, it's a work thing, unfortunately. I hope to be able to spend some time seeing more of the place though. It really is quite picture-postcard, isn't it?'

Peering around, he could see the library from here. It was just along the green where the village ended and the fields took over. The houses that would take its place facing the river would be the most sought after, he was sure, and they were keeping the name Cherry Lane for one of the streets. It was a gorgeous view, especially when the cherry trees were in full bloom as they were now. The houses further back in the development that would look out over the pastures would sell as well. And no one bothered using libraries these days, did they? Each mobile phone was like a tiny computer and everyone had one. Even his gran did. He did so much work on his he almost didn't need a laptop. And all newspapers were online too. Ebooks were cheap and with so many search engines, forums, and online chat groups he couldn't imagine who would ever walk into a library and ask to borrow a book. A tiny village library like this was probably empty ninety-nine per cent of the time. He was pretty sure that the ayes would far outweigh the nays at tonight's meeting, and as the council had already agreed to the sale, he assumed his biggest problem would be technical questions on square footage, which estate agent they were working with, and when they'd be available.

'Well, I hope you enjoy your time here,' the woman said sweetly.

'Thank you. And I really am sorry about …' He motioned to the ground, then the car. 'You know.'

She smiled and began walking away. 'No problem. Enjoy your stay.'

Jacob glanced at her retreating back as he made his way to the driver's seat, still smiling to himself. He hoped that he'd see her again soon as he was staying in the village. Speaking to her had put him a good mood and chased away thoughts of his father. With a final look at her, he eased off the handbrake, and checked the road for ducks before edging down the small, winding lane that she'd pointed out to him.

Hopefully the rest of the village would be as friendly and if not, he hoped he'd be able to win them over. Plenty of times he'd tried to lead public meetings like this only for his father to step in and start talking over him. Without him here, he'd be able to do it all himself. This project would do only good for Meadowbank's community and for his standing with his father. Yet, as always, the possibility of opposition – of conflict – made his stomach squirm.

After parking the car outside Pond Cottage, a traditional-looking place with wooden shutters, he checked his watch. His father had already warned him not to get to the meeting early. Apparently, the less time they had to shoot questions at you, the better. Jacob couldn't help but cross his fingers that those who disagreed with him wouldn't shout at him too badly. There was something so peaceful about Meadowbank and he hoped to enjoy some of that serenity before heading back to London and the luxury apartments he'd be working on next.

Chapter 6

'Elsie,' Gemma said gently. 'Inching the chairs forward by a centimetre to make sure they're all meticulously in line isn't going to help your nerves, you know.'

'It might.'

They'd been asked to set out a few rows of chairs, with three at the front for Rees-Hale and his cronies, but Elsie knew a few rows wouldn't be enough. As it was, half a dozen people had turned up already and were milling about murderously eyeing the council men and whispering in little groups. Everyone had been asking about the notice and saying they were coming to the meeting. There'd be far more people than Rees-Hale expected.

Elsie tugged down her shirt. At least it hadn't torn open when she fell down in front of that guy. That really gorgeous guy. That really gorgeous guy who'd made her stomach flip. He'd apologised so many times she wondered if he was as nervous as she was. She wished she could be more confident with strangers because then he might have believed her that it was fine, and she knew only too well that Meadowbank ducks were vigilantes. God forbid you should try and move one if it got in your way. You'd end up in A & E missing a toe.

Turning her elbow to study the tear, Elsie realised there was a slight graze, but the skin hadn't broken. She thought again of the man's bright blue eyes and silky voice. He had the calming cadence of an audiobook narrator, and his suit was almost moulded to his body. She normally hated gelled hair, but he'd used just the right amount of product, enough to give a pleasing curl at the front where he'd styled it back. It had been a long time since she'd fancied anyone who wasn't in a costume drama. He'd look quite fetching in a cravat. He was well-spoken too, like he'd had a boarding school education.

'You're really nervous, aren't you?' Gemma asked kindly, given that Elsie hadn't spoken for some time. The only good thing about falling over in front of the stranger was that she'd stopped thinking about the library for a second. She inhaled deeply and nodded, letting go of the breath gradually as if it might help slow the wriggling in her stomach. It didn't. 'I'm not surprised after that complete tit drove his car at you. That's the last thing you needed today.'

'I don't think he was a tit,' Elsie ventured. 'He was nice.'

Gemma glanced at her from the corner of her eye. 'What? *Nice*, nice?'

'Yeah.' Elsie gave a one-shouldered shrug, pretending this wasn't a big deal, and watched Gemma's face pull into a wide grin. She was clearly surprised Elsie had finally shown an interest in someone who was alive and kicking. 'He was … chatty and had kind eyes.'

'Well blow me down. Maybe something nice will come out of this awful day after all. I can't wait to run into him then. Check he's good enough for you.'

An unexpected rill of excitement shot through her. She'd never met anyone she'd *wanted* to stay and talk to like that. Someone who caused her stomach to flutter and her heart to hammer in her chest. 'I don't know how long he's staying for.'

'What did he look like?'

'Tall, handsome … sexy.' She felt herself blush as she said the word.

'*Sexy?* Wow. I don't think you've ever used that word to describe something other than the cover of a book.' Gemma grinned. 'I definitely need to find out who he is. Maybe we can catch him in the pub or something? You could go over and say hi.' Though Elsie loved the idea of being that confident, the thought alarmed her, and Gemma laughed at her terrified expression. 'Or not. You can always just be at the bar at the same time he is. From what you said it sounded like he was enjoying talking to you and might come over as soon as he sees you.'

She liked the thought of that better. Much nicer for him to come over to her than for her to have to speak to him first, even though she had felt more comfortable with him, even on that first meeting, than she had with any other man before. What would they talk about? Would he love books and literature as much as she did? Would he love walking? She could imagine them chatting non-stop covering a million topics and ending the night with a kiss. Something sweet and gentle that brushed her lips and made her want more. The sense of dread that had lingered all day was replaced by a moment of hope but as she glanced again at the clock, it vanished.

Seeing that the meeting was due to start in ten minutes, Elsie felt the apprehension fizz in her stomach. Rees-Hale was prowling around like a hyena, with another man from the council. Karen had pointed him out as another senior manager before she'd begun following them, pretending to tidy. After a few minutes she'd come back to Elsie moaning that they'd not said anything interesting and were instead talking about their cars. Both affected an air of superiority. Neither had ever bothered coming to the tiny village library or seen it in action before making the decision to knock it down. Conrad, the short fat man Elsie remembered from yesterday, was nowhere to be seen and she wondered what his role in all this was.

Rees-Hale had asked her to set up a large easel or A-frame, where he now placed a huge board covered with a sheet and stored a box of papers underneath. Elsie presumed that the board held pictures of the new development and the papers details of who was selling the houses. It was all so horribly real she felt sick.

'I'm just going to get some air,' she said to Gemma before heading to the door.

Not being able to tell anyone had been torture. Through the day people had asked her what was going on and all she could do in response was mumble that they should attend the meeting if they could and make their opinions known. When pressed on what they were going to give their opinion on, she shrugged and ran off to hide in the classics section. Every time one of her favourite people arrived – Bernard, Winston, Patricia – her heart tore a little more knowing the hole that would be left when the library was gone.

In the fresh air, she closed her eyes and enjoyed the feel of the evening sun on her face. The cloudless sky above no doubt meant another pleasant midnight walk for her tonight. She hoped exhaustion would take over once relief that the meeting was done had set in, but she wasn't sure it would. She could easily see herself walking by the duck pond trying desperately to tire her racing mind or ease the heartache tainting her thoughts.

Down the lane, a small army of people led by Bernard and Patricia were ambling towards her. Elsie was pleased to see so many of her neighbours and friends from the village, like Amelia Williams, who'd recently returned to Meadowbank from Paris, and her fiancé, Adam, as well as her old primary school teacher Mrs Bostock. The more people who were here to voice their displeasure, the better.

'Can you tell us what's happening yet, poppet?' asked Winston. He was still limping, but it had been a little less pronounced today.

'Not long to wait,' Elsie replied, her voice resigned but as warm as she could make it. 'Please, come in and have a seat.'

'What happened to your elbow?' asked Patricia.

'Just an accident. Nothing terrible.'

'Are you okay? You look tired. It's bad, isn't it? Whatever this news is. Did it keep you up last night?'

Elsie wished she could unburden herself. 'It did keep me up last night, but not long to wait and you'll know what's going on. I wish I could tell you but—'

'It's fine, darling,' Patricia said, resting a hand on her arm. 'We understand. We all know you would if you could. I'd better get a seat before the front row goes.'

More and more people filed in, including their local historian, the eccentric Mr Hoffelmeyer, and when everyone she thought would attend was there, Elsie stepped away from the door and went to the back of the room. All the seats were taken, and Karen had to actually do some work and find some more chairs for those still arriving. As the room filled, Rees-Hale's face soured. His lips pursed and he glanced down at the box of papers as if worried he wouldn't have enough. Elsie revelled in the I-told-you-so moment, though it was a hollow victory given the foregone conclusion.

At the front, facing the banks of chairs now filled with villagers, were the three chairs Elsie had been asked to set out for the speakers. Only two of those were taken and Elsie wondered who'd be arriving for the third. Probably the man from yesterday with the playdough face and stuck-on moustache. When was he going to arrive though? He was cutting it fine.

Rees-Hale stood up in front of everyone after watching the clock tick to the hour. Among the murmurs and chatter, he cleared his throat, demanding attention and the room quietened.

'Good evening, everyone. Thank you for coming this evening. We'll begin the meeting shortly. We're waiting for one more person to arrive and then we can get started.'

'It's bloody rude if you ask me,' Gemma whispered, joining Elsie at the back of the room. 'Keeping everyone waiting like this.'

'I agree.' Elsie's nerves began to burn in her stomach, morphing into frustration. 'It goes to show how little regard they have for the place, and for us. They have no idea how important the library is to everyone. They've completely underestimated how much we love it.'

Just then a figure came through the doorway and Elsie's mind paused. Her heart, however, had done the opposite and sped up to an almost unbearable rate. It was the handsome man from earlier. She hadn't thought she'd run into him so soon and excitement built in her chest. Maybe he was a book lover too and had come to find some reading material. What would he like? Literary fiction? Thrillers? She couldn't wait to find out. Despite her worries, a genuine smile grew on her face as she moved forwards to explain what was happening, but to her utter surprise, the man went straight to shake hands with Rees-Hale, smiling as if they were friends.

Elsie was vaguely aware of Gemma's concerned glance towards her. 'What's the matter? You've gone all white. Do you need some air?'

'It's him! The bloke from the lane.'

'What? The sexy bloke with the kind eyes?'

Elsie nodded, her mind frozen as it tried to process what it all meant.

'The one who was chatty and sweet?'

'Yes.'

'Fuck.'

'Uh-huh.'

Gemma came closer and gently rubbed Elsie's back, her face clouded with concern. 'Did he say what exactly his work was?'

'No. And I didn't ask because well …' *I got so tongue-tied I could hardly breathe*, she thought ruefully. In the warmth of the room she grew suddenly cold and wrapped her arms around her. She was so stupid for finding him attractive and sweet. Her stomach felt like it was full of boiling water and she about to explode with frustration. Though it was unjust, she felt like she'd been conned, whether by him or her own judgement she didn't know. Had he been extra polite to her in an effort to charm the locals before it all kicked off?

'Right,' said Rees-Hale, projecting his voice across the din. 'We can get started. Thank you again, everyone, for your patience. My name is Gareth Rees-Hale and as the Corporate Director for Regeneration and Economy, I'm here to talk to you about our plans for Meadowbank. I'd also like to introduce my colleague Paul Ryan, who is Corporate Director of Environment and Community, which covers housing.' He seemed to add this bit because despite the enormous job titles, no one really knew what they meant.

From the way the muttering burst into a furore of conjecture, the word 'housing' had rung alarm bells. Elsie's chest tightened as she watched the dismay gathering in the room and glanced at Gemma, who from the flash of her eyes was feeling the same. The other council man shifted in his seat.

'We've come to inform you that Meadowbank Library will shortly be closing as the council has made the decision to sell the land for an affordable housing development.'

The cry of outrage that circled around surprised even Elsie and she couldn't help but be warmed by it. The general ruckus was interspersed by cries of 'What?' and 'Outrageous', and a few swear words were thrown in for good measure from some of the more vociferous members of the community like Lynne Noble. Feeling justified in her outrage, Elsie and Gemma shared a look. They'd both known this would be the response. Patricia and Winston turned to her with sympathetic expressions at the burden she'd had to carry.

'I realise this is a shock,' Rees-Hale said, holding his hands up to encourage everyone to quiet down. 'It's always difficult for us to make these decisions when it comes to removing public services, but we feel very strongly this is the right move to ensure a good economic future for the village of Meadowbank.'

'How many times do you think he rehearsed that speech?'

Gemma asked but Elsie didn't get a chance to reply as he bull-dozed on.

'Mr Jacob Yardley,' Rees-Hale motioned to the handsome man who seemed indifferent to the crowd's reaction, 'is here from Conrad Yardley Construction, which will be building the houses, to explain more about what the new development will look like.'

'Hang on a minute. Do we even need any more housing?' asked Lynne Noble, standing up. Adam, her son, tugged on her arm and she sat down with a loud, 'What? It's a valid question.'

'It definitely is a valid question. It's a very good question,' Rees-Hale replied, in such a politician's voice that Elsie cringed. Knowing Lynne, she'd be throwing something at him before long, possibly a chair. 'And the answer is, undoubtedly, yes, we do. In order to improve the economy and skill retention in the area, we need to ensure that we have a range of housing prices available. Recent research has shown that we only really have houses in the upper price categories that most young people won't be able to reach. We want to encourage people to stay here rather than leave for job opportunities elsewhere thereby retaining skills and improving the economy.'

What did that mean exactly? Elsie wondered. Did improving the economy mean having well-known coffee chains or super-markets? What about the little tearooms and village shop they already had? They'd be destroying one person's livelihood for the convenience of others. Okay, a supermarket might employ more local people, but what of Meredith, who ran the shop? She had a family to support too. Elsie couldn't help but shake her head.

As she did so, her gaze turned to Jacob Yardley and his being related to the construction firm owner made it all seem worse. She'd been so stupid to find him attractive. He was clearly a jackal, and she was reminded of Little Red Riding Hood and the Wolf dressing up in Granny's clothes. All that sweet smiling charm hid a cold, black heart, and he was clearly the yah-yah, boring, yuppy, city, sports-car type. God, she'd been stupid.

Unsurprisingly, Jacob hadn't yet spotted her. Men like that – gorgeous, if evil, men – never did. His face was placid, like he'd seen all this a million times before, which he probably had. How many other lives had he destroyed? she wondered. Fury began to mount at the sight of the firm set of his jaw and the detachment in his eyes, especially as she couldn't stop a voice in her head telling her how attractive he was.

'What about the mother and baby group?' asked one of the mums who attended regularly.

'What about the Mingle and Mutter?' asked Mr Dobbs.

Mrs Dalloway stood up, her tall wiry frame matching that of Rees-Hale even though she was probably ten years older. 'What about our book group?'

Rees-Hale cleared his throat. 'There are similar clubs and outreach programmes run throughout the district at other libraries that are easily accessible.'

'But I don't want to go to another library,' replied Mr Dobbs. 'I can't be getting on a bus to another town every week. I can't go galivanting here, there, and everywhere with my gout.'

'We do offer free bus passes to all those over 60.'

'It's not just about the travel though, is it? It's about the friends I've made here. I don't want to have to start all over again some-where else.'

Elsie's heart almost broke for Mr Dobbs. He was much like Winston, only Winston hadn't quite got to the point where he felt he could attend an organised session to deal with his loneli-ness. For him, the company of those in the library was enough. Mr Dobbs had been one of the founding members of Mingle and Mutter after his wife had died eighteen months previously.

The anger that had been building since yesterday surged into a high, insurmountable peak that burst out of her. This was a travesty. She opened her mouth to speak but her shy nature pulled her back. There were enough outspoken people here; she was sure they'd make the points for her, and probably make them better than she could.

'Well, you could think about it as making new friends,' Rees-Hale replied, in such a condescending manner Elsie's hackles rose even further.

Patronising sod. She took such a deep breath in, even Gemma looked over. She'd hoped filling her lungs might extinguish the flame of anger inside but instead it fanned it, making it stronger.

Suddenly Maria, another one of the mums, stood up. She was a new mum, who'd been at school with Elsie, and her baby, Daisy, was only a few months old. 'I don't think you realise how important things like the baby group are, Mr Rees-Hale. For many of us, they, and this library, are life-savers.'

The way Maria's voice caught piqued Elsie's interest. Maria wasn't the most outspoken person in the world and whenever asked, always said she was absolutely and completely fine. Whereas the other mums would happily admit to being knackered or having sore boobs, Maria's static smile never shifted, and a negative word never left her mouth. She always wore a full face of make-up with perfect hair and though she got on with the other mums, Elsie knew they often felt in awe of her and the way she had everything together. For her to stand up and say something – something that, judging by the tone, was important to her – was a surprise to say the least.

'We have looked at all alternative provision and really believe there is enough elsewhere.'

Maria glanced over her shoulder at Elsie imploringly and Elsie pressed her back against the wall. Could she really, in all good conscience, sit back and let these people's lives be torn apart? A shaft of steel straightened her backbone. If she was going to lose her job anyway, she might as well appease her conscience at the same time. Embarrassment tied her tongue and she struggled to form her thoughts and feelings into words. They swirled in her head like paint colours mixing together and before she could say anything, someone else had started talking.

'When will the library close?' asked Patricia. Her voice was also strained, and Elsie could imagine her close to tears. She angled her head to see but couldn't make her out in the crowd.

Rees-Hale cleared his throat again. With everyone's outbursts he hadn't even been able to unveil his silly board and it sat covered in its sheet. 'The library will close to the public in a month's time, giving everyone a chance to return their books and for preparations to be made. Until then, the construction people will begin work on the land surrounding the library.'

The beautiful green fields that encompassed Elsie's second home would soon be a muddy worksite full of heavy machinery.

Once the library closed to the public, Elsie and Karen would sort out the inside, readying the books to be sent elsewhere or thrown out altogether. She'd sat through the meeting this morning unable to form her objections into coherent sentences among the panic and fear eddying inside her. All the protestations she'd listed in her head had vanished. She'd planned on writing a letter tonight, after this meeting, giving a comprehensive list of objections and arguing against every point they made. Still, she felt slightly ashamed of herself now, like she'd let down all the friends in front of her by not defending them. It was clear that a strongly worded letter would never be enough.

Rees-Hale's announcement was met with more infuriated cries and Elsie's attention was drawn back to the room.

'What about all the historical records and the archaeological finds?' Mr Hoffelmeyer was on his feet now, in his linen suit and bright yellow pocket square.

'They'll be moved to Witchbury.'

'Witchbury?' His high-pitched squeak would have been comical if it wasn't for the utter tragedy they were talking about. 'But that's miles away. We need the records here. The old convalescent home was here! This village dates back to the Bronze Age. Meadowbank records should be in Meadowbank.'

'Hear, hear!' some of the older men shouted, nodding. When

Mr Hoffelmeyer sat down, one of the men who'd called out gave him three heavy pats on the back.

Rees-Hale glanced behind him at the other two men, frustration radiating off him. Then Jacob stood up to address the discontented crowd. He pulled down his suit jacket, his chin lifted. Where Rees-Hale seemed exasperated, he was cool and collected. When his eyes scanned the room and finally rested on Elsie, he gave a double-take, and something strange passed over his face. She wasn't sure what emotion it was, but he was clearly surprised at her being there, but he could never be as surprised and disappointed as she was.

'If I may, Mr Rees-Hale?'

Rees-Hale nodded and went back to his seat, giving Jacob the floor.

'Good evening, everyone. Thank you all for coming tonight and making your opinions known.'

He went to the board and pulled off the sheet with a flourish that only annoyed her more. Heads craned to get a better look at the pictures and the computer-generated re-creations of the new development to be named Spring Court. It sounded horrendous. She had to admit though, the new cottages looked quite sweet even with the red-brick, tiled roofs and fake chimney stacks.

Elsie crossed her arms over her chest. His voice was as calm as the duck pond on one of her midnight walks, and her muscles tightened. He was as much of a politician as Rees-Hale. All that charm and charisma had clearly been him trying not to piss off one of the residents before the meeting. Had he really been sorry for her accident? Had there really been a duck in the road? He was probably lying, trying to cover himself for driving too fast. People like him always did. He must think her a complete idiot.

'As you know, my name is Jacob Yardley and I work for Conrad Yardley Construction. We're one of the top housing development firms, working with some of the country's finest architects to develop affordable housing that seamlessly blends into its surroundings.' He reached out a hand to Rees-Hale, who gave him a wad of papers from the box he'd brought in. Jacob handed the stack to the front row, everyone taking one and passing the rest on like they had at school. 'Let me just share these before I tell you more about Spring Court, our fantastic new development of traditional-style cottages.'

He sounded like he was reciting something from a website and before Elsie knew what had happened, she felt a sort of snapping in her brain, like a rubber band stretched too far, and her feet had taken a step forward. Her voice resounded across the room loud and clear but the words didn't seem to come from her. It was like an out-of-body experience where she was watching herself from above. She had no control.

'This isn't about what you build or how much it blends into the surroundings. This is about you stealing our books! Removing our library and what that means to all of those who use it, which is our entire community.'

No one in Meadowbank had ever heard Elsie raise her voice before, let alone shout across a crowded room. She had the librarian's ability to speak quietly but firmly when needed, which she most certainly was not doing right now. Her voice had come out at such a volume even Gemma was staring wide-eyed, but also proud and supportive. Everyone in the room turned to face her and Elsie felt her cheeks begin to burn as she heard her name muttered. Heat rose from her chest up to her neck, turning her skin redder and redder by the second. She must look like a shouting tomato, but Jacob Yardley needed to realise what he was doing to the people of Meadowbank by taking away one of its most important places.

Jacob's body had stilled but he gathered himself. 'I understand that this is a shock to you all but—'

'A shock?! It's more than that.' Egged on by Patricia's nods, and Winston's and Bernard's encouraging smiles, she continued to speak. So what if she lost her job or wasn't redeployed to a position she didn't even want? She had money in the bank. Not a fortune, but enough for a while. She'd never had anything except books to spend her wages on. If she caved and let down the people she cared most about, she couldn't live with herself. The decision she'd been agonising over had been made and she turned her attention from a stunned-looking Jacob to Rees-Hale.

'Mr Rees-Hale, you can say that all the clubs will be accommodated elsewhere but no one connects with the children the same way Patricia does. I don't care how good the other volunteers are at other libraries, they won't be anywhere near as wonderful as she is. They won't have characters she's knitted herself, and for a lot of the mums – who are already tired and worn out from night feeds – the last thing they need is to have to drive three-quarters of an hour to the nearest library. Which is how far away the nearest one is, by the way. I'm not sure you're aware of that.' Rees-Hale's head moved back fractionally, giving him a double chin. 'And that's those who drive. Some of our mums don't, which means packing up everything their child needs – and for little ones that's a lot – and getting a buggy onto a bus and off again at the other end before walking to the library. Then we have those who come here for company because they're lonely.'

Rees-Hales attempted to interrupt but fuelled by anger that had now materialised in her veins like molten lava, she carried on, not giving an inch. 'Yes, there are other groups like our Mingle and Mutter and Mr Dobbs could go to those but despite the reasons he's already given you for it being a bad idea, what about those who come into the library to be with other people?'

'I don't quite understand what you mean,' said Rees-Hale as she paused for effect.

Of course you don't, she thought but managed not to say that out loud. 'I'm talking about all those who maybe aren't ready to attend something structured. I'm talking about those who come here to use the computer or read the paper, just to chat with someone and see and speak to another human being.' Winston smiled at her, and though he knew she was talking about him, he looked at her with such pride that tears almost formed in her eyes. 'Not everything is black and white, Mr Rees-Hale,' she replied, softening slightly. 'Sometimes people need company and that's one of the most important things the library provides. Not only is it full of books that people love to read, it provides a way for people to connect and support each other. No amount of clubs here, there, and everywhere can replace the love and care that come out of Meadowbank Library. It's not just the books that bring people together here. It's not just a place, Mr Rees-Hale. It's the very heart of our community.'

A round of applause met Elsie's ears. Beside her, Gemma's hands blurred they were moving at such speed. Nearly everyone was clapping. Everyone that was except Rees-Hale, who was positively apoplectic. The other council crone (Elsie had already forgotten the name) sat slightly dazed. Jacob's face had changed to one of unflinching indignation. His mouth had turned into a small, thin line and his blue eyes stared at her so coldly, the temperature of her red-hot cheeks plummeted.

'I understand what you mean, Miss Martin,' Rees-Hale said through a tightened jaw. It was the first time he'd addressed her so formally, which definitely meant she was now out of a job. 'But as I've said, we feel very strongly there is significant and satisfactory provision elsewhere.'

'The thing is—' said Jacob, adding on to Rees-Hale's statement. It was almost as if he knew the council man was floundering.

'Why can't you build on the land next to the library and behind it and leave the library alone?' she insisted, cutting him off.

Jacob paused, re-grouping. 'The simple answer is that we want to build as many houses as possible because this is going to benefit the whole community.'

'That's rubbish,' Elsie replied. From the side of her eye, she could see the shock on everyone's faces that she was speaking out so vehemently. 'It's all about profit.'

'Hear, hear,' Winston and Patricia cried.

'What about us who want the houses?' shouted one man, pointing at the board. It was Mr Smith, who had moved to the area a few years before so was still considered to be a newcomer. Elsie hadn't imagined anyone would ever be in favour of it but was spared saying so as Lynne and the others silenced him in a cacophony of dissent.

Jacob threw a hand into his hair, pushing it back. The gel made it spring forwards again. Maybe he did use too much after all. 'Let me be honest with you all. I always prepare for these sorts of meetings, and I've been taught,' he gave an odd sort of chuckle, like everything he'd been shown was now going out of the window, 'to write a whole speech trying to cover all the possible objections, but I can see from what … Miss Martin, was it?'

Elsie nodded. Even with her face the same colour as a fire engine he still only about remembered her name. *Utter swine.*

'I can see from what Miss Martin has said that any speech I might have prepared will sound rehearsed and I want you to know how seriously I take your objections. Let me be honest, I can see that people love this library and the sense of belonging it gives, but let me ask you this—'

He paused for dramatic effect and Elsie had to admit he had charisma. A way of speaking that was captivating and, she had been right the first time, charming. Already, he was soothing the ire in the room as a mother sings a lullaby to a fractious baby. He had the crowd's attention and some of the faces were softening.

'To the mothers and fathers in this room, how many of you have said goodbye to your children because they couldn't afford to buy a house here?' People looked to each other, and Elsie noticed a shade of doubt in their eyes. 'How many of you with young children are going to face the prospect of that when your children grow up? What I'm proposing is not just so some people can buy houses now. What I'm proposing will benefit Meadowbank's community well into the future. This is for your children and your children's children. So you can sit and watch your grand-children grow up, get married, and have kids of their own in the same village as you.'

He emphasised the last part of the sentence by thrusting a fisted hand into his palm. This struck a chord with the attend-ants from the baby and toddler group and Elsie felt her grip on the situation loosening. She had to do something.

'But what about those who love to read but can't afford books?' she shouted again. Jacob paused and as she adjusted her glasses.

'I find that hard to believe,' he said with another laugh. Elsie felt her hands clench at the insulting tone. 'Ebooks are so cheap these days and they can be read on tablets, phones, computers. And you're probably going to say to me, what about newspapers?' His eyes ran over the crowd as if he'd already clocked who was likely to be a newspaper reader. 'I read *The Times* every day on my phone while I'm having breakfast.' She shot a glance to Winston at the mention of his favourite newspaper and though she was sure he didn't agree with Jacob, the idea of it surprised him. 'And what about the children who come in to do homework? Because I can see you've thought of everything, Miss Martin.'

Fury burned within her and for the first time since seeing his handsome face she wanted to smack him and upset his overly gelled hairdo.

'Every phone is like a tiny computer these days and I'm sure there isn't a person here who doesn't have a decent mobile phone. Every teenager has one with internet access so they can do their homework and play games and talk to their friends. Schools have banks of computers, and every possible provision is made. And even if that wasn't enough, as Mr Rees-Hale says, there are other libraries where people can go.'

For the first time he stared directly at her, and Elsie instinctively crossed her arms over her chest to protect herself. His eyes met hers, a distant echo of the softness she'd seen before. She raised her chin, unwilling to let him win.

'You talk about these clubs and groups that you run,' he continued, pacing gently around the space between him and the crowd. 'Let me ask you this, couldn't you, instead of going all the way to a different library to attend a club to ease loneliness – which, in my opinion, is a fantastic idea. I mean, who of us doesn't get lonely at times? – couldn't you instead invite these people into your homes?' A murmur flew around the room and Elsie could see the shame on people's faces that they hadn't done that before. She wanted to tell them that they hadn't done anything wrong, but Jacob was pulling on their heartstrings. 'If you know who attends these clubs and who is feeling a little isolated, why don't you invite them round for a cup of tea? Can't the members of the book group take turns to host and everyone else bring the wine and cheese? To those of you who attend the mother and baby groups, what about taking it in turns to host in your own homes?'

'Because my house is a mess?' shouted Gemma from beside Elsie.

Though it made her smile, Elsie couldn't think of how to rebuff the points he was making and the effect it was having on the crowd was even more disconcerting.

'Isn't everyone's?' Jacob countered and a small ripple of laughter ebbed around the room. 'If you hold it in each other's homes, there's no danger of running out of nappies or baby milk or tea for the mums.'

'Black coffee more like,' one answered.

'Or vodka,' another announced.

'Hey,' Jacob replied, smiling widely, 'however you get through the day.'

Again, he laughed, dipping his eyes as he brushed a hand through his hair. Having a handsome face didn't mean you had a handsome heart or a kind soul. He was an actor through and through. Elsie was absolutely raging. Did he think he was James Dean or something?

'I know you don't know me, but please believe me when I assure you that we've done copious amounts of research before choosing this location. We don't build houses willy-nilly—'

Elsie found herself speaking again. The words slipping from her mouth as soon as they formed in her brain. 'So we should be thankful that you've chosen our tiny village to build in?'

'In a way, you should.'

The bloody cheek! How far up his own backside could one man get?

'I really, truly believe that building some beautifully designed, affordable housing that will benefit this wonderful little village not only now, but in the future as well, is the right thing to do. I believe it's the only thing to do to make sure this village doesn't shrink and wither and get left behind the rest of the world. Building will make your community stronger and ensure families can stay together where their children were born and raised.'

The only relief Elsie could take as she stared around the room and Jacob returned to his seat was that he hadn't received a round of applause like she had, but it was a small and pointless victory. Her heart sank as she saw the village she'd grown up in confused and torn between her view and his. Some of the things he said had merit but that didn't mean they had to tear down the library. Why couldn't they build elsewhere? She was just about to open her mouth to continue the discussion when Rees-Hale got to his feet.

'I think we'll leave it there. Copies of the plans will be available here at the library for the next few weeks and do please take a handout. It contains a useful FAQ. Good evening.'

As soon as everyone began to gather their things and chatter filled the room, Rees-Hale marched over to Elsie. Karen, who had been standing at the back but had edged away as soon as Elsie began her tirade, also came over. 'If you could please close the library as soon as everyone has left. I'd give them ten minutes to get out and then tell them it's time to go. Miss Martin?' He turned to Elsie, pinning her with angry eyes but lowering his voice to a harsh whisper. 'You'll receive a letter informing you of disciplinary action over the next few days. I had thought I'd made it perfectly clear that as council employees you're expected to support the council's plans. What you did this evening was completely inappropriate. I'm afraid you've given me no choice but to take action.'

Elsie tried to speak but her brain had run out of steam. She nodded, tears springing to her eyes. She hadn't so much as nailed her colours to the mast as climbed up and wrapped herself around it and there was no going back now. From the bursts of conversation that floated towards her she could see some were still fully on her side while others were edging more towards Jacob's. Patricia was trying to calm two men who were squaring up to each other and two of the mums were at odds about whose house Toddler Toe Taps should be held in first.

Elsie had never seen the village like this and the thought that she'd made a fool of herself in front of everyone for nothing was galling, if not downright painful.

Jacob was gathering his things ready to leave. Did he know what he'd done to the village? To her? He probably had no idea. She'd never felt a rage like it: a guttural instinct to protect the thing she loved, as a mother protects a child. He'd come in, destroyed everything, and would leave again soon enough. As he neared the door he glanced back at her, his expression unreadable. He probably wasn't even looking at her, just eyeing up the square footage, sizing up the work involved in demolishing the place she loved so dearly. She could honestly say she'd never hated anyone as much as she hated him. Why did the only man she'd felt an attraction to in years have to be the worst person she'd ever met?

Chapter 7

When Jacob exited the library, he cast a hand over his forehead and wiped the thin veil of moisture that had begun to form at his temples. Wandering to the bench by the riverbank he loosened his tie, pulling the knot down as low as possible and unfastening the top button of his shirt. Though he imagined, or at least hoped, his father would have congratulated him on handling the indignation of the crowd, Elsie Martin had made him sweat.

Elsie Martin. So that was her name. He said it again in his head, enjoying the old-fashioned sound. It suited her, and from the depth of her eyes, she had what his mother would have called an old soul. Though she hadn't looked at him kindly once she'd known who he was. She'd looked at him like she wanted to tie him to a stake and set fire to him and his plans.

Why did she have to work here of all places? Why couldn't she have worked at the cute bakery just across from the green he'd spied on his way in. It was impossible to say exactly what it was about this woman that had piqued his interest so quickly, but he hadn't been attracted to someone like this for a long time. It didn't matter though. Whatever it was, she despised him now.

Normally, his detachment stayed in place throughout the myriad objections that always came up, but there was something about the way she spoke that had threatened to tug on his heart-strings and derail everything. If his father's expectations hadn't been weighing so heavily on him, he might have agreed with her. From the crowd's reaction there was clearly something in what she said. Luckily, he'd won some people over, but not her.

The villagers began to file out, mostly in pairs and small groups, chatting away, and it suddenly struck him that no one was on their own. Everyone was walking with someone, eagerly discussing the news. Had Elsie been exaggerating about some individuals' loneliness? It didn't look like anyone could be lonely from the scene before him and he felt justified for his suggestion that neighbours could always support others who were feeling isolated. That was the case now, right before his eyes, as everyone spoke to their neighbours, seeing what they thought of the matter. As they went past him, some tutted and cast cold stares his way, whispering things like 'should be ashamed of himself'. Others, who he assumed supported his plans, nodded and flashed small smiles. At the end of the meeting, the discussion that had broken out had been a fifty-fifty split. Given Elsie Martin's opposition, it was better than expected.

'Thank you for coming,' said Rees-Hale, holding out his hand. Jacob took it and gave it a firm shake. 'I apologise for Miss Martin. I'd expect a member of library staff to act better. She'll be facing disciplinary action for arguing as she did today. All council staff are expected to toe the party line, whether or not they agree.' He tutted.

Alarm bells began to sound in Jacob's head. While he wasn't exactly thrilled she'd tried to derail him, it didn't seem fair she might lose her job over it. 'Is that really nec—'

'I'm afraid it is absolutely necessary,' Rees-Hale barked. A clear warning not to interfere in matters that weren't any of his business. 'I apologise, Mr Yardley. I'm shocked, that's all. I'd never have thought she had it in her, to be honest. She's always been quite a shy, mousey little thing. Every time she's had to speak in front of anyone, she's always turned bright red and clammed up. I really can't get over it.'

Rees-Hale's disparaging description annoyed him. Elsie had spoken with such passion nearly everyone was swept along by the tide of her response. While there'd been a fire in her speech, there'd been an eloquence too, and it had brought colour to her cheeks in a rather attractive way. He had to shake off these thoughts though. It was clear that even if he did run into her again, they wouldn't be chatting about places to visit. He still couldn't believe that she was diametrically opposed to him.

If he hadn't met her before and seen her shyness for himself, he'd never have believed she could be like that. To see her shouting at him from across the room, like Boudicea directing her army, had been quite something. Frustration had flooded within him, but he'd soon realised that she was speaking from the heart and that she believed completely in what she said. It was admirable. He wasn't used to reactions like those. Often there were some heat-of-the-moment responses, but they died down quickly. Most people made one argument and that was it. The way she'd kept going was astounding. Even with all of that though, Jacob was sure he had nothing to worry about.

'Let's not be hasty, Mr Rees-Hale,' he began, feeling the need to try again. 'It's a stressful time for everyone and it must have been a shock for her. I think we won everyone over in the end, and even those who weren't one hundred per cent on our side have been given something to think about.'

Jacob glanced over his shoulder. He could see Elsie inside the library moving chairs around, placing them back where they belonged. The apples of her cheeks were still red as she talked with others who had stayed behind. He couldn't help but admire that she'd carried on despite her evident embarrassment. When he'd first started having to speak to large groups the same had happened to him. It was only with practice, and his father's shouting at him to stop it, that he'd broken the habit.

'Well,' said Rees-Hale, with a slight nod of his head. 'I'll be off, and I'd suggest you do the same before Miss Martin comes out.' He stepped away, then spun back. 'If she does say anything to you, I'd appreciate you telling me straight away. I need to know of any and all breaches of the council's code of conduct.'

Rees-Hale marched away, meeting with the other council man who had stayed silent throughout like a heavy attached to a mob boss. Jacob began walking towards the village green. After a few minutes he heard Elsie's voice again as she chatted with the dark-haired lady who'd been standing at the back with her. He checked over his shoulder to see which direction she was walking in and slowed as she came his way. For a second, he thought about saying something but the frosty glare forced him backwards. If looks could kill … In seconds she'd strode past him and didn't bother looking back.

After all that, he quite fancied a drink in the pub. It looked inviting with the flower baskets hanging outside but seeing that a lot of the villagers were headed in there, it was probably best to stay away. There was no point in inviting trouble.

As much as he tried, he couldn't stop seeing the sheer look of desolation in Elsie's brown eyes. Their toffee colour had been magnified by the lenses of her glasses and when she'd stared at him, defying his words, urging him to make a better point, he'd felt something stir deep inside. Jacob reminded himself of all his friends moving away from the village they'd all grown up in because they couldn't afford to live there. He'd missed them all as one by one they'd drifted away. No matter what Elsie Martin said, he was right in what he was doing. The next generation of Meadowbank villagers needed this housing, and more importantly his father would never speak to him again if he messed this up.

Jacob drew his mind back to his plans for the evening, contemplating a quiet night in, maybe a run, when his phone rang. He reached into the inside pocket of his suit jacket and pulled it out.

It was his father. He should have known his father would call as soon as he thought the meeting was done. As Jacob carried on his way, passing the green now and nearing Elm Lane, he swiped to answer. 'Father.'

'How did it go? I take it we're not going to have any problems?'

'I don't think so,' Jacob replied confidently. For all Elsie Martin's vocal rebuttal, she wasn't likely to do anything more than she had in the meeting. That's all most people did. They bluffed and blustered but then all the frustration faded away. There might be one or two threats – from family solicitors and such like – but even those rarely came to anything. No, as far as he was concerned, everything would be going ahead with no problems, and he told his father as much.

'You say there were one or two objections? What were they?'

'Some were worried about the services they were going to lose—'

'That's for Rees-Hale to sort out,' his father barked, cutting him off before he could say the very same thing. 'What else?'

'Some talked about what a hub the place is for the community. How it helps people who are lonely and isolated—'

'Bah! Again, Rees-Hale can deal with that. They've chosen to sell the land. Those concerns are for him and the rest of his council minions to assuage. I hope you let him deal with them? I know how you like to try and make everyone your friend. You didn't get involved, did you?'

Thinking how Elsie had threatened the success of the meeting, forcing him to speak when he should have sat back and let Rees-Hale carry on, Jacob mumbled a noncommittal response. 'Rees-Hale did very well.'

'Good. Good. Now that the meeting's done, we can sign the contracts tomorrow. For once I can say congratulations on a job well done. So tomorrow you're meeting with Francis and Dominic, yes?'

Francis was the architect and Dominic the foreman for the

building work. Sometimes, Jacob had the feeling his father would have quite happily swapped Dominic for him. Dom loved his job and he and his father could talk about all things digging, draining, and dimensions for hours. They often did, leaving Jacob stood there like a spare prick at a wedding, smiling and nodding and laughing at jokes he didn't find particularly amusing. It wasn't that he didn't have a sense of humour. He did. You just had to really love construction for some of their jokes to be funny. More than once he'd been made to feel inferior for being slow to remember all the jargon and understand the complexities of actually building houses. Though the buildings went up quickly enough, most people underestimated the sheer amount of work involved beforehand.

'Yes, tomorrow at nine,' he answered.

'Good. Listen to Dom. He knows what he's doing. And Francis, obviously. Update me afterwards. I'll be off now.'

Jacob was about to ask him to say goodnight to his mother when his father hung up. It was with relief that the meeting was over and no one else had cursed him that he got to the cottage door and opened it. A sense of peace enveloped him immediately on crossing the worn step of the threshold. The small front garden was blooming with plants, and floral notes carried inside through the unlatched windows. He took a deep breath and immediately loosened his tie. His suitcase remained in the hall as he hadn't had the time to unpack before. Well, he had, but instead he'd lain on the sofa, his feet dangling over the end, and he'd closed his eyes and thought of Elsie Martin's smile.

After they parted in the street, he'd hoped he'd run into her again but hadn't anticipated it being quite like this. Now he hoped he'd see her as little as possible. He still didn't like the idea of her losing her job. He didn't like turning people's lives upside down, but progress had to be made.

Feeling slightly jittery, as he always did after speaking with his father, and from the tension of the meeting, he wandered around.

The small galley-style kitchen was well designed, and the living room comfortable and cosy. A small bookcase in the alcove drew his attention and he stepped towards it, scanning the titles. A book of poetry caught his eye. He hadn't read any since university but oh, how he'd loved it then. When he'd first started studying, he'd hoped to be a scholar: an academic studying literature and writing papers, but his father had made it clear that he'd indulge his wish to study English on the proviso that he joined the firm as soon as he was done. Backed into a corner by the family row that would follow if he refused, Jacob had agreed.

He sat on the sofa, properly this time, and began thumbing through the pages of the book, but his mind kept flying back to Elsie Martin and everything she'd said in the meeting. The way the crowd had reacted to her was incredible. She was obviously well thought of in the village. Guilt began to creep in, but he pushed it down. For the first time in years, he'd had some praise from his father and Jacob stiffened his resolve to make this development a success. Progress had to be made and it was exactly what Meadowbank needed, whether Elsie Martin agreed with him or not.

Chapter 8

'Are you trying to lock your door with a hairbrush?' asked Gemma, from the small gate at the end of the path.

'It looks like it,' Elsie replied with a wry smile before using it for its intended purpose and brushing her hair back from her face. She hadn't realised she'd grabbed it, rather than her keys, from the small table in the hall.

It had been another difficult night's sleep and though she'd had a few hours at the start and end of the night, the middle had involved stressful tossing and turning as her mind raged between the things she'd said and the things Jacob Yardley had responded with. His voice had sounded in her head: the calm cadence she'd found so attractive when she'd first met him tempting her to find the good in him. *Snap out of it!* she chided herself. She had to think about something else, but this morning, racked with tiredness, concentrating on anything proved difficult and her mind wandered like Frodo Baggins on his way to Mordor.

'Does that mean you've locked yourself out again?'

Elsie spun, held the brush in her mouth, and patted down the pockets of her trousers. She removed the brush from between her teeth. 'Umm, yep, think so.'

With a teasing roll of the eye, Gemma opened the gate and

walked to the front door, pulling out her own set of keys. This wasn't the first time she'd accidentally locked herself out and to be perfectly honest, it happened with more regularity than it should for a grown woman. Considering Elsie could recite classic poetry by heart and name some of the greatest first lines in literature, it wasn't entirely her fault. Her brain was clouded with fog and worked in slow motion, though she knew that after a strong coffee, the insomnia-ridden haziness would wear off a bit.

The thought of going to work brought with it the reminder of all she was about to lose, and her heart crumpled. She wouldn't be going to work for much longer because not only had she completely lost her temper yesterday actually shouting across a room full of people (she felt a slight swelling of pride at this as well as astonishment) but she'd also set herself up for the sack. From the way Rees-Hale's voice had grated as he'd said the words, there was no way she'd be coming off with a warning or a slap on the wrist. She'd gone too far for that.

Gemma had been proud but surprised at Elsie's reaction and to be perfectly honest, she'd astounded herself too. Never before had a fire raged within her so fiercely. Never before had she believed in something so fervently it had overridden her sensible brain, and no matter what the future held she was proud of herself. She regretted nothing. Everything she said was true. She hadn't embellished facts or exaggerated. She'd spoken honestly, if somewhat angrily.

Gemma opened the front door, reached inside to the small table in the hall and picked up Elsie's keys, handing them to her before taking the brush and closing the door again. 'Right, shall we get to work? I'm on baking duty this morning.'

Elsie nodded and they waved at the two faces peering at them through the next-door window. Orla and Scarlett, with their matching white-blonde hair, were smiling back, Scarlett's gummy smile seeing them off on their day was a ritual Elsie took comfort in. She'd always enjoyed routine. The prospect of losing the one she'd become so accustomed to sent her shivering and she ran her finger over the edge of the key to focus on a different sensation.

'So,' said Gemma as they exited the small garden gate and began the short walk to the library. 'I take it you had another bad one last night?'

Elsie nodded and let out a sigh. Her eyes were burning and puffy this morning and looked bruised from the heavy shadows. 'It was bad, but not as bad as I was expecting. I don't know if that's because I'm resigned to my fate or because in a way, I'm quite proud of myself.'

'You should be, you were brilliant,' Gemma said, bumping shoulders with her. 'It was like fireworks had gone off inside you.'

'Because I went so red, you mean?' she asked defensively.

'No!' Gemma looked horrified and Elsie reprimanded herself. Gemma wouldn't tease her like that. It was tiredness making her prickly, and she rolled her shoulders back to remind herself to calm down. 'Because you were shining in that room. You light up when you talk about the things you're passionate about, and when you spoke last night it was like you'd come alive. Honestly.'

'Don't be silly,' she replied, unconvinced, but the tone of her voice carried a hint of a question as well.

'It's true. Whatever happens now, you did yourself proud. And the village. And you showed that awful bloody Jacob Yardley what for.'

'It's not going to change anything though, is it?' Elsie's shoulder's slumped and she tried to cheer herself by listening to the birdsong and gazing at the clear blue sky above.

'Why not? It might.' Gemma wasn't a natural optimist, so her reply startled her.

'The deal's going through today. They're not going to change their plans because one red-faced, frizzy-haired lunatic started shouting at them in a meeting.' They strode along the far edge of the village green opposite the ducks paddling lazily on the pond.

'What do you think the village will be like with more people in it?' Elsie asked, trying to picture it in her mind.

Gemma shrugged. 'I don't know really. Busier, I suppose. Fuller.'

'I'm not sure how I feel about that.'

'Me neither.'

'Morning,' Meredith, who ran the village shop, called out.

Gemma and Elsie paused by her side. She was stocking up the wicker baskets that sat outside the shop containing local seasonal produce. They were full of gorgeous tiny new potatoes, crying out to be boiled and coated in butter. Elsie felt her stomach grumble and realised she hadn't had breakfast in her sleepy fug.

'I heard about the meeting,' Meredith said. 'I couldn't manage to get there with the kids, but I heard you stood up for all of us, Elsie. Well done.'

'Thanks.'

'So …' Her eyes were bright and keen. 'What's the next step?'

'The next step?' Elsie's forehead knitted in confusion. Suddenly the shroud of tiredness began to fall away, and her mind sprang to life.

'Yeah.' Meredith gave a forceful nod. 'I assumed you had some sort of plan. I think everyone did after you spoke last night, being that you don't normally – you're not normally – umm—'

'Gobby like me?' asked Gemma, helping her out.

'Yes,' she replied with a grin. 'At least, that's the consensus from those who've stopped in to get their papers this morning. Have you seen anything of that Mr Yardley?'

Elsie felt something akin to indigestion at his name. 'Not since the meeting.'

'Probably hiding out. I don't know how Mr Hawthorne can rent his cottage to him knowing what he's going to do to the place.'

Gemma nodded, then gave her watch a double-take. 'Oh crumbs, I'd better get on. We'll be opening soon.'

They bid Meredith goodbye and carried on their way, only to see Mr Dobbs walking towards the shops. 'I've run out of marmalade,' he said cheerily, as they passed, then paused by Elsie's side, resting a hand on her shoulder in a fatherly fashion. 'I'm so proud of you, Elsie. What a wonderful display of community spirit.'

'Thanks, Mr Dobbs.'

'When does phase two begin?'

Oh lord. What had she started? She hadn't thought beyond getting through yesterday intact and now everyone was hailing her as some protest leader. She wasn't a librarian version of Joan of Arc for everyone to follow. She was probably the least charismatic person she knew. And what more could they do anyway?

But as she opened her mouth to speak, the seed of an idea planted in Elsie's brain. She could start a petition; surely that was the next logical step in all of this. Elsie didn't want to risk instant dismissal, which would definitely happen if Rees-Hale found out she was still not towing the party line, but if the petition was at the bakery, that would solve all her problems. This time, the sensible part of her brain took over and she chose not to say anything until she'd thought it all through carefully. Very carefully. After yesterday, she didn't want to do anything until she'd considered all the options and possible consequences.

'I'm not really sure there will be phase two,' she said, keeping her voice casual.

Mr Dobbs frowned. 'Oh. I think we all assumed you were leading the charge.'

Sensing her hesitation and, she hoped, her fear, Gemma added, 'If there is, you'll be the first to know, Mr Dobbs. We need to have a think about what would be best though.'

Edging away, they were near their usual parting spot when Elsie urgently whispered, 'What have I done, Gem?'

'You've really started something.'

'But I can't! I'm just … just … me! What can I possibly do? If the deal's gone through and the decision's already been made, then nothing I say can make a difference.'

'I don't think that's true,' Gemma replied calmly. 'Like you said last night, those fields are huge. They could build houses on the land behind the library and to the side of it. They'd get loads in there without actually having to knock the library down. The council wants to because then it's one fewer building they have to pay for and two fewer salaries.'

Elsie yanked back her hair, tying it up using the band she'd noticed wrapped around her wrist. On edge and fidgety she rocked from one foot to another. She needed her mind sharp to get through this awful thing and decide what her future was going to look like so she either had to find a way to function while her body was tired or get her insomnia under control once and for all. 'Honestly, all it comes down to is money.' She crossed her arms over her chest then released them immediately, hating the pressure it added to her chest.

Slowly, her thoughts and ideas began to gather momentum. She'd find another job no matter what happened. She didn't know where that would be or what it would look like and she might have to leave the village to find it, but she'd survive. There was a whole world beyond the Meadowbank sign, and more and more she wanted to get out there and see what it looked like. She'd been to Bath and York on holidays with Gemma and Orla (mostly dreaming she was in an Austen or Brontë novel), but many a time she'd planned to go somewhere only to chicken out, staying here and playing it safe. Maybe now was the time to make a change: to break the boundaries she'd placed on herself and step outside the small but wonderful world of Meadowbank she'd inadvertently trapped herself in.

Could she really just stop after last night and go through the motions until the library closed? When she thought of what a difference she could make if she won, the same fire that had burned last night ignited again. From what Meredith and Mr Dobbs said, it didn't sound like it would be just her if she did choose to fight.

'Are you going to be okay?' Gemma asked and Elsie nodded distractedly. 'Then I need to head off, but I'll catch up with you tonight. Don't do anything I wouldn't do!'

Gemma squeezed her tight in a massive hug and then rushed away while Elsie strolled towards the library. The short distance from home had given her a lot to think about. She needed coffee first though. Pulling out her keys she opened the library doors and stepped through. She never bothered to lock them behind her. People knew when the library opened and even if they did turn up early whoever it was would chat while she worked. There was never any danger something bad would happen. Up until recently bad things didn't happen in Meadowbank.

As Elsie stood in the shade of the doorway, staring at the perfect little world she'd inhabited for the last five years, she wondered how anyone could entertain the thoughts that idiot Jacob Yardley had. How could anyone think the low price of ebooks meant people didn't need to borrow actual books? Some people couldn't afford even the lowest price ebooks, Bella's giving tree at Christmas had shown them all that, and some preferred paperbacks to reading on a screen anyway. There was nothing like holding a book in your hands. Yes, newspapers could be read online these days, but that didn't mean people didn't like to buy them as well. And what about those parents who couldn't afford to have fancy mobile phones for their children or computers at home? How were those children supposed to study? Jacob had mentioned schools but the tiny primary school off the village green couldn't afford to keep fixing computers and Elsie was sure other schools would be the same. And then there were the parents who simply couldn't afford to go on day trips all the time during the summer holidays and loved coming to the library and taking part in the activities they organised. He hadn't thought of those, had he?

Suddenly the petition idea didn't seem like a bad one. It wasn't likely to make the situation any worse because how much worse could it get? If she was sneaky enough, she'd get away with it. A steely resolve tensed her muscles, bringing them to life, and she checked her watch. Marching to the desk she switched on the computer, furtively checking the door for Karen's arrival. Luckily, Karen was running late again today. There was also the threat of Rees-Hale turning up with her disciplinary letter, but she imagined he had better things to do first thing in the morning. He'd probably get someone else to write it and post it anyway. That sort of grunt work was most likely beneath him.

Once the screen had flickered to life, she quickly designed a petition and ran it over to the bakery, furtively checking that nobody had seen her.

Gemma had just finished serving a customer when Elsie arrived, clutching it to her chest.

'Hello, you. What are you doing here? I didn't think I'd see you till lunchtime.'

Though she was unlikely to see Jacob or Rees-Hale there, Elsie couldn't stop checking around her. She waited until the customer had left, knowing more would follow soon and her window of opportunity was small. 'I've brought a petition for people to sign. I thought if it was here, I couldn't get blamed for it. Is that okay?' She placed the papers on the counter. She'd even brought a pen. Technically it was stealing as it belonged to the library. She really was turning into a rebel.

'Who are you and what have you done with the real Elsie?' Gemma's tone was teasing but Elsie could tell Gemma was overjoyed she was taking action.

'All I have to do is direct people here, which they're probably coming to anyway. Rees-Hale need never know I started it. As long as I can act natural, that is.' It was going to be a challenge for someone who wasn't a natural rule-breaker, but she'd do her best. She was talking quickly, excited and a little flustered. 'I can't believe I'm actually doing this.'

The person who'd been sleep-walking through life was

suddenly awake and Elsie couldn't deny the exhilaration pushing to the fore amidst the muddle of fear and dread that swamped her body and mind.

Gemma scanned the papers and moved the petition from the corner of the counter, where Elsie had placed it, to the middle. No one would miss it there. 'You're sure?' she asked, raising her eyebrows slightly.

After a deep breath, Elsie nodded. 'Let's do this.'

Chapter 9

After a fairly normal start shelving books, racking that day's newspapers, and helping people to check out their new finds, Elsie noticed things had begun to change. Winston came and sat in his usual seat as did Bernard, but the atmosphere was loaded with a tension that had never existed before. Elsie couldn't stop moving, still jittery and flustered, sure she was going to be found out for placing the petition in the bakery.

'So what of this closure, Elsie?' Bernard said, reading about the spotting of Dwayne 'The Rock' Johnson in the small village of Great Snoring. 'I don't have a computer at home. How will I keep up with the news?'

'It is a shame, Bernard, isn't it?'

Winston flicked down the top of his newspaper. 'You did us proud last night, Elsie. Very proud indeed. Nice to see you speaking up a bit.'

'Thank you.' Secretly pleased at the compliments she'd received she dropped her eyes.

From her seat at the desk, Karen cleared her throat and gave Elsie the stink eye as though Elsie's outpouring had tainted her by association.

'But what are we going to do now?' Winston folded the paper

down to a more manageable size. 'I dread to think what will happen once the library's closed.'

Elsie leaned in and whispered, 'If you wanted to, there's a petition to sign over at Gemma's bakery.'

'Is there?' Winston shouted, causing Karen to look up again. He lowered his voice. 'When did you do that?'

'This morning.'

'All part of the plan, was it?' He tapped the side of his nose as if they were keeping a secret.

'Not really.' Elsie took the seat next to Winston and Bernard spun around in his chair to listen. Her normal duties could wait. There were more important things to do now. 'To be honest, I don't know what came over me last night, but I guess I love this place too much to let it go without a fight.'

'Well, we're very proud of you,' Winston replied, keeping his voice low. Elsie glanced at Karen, who was absorbed in another magazine. 'I'll head on over to Gemma's when I'm finished here. Good girl, Elsie. We'll show them, won't we?' The flash of life that warmed his face lit her heart. 'I take it old stick-in-the-mud doesn't know?' He motioned towards Karen.

'No, she doesn't, and to be honest, I think we should keep it that way or she'll report me to Rees-Hale and it'll be instant dismissal.'

'Your secret's safe with us,' Bernard murmured and as Karen stared at her again, she went about her daily tasks as if everything was fine.

The rest of the morning was spent having similar conversations. Amid her work, Elsie surreptitiously directed people to Gemma's bakery while attempting to look nonchalant. If anyone took one of Rees-Hale's printouts from the pile on the desk and showed a hint of disapproval, Elsie swept in and let them know about the petition. At one point she thought Karen might have been catching on, but Elsie was able to distract her by passing on the gossip that Jacob Yardley was renting a cottage from Mr Hawthorne and Karen immediately launched into a tirade about the ton of photocopying she'd been forced to do for him the other week.

'I wouldn't mind a piece of that action though,' she said lasciviously about Jacob.

Her initial feelings about him threatened to rise again so Elsie beat a hasty retreat to the poetry section. It always calmed her down and she ran her finger over the spines, thinking of her favourite verses. She loved Emily Dickinson and Christina Rossetti the most. A bit of Wordsworth too. Despite herself, she was reminded again of her and Jacob's first meeting. The way he'd helped her up and smiled at her. The feel of her hand in his and his voice. She shook the thought away and ran through all he'd said last night. *Bloody hateful man*. Wanting to close a library meant he had something seriously wrong with him.

'Hi, Elsie,' Maria said, pushing her buggy towards the parenting section. Her make-up was intact as usual and her hair perfect. Elsie eyed the long strands of her own frizzy hair and wondered how Maria did it when she had a baby to look after as well.

'Hi, Maria.' Elsie kept her voice at its normal tone but thought again of what she'd said last night and her concern for Maria grew. 'How are you today?'

'Fine. Absolutely and completely fine.'

Edging closer, Elsie said, 'Thank you for speaking up last night. I really appreciate your support.'

'And we appreciate yours. I don't think people realise how lonely it can be being a mum. For some people,' she added quickly, brushing off the comment as if it didn't apply to her, but Elsie had seen the sadness that had dulled her eyes. Maria turned back to the shelf and searched the titles.

'Can I help you with anything? Are you looking for something in particular?'

'No, no, that's fine.'

'Are you sure?' Elsie ensured her voice was even, calm.

'Oh, umm—' Maria began to rock the buggy where Daisy was

fast asleep. 'I just thought I'd read up on babies and what they do at this age.'

'Oh, right.' Elsie moved to the same bookcase and pulled a book down before handing it to Maria. 'I know a lot of the mums who come to Toe Taps have read this book and recommend it.'

'Have they?' She seemed startled that other mums were reading these sorts of reference books and examined the cover. It was one that detailed what your child should be doing at different ages.

'Yes. It's one of the most popular ones we have. Was there a specific thing you wanted to know? We've got books on teething, motor skills, helping your child learn.'

'No, no. This'll be great, thanks. I'm just curious, you know.'

'I think that's perfectly natural and sometimes reading books is better than going online. The internet isn't always that helpful. There's almost too much information—'

'And some of it's quite scary.' Maria's eyebrows drew together before she caught herself and plastered on the smile that to Elsie had the feel of a mask about it. 'Okay, I'll take this one. Thanks.'

Maria left to check it out and Elsie carried on with her work. There was definitely something going on that Maria didn't want to talk about. She'd always been a private person and it wasn't in Elsie's nature to pry but she didn't want her suffering or worrying alone. Perhaps she should talk to Patricia. She had a way with people and elicited confidences without even trying.

The clock above the door ticked on to twelve and Elsie finished her last job of the morning before going for lunch. Rather than sit on the bench outside and watch the river roll by as she normally would on such a beautiful day, she headed to Gemma's to see how many signatures had been gathered. She hoped for sheets full and her stomach muscles tightened with every step towards the bakery.

As usual, it was busy with lunchtime trade and Elsie had to squeeze through to speak to Gemma, who was stood behind the glass counter. The aromas coming from the large ovens at the back were mouth-wateringly good and Elsie's stomach rumbled again. She'd completely missed breakfast. At least it meant she could treat herself to something from the trays and baskets in front of her.

Protected by the glass were the freshly baked farmhouse and sourdough loaves, and pretzels and bagels. Elsie remembered the first time Mr Dobbs had seen the large New York–style pretzels. He'd been suspicious of them, never having had one before, and Orla had cut one up for him to try. He'd been won over by the chewy dough and hit of sea salt and had also fallen for Orla's chleb pszenny; a type of Polish wheat bread that tasted divine. At the side of the counter were wicker baskets full of golden crusty baguettes and Elsie could imagine one of those with some of the ripe, juicy tomatoes from the village shop. She could even add some Italian mozzarella from the deli too. Her stomach rumbled.

The bakery was tiny but had room for a couple of small tables, each big enough to seat two people, near the wide window. They were nearly always occupied as theirs was the only place you could get Orla's amazing sweets, including the delicious apple and cinnamon szarlotkas that Elsie was quite partial to.

'How many signatures have we got?' Elsie asked anxiously, before eyeing up a warm pretzel and szarlotka for her lunch. She might even add one of Gemma's enormous chocolate chip cookies to keep her energy levels up.

Gemma gave a wry smile and checked her watch. 'You're thirty seconds later than I thought you'd be. What kept you?'

'I had to sidestep a duck,' she teased, not realising that the mention would bring Jacob Yardley back to mind, and the version of him that had been nice, rather than evil. Thinking of him she was suddenly aware of the strength of her heartbeat. 'So, tell me, how many have we got?'

As Gemma glanced at the list, Elsie congratulated herself on having the foresight to number the rows. Gemma took the petition from a woman who had signed it and flicked though the pages. 'Just over forty.'

'Is that all?' Elsie's heart fell. There was no way that was enough to make a difference. She didn't know how many it would take but she was sure forty or so was short of the mark. They'd probably need all the village to sign it.

Gemma chuckled. 'Elsie, calm down. It's only been there for a few hours and not everyone has heard the news yet. There's loads of time for people to come and sign.'

'You're right. What's the feedback been so far?' Elsie pushed her hands into the pockets of her trousers.

'Most people are keen to sign. I had a few who said they thought there should be some more housing, but I had to serve them quickly and get them out before a fight broke out. It was Mr Applebaum, who has those 20-year-old twin boys, so I'm guessing he sees Jacob Yardley's point of view and doesn't want them to have to move away.'

'What do you mean a fight nearly broke out?' Elsie squeaked. 'You are exaggerating, aren't you?'

'I wish I was. Mrs Dalloway was in getting her usual pastries and you saw how she was last night. Both she and Mr Applebaum had quite firm views. She'd bought a baguette and was squeezing it so hard I'm surprised it didn't have fingerprints in it by the end.'

'Gosh. Are you sure you don't mind having it here?'

'Of course not. Did you want any lunch while you're here? I noticed you didn't bring anything with you this morning.'

Elsie nodded at her friend. 'Can I have a—'

Gemma reached behind her to a large brown paper bag and handed it over the counter. Elsie opened it and a smile spread over her face. A pretzel studded with crystals of sea salt, a szarlotka, and a huge chocolate chip cookie sat inside. Closing the bag up again, she thanked Gemma. 'You read my mind.'

'I could tell it was a chocolate chip cookie kind of day.'

As a family entered, the children pressing their noses against the glass and asking for some of Orla's delicious-looking kremówka, a cake like a mille-feuille, Elsie waved and made her way out. As she left, she heard Gemma asking if they'd heard the news about the library and would like to sign the petition. Thankfully, they were quick to, and Elsie went back to work feeling hopeful, yet still a little perturbed.

It was only natural that there would be different views in the village, but it was disturbing to think that her neighbours were actually arguing with each other. Hopefully, it was a one-off as both Mrs Dalloway and Mr Applebaum were known to be quite forceful when they had an opinion on something.

Resting on the bench, she watched Meadowbank River trickle by, the taste of the pretzel cheering her up as she ate. Being hungry always affected her mood. The amount of sugar in the szarlotka and cookie should see her through the afternoon. The gentle movements of the water relaxed her worries over the disagreement Gemma had mentioned. Mrs Dalloway wasn't backwards in coming forwards and once she'd even caused a ruckus in the book club because she was so unyielding in her opinions. It was just her way. Finishing her lunch, Elsie enjoyed the warm sun on her face before she headed back inside.

Her goodwill vanished when, on entering, she spotted Jacob and Rees-Hale talking in the corner where pictures of the new development were displayed. The way they were snooping around the place, deciding its worth in pounds and pence and not seeing beyond the money signs annoyed her. As the burst of anger increased, and Rees-Hale noticed she'd arrived, he began moving towards her. With a shot of fear, Elsie realised what he was here for.

'Ah, Miss Martin.' His hand slipped inside the pocket of his jacket and pulled out an envelope. The label that had been stuck to it had her name printed formally and her full address, testament to the seriousness of its contents. 'As I was coming to the library, I decided to deliver this in person. As I said last night, I'm afraid you've given us no option but to instigate disciplinary action. Here's a letter outlining the grounds on which we've done so and the next steps. It's a shame, but there it is.'

Jacob had been lingering around the poetry section and for some reason it felt like he'd invaded her space, as if he'd tramped into her house uninvited. She was aware of his eyes on her as Rees-Hale spoke and made an effort not to look at him. He was probably congratulating himself that she was being punished for speaking against him. Was he just pretending to look at the books to see her get a bollocking? If so, why was he running his hands over the spines as Elsie always did?

'Right,' Elsie replied, forcing herself to take the letter, holding her fingers rigid so he wouldn't see them shake.

After giving her another disapproving look, Rees-Hale marched out of the library, leaving Jacob behind. He moved out of her sightline, but then his head poked around the side of a stack, like a turtle coming out of its shell. Elsie ignored him and turned her back before opening the letter, steeling herself not to be surprised at its contents. At least Karen wasn't there to watch her. She'd disappeared to her office for lunch as soon as Elsie had returned to the building.

Now her fingers were relaxed, they trembled slightly. There was to be an investigation first. Well, that wouldn't take long, considering there were about fifty witnesses who saw her spouting off last night and it's not like they could confuse her with anyone else as she was the only one with a face as red as a raspberry. Still, she supposed there were procedures to follow and at least it bought her a little more time. She doubted anyone who'd seen her at school would have imagined her ending up in this position; being disciplined for arguing with her boss. She could hardly believe it herself.

Jacob appeared in her peripheral vision, and she thrust the letter back into the envelope and tucked it under the keyboard.

'Miss Martin?'

She took a deep breath in before making eye contact. She wanted to stomp away and ignore him but couldn't bring herself to be that rude again. Even to him. 'Can I help you with something, Mr Yardley?'

Her harsh tone had taken him off-guard, but he couldn't expect her to be the same with him as she was with Winston or Patricia. For a start she liked them, and she certainly did not like Jacob Yardley. 'I – umm – I wanted to say that I'm sorry. Really sorry, that you're now – umm …'

His voice faded into thin air but the time the sentence remained unfinished merely fuelled her anger even more. 'What?'

'Well …' He pointed at the letter then placed his hand over his heart, as he'd done in the street. 'Facing that.'

Just being around him seemed to trigger some sort of dormant rage within her and as at the meeting last night, his words had provoked her before she could control herself. 'Why do you keep doing that?'

'What?'

'That?' She pointed to his hand where he'd pressed it to his heart.

'Well, I wanted you to know that—'

'That you're glad I'm going to lose my job? Because I am, you know. Going to lose my job. Either by your design or the council's I'll be out in a month, or sooner if they decide to sack me for speaking up for this place. Why press your hand to your heart like bloody Napoleon? Is it supposed to show that you deeply mean what you say? That your sentiments are heartfelt? Because it doesn't work. It just makes you look like a really hammy actor.'

Jacob opened his mouth to speak, clearly surprised at her response, but stumbled over his words. 'I wanted you to know that I mean it.' After a second, he rucked a hand through his hair and then rested it on his hip, pushing back the tails of his suit jacket – another one that looked more like a second skin, clinging to his body – revealing a taut shirt-clad stomach. She drew her eyes up. His gaze could be unnervingly piercing and the implacable mask came down again.

'Look, I know you dislike me, and I am sorry, but this place needs housing. I think the last house that was built here was probably in about 1883 or something. Whether you believe me or not, new, *affordable*' – he emphasised the word, too much in Elsie's opinion – 'housing needs building and this is the best location. The fields are flatter here. I don't believe anyone should face something like this for saying what they think is true but—'

What they think is true? The patronising arse.

'But neither is it my fault, Miss Martin. You chose to speak out against your employer's warning.'

How did he know she'd been warned not to speak?

'The sale was finalised today,' he continued. 'And all documents signed. I'm afraid there really isn't anything more you can do.' The fire that had blazed inside him seemed to fade a little as his eyes travelled over her face. 'Good afternoon.'

He walked past her, leaving the scent of his aftershave on the air, expensive but not altogether unpleasant. Lemony with the warmth of something woody. On another man it might be an attractive feature but on a complete and utter philistine it stank.

Elsie put the fierce beating of her heart down to her temper and the heat of their exchange. Gritting her teeth, she straightened her arms to release the tension within them. 'There's nothing more I can do?' she whispered to herself, turning to see the envelope on the desk once more. 'Mr Yardley, I haven't even started yet.'

Chapter 10

Jacob left the library, his heart pounding. He shouldn't have gone over and apologised to her. If his father found out, he'd see it as weakness and at best call him an idiot, or at worst, swoop in to take over the project. It hadn't even done any good. To be honest, that body-language coach needed sacking. And then he'd have put another person out of a job. Guilt prickled the back of his neck.

Why couldn't he be doing something he loved? If he had his way, he'd be doing something for charity. He should have just said no to his father's wish for him to join the firm all those years ago. He'd pretended he wasn't signing himself up for a life of doing his father's bidding, but deep down he'd known he was. He'd always thought there'd be time to get out, but it never arrived. Something about Meadowbank was making him question if it was all worth it. He'd felt a strange sense of calm in the library and had enjoyed looking at the extensive collection. There'd been a number of books he'd fancied and the urge to hold one in his hands had been stronger than ever before, probably because he didn't get a chance to go into bookshops anymore. Feeling disloyal, he shook the thought away, not wanting to be a hypocrite. The quiet peace of the place was getting to him, that was all.

He'd woken up this morning to the sound of birdsong. It had

almost been too loud as the birds hopped from tree to tree right outside his window, but he'd enjoyed the tranquillity he'd felt for the first time in years. It had been a wonderful way to start the day rather than early morning site meetings. Then his father had called. Jacob hadn't even dressed yet, but Conrad wanted to double-check some of the housing designs Jacob had worked on with Francis, questioning some of the decisions Jacob had made, even though he'd already vetoed a lot of them. It was some sort of a test and as usual, he'd failed. Especially as it had been a video call and he'd hastily thrown on a shirt and tie and made sure the camera didn't go lower than his waist because he hadn't had time to get his trousers on.

Now, Elsie Martin had reminded him of the human cost to progress and he'd bungled the apology quite spectacularly. He walked to a bench by the library and sat down, watching the gentle flow of Meadowbank River. Down the way, he could see some of the ducks paddling along from the main pond by the green, and the sun dappled through the cherry trees that were in full bloom. Whenever he saw them on leafy streets, cherry blossoms lasted for only a few days before the wind blew them all off, but here in Meadowbank they seemed to be living longer. It could be the unseasonably warm weather and the lack of wind, but a sort of magic permeated the air here. He'd felt it the first time he came. His father hadn't noticed it and had laughed when Jacob had mentioned it.

'Jacob!' A woman's voice called from the other side of the green. She waved at him, and his spirits fell further. *Leah.* What on earth was she doing here? She'd started in the firm as his father's assistant but had soon been promoted to junior project manager. She was a rising star in the company. Intelligent, good with clients, focused. His father clearly didn't trust him to run this project no matter what he'd told him only days ago. Jacob waited as she dragged a large, impractical suitcase, with a smaller one nestled on top, down the lane. He would have offered to help but she was already stopping in front of him. 'So this is the site, is it? Good choice. I've seen it in photos of course, but nothing quite matches seeing it in person, does it?'

'Leah, what are you doing here? I wasn't expecting you.'

'Your father sent me down.'

'Father?' Among the shock, he could picture his father's face as he told Leah to come and 'support' him. 'When?'

'He rang me last night telling me to get the first train down this morning. I had to get a cab from the station though. I've no idea where my cottage is. It's in Flower Lane or something ridiculously twee like that.'

'Right. And how long are you here for?'

'For the duration of the project of course.'

Jacob felt himself shrinking like Alice in Wonderland. His father always managed to make him feel small. Leah had a knack of doing it too. His father really didn't trust him to run the project on his own after all. But why? Perhaps Rees-Hale had said something to his father. It would hurt his already bruised pride too much to ask Leah the reasons his father had given. On the other hand, the support would be quite useful. He couldn't deny she was brilliant at her job, destined for great things.

'This place is a bit chocolate box, isn't it?' Leah said, removing her sunglasses. She had on tight, well-cut black trousers that ended at her calves and shiny black high heels. A bright red shirt was the only splash of colour under a black suit jacket. Her expensively dyed blonde hair was fastened in a long ponytail with not a strand out of place. 'Good idea to build here. I can see the units selling quickly.' He'd have said 'idyllic' rather than 'chocolate box'. Whether she intended to or not, she managed to make it sound like an insult.

'Right. I'd better get to my cottage.' She swiped at her phone, finding the directions. She twisted on the spot, turning this way and that until she was facing the direction Google Maps told her, and began to march ahead, pulling her case behind her. 'Shall we have a debrief about the meeting once I've settled in? It won't take me long. I just need to freshen up and check some emails.'

'Yeah, sure.' Jacob kept his voice light, determined not to give away his disappointment. 'I'm pretty sure it's this way.'

Leah began to walk off, then paused, clearly expecting Jacob to take her bags for her. He did, because his mother had always taught him to be a gentleman but as he turned, he spotted Elsie Martin at the door of the library. Her arms were crossed in front of her. It was clear she was watching them and yet again, a feeling of guilt at what he was doing to her hit him in the chest.

'We're being watched,' Leah said, pointing directly at Elsie. Elsie spun on the spot and darted back inside the library. 'Who was that frizzy-haired woman?'

Why was her bag so heavy? What did she have in here? He hefted it along the bobbly lane. 'She's the librarian here so, obviously, she's not very happy at the plans.'

Was frizzy the right way to describe Elsie's hair? Maybe that was the technical term for it, but he preferred untamed.

'Well, she'll have to get over it, won't she? It's not exactly the end of the world.'

Jacob thought Leah sounded like his father: cold and uncaring. Would that happen to him one day if he continued to work for Yardley Construction? Would he become like Conrad, only interested in profits? A sinking feeling settled in his stomach, and he ignored the thought. It was too scary to contemplate.

* * *

Jacob walked Leah to her cottage and waited while she called the lady she was renting from. As soon as the woman was on her way with the keys, which would take all of about two minutes in a place as small as this, Jacob made his escape. He had work to do on the project and his father would expect another update at the end of the day.

He had just got himself a cup of tea and settled down at the pine kitchen table when a frantic knock at the door forced him to get up again. The knocking continued, incessant and expectant, as he unhooked the old-fashioned latch before turning a handle further down.

'They wouldn't let me stay!' Leah wailed, in a mixture of anger and dismay. 'Can you bloody believe it?' She marched inside the cottage, suitcase in tow.

'What did they say?' He stepped back to let her in. What else could he do? He couldn't leave her outside. 'Was there a problem with the cottage? A leak or something?'

Leaving the suitcase just inside the doorstep, she thrust her hands onto her hips. 'It was all absolutely fine until she asked me if I was here for a holiday and I said no, work, and she asked me if I was with Yardley Construction or the council and as soon as I said yes, she went ballistic. The old crone said if I was only here to close their lovely library and ruin their lovely village I could, and I quote, sling my bloody hook. Can you believe it?'

'No,' he replied with a shake of the head. He hadn't thought it was this bad. The reaction was more than worrying. A rush of unease shot into the base of his skull, pounding at his brain like a hammer. Though there'd been dissent at the meeting, he'd expected it to blow over quickly. Those type of meetings were full of anger that never materialised into action. But this was different, this was the rental of a holiday let. Didn't they want the money?

'It's insane,' Leah muttered, making her way towards the kitchen. 'Who does something like that? I mean, we paid and everything. And when I told her I'd already paid in full, she said she'd refund the money immediately because she didn't want my type staying in her cottage. I mean honestly … my type? What does that even mean? Young and successful?' She turned to face Jacob. 'I'm going to have to stay here with you.'

'What?' He spun to face her.

'I haven't got time to faff around finding alternative accommodation and this place has two bedrooms. I remember. I might as well stay here, and it saves a little bit more money. Better to keep costs as low as possible in case of an emergency or delay to the build. To be honest, we might have to see how things are tomorrow and update your father.'

The idea of that sent an icy chill down his spine. He needed to keep a firm hold on this situation and not let it get out of hand. If Leah went to his father, he wasn't sure what kind of light he'd be painted in. She was ambitious, a workaholic, and even when she wasn't trying, she made him feel small.

Jacob wasn't sure what was most unnerving, the fact that Leah was staying in the same cottage as him, or that feelings were running higher in the village than he'd imagined. 'Who were we renting these places off?' he asked.

Leah opened her handbag and pulled out her phone. She swiped and tapped at the screen before speaking. 'Yours is rented from a Mr Hawthorne and mine is owned by a Mrs Dalloway.'

'Let's hope Mr Hawthorne doesn't decide to kick me out as well. Okay, we'll see how people are with us tomorrow and if they're okay, I think it's still worth you seeing if there's somewhere else you can say. I'm sure you'll want your privacy too and we could be here a while. Look at back-ups too, in case I'm kicked out as well. There must be a hotel nearby or something.'

'I've already thought of that,' she said without looking up from her phone, as she was now answering emails, typing furiously.

The last thing he wanted was to be in such an intimate position as sharing a house with Leah. The last person he'd lived with had been his ex, Allegra, and perhaps that had been their downfall.

Like some old-fashioned novel, both their parents had wanted them to get together – Allegra's parents were established landed gentry and the perfect in-laws for his socially ambitious father – but it had only been when she'd come back from abroad, five years ago, that they finally had. She'd been working in Italy for a year, teaching English as a foreign language, and she'd changed a lot during that time. On her return, he'd been swept along by her beauty (and a generous shove from his mother and father). She'd no longer been the girl he'd grown up with, and, he was sure, the subtle pressure from her parents had played a part in her falling for him.

But, eighteen months ago, Jacob had decided enough was enough. It was clear they were more friends than lovers and though it had been an amicable parting for them, the news hadn't been taken well by his father. Jacob had recovered quickly enough after the split, as had Allegra, as they both acknowledged they'd been pushed together by their parents. His father, however, still treated him like it was a bitter blow to his, and his son's, prospects. Why did he always work so hard for his father's approval when it was never given?

Jacob's heart hadn't stirred once since. Until his chance encounter with Elsie, that is.

'I wasn't sure what would be happening about food so organised a delivery to my cottage. Luckily, I've been able to divert it to here after a bit of screaming and shouting. I had no idea if there'd even be a shop. I see now there is but it probably only stocks that awful cheap brand you get from cash and carries. Anyway, I've got a few meals from Gennaro's in town. There's more than enough for both of us.'

He had to admire her organisation skills, even though they were vaguely terrifying. He hadn't even thought about what he'd eat tonight. Given Mrs Dalloway's behaviour, there was every chance the village shop might refuse to serve him. He tried to dislodge the treacherous thoughts. Had he completely misread the room yesterday? Had he underestimated the strength of feeling in the village from those who agreed with Elsie? A sinking feeling told him perhaps he had.

Elsie's words had stirred up a whole load of trouble and now he had to deal with the consequences. As much as he was drawn to her, if she hadn't been there, everything would have been fine. He was sure he'd have been able to win them all over. Elsie had whipped the world of Meadowbank into more of a frenzy than he'd given her credit for. Would he ever have imagined the woman who wanted to melt into the background contained such a fire? A glimpse into her eyes – her pretty, almond-shaped eyes – last night had told him there was a strong character there, but all this? If the circumstances had been different, he'd have found that incredibly attractive. He had to forget the effect she'd had on him and treat her as the enemy because if he wasn't careful, Elsie's outburst would ruin his one chance to prove himself to his father and get him off his back. For a while at least.

He'd have to deal with it tomorrow – first thing – that and finding Leah another place to stay. He wasn't quite sure how yet. All he knew was that he had to make sure his father did not find out. Of course if he did tell his dad, he'd be down in an instant and though Jacob wouldn't be allowed to forget the disappointment he'd caused, he couldn't imagine Elsie standing up to the likes of Conrad Yardley. If Jacob himself had never quite managed it, there was no way in hell Elsie Martin could.

Chapter 11

As soon as Gemma opened the door, Elsie marched through, carrying Keats who was slightly confused at his change of location. She hadn't realised she was still holding him, having first gone to her own cottage, but she simply had to talk to Gemma and Orla about her latest exchange with Jacob bloody Yardley. 'That absolute, complete and utter—'

'Shhhh!' Gemma and Orla replied in unison, pressing their fingers to their lips.

Elsie closed her mouth and grinned. Baby Scarlett was falling asleep in Orla's arms. She looked so peaceful with her eyes closed and her tiny pink mouth sucking on the dummy that pulled rhythmically in and out. Orla stopped rocking, but as soon as she did Scarlett's face wrinkled, preparing to cry, and Orla immediately started again. Elsie found the motion soothing and without realising it, had begun to copy her. Keats stared at her with an incredulous expression until he decided he wasn't impressed and fidgeted to be put down. He ran out of the open back door, no doubt to go back through the cat flap and into his own home.

'She's only just gone off,' whispered Gemma. Her angular face always softened somehow when she spoke of her daughter. 'Every time we put her down, she starts crying. She's so tired I know if we can get her to sleep, she'll go through the night. It's just getting her off properly. Every time we've tried, she cries as soon as we take our arms out from under her.'

'Teething?' Elsie asked. She had no idea if it would be teething. She didn't know very much about babies. All she knew was that children Scarlett's age did teethe and made a mental note to recommend *Tiny Teeth and Easing Earache*, which one of the mums had mentioned.

'Think so,' Gemma replied tenderly.

Scarlett's face had softened again, the peachy skin smoothing out, and Orla made her way upstairs, moving slowly and carefully so as not to wake the beautiful sleeping baby. Scarlett's fine blonde hair splayed out in tiny threads over Orla's pale arm.

Elsie was reminded of a poem by Emily Dickinson, 'The Child's Faith Is New'. Scarlett's innocence was written all over her peaceful face. In the poem, the child lost its naivety and grew up to be cynical. She hoped Scarlett wouldn't be liked that.

People had always assumed Elsie was naive because she was a shy bookworm and no fun because she liked poetry. But they were people who didn't know her. People who didn't realise that after a few glasses of wine, and it had to be after a few glasses of wine because she couldn't even think of it before then, she loved nothing more than singing and dancing around the living room with her friends. She could belt out a pretty good rendition of 'Independent Woman' (her love of Beyoncé ran deep) with Gemma and Orla either at home or in the pub and last Christmas Eve had been a fine example. Nearly everyone in the village went to the pub on Christmas Eve and as soon as last orders were called, a singsong would start to delay being kicked out until the very last minute. At that time of year, they normally sang Christmas carols and went home only when Dean turned the lights out and they had to fumble away in the dark.

Okay, she'd never been one to go to Ibiza or one of those holiday destinations full of bars, but that was because she was terrified of flying, not because she didn't know how to have fun. Only people who didn't know the real her thought she was boring. Cynical people who only ever judged a book by its cover. People like Rees-Hale and Jacob Yardley.

Every time Elsie thought of Jacob her stomach knotted with anger and frustration. At least, she assumed it was anger. It couldn't be attraction because since the public meeting, and their run-in this afternoon, she'd promised herself she'd never be attracted to him again. The connection she'd felt the day they'd met would fade soon enough, and in fact, it was disappearing already to be replaced with a sharp, stinging irritation.

Only once Orla carefully laid Scarlett in her cot, Elsie began to speak. Keeping her voice down was going to be difficult given how much she'd stewed on it all afternoon.

'Jacob Yardley is the most insincere, rude, evil man I've ever met,' Elsie started. Gemma picked up a bottle of wine, showing the label to Elsie. 'No, thanks. I'll stick to tea tonight. My brain's fuggy enough without adding alcohol into the mix.' As Elsie's anger abated slightly from the peace of the cottage and the knowledge that she was surrounded by friends, she took off her glasses and rubbed her eyes. 'I desperately need a good night's sleep, but you go ahead if you like.'

'Nah, I'm all right with tea as well, but what's happened now?'

Elsie told her about seeing Jacob at the library after she'd had her disciplinary letter hand-delivered by the even more evil (perhaps 'demonic' was a better word) Rees-Hale. 'Jacob acted like it was all over and I should accept it and run off home like a good little girl. And that's after he gave me a lecture on afford-able housing. Bloody sanctimonious … urgh!' She balled her fists. 'He's so irritating.'

Elsie moved to the sofa and flopped down as Orla descended the stairs in her pink fluffy rabbit slippers and took the tea offered by Gemma. Gemma then set a cup in front of Elsie on the small coffee table in the living room.

'And now some woman has turned up who's clearly his girl-friend.' *Not that I care*, thought Elsie, though she didn't say anything out loud. If that was the type of woman he went for – someone toned and … well dressed – then that was down to him.

'She's not his girlfriend,' said Gemma, knowingly. 'She's another project manager.'

'How do you know that?' For some reason that fact made Elsie feel a tiny bit better, then it was swallowed up by annoyance and anger. 'I don't care.'

'Yes, you do. Apparently, Mrs Dalloway had unknowingly rented her other cottage to this woman who also works for Yardley Construction. When she went to meet her and give her the keys, she threw her out as soon as she said who she worked for!'

'No!' Elsie's eyes were wide, but all she could do was look between Gemma and Orla. 'Where is she staying then?'

'With him. If you ask me though, there's something going on there.'

'Gemma,' Orla said softly.

'What?'

Orla nodded towards Elsie.

'It's fine,' Elsie said, though inside she was reeling. 'So he's knocking off his secretary as well as knocking down our library?' Swirling scorn tied a knot in Elsie's stomach. She disliked him intently.

'There were a few arguments in the bakery today,' Orla said. 'I didn't want to say anything earlier, but I can see a bit what this man is saying about housing.'

Gemma turned full-on to face her. 'How can you say that?'

Despite it being a warm evening with nothing but the gentle breeze blowing in through the open window, the room grew chillier.

'I just think that when Scarlett grows up, we may want her to stay in the village and she cannot live with us forever. She'll need her own house and how will she afford one? Where would she live? There are only the old cottages and farmhouses that are too expensive. If they are designed nicely, some new housing might not be such a bad thing.'

'I can't believe you're siding with them,' Gemma said, turning away slightly. She'd always been good at flying off the handle.

'I'm not siding with anyone, but I think it's true.' Orla reached out and put a hand over Gemma's. Elsie watched their fingers intertwine but could tell from Gemma's face she was annoyed. 'It took us so long to save up for this house to buy your parents out, didn't it? Not everyone will be as lucky as us. I can see why Mr Applebaum got upset earlier today. And having more people in the village could be good for business, but I'm not saying they should knock down the library.'

'Is that why you weren't asking everyone to sign the petition?' Elsie didn't know if Gemma was aware of how accusatory her tone was, and shifted in her seat. She'd never seen Gemma and Orla fight and hated being witness to it now. Should she say something?

'No,' Orla replied calmly, ignoring Gemma. Orla understood her as well as Elsie did and knew she would cool down in a moment. 'That was because I was busy trying to serve and cook. Sometimes I forgot.'

'He still doesn't have to knock down the library,' Gemma grumbled.

Elsie decided to cut in before the disagreement escalated further. 'The point is, he thought he was doing me a favour by telling me to leave things alone but all he's done is made me more determined to save the library. No matter what the cost. I understand what you're saying, Orla,' she added diplomatically. 'And it's hard to disagree with some of it, but then, as Gemma said, they could build behind the library or next to it. They don't actually have to knock it down.'

'What about your job?' Gemma asked, unclasping her hand from Orla's and wrapping it around her cup. Pain shot over Orla's face, but Gemma didn't seem to notice and may not even have realised how it came across. Elsie made a mental note to mention it to her. 'You're already on thin ice with Rees-Hale. If he finds out you're doing more, he could suspend you or sack you on the spot.'

'I've been thinking about that all afternoon. There are some things I can do while I'm working there and if I get sacked, then I actually have the freedom to do more.'

'Like what?'

'For a start, I want to organise a big author event straight away. There's that woman who lives outside Meadowbank who's a best-seller: Neve Chapstone. The recluse. She writes lovely romances with down-to-earth heroines, and readers love her. We've been trying to get her to do an author talk for ages, but she's always been too busy. Plus, she's notoriously shy and never does these sorts of things.'

'Never?' Gemma asked.

'Never, but it's worth a shot now, don't you think? If I can get loads of people to come, maybe even the local papers, and casually drop in that the library is closing, they might run something, which could cause an uproar.'

'Good idea,' Orla replied, and her enthusiasm warmed the cold atmosphere in the room. 'You could embarrass them into changing their minds.'

'Exactly.'

'I like the idea too,' said Gemma, taking Orla's hand once more, the slight tension forgotten. 'But that's going to take a bit of time to organise and what makes you think she'll say yes this time?'

'All authors love libraries!' Elsie said. 'Plus, she's just had a new book out. Her latest book came out yesterday, so the timing is perfect and wouldn't look suspicious. We just need her to agree.' Gemma's gaze sharpened and Elsie wondered what she'd said. 'What?'

'It won't look suspicious?' She and Orla giggled and the last drops of pressure in the room dissipated.

'It might not.'

'It will look *totally* suspicious, Elsie. Rees-Hale's not an idiot, and that Jacob might be a lot of things but a fool he is not. You'll have to pretend it was in the pipeline but unconfirmed or something.'

'Okay.' Elsie nodded to herself. 'That's probably a better idea.' She knew what a bad liar she was, but saying it was something they were thinking about but hadn't confirmed yet wouldn't be a total lie. And if telling a little white lie helped her to achieve her ends then so be it. There was no way Karen would ruin it either because she had no idea what Elsie was up to half the time. Her annual appraisals and monthly one-to-ones were mainly spent with Elsie listening to Karen moan about her love life. 'I'll have to interview her. That's how these things normally work.'

'You'll be brilliant,' said Orla, as terror spread over Elsie's face. But she'd have to do it. She had no choice.

'In a way, I wish Rees-Hale had sacked me on the spot. It would mean I could do what I liked, but then I think it might be better to stay on the inside for as long as possible so I can hear what's going on. Right now, if they want to have site meetings, we've been told to let them use Karen's office, which means I can earwig.'

'Elsie Martin, what's happened to you?' Gemma asked with widened eyes. 'Where's this new mischievous version come from?'

She felt her cheeks colouring.

'You tease too much, Gemma,' Orla said, standing up to make another cup of tea. 'She has always been there, she just never had something to fight for before. Do you remember when Winston and Bernard fell out over that celebrity he said he spotted in Little Thrumpton? Elsie was like the United Nations brokering peace.'

'Well, now she's more like an MI5 spy sneaking around. If you get the sack and keep kicking up a fuss, Rees-Hale could ban you from the building.' Elsie's face froze in terror. She hadn't thought of that. 'I'm joking!' Gemma replied, her hand shooting out. 'I can't imagine they'd do anything that extreme. So, what's the first step in your official save our library campaign?'

'It's my turn for a Saturday off this weekend as the volunteers are in, so I'm going to go and see Neve Chapstone, and convince her to come and hold a book launch at the library. I figure that the investigation hearing is next Friday so I probably won't hear officially if I've got a case to answer, which we all know I have, until the start of the week after. Then they have to give me notice before I actually hear the results of it all.' She swallowed, imagining how it would feel to be torn from her beloved library, but put on a cheery tone. 'So as long as we hold the launch within the next two weeks, I should be okay. What happens after, we'll have to wait and see.'

Orla put a fresh cup of tea down in front of Elsie and touched her knee. 'I'm sorry you're going through this, Elsie. It's so horrible.'

Elsie felt tears sting the back of her eyes. 'It bloody well is.' An image of Jacob with his hand pressed to his heart like he was accepting an Oscar shot into her brain and stoked the fire once more. 'But I haven't even begun to fight yet and if I do lose, it won't be for a lack of trying.'

'What else can we do?' asked Gemma. 'The petition now has over two hundred signatures, and I'm sure it will get more over the next few days. When will you, or should I say, we present it?'

'I don't know really. I want to wait as long as possible.' An idea tickled the back of her brain but it wasn't fully formed, and she wanted to think it through before saying anything to Gemma. 'Once I'm no longer working at the library though, we could organise a picket as well, couldn't we? I can just see Mrs Dalloway walloping workmen with a wooden sign.'

Gemma nodded vehemently. 'That's a great idea. Mrs Dalloway is pretty fierce. I wouldn't want to be on the receiving end of her temper.'

'But I don't think we should do it yet. I like the idea but it's a pretty bold move and I think we should keep that in reserve until we need it. I've no idea when they're going to start work. Disrupting the site once the builders arrive could be really effective and I don't think we should do it until then.' She sighed. 'I am worried about dividing the village even more though.'

'There's nothing you can do about that,' Gemma said. 'Everyone's entitled to their opinion.' She flashed a conciliatory smile at Orla and Elsie relaxed even more. 'You haven't made this happen. You're trying to save your job, which anyone would do.'

'Trying to save my job while also nearly getting sacked seems a stupid way to go about it, but I know what you mean.'

'So picketing will be phase two, will it?' Gemma joked, referring to Mr Dobbs's question that morning.

'Yep. Phase one is the petition. I put one in the village shop and the deli too, but I haven't checked their signatures yet. With that and the book launch, it'll definitely put the pressure on. Hopefully enough to make them change their plans. Phase two is picketing and kicking up more of a fuss.'

It hadn't escaped Elsie's notice that even though Orla was normally quiet she'd seemed distant during much of their conversation. Were the divisions in the village running closer to home as well? The idea that she was dividing the village further left a cold, hard lump sitting in her throat. Saving the library for herself and her friends might mean disappointing others and she didn't like that at all. She hoped they'd see that compromise was possible: that they could have new housing and still save the library.

With a yawn, she said goodnight to Orla and Gemma. With any luck, the lack of sleep from the last few nights would catch up with her tonight. She felt tired through to her bones and every muscle was slow and lethargic. She needed to be alert and ready for the next two weeks, to strike while the iron was hot, and deep down she knew that these first weeks of high emotion in the village were pivotal and would most likely decide the rest of her future.

Chapter 12

'What's the state of play?' Conrad Yardley barked through the screen at his son.

Leah had organised a catch-up from the cottage and now Conrad's face loomed large and angry from the laptop screen on the kitchen table. Her attempts at finding an alternative residence for the duration of their stay had come to nothing and Jacob was thinking he might have to go somewhere else and commute into the village, which his father wouldn't like. He'd made it plain he expected Jacob to be on site to deal with any problems as it was his first solo project, but he couldn't help the nerves he felt around Leah. She exuded a kind of pressure that was even more forceful than his father's.

Jacob cleared his throat to get rid of any niggling nerves. 'Since the meeting on Tuesday, the village seems to have quietened down. The land deeds are being transferred and the building work is due to start on Monday. All's going to plan.' Though he'd been concerned after Elsie had spoken out at the meeting and Leah had been kicked out of her cottage, Jacob had decided everything would be fine. He wanted his father to congratulate him and at the moment, nothing else had happened. Of course, his father didn't bother to say job well done.

Conrad made a low growling noise that ended with him coughing. 'Don't get above yourself, boy. You've got a long way to go yet. You'll learn that the more projects of your own you run.' Jacob cast a glance at Leah, feeling embarrassment inch up his neck. She either pretended not to see or was busy making notes as she kept her eyes down on her notepad.

He'd have to take what he could from it. It at least meant his father now recognised he could run projects himself. If only he was actually enjoying it. He'd hoped that with this project being the most interesting he'd worked on, he would have, but it hadn't happened yet. The slim compliment should have cheered him, but no matter what he did it was never enough for his father.

'What do you make of Leah getting kicked out of her rental?' Conrad barked.

'An unfortunate response from one individual,' Jacob replied, shrugging it off.

'Hmm.'

'It was one batty woman,' he added, hoping to assuage his father.

Conrad narrowed his eyes at the screen. 'Did I tell you Allegra was back from her trip to the Caribbean? She suits a tan.'

'Is she?'

'Yes, she is. And she's still single. It's not too late, Jacob. You could—'

As humiliation swelled within him, he risked interrupting his father to say, 'I'll let you know how I get on with Dom, okay?'

'Don't interrupt me, boy!' Conrad shouted, then he cast his eyes to Leah and growled again. 'She's still single and too good to let go of again.' Jacob didn't reply. 'Right, well, I must go. Your mother and I are having dinner with the Popplefords this evening.'

'Say hello to—'

Conrad ended the meeting.

'It's nothing personal. He's always doing that,' Leah added. 'Closing the meeting before anyone can say goodbye. I don't think he's used to doing them online.'

Jacob tried to not let it irritate him that Leah was explaining his own father to him. And it still felt personal. His father was always ending their calls as quickly as possible, cutting him off like he couldn't wait to get away.

'So, I was thinking,' Leah said, closing the laptop and placing her notepad on top. 'We should really be thinking about ...'

Leah spoke at length about things they should check up on, contracts they should chase. Didn't she ever relax? All Jacob was thinking about was signing off for the day and letting his mind relax.

'Why don't you take the evening off, Leah? It's been a hectic few days.'

'I'm fine,' she replied, without stopping whatever task she was performing.

'Okay, well, I think I'm going to go for a run first.' The hobby had saved him from internalising the disappointment he often felt after dealing with his father, and he could feel the unspent energy buzzing around his system, twitching his muscles and lingering in his brain.

'Sure,' Leah said, but there was a disapproval in her voice. Like he wasn't giving it one hundred per cent like she was.

When he came back down in his running gear and reached the door, ready to begin, she called out, 'Do you have some money on you? Would you mind grabbing a bottle of wine on your way back? It's such a nice evening I quite fancy a glass while I work.'

'Yeah, sure.' He had some in the little zip pocket inside his shorts, where he also kept his keys. His phone was strapped to his arm, though he wouldn't answer it. This was his only escape from reality. His time to think about the things he'd prefer to do, or would do one day, like work for a charity and make a difference somewhere. His way of coping with the idea of working in his father's firm for all eternity was that someday he might be able to start a charitable side that built schools and orphanages in places desolated by war, or lacking the infrastructure to do so themselves, but those dreams were a long way off yet.

Closing the door behind him, Jacob took a deep breath and began his run. He had no idea where he was going. He wanted to flee from everyone and everything, and simply be in his body, feeling the power in his legs and the burning in his lungs. It wasn't long before the scenery took his breath away as he ran along dirt tracks at the sides of fields and down bridleways.

Pastures spanned the distance as far as the eye could see. Wheat was beginning to grow, and he inhaled the subtle aroma and the fresh air, taking great deep breaths as he sped on. It wasn't long before his body was warm and he was at that point when the energy in his limbs increased rather than decreased, edging to where he felt like it was gloriously on fire. The scenery was far more beautiful than anything on his usual run at home. Before long, the track he followed led him away from the wheat fields and the colour palette changed to shades of green, from enchanted emeralds to yellow-toned chartreuse. The sweeps and curves of the horizon outlined the different meadows, and some contained cattle or sheep, while in others, horses lazily cantered around.

Jacob passed through a wood, pausing in a coppice to catch his breath and admire the view. The branches met in a canopy above his head, sheltering him as he slowed his heart rate. It was stunning but also calming. In a ponderous mood, he leaned against a stump, bracing his hands against his legs as his energy recovered.

The boughs and leaves of one tree intertwined with another as if they were holding hands. It was almost as though they needed each other, to forever be joined. His relationship with Allegra had failed because they lacked that fundamental need: a desire to grow together, wrapping one's life around the other's. It was the type of love he longed for deep down, but on a day-to-day level felt so out of reach. If he found anyone he loved that deeply, they'd have to take him and his family. Would anyone ever want to put up with his father? There wasn't much chance of that. His mother was a different story. Georgia Yardley was kind and steady, the complete opposite to her husband. If she was the tranquil, gently flowing Meadowbank River, then Conrad Yardley was the sea during a storm. They were polar opposites, yet for some reason she put up with him. Love was a strange thing.

The problem with finding a girlfriend was that his father wanted someone from the same 'set' as them, which was utterly prosperous in this day and age. His father was a snob. Jacob's mother had always said that it wasn't enough for his father to have the money of the upper classes, he wanted to be accepted by them too. He was like some Regency mama intent on her daughter marrying up. It would no doubt be another disappointment to him when Jacob didn't, especially as their only child. Any woman worth her salt wouldn't put up with his father's rudeness, and Jacob knew full well he would be rude in the extreme until Jacob brought home the right girl.

After a last glance at the coppice, Jacob began to jog, following a well-trodden track. The dust on the ground sprang up with every step until he was back to a running speed, at which point he didn't even notice it. The woods receded, and pretty thatched cottages came back into view. As he approached the edge of the village green, he slowed his pace, using one of the park benches to stretch his hamstrings and quads. The release in the muscles made him sigh with relief and he stretched his neck up to the sky. The evening sun was still warm and dried the sweat on his forehead before it could trickle down the sides of his face.

In the shade of the high reeds that shielded this side of the duck pond from the rest of the green, he listened to the birds singing. Their gentle songs chimed together in a musical chorus underpinned by the tinkling of the water. With the ducks quacking as they paddled about in the pond, dipping their heads and splashing water over their backs, he reached inside the waistband of his shorts for the little zip pocket that contained a ten-pound note.

'What on earth do you think you're doing, young man?'

exclaimed a woman with thick grey hair and glasses. She was clad in a huge cotton dress that swung off her tall frame. He recognised her as the woman from the book group who'd spoken at the meeting.

Just as he was about to answer, Elsie Martin came into view. She was walking from the direction of the library wearing a cute summer dress. The pale beige stripes on the white linen emphasised her untanned skin and the tie at the waist accentuated her curves. The warm air had made her hair curl and though she'd tied it back, wavy tendrils fell around her face. Why did it have to be her! Why couldn't it have been anyone else?

'Elsie!' shouted the woman. 'Elsie, come here. This young man was going to wee in the bushes!'

'What?' Jacob yelled, turning back to the woman. 'I wasn't. I was just getting out my—'

'I know full well what you were getting out, young man. My husband might have been dead these five years, but I know what's tucked inside your shorts.'

Feeling his cheeks burn and the heat race over his neck, he was grateful to be hot and sweaty already so Elsie wouldn't notice his blushing. She came closer but kept her distance and her eyes darted between him and the woman. She looked at him with such disdain he could taste it. 'I wasn't,' he said again to Elsie. 'I was trying to—'

'There are public conveniences at the library, young man. For as long as it's there for,' the woman added sarcastically.

'Honestly, I was—'

'You've clearly got no respect. If you respected this village and the thoughts and feelings of its residents, you'd have changed your plans and be out of here already. Nobody wants your new housing. We want our library.'

'If I could just finish my sentence, I can explain that—'

'*Finish your sentence?* Don't you cheek me, young man.'

'I really would like to say that I was trying to get out a

118

ten-pound note, that's all. I need to stop in at the village shop. I assure you I had no intention of ...' He didn't want to say the words out loud. 'Doing anything else.'

He turned to Elsie. There was a glimmer in her eye and a pull at her mouth. She was almost giggling at the craziness of the situation. He paused, enjoying seeing her smile, but unable to decide what to do. He couldn't put his hand inside his shorts with these two women watching him, but neither could he walk away; that would be even ruder and would no doubt start another row. He already felt like he'd been told off by a teacher. Against a strange, peaceful backdrop of ducks quacking and birds singing, the three of them stood in a standoff. He couldn't stay there forever and tried to summon some of the advice the body-language expert had given him. Elsie had said he looked like Napoleon with his hand over his heart, so not knowing what to do, he gave a weird sort of bow as he said, 'Right well, I'd better get going. I've got to get back to—'

'Your *assistant*?' Scorn and innuendo dripped from the woman's voice. 'Still sharing a house together, aren't you? And she's been gallivanting around like she owns the place. Told me book clubs can be done from anywhere.'

Had she? Leah hadn't mentioned anything to him.

'When was this, Mrs Dalloway?' asked Elsie, her brows knitting together, all trace of amusement lost.

Mrs Dalloway? So this was also the woman who'd kicked Leah out of her cottage. 'Mrs Dalloway, I'm sorry that—'

'While this one and another bloke were wandering around outside the library earlier, she was inside making comments. Apparently, no one likes book clubs, and she has no idea how people enjoy sitting around talking about made-up stories. Idiot.'

Elsie pinned Jacob with a sharp stare. 'These people don't care about the things that actually matter, Mrs Dalloway. They only care about money and profit, and shiny red sports cars and getting their own way—'

Jacob tried again, speaking without thinking. He just felt a need for her to think that he was better than a person who'd pee in the bushes or hate books. 'I really am sorry that—'

'Well, they've got a shock coming, haven't they?' Mrs Dalloway replied, and he was sure Elsie flashed her eyes in warning before she turned and moved away.

Mrs Dalloway followed her, and Jacob was now free to go to the village shop, but he wasn't sure he dared to. After that exchange he could really use a glass of wine to steady his nerves, once he'd had a shower of course. Mrs Dalloway was incredibly scary but the thought of returning to the cottage was less than appealing. With no other choice he headed on.

The wicker baskets on either side of the shop door contained tomatoes and new potatoes. All marked with a small chalk sign saying local produce. He smiled at the woman behind the counter when he walked in, and though she smiled at first, it quickly faded when she recognised who he was. She grabbed some papers from the top of the counter and hid them underneath. Jacob frowned, but perhaps she was looking at something personal. His mind flashed back to Mrs Dalloway's comment a few moments before and Elsie's reaction. Was something going on? No, it couldn't be. Even though Elsie had spoken at the meeting, he couldn't imagine her, or this sleepy place, doing anything.

Jacob moved to the back of the shop and, as he was alone, took this opportunity to retrieve his ten-pound note. After perusing the selection of bottles, he grabbed a white wine with the picture of a koala on the front. He liked koalas, and nice labels were his main way of choosing wine as he knew nothing about the different types.

When his father had made his first million, he'd gone on a wine-tasting course to learn about the varieties and where they came from, thinking that this knowledge would come in handy one day. It never really had, though his father always tried to shoehorn some of it into conversation. All Jacob knew was that with the hot weather he quite fancied the cold, crisp taste of white rather than a rich, filling red. He took the bottle from the fridge and moved to the counter. The owner fiddled again with the papers, moving them even further down but he still couldn't see what they were.

'Is this everything?' she asked. She flashed a smile, but it was more because she had to than because she wanted to.

'Yes, thanks.' He handed over the money and was about to leave when another person paused in the doorway.

'Are you serving the likes of him?' asked the man gruffly. He was about the same age as Jacob, but his build was very different. He had large broad shoulders and hands like shovels. Jacob didn't fancy getting into any sort of altercation with him.

'I'm a business, Rob, just like you. I can't pick and choose who I sell to. If I did, I wouldn't be selling to you after you cheated on your girlfriend.'

The man blushed. 'Yeah, but he's an outsider. You don't have to worry about upsetting him and I'd have thought that you of all people would stand up and fight. You've always said the library saves you every school holiday.'

The woman behind the counter dropped her eyes. 'I know what I said, Rob, and I'm doing my bit.' She glanced down at where she stuffed the papers.

Jacob moved to the doorway and the man looked him up and down before stepping aside and letting him pass. His relaxing run hadn't been quite as calming as he'd hoped it would be. He was used to people not taking the news of a development very well, but this time was worse than anything he'd ever seen before.

When he'd returned from the shop, Leah hadn't moved from her spot. She was still head down working.

'I got the wine,' he said, taking the bottle to the kitchen and putting it in the fridge. She didn't answer. 'I'm going to go and have a shower.' He waited for a minute and after a second, she lifted her head.

'Hmm? Sorry?'

'I said I was going to have a shower.'

'Okay.' She was completely uninterested, looking at him as if she had no idea why he'd shared that information.

Staying with strangers was always awkward and difficult for him but Leah's focus on work made life even harder. He wondered how she switched off. He had running, Elsie clearly loved books. He turned the shower to cold, hoping the freezing water would drive out thoughts of her and what an evening with her would be like. He really wished Elsie hadn't seen the encounter earlier and hoped she didn't think he had been about to take a leak in the bushes.

Why couldn't he be attracted to someone unconnected with the project? He hated how much he cared what she thought of him.

The cool water of the shower pummelled his back and neck, easing the tension in his muscles and releasing the strain from his run. In a burst of magnificent sunshine, the evening had grown even warmer, and he turned the temperature down further to let the cold water enliven him. All he wanted to do now was eat and then read the news on his phone. He might think about reading the poetry book he'd found on the shelf to help him sleep, but he'd see how tired he was first. Would he get to do that with Leah there? He wasn't used to sharing his space like this and knew he'd find it even harder to switch off with a relative stranger around.

When he came downstairs, Leah had a glass of wine but was back at her laptop, glancing between it and some papers to the side. As he poured himself a glass, it put him in mind of the village shop and its owner moving those papers from the top of the counter to the bottom. She was so eager to get them out of his sight he wouldn't have been surprised if she'd stuffed them down her top. He also thought of Mrs Dalloway's comment that he had a shock coming. 'Something strange happened on my run this afternoon.'

'Oh, yes?' Leah replied, slightly annoyed he was interrupting her. Jacob outlined the two incidents, but she didn't seem fazed. 'I wouldn't worry. I've worked, I don't know how many projects with your father, both now and as his assistant, and whenever something's announced there's always a feeling that something might happen for the first few days, but nine times out of ten it never does.'

'But I'm sure they're planning something.' The shop owner eyeing the papers and saying she was doing her bit concerned him.

Leah laughed. 'Jacob, relax. I can't imagine this village is planning anything. It's so quiet. Eighty per cent of the population are over 60 and the other 20 per cent are too busy with families and lives to actually do anything. The most opposition this place has had to offer is an angry librarian and I'm pretty sure she's run out of steam by now. She didn't seem the type to do much. Far too quiet and mousey. I'm sure you're being paranoid, which is natural given this is your first project.'

Did she have to keep reminding him? He tried to take some comfort from her words.

The air drifting in through the open kitchen window carried the aroma of flowers and he took a large drink from his glass. She was probably right, and he had to admit she had more experience with these things. At least he had the weekend to look forward to. Perhaps he'd go for a drive out on his own and run somewhere different. He didn't fancy a repeat of earlier.

Roll on next week when they'd put the fence up and begin marking out the ground. The sooner this project was completed the better.

Chapter 13

Whether it was sheer exhaustion from the lack of sleep over the last few nights, or that her mind had relaxed after finally settling on a course of action, Elsie had managed an entire night's rest and felt like a human being rather than a zombie for the first time since hearing the news. Feeling refreshed, she drove to Neve Chapstone's house, eager but nervous about organising phase one of her plan.

With Saturday being one of the busiest trading days for the village shop and the bakery, she was sure the petition would be full by the evening, and she couldn't wait to present it to Jacob Yardley. Even if they still built some houses, she had to convince him to keep the library safe. She had no idea how much chance there was of doing that but try she would.

Neve Chapstone lived in the next village over and Elsie had the window open as she wound through the country lanes connecting Meadowbank to Great Bingham. Nerves built in her stomach with each passing mile. So much was riding on this, and the reality was she had to convince a virtual recluse to finally come out in public. Not to mention sit in a room full of people and interview her herself. It was a tall order by anyone's standards. By Elsie's it was phenomenal.

Thanks to local gossip, Elsie knew exactly where Neve Chapstone lived without having to try and find her address. She hadn't had to contact her publisher or agent or even go through her website. The whispers had started after the postman had seen her name on a letter. The postman's wife was a big fan and with Neve being such an unusual name, he'd recognised it immediately. There was also the fact that Neve had moved in with her son, or a much younger husband. No one really knew for sure because they kept to themselves. Still, before long everyone within a ten-mile radius knew who'd moved in and where. Elsie wouldn't put it past the village gossip network that it was known what Neve's favourite meal was or what brand of washing powder she preferred. Poor Neve Chapstone couldn't have put her bins out without someone knowing about it and passing it on to everyone they knew.

The sweeping fields on either side of her gave a sense of peace that calmed the anxiety a little. As it was nearing ten o'clock on a Saturday morning, the lanes were quiet. So far, she'd been able to amble along in her old, hardly ever used car, happily glancing out of the window and enjoying the view. A flock of birds swooped and soared over a field and Elsie leaned forward to watch them, flicking her eyes back to the road to ensure she stayed safe. The flock moved with a mesmerising majesty. They dipped and reared as one, the individual birds small swirling specks in the sky. Nature was remarkable, and it was one of the things she loved about Meadowbank: the village was somehow in tune with the world around it.

As she looked ahead, Elsie spotted someone on the side of the road. They were sitting on the ground, just down the bank from one of the passing places. The view from that spot was rather lovely, stretching out over the fields all around them, but as the person had their back to her, she couldn't tell if they were okay. Worried it was someone from the village who'd had an accident, she slowed down and pulled onto the verge.

'Hello? Are you okay?' As she rounded the front of the car,

the figure stood and she paused, wishing she hadn't followed her conscience after all. 'Mr Yardley.'

'Elsie – I mean, Miss Martin.' Jacob's voice wavered, but she couldn't tell if he was out of breath from his run, or just surprised to see her.

'I didn't know it was you,' she said quickly. 'I thought you might have been in trouble.'

'Ah. And if you'd known it was me, would you have driven on by?' He smiled awkwardly. Was that a joke?

'Of course I wouldn't!' Her voice rang with outrage. 'If you needed it, I'd help you no matter what.' Jacob dropped his eyes and she felt a surge of embarrassment at speaking to him like that. She couldn't always help her responses when they were in the library – the place fired something inside her – but they weren't there now and he hadn't even done anything.

'Yes, I know. I'm sorry …' He shook his head seeming somehow disarmed and yet again she felt riddled with guilt for being rude to him.

'What are you doing here?'

'I was out for a run. I think I might have got a little lost.' He looked about him, turning left and right, trying to figure out where he went wrong. 'It really is breathtakingly beautiful here, isn't it?' Was he just trying to win her over? Before she could figure it out, he glanced back to her, taking a step forward. 'I know you probably don't want to talk to me, but I don't suppose you could tell me which way heads back to Meadowbank?'

If they could go back to that first meeting, if he was here to do something other than destroy her library, then she'd happily talk to him. She'd happily walk the fields hand in hand— The thought sent a tingle up her spine but she pushed it away. 'It's that way,' she said, pointing in the opposite direction she'd been driving, and before she could stop herself added, 'You're probably better off following the road so you don't get lost again. There's a path that runs along the edge of the fields all the way there.

126

Sometimes people drive too fast on country lanes and …' *And she didn't want him to get hurt.*

'And?' he asked hopefully. The air seemed to sparkle between them. She hadn't realised until now how close they were physically. When exactly she'd taken a step towards him she wasn't sure. She could see his chest rising and falling under the fabric of his T-shirt. Did he know what she was thinking because he'd stepped towards her too? Regardless, she shouldn't care about him at all. Their chance had gone.

'Nothing,' she said quietly.

Whatever had existed in the air between them was swept away by the breeze and he took a tiny step back. 'Right. Thanks. Is it your day off today?'

The question surprised her, and as she thought of what she was doing, her cheeks began to burn. 'Yes, it is.'

'Well, I hope you have a lovely day.'

With a smile that was almost as disarming as the one he'd flashed when they first met, Jacob began to jog steadily in the direction she'd told him, making his way back to Meadowbank, probably to work on plans to destroy the library. Why, oh why, did he have to be evil incarnate, here to steal the village's soul? Overly dramatic? Possibly. But not by much. A nice smile didn't mean a nice man. Elsie reminded herself of why he was here and, no matter what, she had to do everything in her power to save the library for Winston, Bernard, and Patricia. Even if she had to stage a sit-down protest in Neve Chapstone's living room or hang on to the author's ankles so she couldn't kick her out, she wasn't leaving until Neve agreed to hold a book launch at the library.

Climbing back into her car, she shoved it into gear and continued on her way. It was a gorgeously bright and sunny day and the clear, cloudless sky reached out over the fields.

Elsie wondered if she should have given Neve some warning of her request and a slight twinge of guilt tensed her muscles. If she'd done that, Neve would have had time to think of an excuse and say no and there was no way Elsie could afford for her to do that. Whether it was rude or unorthodox to turn up on her doorstep and ask, she had no choice.

Circling the large war memorial in the centre of the village, Elsie followed the road to the left, passing the tiny church and turning down a short drive shaded by large trees. The red brick of the house had paled to a gentle pink and the bright white door, framed by two columns, glistened in the sun. Elsie's nerves rattled around her stomach like an enthusiastically shaken maraca as she got out. With a deep breath, she stepped forward and knocked.

The door opened and Elsie was momentarily taken aback by the tall, dark-haired man with full pale lips. He seemed around the same age as her and the gentle lines around his eyes and across his forehead added to the sense of masculinity emanating from him in waves. His hair lay longer than Jacob's and he tucked the dark and curly strands behind his ear. Again, Elsie cursed Jacob for pushing his way into her thoughts.

'Good morning,' Elsie said, clasping one of Neve's books in front of her. Perhaps because she used books and stories to shield her from the world, she'd subconsciously taken that armour with her.

'Good morning,' the man replied with a slight chuckle. 'How can I help you?' He glanced down at the book. 'Oh, a fan! Are you wanting an autograph from Neve?'

Still in shock that this man had been living nearby and no one had thought to mention how attractive he was, Elsie glanced down at the book. It was actually a library copy and in general she didn't approve of writing in books. Any time she'd had to underline a passage at school or university she'd wince and secretly apologise to the page, promising to rub it out when the term ended. This time, she didn't want to seem rude by saying no and anyway, an autograph by the author was slightly different. 'Oh, right. Umm … yes, please. But—' She swallowed down the nerves threatening to send her voice wavering. 'I was wondering if I could talk to Neve for a moment, please?'

'I'm sorry, I'm afraid she's busy, but I can take the book and get it signed for you. It won't take a moment.'

'No,' Elsie screeched, hugging it closer as he reached out to take it. Surprised, he frowned but it didn't detract from his good looks. 'I really, really need to speak to Neve. Please? It's important. It's about Meadowbank Library.'

'Meadowbank? Oh yes, I heard it was closing.' The man shook his head. 'It's always a shame when libraries close. I think my heart breaks a little each time.' He flashed her a smile and Elsie's heart gave such an uncomfortable flutter it almost burst against her ribs. If anything was going to push thoughts of Jacob Yardley away, it was this man. Such a shame he was Neve's husband. That's if he was. She noted the absence of a ring. 'But I am so sorry. Neve's right in the middle of something and is painfully shy.' Reaching out for the book again, he said, 'But she'll be more than happy to sign this. So who shall I ask her to make it out to?'

'I know a thing or two about being shy,' Elsie said, not sure where this conversation was going. She hadn't intended to talk about herself, but she needed a way in. 'I'm sure if I could speak to her, she'd see I'm not that scary, and it really is very important. I was hoping that she might come to Meadowbank Library for a book launch. I'm aware her latest book came out a few days ago.'

'But I thought the library was closing?' As she still hadn't given up the book, he finally dropped his hand from where it had been dangling in mid-air.

'It is, but …' Her words failed and the dark-haired man scrutinised her. Elsie opened her mouth to speak but found herself stumbling. She'd thought it would have been easy to at least get inside the house and then she'd be able to convince Neve. Talking to this man – whoever he was – on the doorstep was proving even more difficult.

He leaned against the doorframe and Elsie felt the intensity of his gaze. 'I'm sorry if I'm being thick, but what exactly are you hoping to do?'

She needed to choose her words carefully in case Rees-Hale found out. 'I know Meadowbank Library is closing but we were still hoping to hold events until that actually happens. As a local author, Neve would be perfect. I know she's never really done an event like this before, but we thought it would be a fabulous goodbye for the library to have someone of her calibre.'

He watched her for a moment as if reading the lies – or at least half-truths – on her face then shook his head. 'I'm being rude. If Neve knew I'd left a fellow book lover – especially such a pretty one – on the doorstep instead of inviting her in, she'd never forgive me. Please, do come in?'

Elsie hesitated. She always felt on edge when people paid her compliments, especially as she didn't know who this man was. Was he the younger husband everyone had talked of, in which case, shame on him, or was he her son? Elsie didn't think of herself as pretty or remarkable in anyway. It wasn't that she had low self-esteem; it was more that she was perfectly aware of her own insignificance in the grand scheme of things and accepted that fact with pragmatism. Plus, over the years, men had never really sought her company over that of her friends.

'I'm Liam, by the way,' the man said, stepping aside. He opened his other arm to welcome her in before leading the way to a large conservatory that was more like another room. It ran the entire length of the back of the house. At one end was a large oblong table and at the other, a settee and armchair with a bookcase full of books. Elsie, unable to stop herself studying a bookshelf when she passed one, couldn't help but glance over and was surprised to see an incredible number of thrillers and horror novels. She'd imagined seeing rows of romances and maybe some of Neve's own books, but perhaps they were in her study.

Even with the doors and windows open, the heat of the day warmed the atmosphere. It wouldn't be long before the room became uncomfortable and already Elsie could feel her armpits moistening or was it the attraction she was feeling towards Liam?

She clamped her arms down by her sides, hoping he was about to say that he was off to get Neve for her to chat to. Instead, he sat down on the sofa and motioned for Elsie to take the armchair.

'So, tell me more about this author talk at the library.'

'It would be such a good cause. It would be to—' She nearly said *save* the library but managed to hold back. 'To really go out with a bang. I realise Neve's very busy, but if I could talk to her—'

'It's fine,' he said, waving his hand dismissively. 'You can talk to me. I'll pass everything on.'

Feeling frustration mount, she breathed deeply before carrying on. 'This would mean so much to the village. We're about to lose our library, we really want to have one last amazing event for us all to remember.' She tried to sound cheerful even though saying the words out loud broke her heart. 'We've always loved author talks … and I know Neve isn't that keen on them and that she must be really, really busy, but …' She was rambling, her words tumbling out, without any idea of where she was going, and she hadn't even thought about her interviewing Neve. As she did, her nerves bubbled so fiercely she thought she might be sick. 'I know how respected Neve is. I just know that everyone would turn out to support her and it would be a lovely way to say goodbye. Our library is very important to our community,' she added somewhat meekly.

'That's very flattering.' Liam leaned forwards. His elbows were now resting on his knees and she could see a hint of the dark hair on his chest from the open top of his shirt. 'But I'm afraid Neve is incredibly busy. She's halfway through writing her new book and it's not been going very well, to be honest.' He scratched the back of his head. 'I really don't think she could spare the time.'

Elsie placed the book on her lap, flicking the pages back and forth to feel them beneath her fingers. She couldn't hear any noise in the house and wondered where Neve was and why this man was being so protective of her. Somehow, she had to speak to Neve. Some of the steel backbone that had appeared during the

131

public meeting strengthened again and Elsie's confidence grew. 'If I could speak to Neve myself, I might be able to explain a little more about the situation.'

She wasn't exactly sure what that meant. She'd covered pretty much everything without telling the actual truth, but all she knew was that she needed Neve to say yes – not this man – and the only way that was going to happen was if she spoke to her directly.

After another penetrating glance that read her like a book, Liam sat back, crossing his arms over his chest. 'Why don't you tell me what's really going on, Miss …?'

'Elsie. Elsie Martin.'

'I get the feeling you're not being straight with me and as you're asking Neve to do something she's never done before, I feel like you need to tell me the truth.'

Elsie froze. Even her breath paused, flowing neither in nor out. How could she answer that? Could she trust him and tell him the truth? His gaze hadn't shifted from hers and she was sure he had an idea already.

'Let me see if I can guess.' He pointed at her. 'I think you're hoping Neve Chapstone will hold a book launch at the library because you want to prove to the council and the new developers just how important it is. Show them how many people attend and value the place and try and convince them to change their minds. Am I right?'

She didn't answer with words but felt her cheeks doing it for her. She didn't even bother feeling to see if they were hot because she'd scorch her fingers. Her face had become a supernova.

'I see that I am.' He chuckled. 'Why didn't you just say that?'

'Because if I do, I might lose my job,' Elsie blurted out, then drew back. 'I'm not supposed to go against the council's decision.' As he'd guessed so much, it seemed easier just to come clean. In for a penny, in for a pound, as Mrs Dalloway would say. 'And I'm already facing a disciplinary for speaking out at the public meeting. If I'm caught doing anything else it could be—'

'I'll come.' He sat back, running his finger back and forth over his chin as if deep in thought.

'I'm sorry, you'll …?'

'I'll come.'

Elsie gazed around wondering what was happening. Had he gone mad? Had she? Had Neve appeared somehow, and she hadn't noticed? 'I'm sorry I don't understand.'

Liam laughed. 'I see you haven't twigged. I'm Neve Chapstone. Well, that's my pen name, anyway. As I said before, my name's Liam.'

'It's a pen name?' Elsie almost dropped the book from her lap.

'It is. Well, not exactly. It's my mother's name. She moved in with me when we came here after my father died.'

'I'm so sorry.'

He waved the remark away. 'That's kind but it's fine. When I started out, I found it hard to get a publisher, so I used her name and Bob's your uncle – or should I say Neve's your mother – and here I am.'

Elsie was aware of her incredulous stare and the confused tilt of her head. 'So you're Neve Chapstone?'

'Yes.'

She let that sink in for a moment. 'But won't it blow your whole' – she moved her hand around in a circle that encompassed his rather attractive form – 'thing if you come? I don't want to ruin your life.'

'That's very kind of you, but it won't ruin my life. Actually, I've been thinking about coming clean for a while. Whenever Mum goes into the village, she's always getting asked what she's writing and what's going to happen to this or that character. She hates lying to people. More than once we've been caught in a lie and had to pretend we're talking about different projects. I was also thinking of branching out into thrillers and writing under my own name, so it was all going to come out eventually. It might as well be now and for a good cause.'

'Are you sure?' Elsie asked, her mind slowly beginning to work as the shock wore off. Considering his initial reticence, he'd decided very quickly.

'Definitely. I've always wanted to do author talks and found it quite sad that I couldn't. It can be a bit of a lonely life being a writer.'

He was so genuine, unlike Jacob, that she found herself warming to him, and he was willing to make a big sacrifice to help save the library. 'I can't even begin to imagine the amount of work that goes into writing a book,' Elsie said, looking at the one in her lap. Maybe that could be one of her questions. How do you even begin? 'I love stories and reading but I wouldn't know where to start with actually writing one.'

'It is quite gruelling sometimes. But of course, I'm blessed to be able to do my dream job.' So had she, up until recently. 'When were you thinking of holding this book launch if the library closes in a month?'

Elsie straightened and replied with confidence. 'I was hoping for two weeks' time. On the Friday.'

'Is that enough to really market the event?'

'I promise it will be. Even if I have to print and deliver flyers myself. I'll be organising everything and I can assure you we'll have lots of copies of your book for people to buy and they'll definitely want you to sign them. I thought we could do a short interview with me asking you a few questions.'

She'd much prefer it to be someone else but there wasn't anyone.

'I know you'll do your best; you seem that type of person. If you're really sure you can make it work, then, Elsie, I'm happy to come along. It would be lovely, and it is such a shame another one of our libraries is closing. I already know I'm free for that date. Shall we say 7 p.m.?'

Elsie couldn't believe her luck. 'And you really are sure? I mean – you're sure that date works for you?'

'Perfectly.' He stood. 'It's all settled. But I warn you, Miss Martin, I'm rubbish at organisation so I'll be relying on you to have everything ready. I'll just turn up and do the talking.'

She smiled, standing too, and despite her own nerves she was looking forward to it already. 'That sounds absolutely perfect to me. We'll start advertising the event immediately.'

Liam put his hands in his pockets and rocked on his heels. 'I'm quite excited about it and I admire your plan. Did you come up with it yourself?'

'Yes, I did.'

'I'm very glad you picked me.' His eyes warmed as she met his gaze.

She had to resist the urge to hug him she was so grateful. He smiled at her, and she felt slightly giddy, then he thanked her again, even though it should have been the other way around.

'Can I convince you to come into the kitchen for a coffee?'

'Oh, umm. Yes, that'd be nice, thank you.' She couldn't believe she'd agreed so quickly, surprised that the nerves in her tummy were egging her on rather than holding her back.

'Follow me then. I don't get many visitors whom I can actually talk to since moving out here. My friends are all in London. Oh, and thinking about it, I'd appreciate it if you could keep my identity a secret until the night of the talk, if that's okay. I need to square everything with my agent, and let Mum know.'

'Of course. It'll only make the night more memorable. Is your mum here now?' Elsie hoped she wasn't. She quite fancied talking to Liam on his own for a while.

'No, she's off shopping in Witchbury, spending my latest royalty payment.'

Elsie smiled and followed him through to the kitchen, where they sat and talked about books, reading, writing, and everything related to her favourite subjects. Liam was kind and inquisitive, funny and charming. Truly charming, unlike Jacob, who simply acted like he was.

Elsie climbed into the car an hour later and drove off as Liam waved from between the two columns that framed the front door. There was still a long way to go in her campaign, but at least she was a little bit closer than she had been this morning. The petition was all well and good, but everyone launched petitions. They were to be expected. And unless there were thousands or millions of signatures, they were easily ignored. But something about this felt right. Like it might actually have a chance of succeeding.

From the research she'd been doing on Conrad Yardley Construction and the man himself, she could already tell he was a snobbish, pompous millionaire who only cared about reputation and revenue. Hopefully, the newspaper coverage of the event would put a dirty great dent in that reputation and be just the thing to make him change his plans.

Chapter 14

The days that passed at work were, for Elsie, far more exciting than she'd ever thought possible under the circumstances. Something about the situation, and what she was doing to fight it, made her feel more alive than she ever had before. Her confidence was growing – as long as she didn't dwell on interviewing Liam in front of everyone – and, dare she say it, she was actually enjoying the pressure, the need to act.

Books and the library had always been her sanctuary. They made her feel safe and secure when the rest of the world proved too much. In her early twenties, they'd helped her battle the demons of shyness and introversion that had threatened to overwhelm her. At first, they'd been crippling. She couldn't sit in an interview or speak to a stranger without turning pink and stuttering, and dating had been entirely out of the question. She relied on Gemma to tell her if someone fancied her because she was never able to pick up on the signals. The ground she constantly stared at never gave anything away and she'd often been told she'd missed lingering glances or sweet smiles. But over the years she had learned to manage her shyness thanks to her heroines such as Cathy in *Wuthering Heights* and Lizzie Bennet in *Pride and Prejudice* and even Bridget Jones from *Bridget Jones's Diary*, not to mention the women who wrote those stories, and of course, there'd been the unwavering support of the Meadowbank villagers: those regular customers who over time had become like family, making the library feel more like a second home than a place of work.

As she shelved a pile of books, dancing around among the stacks, her nerves fizzed and tingled with excitement. She had already contacted Neve Chapstone's publisher and the books were due to be delivered by the end of the week. She'd printed out a poster and pinned it to the noticeboard outside and the one in the village green. Notices had also gone on their website.

Her brain was firing at a million miles an hour as she imagined Jacob's reaction when he saw how popular the library was, and the big-name authors who lived nearby and supported her cause. She just hoped the local papers would come. She'd sent them an email and even knocked up a professional-looking press release, but it wasn't simply the way she was fighting this that made her jittery with exhilaration, she was exploring a side of her character she had never known existed, and for once that feeling overcame all others. She'd never scurried around behind people's backs before, told half-truths to her boss, or even defied direct instructions. The defiance she was showing – made all the more justified by her being right – made her feel naughty and proud at the same time. It was invigorating.

'I wish aliens would land and whisk away this bloody lot,' said Bernard, peering out of the window behind his computer screen. A few of the Mingle and Mutter group gathered too.

Elsie placed the last book on the shelf and came to a stop behind him. Since yesterday morning, at exactly nine o'clock, the fields had been encompassed by six-foot metal fencing fastened into vast concrete blocks that had been unloaded from the back of a truck. Now someone was walking around with a can of spray paint writing things on the ground. Elsie didn't know what, she couldn't see from here, but no doubt it was instructions for people

138

to start digging. Jacob, clad in a dark blue suit with brown shoes – not appropriate footwear for stomping through a field – was chatting with another man who she assumed from the enormous rolled-up paper under his arm was an architect. Rees-Hale was also there. Despicable man that he was.

'No celeb sightings today?' asked Elsie, trying to cheer Bernard up. He'd been angry these last few days, wanting to scale the fence and draw over their markers, but she'd managed to calm him down before he went home.

'Apparently Henry Cavill, the man who played Superman, was seen in Waitrose in Witchbury, but nothing else. And to be honest, I don't believe it. Why would he go to Witchbury? Bloody awful place.'

'Never mind,' Elsie said, patting his shoulder. 'I'm sure someone else will be spotted soon. Perhaps Michael Caine will pop down to the garden centre again, or who was that footballer seen at the kids' playpark?'

'Lionel Messi.'

'That's the one.'

Winston flicked his paper down and smiled at Elsie. 'You're very chipper today considering.'

'Am I?' She had been trying to act normally.

'You are. What's going on? Are you handing in this petition today or something?'

'Shhh! It's still a secret. And not today, no. I've got a plan for it.'

His eyes misted a little. 'I don't know what I'll do when I can't come here every day and chat to you.'

'Oh, Winston.' She stood behind him, resting her hands on his shoulders and her cheek against the top of his head. 'Don't worry. Whatever happens, I'll come and see you at least once a week. Even twice a week. Maybe every day if you like. And I'll even bring cake.'

He reached up and patted her hand. 'You're a good girl, Elsie.' With a final squeeze she went back to the desk.

'I can't wait to work somewhere different,' Karen said, turning the page of her magazine, whose cover story was on dog kennels for pampered pooches of the rich and famous. 'I hope they move me to Customer Services in the new office in Witchbury. They've got air-conditioning and a really nice canteen. My friend who works in Finance told me about it. No more crappy packed lunches for me.'

She didn't have to eat crappy packed lunches now, Elsie thought. Not only could she make herself something nice, as Elsie did, but if she didn't fancy doing that she could nip to Gemma's bakery and get something delicious or visit Annie's Tearoom. If she wanted something a bit different there was always the deli. There were plenty of options within Meadowbank that could satisfy her, but she preferred to look down her nose at the tiny village. Why some people thought the big city lights were so much brighter and better was beyond Elsie.

Patricia whirled into the library, pausing to read the A3 poster Elsie had printed up and pinned to the door advertising the book launch.

'What's all that about?' she asked, pointing over her shoulder.

'It's something we've been hoping to do for ages, but Neve Chapstone never agreed.'

Karen's head lifted but she didn't speak.

'I heard she never does interviews,' Patricia replied. 'I've always wished she would. She's one of my favourite authors.'

'Well, for some reason she said yes this time!'

A thrill shot through Elsie at the truth that only she knew. Not only was Neve Chapstone a man, and a kind-hearted, handsome one at that, but she – Elsie Martin who everyone thought wouldn't say boo to a goose – had organised this. She had made it happen and though she didn't want to toot her own horn, she had a good feeling about how this was going to pan out. Something about it felt right and she was sure with Liam Chapstone speaking eloquently on the subject of how important libraries were in front of the local media, Jacob Yardley was virtually guaranteed to have to change his plans and build next to the library rather than over it. She hoped Liam used the same line he'd said when they'd met: that a little bit of his heart broke each time a library closed. That was sure to win people over.

'That's a coincidence, isn't it?' Karen piped up, eyeing Elsie suspiciously. 'I didn't know we were trying to get her for a book launch.'

'I'm sure I told you,' Elsie said, feigning innocence. 'I probably didn't make a big deal about it because I didn't think she'd ever agree. Like Patricia said, she doesn't normally.'

Secretly, Elsie congratulated herself on not slipping into 'he'. 'Hmm.'

'Well, if I were you,' said Patricia, bouncing on her toes in excitement. 'I'd contact *The Bookseller* and all the industry press. If she's never given an interview before, they'll all want to be here to hear what she has to say. That'll show—'

'Shall we get set up for story time, Patricia?' Elsie spoke rapidly, cutting her off before she could say anything else incriminating.

Luckily, Karen had returned to her magazine and was too wrapped up in a feature on the latest trend in home décor (cushions shaped like body parts) to notice. Elsie grabbed Patricia's arm and pulled her deep into the children's section.

'What's the matter?' asked Patricia, rearranging her sleeve once Elsie had let go.

Elsie leaned in and whispered, 'That's exactly why I've organised this book launch. To embarrass Jacob and his awful father into changing their plans.'

Aghast, Patricia drew back, her mouth hung slightly open. 'You have?' Elsie nodded. 'You clever girl! I was so proud of you when you spoke up at the meeting, and then organised the petition, but I had no idea you were so crafty. There's a new-found confidence about you, Elsie, and I like it.'

Elsie beamed at the compliment. 'Do you really think I should contact the industry press?' It would mean more people here watching her speak and the thought terrified her.

'Yes, definitely. I'd go for anyone even remotely interested in romance and books or literature. Have you spoken to Mrs Motley up at Highfield?'

'Mrs Motley?' Elsie's forehead creased in confusion. 'No. Why?' Suddenly it dawned. 'She's a freelance journalist, isn't she? Do you think she'd be interested?'

'I do,' Patricia replied, nodding emphatically. 'Amelia Williams at Meadow Farmhouse told me she was lovely when she visited with her family, and she really likes the village. I'm sure if you contacted her, she'd try and help if she could. She'd definitely want to get a piece on Neve Chapstone finally giving an interview. Do you think if I text my daughter the news, she'll come to the launch?'

'It's worth a try,' Elsie replied, not wanting to get Patricia's hopes up.

'I always hoped I'd be sitting with my grandson doing Baby and Toddler Toe Taps and bouncing him on my knee. It breaks my heart to think I won't get the chance to do that, not just because my daughter will never forgive me, but because the library won't be here anymore.' Tears pooled in her eyes. 'With the library going, it feels like it's the end for me and Aimee.'

'I'm sure that won't be the case, Patricia. It'll be okay.' Elsie patted her hand. 'Actually, I was hoping to ask you something about Maria.'

'What about her?'

'She spoke up at the meeting about how the mother and baby group really helps people and then the other day she was in here getting a parenting book, but she was acting kind of odd about it.'

'Maybe she was embarrassed? Some people get that way about self-help books.'

'Maybe, but I had the feeling there was something bothering her. I was wondering if you could keep an eye on her during Toe Taps and see if you can spot any signs of anything.'

'Like what?'

'I don't know. I just have a feeling that maybe she doesn't have it as together as she makes out and could use someone to talk to.'

'Okay,' Patricia replied. 'I'll keep an eye.'

'They're coming over,' shouted Bernard. He'd given up looking at the monitor and was now standing up, staring out the window. 'In fact, I think they're coming in.'

'They're using Karen's office,' Elsie said. The poster! She ran to the door and stood in front of it, stretching herself as tall as possible.

As Jacob and his motley crew rounded the doorway, she pressed her back against it. He frowned quizzically but didn't say anything and moved towards the desk, followed by his assistant, who gave her a snarling glower. The architect, who was shorter than Jacob by a good foot, scrambled to keep pace with Jacob's long, marching stride, like a medieval peasant struggling to follow his despotic master. Jacob paused at the desk and spoke to Karen, who batted her eyelids. Elsie was surprised she didn't curtsey.

When they were far enough away, Elsie walked back to Patricia. 'Come on, we'd better get set up for Baby and Toddler Toe Taps.'

Patricia opened the hidden cupboard and began pulling out the story blanket and instruments she wanted to use for the day's session. 'Meanie, meanie, tiny weenie,' she muttered, and Elsie couldn't hold back a giggle.

'You're not in Toddler Taps now, you don't have to rhyme.'

'And,' said Gemma, who'd come in bearing the cake tray, 'from the way he stood at the public meeting I don't think that's true.'

'It could just be the cut of his trousers,' Elsie offered, and Gemma chuckled too.

'It's a shame he's so handsome,' Patricia said. 'If he were a nice man, he'd be quite a catch. Too bad he's such a tosser. I mean, he's clearly rich, clever, has lovely blue eyes and, I have to admit, he was quite charming the other night at the public meeting. Even though he is—'

'The evillest man of all time?' Elsie answered. 'Well, regardless of his … inside leg measurements, he's a philistine and I hate him. What cake have you brought for us today, Gemma?' She turned to her friend, wishing that the image of his smile wouldn't keep popping up whenever she thought of him. She needed to think of Liam Chapstone's smile instead.

Gemma's grin showed Elsie that she knew her real thoughts about Jacob but she didn't say anything. 'It's a delicious banana and toffee cake. It's like banoffee pie but in cake form, and I've got some oat cookies for the kids.'

'Speaking of which,' said Patricia. 'I'd better get a squiggle on or I won't be ready.'

Elsie turned to Gemma. 'You're early today. You don't normally come until Toddler Taps has finished.' Gemma's expression tightened. 'Is everything okay?'

She checked around for Karen, then whispered, 'It's Orla. She's being really weird.'

'How do you mean "weird"?'

Together they moved to the desk and Gemma put down the tray. Karen was probably pretending to tidy the W section, earwigging on Jacob's conversation. Elsie had been hoping to do the same, but she'd have to wait. Gemma was more important.

'She's really withdrawn and … Oh, I don't know.'

'What like one-word answers?'

'No, she's talking to me like everything's fine, but I feel like something's bothering her.'

Elsie had been hoping for an opportunity to speak to Gemma and it looked like it had arrived. 'You were a little brisk with Orla the other night when we were discussing plans. She is entitled to her own opinion. If all she did was agree with you, you'd hate it.'

'I know and I've apologised for that. After you'd gone, I knew I was being unfair because she's right; in some ways more people here would be good for the village and for our business. I told her I was sorry for being moody and I thought we'd put it all

144

behind us, but ever since then she's been really subdued. She seems fine with Scarlett and she's smiling at me and assures me everything's okay, but then there's this atmosphere around her.'

'And you've tried talking to her?' Gemma pulled a face. 'All right, I was only checking. What could it be? Scarlett's okay, isn't she?'

'She's brilliant. And I mean literally brilliant. She's been sleeping through the night and hasn't been as wingy with her teeth.'

'Still, maybe looking after her and trying to run the café are both getting to Orla?'

Gemma nodded, but to Elsie it was unconvincing. 'That's all I can think of.'

'I'm sure if it's anything else she'll tell you when she's ready. Try not to worry. I don't know anyone as in love with each other as you two are. We're all tense at the moment. Has anyone else signed the petition?'

'A few. But we've also had a few more arguments in the bakery. We've never seen anything like it. Some people have asked we take the petition down because they believe the development is the right thing for the village and said we shouldn't be pushing our opinions onto them.'

'What did you say?'

'I told them it's my shop, my rules, and if I want to display something I will. Whether it's a petition or a poster.' That was typical of Gemma, but warning bells sounded in Elsie's head.

'Gemma, I really don't want you damaging your business over this. This is my fight and if it's putting you in a difficult position then I can find somewhere else for the petition to go. Do you think that's what's bothering Orla?'

'Maybe. She hates conflict. Especially after her family were so horrid about her moving away. Yes, I bet that's it. Are you sure you don't mind if we just have it at the shop and the deli? I think most people who want to sign it have already.'

145

'Of course not. I'll pop in and grab it on my way home then it's gone.'

'Thank you. Right, I'd better get back to the bakery. Are you coming round tonight?'

'No, I don't think so. I've got some more emails to send about the book launch.'

'Okay, catch you tomorrow then.'

Gemma left and Elsie hoped this small change would make Orla feel better. She loved Orla as much as she loved Gemma and would never want them to fall out. As the mums and children began to arrive for Toe Taps, Elsie made a mental list of all the people she needed to email tonight. With only a week to go, she had to contact them quickly. Perhaps she should supply directions to the village. Most people wouldn't know where it was, and she didn't want a single one getting lost. Karen came back to the desk and began reading her magazine again, clearly bored. They couldn't have been discussing anything of interest to her, but Elsie wanted to know more about the project and what their next plans were.

Seeing her chance, she moved to the back of the library, closer to Karen's office. If she dusted the spines of books rather than moved around, she could just about hear what was being said. Jacob's voice was a low rumble that contrasted with his colleague's higher pitched squeak.

'So when did this bloody book launch get arranged?'

Damn! He must have seen one of the posters or read the website. Elsie made sure she couldn't be seen through the tiny window in the office door.

'Apparently,' Leah said in slightly hushed tones, 'it's been in the pipeline for ages, but Karen told me that Elsie Martin, that frizzy-haired librarian, has organised it all.'

Well, that was rude, Elsie thought, pulling one of the wavy tendrils around her face and examining its frizziness.

'Why?' Jacob asked incredulously. 'It won't make any difference. And who is Neve Chapstone anyway?'

146

'She's a romance writer,' Leah said somewhat disparagingly. Elsie bristled. Romance was one of her favourite genres. It always annoyed her how people sneered at romantic fiction as if it wasn't as good as other genres. To Elsie, nothing captured life as well as a romance novel and who didn't need an uplifting, happy ending now and then?

Leah continued and Elsie could picture the sneer on her face. 'I doubt many people will come. It's not like it's a big-name celebrity. I'm guessing she's like Barbara Cartland but less pink and way less famous.'

'Okay,' Jacob said, and Elsie caught a glimpse of him striding around the office with his hands on his hips. Her eyes roved to his flat stomach and the muscles of his chest. Then she dragged them up, annoyed with her body for its visceral reaction. 'Then it'll probably only be a few people from the village. We can handle that.'

Can you? she thought, because it sounded to her like he was rattled.

'We don't need to mention this to … anyone.'

Ha! That meant he didn't want it mentioned to his father, who, according to what she'd read, held the reins rather tightly. She lifted a book off the shelf and dusted the cover before returning it, all the while smiling at the little win. Just as he had at the meeting, he and Rees-Hale had completely underestimated her.

She heard them approaching the door and launched herself around the stack, jogging back to the desk.

'Where've you been?' asked Karen. 'And why are you jogging?'

'I was just tidying the poetry section and I umm …' Elsie hated exercise and hadn't run since school. 'I was just seeing how bouncy my shoes were. I think they've got less bouncy and I don't want to get a bad back from no arch support.'

What on earth was she talking about?

The door handle of Karen's office was yanked open with such force Elsie could hear it from the front of the library. Jacob marched passed in his usual efficient manner, pausing only to stare at her before walking on. He was clearly frustrated but there seemed to be something else in his gaze, something she couldn't read. The look he shot her only made her more determined to invite as many people as possible to Neve Chapstone's book launch. With the added surprise Neve, or should she say Liam, had in store, there was no way it couldn't work.

Elsie pushed her glasses up the bridge of her nose. Jacob was in for one hell of a shock if he thought her nothing more than a frizzy-haired bibliophile. He probably didn't even know what bibliophile meant, she thought with a grin, but he'd soon find out.

Chapter 15

Elsie buzzed around the library on the evening of the book launch checking her watch every two seconds for Liam Chapstone to arrive and wondering if Jacob would also attend.

After arranging the seats and tea and coffee things, and making a nice display of paperbacks on the signing table, she found there wasn't much else to do. Every now and then her brain liked to frighten her with the idea that Liam had changed his mind and wasn't coming: that he'd decided not to reveal his true identity and preferred to continue writing as Neve Chapstone. They'd swapped numbers and the text messages they'd exchanged hadn't hinted at anything like that, but it didn't stop Elsie worrying anyway. She shuddered as it ran through her head once more. She had images of him stepping outside his house and opening his car door, only to pause and turn around to head back inside as he suddenly realised this wasn't a good idea for his career after all. She had to hope her mind was running away from her. It wouldn't be the first time.

'It's going to be fine,' said Gemma, bouncing Scarlett on her hip, as Elsie ensured the cups and saucers were perfectly in line. 'This is going to do the trick. Have you seen the number of people who are here already? There's no way this won't work.'

Strangers had been arriving in the village throughout the afternoon and every time someone had come into the library making sure they were in the right place, Elsie had congratulated herself on her bravery. 'I'm ridiculously nervous though. I honestly don't think I've ever been this terrified in my life. I can't believe I'm going to sit in front of everyone and ask Neve questions.'

'You've shouted your head off in front of everyone, so sticking to a script of questions should be easy-peasy.'

'Nerves can be good,' Patricia said, joining them at the refreshments table. 'They keep you focused. Keep you alert.'

'And I'm going to have to be tonight. Since he found out, Rees-Hale's been trying to trap me into admitting I'd organised it after the closure was announced.'

'Did you admit it?' she asked.

'No. I don't really know how I managed it. I was so hot and flustered and my cheeks were on fire. I must have looked as guilty as sin. I suppose the only good thing about always blushing is that it's not a tell when I do it while lying. I've got to see him on Monday about my madness at the public meeting. I don't think it's going to be fun.' Tapping into some of her new-found confidence she stood a little straighter. Whatever happened to her didn't matter. All that mattered was saving the library for the people she loved and for Meadowbank. 'He said he'd be attending tonight.'

'And look who else just walked in,' Gemma said.

Patricia and Elsie turned around as Jacob and Leah appeared. They were standing so close to each other their arms were touching. For a second Elsie wondered what it would be like to make contact with him like that. She gritted her teeth, banishing anything other than evil thoughts. She'd probably catch his idiocy. His blue eyes caught hers and she held herself firm, willing for her cheeks to remain cool. Why did he keep looking at her? Was he checking she wasn't about to start shouting again? He lifted his chin a little before dropping his eyes away. Leah then spoke to him, and he looked at her before breaking out into a grin. Was there a note of tension in his jaw though? She fervently hoped so.

Journalists were all huddled together in the corner where Bernard and Winston normally sat. Elsie had surmised that most of them already knew each other from the way they'd formed little groups and cliques. Jennifer Motley, the freelance journalist who lived at Highfield, the large manor house on the outskirts of the village, waved to her and Elsie went over.

'Is everything all right, Jennifer?' she asked the tall, elegant lady.

Elsie had been so pleased when Jennifer had expressed interest in the story. She'd been as nervous about calling her as she was about going to see Neve Chapstone, all because Highfield was such an imposing house. Mr Motley, Jennifer's husband, was a well-respected human rights lawyer and was often in the public eye. Because of that, Jennifer explained, they didn't go into the village much, but this story was definitely worth pursuing and Jennifer had hopes of selling the story to one of the national Sunday supplements. Tonight, Jennifer was standing next to another reporter who on arrival had introduced herself as from *The Writing Edit*, one of the best-selling writing magazines of all time.

'Do you know when Neve is going to arrive?' Jennifer asked.

'We said seven-thirty so that everyone has time to get here and get settled.' She quickly checked her watch. 'Only five minutes to go.'

'How did you manage to secure her?' the woman from *The Writing Edit* asked. 'We've been trying for ages, but she's always said no.'

'I can only suppose it's because she knows the library is closing and wanted to support us in our last ever event.' She'd rehearsed this line a number of times, tinkering with it like a writer toys with a story, to make sure she said nothing that could get her in even more trouble if it appeared in print.

'Well, it's wonderful of her, isn't it? So you've met her already?'

'Yes,' Elsie said, eager not to say more than necessary.

'And what was she like?'

'Very nice. Very nice indeed.'

'And when is the library due to close?' the woman asked, making a note on her phone. Elsie had expected them to have pencils and notepads, but it was all phones and iPads these days. 'In two weeks.'

'It's a tragedy,' Jennifer said.

'Could you excuse me?' Elsie replied. 'I must get everyone seated, ready for Neve to arrive.'

During their conversations, they'd decided that Elsie announcing Neve was here and then Liam walking in would create the most impact and the biggest splash with the reporters. He was going to call her when he had parked up outside, which should be at any moment. Elsie made her way towards the groups of villagers in the centre of the room. So many people had turned up that Patricia had to find more chairs, and as she scanned the room quickly counting, Elsie realised they wouldn't have enough. The thought of speaking in front of so many people sent her heart palpitating. It would be standing room only if anyone else came now, but it was all for the good. It showed how important the library was and how these events were well attended. She couldn't imagine what a disappointment it would have been if only a few people had bothered to turn up.

As she hurried to the door, a voice as smooth as she wished her hair could be halted her.

'This is quite a turnout,' Jacob said, nodding towards the room.

Leah had gone to get herself and Jacob drinks, judging by the two cups she was holding over by the refreshments table.

'Meadowbank villagers love their library,' Elsie replied coolly. His gaze shifted from the crowd onto her, and his stare intensified. He crossed his arms, the material of his shirt tightening over his biceps. Why did he have to have such nice arms? She mentally told her body to calm down. The confidence she'd been finding made her lift her head and meet his gaze.

152

'How did you organise this so quickly?'

'I didn't. It had been an idea for a while, but we hadn't heard back, that's all.' For some reason, she decided to press her luck. 'But if I had to hazard a guess, I think hearing the library was to be torn down to make way for housing we don't need made Neve say yes.'

'Housing we don't need?' he echoed, and she nodded. With a sad shake of the head, he said, 'Elsie, I wish you could understand my point of view. This place does need housing. I never had you pinned as someone so short-sighted.'

'Well, that's why I wear glasses,' she replied smugly. It wasn't a great joke, but it was better than turning beetroot red and opening and closing her mouth like a bemused goldfish.

'You know what I mean. When I first met you, I imagined you as more …'

He searched for the words, and predicting something derogatory, Elsie opened her mouth. 'What? A pushover? A nobody who would let you drive into town in your ridiculous sports car, acting like you've come here to save the village when what you've really done is destroy a vital part of it.'

'No, I was going to say—' A panicked look had come into his eyes, but she couldn't stop the lava-like flow coming out of her.

'Something even worse, I should imagine.'

He stared, dumbstruck, and she couldn't exactly blame him. She hadn't intended for that tirade to come out. Why did he have this effect on her? Before he could gather himself and insult her anymore, she said, 'Excuse me', out of some ridiculous prim English politeness and walked on to the door. Her phone rang and excitement raced as she answered. Hearing Liam's voice calmed her anger after her encounter with Jacob but fuelled her anticipation even more. She couldn't wait to see the look on everyone's faces.

'I'm outside,' Liam said cheerfully.

The difference between his voice and Jacob's was stark. Liam's was jovial and light, like a breath of fresh air after the thick, doom-ridden atmosphere that Jacob brought with him.

'Okay, I'll be there in a second.' Turning around to face the room she felt nerves bubble up, and swallowing them down with a deep breath was almost impossible. 'If you'd all like to take your seats, Neve is just arriving.'

Everyone hustled to find a chair and not be one of those left standing. Unfortunately, Mr Farmer and Mrs Collins were arguing over their seats.

'I got here first,' Mrs Collins said. 'I put my coat there and then went to get a drink.'

'You put your coat on one chair and your bag on another. You can't hog two chairs when there's only one of you.'

'I wanted to make sure I got a seat, knowing that people like you would steal it given half the chance.'

'People like me?' Mr Farmer's eyebrows shot up so high they met his fringe. 'It's people like you who are the reason my son has got to move to Witchbury.'

'What on earth do you mean?' Mrs Collins replied, grabbing her coat and plonking herself in one of the chairs she'd saved. 'Your son moving has got nothing to do with me.'

'It's because people like you who signed that pet—'

Knowing he was about to say the word 'petition', Elsie shot forwards. 'Here's a seat, Mr Farmer.' She grabbed the office chair from behind the desk and wheeled it out for him. She didn't mind standing. The exchange calmed down as they each muttered to the person next to them and Elsie went to the door. She couldn't stop her eyes drifting to Jacob to see what effect that had had on him too. He was probably pleased the villagers were at odds. Probably thought it was a good thing and would mean more sales of his horrible houses, but surprisingly, the look on his face was one of confusion. Elsie cast her eyes to the doorway, where a shadow suddenly obscured the light filtering through.

'Mr Rees-Hale, good evening.'

He paused, before eyeing the cluster of journalists and marching off to Jacob and Leah. He gave a small grunt in reply, as Elsie carried on outside.

Liam had his hands in his pockets, and gently nudged a tuft of grass with his foot as Elsie approached him. At their previous meeting, she'd never really appreciated how tall he was or how broad his shoulders were.

'How are you feeling?' Elsie asked.

His smile was wide and carefree. 'Nervous. Excited. I feel like this is the beginning of a new chapter for me and my writing. It's very …'

'Exciting?' Elsie offered, unable to think of anything better.

'Terrifying! But in a good way.'

Elsie laughed. He looked even more attractive today than he had the last time she'd met him. He was wearing a pale cream shirt with birds on it and dark denim jeans, turned up over scruffy high-top trainers. The writing world was in for a shock when they saw him.

'Will I get run out of town for being a man?' he asked.

'Everyone will be thrilled. Surprised, but thrilled.' The space between them filled with warm spring air. 'I've been worrying you were going to change your mind.'

Liam laughed. 'I wouldn't do that. I said I'd come, so here I am. I wouldn't let you down.'

Elsie looked up to meet his eye and a rumbling began in her lower tummy. Was there something between them? It wasn't as immediate as it had been with Jacob but look where those feelings had got her. There was no future there, but with Liam, she had the distinct impression that if he was interested in her, and she didn't know for sure he was yet, she'd be more than happy to see where it led.

'Come on,' Elsie said. 'I'd better get you inside before they come out here looking for you.'

'I can already see some faces at the windows. Let's go before they twig and ruin the surprise.'

Elsie led the way and at the doorway, made her announcement. 'Ladies and gentlemen, please welcome Neve Chapstone.'

Chapter 16

A round of applause started and Elsie stepped aside to reveal Liam. There was a slight lull as realisation dawned and everyone understood what she and Liam were silently telling them. After the initial shock, manners took over and everyone clapped until Liam had gone to the front and stood before the signing table. Elsie had set out two chairs: one for her and one for him and she made her way to the front, fear shaking her legs as she went. She was aware of Jacob watching her. Could feel his eyes somehow. But she forced herself to be brave. She could do this. She had to.

'Thank you, everyone, for coming,' she said, her voice wavering, but gathering strength as she looked at Liam. 'If you haven't guessed, this is Neve Chapstone—'

'Well, actually, my name's Liam Chapstone but I've been writing under the pen name Neve – my mother's name – since I began writing romance.'

The journalists were typing furiously, unable to contain their shock but certain of a good story. Elsie swelled with pride. Everything was going perfectly. Expectation hung in the air, building to the crescendo she and Liam had already planned. They both took their chairs.

'I wonder,' she began, feeling more at home now she was sat

down chatting, 'if you could tell us why you love writing romance novels and why you chose to use a pen name.'

The audience listened, enraptured.

'I think romance is such a unifying genre, don't you?' Heads nodded in the crowd. 'Every story has some romance in it, no matter if it's fantasy, science fiction, horror. Watch any movie and romance is certain to be a key thread.'

He spoke eloquently and glanced at Elsie throughout. This time, her eyes were up and focused rather than staring at the floor and she didn't need Gemma's help to know there was an attraction between them. Without a hint of shyness or embarrassment, she smiled back, encouraging him to continue and be brave. The journalists were itching to ask questions, and some shouted them out, but with poise and grace, Elsie asked them to wait until the end.

The only time her smile wavered was when she caught Jacob's and Rees-Hale's eyes. Rees-Hale looked like he was about to explode. His cheeks had turned a deep ruddy red and splotches were visible above the collar of his shirt. He glared at her with what can only be described as murderous intent. Jacob had grown pale. His eyes darted from the frenzied journalists to Liam and her. His words of earlier rang through her head. He'd never taken her as being short-sighted. Well, she wasn't. He was. He was the one who couldn't see the value in the thing he was destroying. Perhaps now he'd sit up and pay attention.

Elsie asked more questions about how he became a published author, where he got his inspiration from, and how he found living in such a beautiful area. Liam continued and there wasn't a woman in the room who wasn't in love with him, or a man who didn't want to befriend him. He was charming, charismatic, genuine. In contrast, Jacob had bitten back his lip and frustration was etched deep into his brow.

Finally, Liam announced why he'd chosen now to reveal his identity. 'I know many of you, particularly my journalistic friends here, will be wondering why now? Why did I decide today, and

Meadowbank Library, as the right time and location to reveal the truth? Well, the first answer is I'd been thinking about it for a while now. I love writing romance, and I have every intention of continuing, but I've also been wanting to branch out into the world of thrillers and suspense.'

A whisper flew around the journalists, who all knew they'd struck gold this evening.

'And the second answer is—' He stood up and Elsie followed suit. 'Because when I heard that Meadowbank Library was closing, and I saw that some time ago Elsie Martin had got in touch with me—'

She flashed him a grateful smile for keeping up her story before dropping her eyes, aware of Rees-Hale and Jacob's stares.

'I knew I had to be here.' He paused and took a breath. 'Because a little piece of my heart dies every time a library closes.'

For a second, Elsie wondered why he'd chosen to use the exact same words and the exact same tone he had when he was talking to her on the doorstep, but seeing the effect, she relaxed. It was a good phrase and conveyed so eloquently his, and her, thoughts on the matter.

'If Meadowbank Library does indeed have to close, then I hope we've been able to go out with a bang, but—'

Now it was time for the pièce de résistance. Elsie went to the desk and gathered the petition before boldly making her way back to the front. 'Liam, would you like to sign the petition we've mounted asking for the developers to change their plans and *not* destroy the library?'

'I'd be delighted.' He theatrically plucked a pen from his shirt pocket. He took the papers from Elsie and laid them on the table, signing under everyone's gaze.

The whispering of the reporters had grown to eager chatter, and from their expressions they were enjoying the show.

'Here you are, Mr Rees-Hale, Mr Yardley.' Elsie marched to where they stood at the back and placed the petition in Jacob's hands. Her finger touched his and something akin to a static shock raced up her arm. Elsie put it down to stress and, though it had left a pleasant tingling in her body, ignored it. Rees-Hale had turned from red to a purplish-beetroot colour and Elsie marvelled at the strange hue. Even she hadn't turned that colour before. She hoped he wasn't about to have a heart attack. Jacob's eyes focused on the document in front of him before locking on her, anger radiating off him in waves she could almost feel. 'Perhaps now you'll reconsider your plans. With Mr Chapstone we now have over 1,600 signatures. I think that should illustrate the strength of feeling within the village.'

Worryingly, that still meant roughly half the village hadn't signed it, but Elsie didn't say so.

'Now,' Liam said cheerily, clapping his hands together to break the awkward silence that had descended. 'Would anyone like me to sign a book for them, considering this will be my one and only signing as Neve Chapstone?'

A throng of people rushed to the front while others eyed Elsie as she made her way back. It was disconcerting to see the mixture of pride and disapproval on the faces before her. Some of Elsie's own neighbours didn't seem happy at what she'd done and watched her with open condemnation. She pulled her arms around her, holding tightly on to her elbows, aware that, subconsciously, she was raising a shield.

'He fancies you, you know,' Gemma said, edging closer to her ear to be heard over the rising noise.

'Jacob? Well, after everything, I'm not interested in him at all.' She pulled her eyes away and focused back on Liam.

'No, not that twit. Liam.'

The last time Gemma had pointed out someone fancying her was when a visitor staying at the Drunken Duck had taken a shine to her while researching his family history. Elsie hadn't noticed until he'd left the village and the chance had gone. She hadn't been too upset; she'd noticed he had a habit of chewing his pencil, which was terribly unhygienic, but he had been quite cute.

She watched Liam for a moment and had to admit that she'd been hoping he might like her. But could he really be interested in her? Throughout his talk, he'd glanced over so often she'd assumed he was checking to see when his time had run out. But why shouldn't he? she thought suddenly, and it was as if a new voice was speaking in her head. She wasn't gorgeous but she wasn't too bad looking and they had a lot in common.

Liam had a nice smile and dark hair that would probably feel quite nice under her fingertips. She cocked her head as she imagined a kiss. It was a very nice thought. Then, for some reason, her treacherous eyes shot to Jacob. For a second she imagined kissing him instead, but when he looked at her with his icy-cold stare, she froze, feeling something quite undefinable. Liam loved words and books and made a living using them, bringing pleasure to those who were wise enough to read his novels. Beautiful, brilliant, uplifting stories of love and hope and friendship and romance. If Elsie the bookworm was going to have a decent relationship with anyone, it would be him.

'What do you think will happen to the petition?' she asked Gemma, keen to change the subject.

'I don't know. We just have to wait and see what the papers print over the next few days, I guess. Did you see Orla's face at all?'

'No.' That was a strange question. 'Why?'

Gemma shrugged. 'No reason.'

Were they still having problems? 'Gemma, is everything—'

'I'm going to grab Orla and we'll head off, okay? Scarlett's tired.' She drew her in for a hug. 'See you tomorrow. I'm so proud of you, Elsie.'

As the evening drew to a close and the villagers began to leave, Rees-Hale cornered Elsie while she was stacking chairs. Liam was still talking to the journalists, which could only be a good thing as far as Elsie was concerned. The more time he spent talking about why he was here the better.

161

'You haven't forgotten our meeting on Monday, Miss Martin?'

'No, I haven't,' she replied, unable to hide the note of fear in her voice.

'Good. See you at three o'clock.'

He stomped out of the building, followed by Leah and Jacob. Jacob lingered for a moment, casting his eyes over Elsie as though he wanted to speak to her, but then he glanced at Liam and departed. He probably hated him as much as he hated her now.

Elsie made her way over as the reporters were wrapping up their questions. After one had left, the others followed in a stampede and before she knew it, she and Liam were alone in the now-empty library. The late evening sunshine shone through the windows, spreading a golden glow across the room.

'That went well, don't you think?' Liam said, coming over and helping her stack the chairs.

'You don't need to do that. I can tidy up.'

'I don't mind, especially as your supervisor left as soon as she could. Is she always like that?'

'Always. She doesn't care at all that the library is closing.'

'I hope that my signing the petition in front of everyone makes a difference.'

They continued stacking chairs in silence until there were only two left. Elsie took a rest on one, feeling suddenly tired. It had been a long and stressful day. It had been a long and stressful two weeks and with only a few good nights' rest she felt swamped with exhaustion.

Liam sat beside her, and she felt her body tense at the proximity. They were shoulder to shoulder as she'd had to pack the chairs in so tightly. If he splayed his leg out, it would touch hers. She wondered what it would feel like if his body did touch hers. Would she feel the same thrill she had when her eyes had first met Jacob's? She refused to think about him anymore and focused on the lovely man beside her who had spoken about the need for happy-ever-afters in a world where, unfortunately, things didn't always work out how we wanted them too.

'You're really quite amazing, you know?' Liam said, his voice soft. 'Not many people would put themselves out there like you have.'

'I don't think I'm amazing. I think I'm doing what anyone in my position would do.'

He laughed and embarrassment inched up her spine, tingling her cheeks. 'Karen's in the same position as you and she hasn't done anything. Half of your village don't want to lose the library but they're not mounting petitions and launching secret resistance campaigns. You're doing something very special, Elsie. Because you're special.'

The tingling mounted to full-on pins and needles, but her brain stalled. She turned to face him, wondering if he was going to kiss her. The peace and quiet of the library, her normally happy place, had been replaced with a dense, heavy atmosphere loaded with a sense of possibility and she wasn't sure how she felt about it.

'I should put you in a book,' Liam said. 'The perfect feisty heroine.'

Elsie tucked a lock of hair behind her ear and pushed her glasses back up her nose. As usual with her frizzy mane, it bounced back and as she raised her fingers to push it behind again, Liam lifted his hand and his fingers brushed hers as he took the strand of hair and wrapped it around her ear. His eyes swept down her face, coming to rest on her mouth, and he kissed her.

Liam might have said he should put her in a book, but right now, Elsie felt like she was already in one. The gentle pressure of his lips, as well as their melting softness, sent a wave of emotion through her. As her willingness became clear, Liam kissed her harder and for a few moments time stopped. Eventually, he separated from her.

'Wow. That was quite something. I normally only get to write about those types of kisses. I never thought they really existed.' He smiled so warmly she wouldn't have been surprised if she'd melted into a puddle. 'I'd better stop, or I won't want to leave.'

'Right.' It wasn't a particularly sexy response, but she didn't know what else to say. It felt like something was missing and she ignored the thought, putting it down to her lack of experience and extreme tiredness. Elsie straightened her glasses as Liam sat back. 'What's next for Neve Chapstone? The journalists were very interested.'

'They were. This might be the most media coverage I've ever had. I also spoke about my thrillers and there was a lot of excitement for them. My agent will be pleased. Shame she couldn't make it tonight, but there you are, I suppose,' he said, standing up and picking up his chair. 'I should get going. You must be tired after today, but I think it went well.'

Without knowing what else to do, Elsie stood and took her chair too. Was that it? One steamy kiss and then back to a more professional relationship? She felt winded and not a little confused.

'This whole thing has been quite exhausting,' she replied, keeping her tone light.

'Perhaps …' He paused and Elsie waited to hear what he had to say. 'Perhaps I could call you tomorrow and we can meet again? Have a coffee or something? You must know I'm pretty mad about you?'

Mad about her?

'I'd like that.'

Liam Chapstone had not only kissed her but asked to see her again too! Her instincts had been right, and thankfully, this time she'd listened.

'Good.' He nodded and anchored his hands in his pockets. 'Then I guess I'll call you.'

He headed to the door and left with a quick wave. Once he'd gone, she assessed the debris and detritus left from the launch. All of the books had been sold and the till sat full of cash. Money that would go into the council coffers for them to use somewhere else, she thought bitterly, but her point had been made and made well. Even if she was for the sack on Monday, which she would be judging by Rees-Hale's splotchy face, at least she'd done all she could. The fear of finding a new job was tempered by the idea that the library would at least still be here because she was absolutely sure she'd been successful. There was no way this couldn't have worked.

Chapter 17

'Why didn't you tell me about this bloody book launch, Jacob?' Conrad shouted through the computer screen. This was not how Jacob wanted to spend his Saturday afternoon. His father's face was puce and so close to the screen, Jacob could see the new, smaller hairs growing at the top of his moustache. 'I could have stopped all this nonsense from happening. Now look—' He held his phone up, showing some sort of news article, but from the glare, it was difficult to see.

He didn't need to read it. He already knew what it said. He'd completely underestimated Elsie Martin and the effect this innocent-sounding book launch would have. It hadn't just been some author he'd never heard of and a few of the villagers, it had been a media-attended, packed-out gig. The local paper was full of it. They'd dedicated the first five pages, including the front, to the fabulous author revealing his true identity in the library due for closure. After seeing all the journalists there, Jacob had also kept an eye on the social media channels, and the publishing world was ablaze with the fact that best-selling romance author Neve Chapstone was actually a six-foot-tall man called Liam.

The one thing he could say for Elsie Martin was that she had an amazing poker face. Never once when he'd spoken to her before the book launch began had he suspected she was harbouring such a secret. She was certainly an enigma. The trouble was, no matter how much this enigma consumed his thoughts, and she had been, far more than was necessary, she was causing him trouble and threatening everything. He couldn't afford for his father to lose faith in him when he'd only recently made so much progress.

Then there were the doubts she'd cast in his mind. The event had been packed out and more than once he'd heard the villagers saying it was like this or that event they'd attended before at the library. A seed of doubt had been planted that maybe this place was more of a hub for the community than he'd realised. He'd thought libraries were outdated but maybe it was his opinion of them that was?

'Well?' his father barked. 'What do you make of all this? You've really let us down here, Jacob. I hope you've got a plan to bring things back in line.'

'Yes, of course I do,' he replied, though in actual fact he didn't. His brain scrabbled around for something tangible, leaving behind a mass of self-doubt.

'Because if you don't, we could be in a whole heap of trouble. This is a PR nightmare. If some of the nationals pick this up, we could be in real trouble.'

He had to play things down as much as possible or his father would be here like a shot. From the corner of his eye, a headline on his phone caught his attention. 'If you look into the different articles, most are focused on the fact that this guy is writing really successful romance novels. They're more interested in the fact *she* is a *he*, and a lot of them are looking at the question of whether the romance industry is biased towards female authors. Not many of them focus on the fact the library is closing, it's more of a footnote, if indeed it's mentioned at all.' His words seemed to be working, and he spoke with increasing confidence. 'Maybe a line or two about what a shame it is another library is closing, but it's a given fact the country is losing libraries left, right, and centre.

None of them question it. The only ones that mention the closure in more detail are the local rag, which won't make any difference to anything, and the paper from Liam Chapstone's home village, which is hailing him as the best thing that's happened to them in about a hundred years.' He cast aside the paper, which some unknown person had posted through his letterbox this morning.

There were one or two more that had focused on the closure as much as Liam Chapstone revealing his true identity, but with any luck his father hadn't seen those and wouldn't notice that Jennifer Motley's name was at the bottom of one of them. His father had been hoping to befriend Hugh Motley for some time and had assumed he'd be on board with their plans.

Conrad grunted. It probably didn't help that this conversation was happening at three in the afternoon, so his father had been stewing all day. No one could work themselves up into a frenzy as well as his father.

'Who's behind all this nonsense, hey? Who's the ringleader and what do you intend to do about them? We don't want the name of the business appearing in the paper unless it's linked to something good. We're being painted as the bad guys, which isn't a surprise—'

Because we are, thought Jacob with a shudder.

'But it's your job to minimise negative coverage, Jacob. Get this under control.'

'We believe,' Leah said. 'That the woman doing this is—'

'A woman?'

Jacob resisted rolling his eyes. It was clearly inconceivable to his father that a woman would have the brains and brawn to do something like this.

'Yes,' Leah said, edging forwards, either ignoring his tone or so used to it, it didn't even register anymore. 'It's a woman who works at the library called Elsie Martin.'

'*Elsie*?' he echoed. 'Sounds like my grandmother.'

She doesn't look like a grandmother, Jacob thought wryly,

thinking again of her curves and wild hair. She carried herself as if she had the wisdom of an entire life inside her, of a heart that wasn't swayed by money or possessions – or looks for that matter. A spirit that required more than material things to make it happy. His English degree hadn't been wasted after all, he thought. That was the most poetic he'd been in a long time. The tightening in his stomach meant he was more attracted than he'd been to anyone in a long time, but there was no way he could do anything about it. She'd never be interested in him now, and if his father ever found out, he'd kill him for consorting with the enemy.

Leah continued, 'She's nothing more than an inconvenience though, Conrad. And I've been assured she'll be out of a job come Monday.'

Jacob's head shot round, and sympathy pierced him. Elsie clearly loved the library and believed in what it stood for, and though he'd disagreed with her opinions (he ignored the doubts niggling in his mind from earlier), he could only imagine how heart-wrenching it must be to be fired and unable to work there until its last day. His father would call his feelings a weakness, and he was right. There was no place for emotions in business, but he still couldn't easily shake them off.

'After the petition was brought out—'

Conrad cut Leah off. 'How big was this petition?'

'About half the village,' Jacob said, trying to take some control. Sometimes his father and Leah would discuss things as if he wasn't there. It made him feel small and like a part-time office boy rather than the owner's son. The man who would one day inherit this vast, million-pound business.

Conrad made a guttural noise in his throat. 'We've had worse.'

'Rees-Hale couldn't contain himself,' Leah said with a wolfish grin. 'He told me he was sure she was behind all of this. He didn't believe the book launch had been in the pipeline for ages, though he couldn't prove it without asking Liam Chapstone and he didn't want to risk him getting even more involved.'

Jacob's mind wandered away from his father's phlegmy noises towards this Liam fellow. He'd seen the way the author had watched Elsie throughout the evening, and it had made him uncomfortable. Jealous.

Leah continued happily, 'He said when he sees her on Monday it'll be gross misconduct. Apparently, she's worked there for forever. Never even left the village.'

An icy blast shot over Jacob's skin. She really was sacrificing everything to stand up for what she believed in, and he didn't like the mocking tone Leah had adopted. It was unnecessary but his father was enjoying it.

'What an idiot.'

Jacob clenched his jaw. It wasn't idiotic at all. As much of a pain as it was – and it was proving much more of a pain than he'd ever experienced before – it was courageous. Principled. Even more disturbingly, he was starting to wonder if there was something in what she'd said at the meeting. Every time he'd been in the library it had been full of villagers and last night had shown that special events were well attended too.

'She'll be out of our hair by Monday,' Leah reassured Conrad, then flashed him a smile. Jacob knew he should have been grateful for her support but the whole thing left a bitter taste in his mouth. 'And with two weeks until the library officially closes …' She looked to him to continue.

'I don't foresee any further problems,' he finished.

'Sure?' Conrad growled.

'Definitely.'

'One more chance then, and that's it. Any more fuck-ups and I'll be down there quicker than you can say Meadowbank.'

'Understood,' he replied as his father clicked off the call. This time Jacob didn't even bother to ask if his well wishes could be passed on to his mother.

Leah closed the laptop. 'That went about as well as can be expected. Your father managed to keep his temper under control.

I once saw him knock a foreman's hat off over something much less important.'

'Good thing he wasn't actually here then.' Jacob sat back, raking a hand through his hair. 'I guess it could have gone a lot worse. There's been far more media coverage than I ever expected.'

'And me,' Leah replied, swiping at her phone screen. 'I'm keeping records of everything in case we need them in the future.' He hoped that was all it was for and not so she could go scurrying to his father if the situation worsened, absolving herself of any responsibility. She slid her phone into her back pocket and began working again on the laptop.

'I thought I might go for a run,' he suddenly announced. He had no idea why he felt he should report to Leah. He wasn't exactly giving the impression of someone capable of running a huge company. To be honest, he had doubts about that himself. She nodded, but didn't really respond, eyes down on the screen.

How Jacob wished they weren't living together. The last few evenings he'd spent his time reading that poetry book he found on the shelf while she worked or did something on her phone. Time had passed slowly, awkward and uncomfortable. He supposed that one day, when he did share his life with someone – someone he loved – evenings would feel contented rather than difficult. He was nearing the end of his book now and wanted another, but the only option was the library and he couldn't go in there: it would be like admitting he was wrong. He'd have to buy one.

He quite fancied a pint as well, but he couldn't imagine the embarrassment of going into the pub and being refused in front of a roomful of strangers. Especially strangers who'd be glad to see him fail. They had no idea what was at stake for him. The years he'd waited to hear some form of approval from his father. Words that, if he played his cards right, would come and, he hoped, fill the dark void that sat in his soul.

With muscles itching with energy, he headed out of the door half an hour later ready to work his legs and feel that strangely addictive burning in his chest. Just as he was about to turn down the road from his rented cottage, he saw an old man on a bicycle up ahead. He was wobbling precariously, and though he knew he should mind his own business, he felt the need to make sure the man got to his destination safely. The wobbling grew stronger, and the man lurched from side to side. He'd probably do better if he picked up some speed, but Jacob wasn't sure he was capable of that. As he'd feared, the bike leaned too heavily to one side and the wheels slipped out from under him. The old man tumbled to the ground and Jacob found himself sprinting towards him, his tired legs burning with the effort.

'Are you okay?' he asked, untangling the bicycle from the man's limbs, and propping it against the wall. 'Don't move yet. I'll help you up in a second.'

'I don't need any help from you, thank you very much.' The old man's sharp tone took him by surprise. His thinning grey hair that had been combed into an old-fashioned style had fallen forwards and the man pushed it back with an age-spotted hand. Luckily there didn't seem to be any cuts or bruises on his arm.

'Please let me help you. You've hurt yourself.'

The old man pushed himself up onto his forearm and with the other hand, felt his forehead. Blood trickled from a small cut, leaving a stain on his fingers, but he didn't seem concussed or confused.

'Don't move too much. Have you hurt your neck? Please, I really think you should be lying still. We should call an ambulance.'

'Get away with you. I'm fine, stop fussing.' The man began to climb up onto his feet and Jacob helped by supporting him under his elbow. 'I don't need *your* help. Why would I want the likes of you to help me?'

'I'm sorry?'

As soon as the man was upright, he wrenched his arm away as if Jacob was trying to kidnap him.

'Winston?' A soft voice laced with concern carried on the

breeze and Jacob looked up to see Elsie running down from the library. Jacob realised that despite everything, he was glad to see her. A slightly stronger breeze took some of the cherry blossoms from the trees and sprinkled it like confetti behind her. His heart almost burst at the sight. She stopped by Winston's side and put a protective hand on his arm. 'Winston, what happened?'

'Oh, nothing. I lost my balance, that's all. I thought with my bad leg I might ride to the library because it wouldn't take as long, but it's being an absolute bugger – my leg, not the bike – and I fell off.'

'Are you all right?' She tilted her head, studying the cut on his forehead.

'Just some bumps and bruises. My pride's hurt most of all. I used to be able to ride to Witchbury and back when I was younger. When did I get so old?'

There was such fondness in her eyes and concern on her face, Jacob felt he had to speak. 'I know you said you're fine, but we can call an ambulance if you like?'

'I've already told him,' Winston snapped, speaking to Elsie. 'I don't need one.'

'I'm sure he's only trying to help,' Elsie replied.

'By stealing our library and knocking down the place we all feel so at home?' He shook his head. 'I don't think so.'

With all his heart Jacob wished he could dematerialise and reappear somewhere else. An island in the middle of nowhere maybe. The seed of doubt grew a little bigger. 'If you're all right, sir, then I'd better get going.'

'Sir? Ha!'

'Do you want me to take you to the doctor's, Winston?' Elsie gave Jacob what looked like an apologetic smile. 'Or get him to come and see you?'

'No, no. Honestly, I'm absolutely fine.' He went to walk but his bad leg gave way, causing him to drop to one side again. Instinctively, Jacob reached out to support him. 'I can manage.'

'Yes, of course. Sorry.' He let go.

Seeming surprised at his reaction, Elsie said, 'You don't normally come to us on a Saturday, Winston. What made you decide to today?' She smelled of vanilla and fresh air and her hair carried a note of berries. It filled all of Jacob's senses, wrapping around his brain.

'I thought I'd better make the most of it before this young man destroys my home from home.' Though she looked uncomfortable at Winston's remark, the fire he'd seen in her eyes on previous occasions sparked again. 'I was sitting at home and all I could think about was how much I'm missing my Lillian and I knew I had to get out and do something before it all got too much again. So, I thought I'd come and see you and maybe find a new book to read.'

The pain in Winston's voice had been reflected in Elsie's face and Jacob felt more than just a wavering in his belief that libraries were outdated institutions. Then he imagined the ruddy, angry face he'd seen this morning. The one he had to live with day in and day out. Even the thought of his father's disappointment cut deep.

In a cheerful tone, Elsie rallied Winston. 'What do you fancy today then? Something chilling and blood-curdling or something a bit more suspenseful? Maybe sci-fi to take you away from the world for a while?'

'Let's find something exceptionally gory, shall we? That always cheers me up.'

Elsie took his bicycle from where it had been resting against the wall, but Winston took the handlebars from her.

'I can manage, poppet.' He walked slowly towards the library, and to Jacob's astonishment, she lingered behind.

When Winston was far enough out of earshot, she glanced at him and dropped her eyes as she said, 'Thank you for helping him', then turned to head back to the library.

A powerful force inside him made him speak, though he didn't know what he was going to say. All he knew was that he wanted her to stay a while longer. 'I hope your friend is okay.'

'I'm sure he'll be fine. I'll make him a cup of tea in a minute.'

That the librarian would be making a cup of tea for the old man only cemented his worries. Was he wrong about all libraries or just Meadowbank? It did seem to be a world unto itself.

'Thank you for your directions the other day. I made it back in one piece and didn't get lost again.' She nodded but didn't speak. 'The world feels very different here sometimes. Like time has stopped working or slowed down.' What was he even saying?

She stared at him for a moment. 'There's a beautiful route between here and Little Thrumpton that takes you over the top of the highest fields so you can see for miles.' As she finished the sentence, the softness her eyes and voice had carried faded, as if she was angry at herself for being polite to him. 'I'd better go.'

Elsie walked quickly to the library, but before she stepped inside, she glanced at him one last time. It really shouldn't have, but it set his soul on fire.

Chapter 18

Jacob rolled over and checked the time on his watch. With a sigh, he rammed his head back onto the pillow and pressed the heels of his hands into his eyes. They were gritty but no matter what he did he couldn't get comfortable, and sleep wouldn't come. He must have dozed a little, unable to recall every ticking of the clock, but for the most part he hadn't slept, and his mind was now well awake.

Things were bothering him. So many annoying and confusing things. His father first and foremost played on his mind. The words he'd said about no more fuck-ups ran round and round his head. Leah's joy at Elsie losing her job concerned him as did the way he felt pressure build in his chest whenever Elsie looked at him. But even as the image of her face flew into his mind for the millionth time that night, he knew it was more than a physical attraction. More than just admiration for her courage. There was something else within him and he couldn't help wondering what might have been had they both been on the same side.

Jacob rolled over once more, pushing the book of poetry he'd tried reading to the edge of the bed. He'd hoped that turning to face the open window might calm him down, but all that happened was the bedsheet wrapped around his legs, tying him in a knot. With an angry sigh he kicked and pushed it down with his feet.

This was hopeless. He might as well get up and go for a walk. He felt the need to get out of the cottage and away from Leah, his job, his doubts, his father – all the things clouding his mind and stopping him from sleeping. He felt trapped by his life and the expectations on him. It should have been so simple; turn up and build some houses. His father had even described this as an easy one. And now look. A divide had opened in the village, and he was responsible for it. Perhaps a walk in the dark, without the villagers being rude to him and without the fear of running into Elsie, would clear his head enough for him to actually fall asleep.

Through the open window the night was still and without the flutter of leaves in the breeze or the hum of traffic, there was nothing but a deep, dense silence. The ducks had fallen asleep hours ago and Jacob felt like the only person in the whole world who was awake. He pulled on a T-shirt and his jeans over the boxers he slept in and padded quietly downstairs before slipping on his trainers. Grabbing his keys, he stole out of the front door, closing it quietly behind him.

The streetlamps that dotted the lanes here and there were in the old Victorian style but weren't evenly placed and as Jacob made his way towards the village green, he stumbled into a large bush growing over a garden wall. Brushing his arm to ensure he hadn't taken any of it with him, he reached the end of the lane that opened onto the wider road circling the green and duck pond. He could only imagine the fêtes and fairs that were held there every year. Surely the community spirit Elsie was so fond of would endure despite the divisions he'd created.

In the corner of the pond, the ducks slept huddled together on a small bank. Every light in every house was out. He really was the only person awake in this little world. The sheet of black motionless water reflected the bright full moon. A circle of brilliant silver light shimmered at him. There was something incredibly peaceful about the place. More so than he'd found anywhere else he'd lived. Even in his hometown, which wasn't that dissimilar to Meadowbank, and certainly not in the city. Yet the air was special here. He felt that magic again, just as he had the first time. If things were different, he'd be happy to stay. To one day become like Winston and grow old here, but that would never be for him. Not after all he was doing. He still believed the housing was needed, but the location? It was too late to change things now. His father would never countenance it.

Jacob glanced over his shoulder towards the library in the distance. The little seeds of doubt sown by his own mind but magnified by Elsie Martin and an old man who'd fallen off his bicycle had grown in the small hours of the night as the world had shrunk around him. He'd been so sure when he arrived, but now the feeling of uncertainty expanded and all he could do was hope it would disappear by daybreak. The wire fencing surrounding the land adjacent to the library appeared industrial and stark compared to the picture-postcard cottages, but at least the ones he'd designed would fit in.

After taking a deep breath of the fragrant night air, Jacob headed over to the library. He knew there were benches opposite it on the riverbank and it'd be nice to sit there for a while before going back to the cottage. He was beginning to feel drowsy but didn't want to return until his body and mind were tired enough to guarantee sleep.

He didn't see the figure sat on the bench until he rounded the corner, and they looked up, startled. The lenses of her glasses reflected the moonlight, and he could tell from the cascading hair who it was. The woman who was causing him all these problems; the woman who despised him. Jacob wondered whether to turn around and go back to the cottage. It would be easier. He couldn't face a barrage of abuse about the library right now, he was too tired. Too raw. Too torn. But would turning on his heel and running away solve anything? It might even make things worse. Tentatively, he continued his walk to the bench.

The first time he'd seen her she'd been so shy, not wanting anyone to notice her. He'd never believed in auras and all that nonsense, but a strange energy radiated off her. It was ironic that her attempts at inconspicuousness had made her all the more memorable to him. Then the version at the meeting had emerged, and the one he'd met since was so different. What version would he see this evening?

Jacob sat on the bench, his hands in his pockets. The night seemed to have grown chillier and the hairs rose on his arms and the back of his neck. Instinctively, he put his hand there. 'Hello.'

Elsie dropped her eyes. She was wearing tracksuit bottoms and a T-shirt, but she looked far from slobbish and he had to draw his eyes away.

'Hello. Fancy meeting you here.' He chuckled, not knowing what else to say but no smile passed over her lips. He should have cut his losses then and sat in silence or said goodnight and headed off on his own. Only, just as earlier in the day, he couldn't quite bring himself to go. 'You couldn't sleep either?'

'No. But this isn't a rare occurrence for me. Is your conscience keeping you awake?'

He should have expected some sort of remark. Just because she hadn't immediately left didn't mean she wanted to talk to him. 'My conscience is fine, thanks,' he replied defensively. He couldn't exactly admit to his doubts. What if it got back to his father? They sat in silence for a moment. Knowing how much she hated him, he felt he needed to say more. To do something to try and convince her he wasn't completely bad. 'Look, I'm not entirely evil, you know. I really am sorry we don't agree, but it doesn't mean I'm a bad guy.' This time, he didn't bother thinking of the body-language coach and left his hands clasped in his lap. She stared ahead at the slowly trickling water of Meadowbank River. 'How was Winston after his fall?'

At this Elsie finally looked up but her expression was different, softer somehow. 'He's okay.' He was about to ask another question when to his surprise, she continued. 'I cleaned the cut on his head, and we chose some books. He stayed until closing time then I took him back to his cottage.'

'I'm glad he was okay. When did his wife die?'

She toyed with her fingers, rubbing one thumb over the other, surprised by his interest. 'Nine months ago. He fell into a depression for the first few months. We all had to take him food because he wasn't eating anything and he lost a lot of weight. Getting him back into the library and talking to people every day has really helped him deal with living without her.' Elsie had said far more than he'd thought she would and she seemed to think the same from her reaction. She shuffled then crossed her legs. 'Anyway, thank you for helping him.'

'Like I said, I'm not entirely evil.'

'Just mostly?'

'You really hate me, don't you?' The words were painful to speak, and he could hear his father's voice in his head calling him pathetic.

'I hate what you stand for. You're asking me about Winston now you've seen him vulnerable, but what about all those you haven't seen upset or scared or lonely?' Thanks to the pale moonlight, he could see the fire burning in her eyes behind the lenses of her glasses. 'If he hadn't fallen over and admitted to being lonely, would you care now? Would you be asking about him? Because, he's not the only one, you know. Bernard, for all he pretends to care about megastars being spotted in supermarket car parks, just wants to talk to other people. That's why he comes into the library. And it's the same for so many others.'

This time, Jacob was the one to drop his eyes. Hearing his own doubts said out loud to him was physically painful. When he spoke, his voice was resigned. 'I wanted to get some fresh air because I couldn't sleep. I didn't want another row with you.' She turned slightly away, and the pale skin of her arms shined in the light. 'I can understand it's hard for him. I get the impression he and … was his wife's name Lillian?' She nodded. 'They must have been married for a long time. I can't imagine what it must be like to have spent a lifetime sleeping in the same bed as the woman you love and then being suddenly alone.'

Judging from her surprised reaction, Elsie must think him the most uncaring, heartless man in the world. They sat in silence for a moment, the only sounds around them were the babbling of the water and the odd rustle in the hedgerows.

'Did you try reading?' Elsie asked quietly. 'To help you sleep?'

'I did, but it didn't help.'

'The first things to try are warm milk – even on a night like this – and reading.'

'You seem to know a lot about it. Does this happen to you often?'

She brushed her hair back from her face. 'I suffer from insomnia. There's no rhyme or reason to it. Just sometimes I don't sleep. At all. For days – well, nights – on end.'

'That sounds exhausting.'

She removed her glasses and rubbed her eye with a fingertip. 'It is.'

He wondered how, with that to contend with, she found time to start petitions and surreptitiously organise book launches to scupper his plans. He shouldn't have been impressed, but it grew among the frustration. 'What do you read to help you fall asleep?'

'Poetry.'

'Really? I always thought people only read that at school because they had to—'

'It's an acquired taste.' He could see the blush coming into her cheeks. He hadn't meant to upset her, especially as he was reading some too.

'I found a book of poetry at the cottage, and I've quite enjoyed reading it again. I don't know if it's because I'm older and have

181

experienced more in my life but a lot of the things that didn't make sense to me before do now.' Embarrassed, he watched his hands. It wasn't until he raised his head to glimpse the moon, he realised she was observing him.

'I'd better go,' she said after a moment's silence, standing up and crossing her arms over her chest. The pale moon outlined her body and cast shadows behind.

'I hope you sleep better.'

'I doubt I will.' This time, all the anger had left her voice and in its place was a hollow desolation that punched his heart. 'I'm going to lose my job on Monday and the library that I've loved and basically lived in for the last five years is going to be torn down to make way for housing. Unless you change your mind and build your houses somewhere else, or don't knock it down and build beside it.'

His speech stumbled as for a millisecond he calculated how many plots they'd lose if they kept the library. It was insupportable. He couldn't even entertain it. His father would— He didn't even finish the thought. 'I-I'm sorry. I can't.'

'You might when you've read the papers. Liam Chapstone caused quite a stir and with him signing the petition, you might have to rethink your plans.' She straightened her back, defiant.

Little did she know how close to the truth she'd come. Thank God he'd played things down when he'd spoken to his father. He felt vulnerable, exposed, and thought back to all his friends leaving the village, to missing them and ending up alone. 'It was well played,' he admitted. 'But I'm sorry, Elsie. Most of the articles I've read have focused more on Liam Chapstone's revelation of being a man with a female pseudonym than the library closing. I'm not sure it's going to change my father's mind.'

Elsie's face hardened. 'I wouldn't be so sure about that,' she replied before turning on her heel and marching off towards her cottage.

For a moment, Jacob watched the water glide along. The stream rippled as stones and rocks interrupted its flow. He was beginning to wonder if following in his father's footsteps was worth it. Was he really going to be doing this for the rest of his life rather than something more rewarding? It looked like he was, unless he was going to break his father's heart and be disowned. As for Elsie's heart, he supposed he had to get used to upsetting people. He shuddered at the thought.

Time for bed too, though he still wasn't sure he'd get any sleep. Right now, he wasn't sure it was even worth trying.

Chapter 19

As she turned down the lane on Monday afternoon and parked outside her cottage, Elsie hadn't even pulled on the handbrake before the net curtain next door ruffled. Within seconds Orla had launched herself out of the house towards Elsie as she exited the car.

'What happened? Did they let you off with a warning?' Orla's pale blue eyes were wide with worry but all Elsie could do was shake her head and wipe away an escaping tear. Orla's arms encompassed her in a soft but reassuring hug. 'Oh, Elsie.'

'They sacked me, Orla. On the spot. I knew there was a chance – a big one – so I don't know why I'm so upset.'

'It's natural to feel the way you do, but I'm so sorry. It will all be all right. I promise.'

'How can it be all right? The library's going to go and then what will Patricia and Winston and Bernard do?'

Jacob's words from Saturday night had rolled around her head for the remainder of the weekend and though she'd hoped he was bluffing, when she went back over the articles, scouring the internet and social media for them, she saw he was right. Many of the stories focused on the revelation that Neve Chapstone was an attractive man called Liam and that he planned a bold move into writing thrillers under his real name. She'd been crushed, and even Gemma and Orla's company hadn't lifted her spirits. In fact, they'd made them worse. There was an atmosphere in their sweet cottage that had always been a home from home for her. A tension had permeated the air and after they'd started sniping at each other, which had resulted in Orla taking Scarlett for a walk, Elsie had beat a hasty retreat too, knowing Gemma was best left alone.

How had her plan backfired? She'd been convinced that Liam's reveal would add to their success, not take away from it. She guessed it was all in the writing. Jennifer Motley had focused on the library closure, but those who hadn't were getting more attention than her article.

'We'll look after them,' Orla promised, holding Elsie at arm's length and tilting her head to make eye contact. 'We'll find other ways of helping them. Have you told Gemma yet?'

'No. But I'll head over there now. I could do with one of your amazing apple cakes.'

'Gemma thought you might say that and put a szarlotka aside for you out of the last batch I cooked.' Her hand, which was wonderfully soft even though she cooked for a living, cupped Elsie's cheek. 'We'll help you through this, Elsie. It'll be okay.'

'Gemma's very lucky to have you,' she said in response, then sniffed back a tear and wiped her face. 'Right, I'd better go and see her now, then I can hide all evening.'

'Did you want to come for dinner?'

'No, thanks. Not this evening. I think I'd prefer to watch Jane Austen adaptations and eat cake.'

'Well, we're next door if you need us.'

With a final squeeze, Orla let go and Elsie made her way to the bakery. Her legs were leaden, and her heart, bruised and sore. Every time it pounded it reminded her of all she'd lost today. If it was this hard to break the news to Gemma and Orla, how hard was it going to be to tell Patricia, Bernard, and Winston? As it was now half past four and the school rush had finished, Gemma was busy wiping down the counter, clearing out the empty baskets that had previously contained breads and other treats, and starting to pack up for the day. Though she didn't close until five, they'd nearly always sold out by then.

The door was open and as soon as Elsie entered, Gemma looked up. She didn't have to say anything. They'd known each other so long that she could immediately read Elsie's face. Gemma sprang out from behind the counter and rugby-tackled Elsie into a hug. The wind was knocked from her lungs and she was in danger of breaking a rib, but Elsie relaxed into the safe bubble of friendship. The pesky tears that had come and gone throughout the afternoon returned with a vengeance and this time Elsie let them fall.

Gemma eased herself back and said, 'We always knew it was a possibility. Now we have to look on the bright side and plan your next steps.'

She was always so practical. Sometimes people mistook her attitude for a lack of empathy, but Elsie found it reassuring. Gemma was fiercely loyal and having someone like her on your side was a good thing, especially if you were prone to going over and over things in your head, as Elsie was. Though she'd tried her best not to replay the meeting in any great detail, one thing that kept popping up was Rees-Hale's revelation that Jacob Yardley had defended her and didn't feel she should be punished for speaking out at the meeting. She wasn't ready to talk about that yet and had no idea how she felt about it, but her heart had quivered when Rees-Hale had told her.

Why would Jacob do that? She'd done nothing but cause him problems. His expression, his body language – everything about him – pointed to him hating what she'd said. And his behaviour afterwards, except for perhaps his run-in with Winston, had shown him to be concerned with the housing development and not with the community she loved so much. It made no sense. He was such a confusing man.

The other night, sat in the pale moonlight and thick silence, she'd thought he might have had a soul. She'd seen a flash of a real human being beneath that posh, businessman exterior. When he'd spoken of Winston, there'd been a tenderness in his voice that had connected with her heart and she'd been tempted to soften towards him, but no sooner had she thought that than he'd been happy to tell her, her plan hadn't worked.

'Sit down. I've got something for you.' Gemma moved behind the counter and took out the szarlotka she'd been saving. Elsie sat at one of the small tables in the window, where she could see out onto the green and the schoolchildren still playing. Life will go on, she told herself. Life *will* go on. The cinnamon and apple flavour hit her taste buds, sending with it a shot of relief. Her temples throbbed with the stress of the day as she took comfort in the small things her life offered, like the delicious cake.

The revving of a powerful engine interrupted the silence and Jacob's red sports car pulled into the village. Gemma leapt to the doorway, only one step short of waving her fist in the air.

'I'm in half a mind to march out there and stop his car to show him your face and let him know what he's doing to you and this village. I bloody hate him and his shiny, tiny-penis-replacement sports car. Not to mention his snobby, awful colleague. Do you know she's still living with him? Admittedly, most people won't rent to them now they know why they're here, but still. I bet they don't stop bonking.'

Elsie's head shot up of its own accord. The thought made her cheeks burn and something fierce rise up inside. To her shame it was jealousy. She shook her head to push the thought away.

'Why are you shaking your head? Don't you think they are?'

She'd only meant to metaphorically shake her head and quickly tried to cover herself. 'I had something in my teeth.'

'So you shook your head to get rid of it?' Gemma narrowed her eyes in puzzlement. 'Bit odd. You've never done that before.'

'Never mind. You were saying?' Elsie shoved a large piece of cake into her mouth so she didn't have to speak any further.

'What *was* I saying? Oh, yes, I was ranting about them bonking all the time. I bet that's all they do when they're not tearing down libraries and ruining people's lives. Bonk, bonk, bloody bonk.' She turned back to Elsie her voice softening again. 'So what now?'

Looking out of the door and the large front windows of the bakery, Elsie watched the people of Meadowbank meander back and forth. The scene was so idyllic. So peaceful. The people she cared about most in the world were out in that space. She couldn't stop now, no matter how heartbroken she was. She turned to Gemma, feeling the confidence she'd experienced over the last few weeks returning. For Elsie it was a surprise to know the self-belief that had ebbed and flowed throughout her life was here stronger than ever, and apparently, here to stay. 'I'm going to have tonight to feel sorry for myself, eat chocolate, and come to terms with what's happened, and then tomorrow I'm picking myself up and coming for dinner so we can discuss phase two. Remember phase two?'

She nodded. 'Picketing.'

'Yep. I said if I was sacked I'd be free to do what I wanted and now I am. There must be other things we can do apart from that. This is far from over. I just need a little time for today's bruises to heal.'

Before, when she'd thought about this outcome, she'd presumed it would give her even more freedom to work to save the library. Now the chance had come, was she really going to slink away into the shadows, licking her wounds, defeated? No, she wasn't. Some of her dearest friends needed her to keep going until the day the wrecking ball actually knocked the place down and that was exactly what she was going to do.

'But first I'm going to nip to the deli and get a box of fancy chocolates for my costume drama marathon tonight.'

'Sounds like a plan. Are you sure you don't want to come for dinner?' Gemma's voice rang with concern and Elsie smiled at the repeat invitation.

'Honestly, it's fine. I'll see you tomorrow.'

She made her way to the deli and was instantly hit by the strong smell of cheese and salty prosciutto as she walked in. The glass counter that ran the length of the shop overflowed with different varieties of cheeses and meats from all over the world and she was tempted to treat herself to some for supper. Why shouldn't she? She'd had a rough day and deserved something nice to help her rally. She took a box of delicious-looking Parisian chocolates from one of the thick wooden shelves on the side wall and made her way to the counter, ordering some prosciutto and pecorino. After a short conversation about the library, (happily they were on her side) she turned to make her way outside and saw Jacob holding the door open for her.

She stepped through back into the fresh air and for a moment, Elsie planned to ignore him, not even saying thank you. Then she remembered Rees-Hale mentioning Jacob had tried to save her job. She still couldn't figure out why he would do that, but she had been brought up to be polite and if he had, then a thank you for holding the door open for her felt necessary.

'Thank you,' she murmured before hurrying off.

'Miss Martin?' Jacob called and she paused as he caught up with her. 'I just – umm – I heard you were seeing Mr Rees-Hale today. I hope that – well …' He let the sentence trail away, clearly unable to say out loud whatever it was.

She felt herself bristling. 'That what?' He'd known what the likely outcome would be so why was he saying anything?

'That everything was okay, I suppose.' He scratched the back of his neck, unable to meet her eye. His gaze darted to the trees and the ground and the children heading down to the green. One of the boys dropped a ball and it rolled towards Jacob. He flicked the ball up into the air with his foot then stopped it again before gently kicking it back. A wide smile that brought warmth to his face made her heart pulse, but the way he was pretending everything was all right irritated her.

'No. It wasn't all right,' she replied, trying to keep the emotion from her voice as she thought of the boy who'd kicked the ball. He loved to read books about space and he wouldn't get to do that anymore. She thought of Bernard and Winston and not seeing them in the library every day. 'I'm out of a job.'

His eyes finally lifted, meeting hers, and her breath caught at their brightness and intensity. A small line formed between his eyes as he frowned. 'I'm sorry. I really am.'

The lilt in his voice nearly persuaded her but she hardened herself. 'Was there anything else, Mr Yardley?'

She could have been mistaken but sadness flashed across his eyes. 'No. Nothing. I'm sorry to disturb you.'

A small voice in her head wanted to ask him if he'd been sleeping better since their midnight chat. He had dark circles under his eyes and now she thought about it, melancholy lingered in the air around him as if deep down he was unhappy. She began to feel sorry for him again and found herself saying, 'If you're having trouble sleeping and need another book to read, Keats is very soothing.'

Once again, she was reminded of their first meeting. The sun had shone just as it was today and the attraction she'd felt then came back harder. He was the first man she'd fancied in ages, someone she'd felt a connection with and had known that connection would grow and grow. Yet this was how things were. Her heart almost ached at the loss of it. 'There's a copy in the library.'

She'd meant to be helpful, but the mention of the library was an insurmountable object between them so that any reference to it sounded like an attack. Jacob had obviously thought so as his jaw twitched. She pushed her glasses up the bridge of her nose out of nervous habit and turned and walked away. This time she didn't say goodbye but just as she had after he'd helped Winston, she glanced back and was surprised to find him still there, watching her, a look of utter desolation on his face.

Chapter 20

The evening sunlight spilled in through the open front window of Elsie's cottage and the warmth of the air blew over her face. With a glass of wine in hand, she contemplated the sunset. A bright white disc of sun lowered in a pale-yellow sky. Shimmery rays of light pushed through the branches of trees, and all was peaceful and quiet. The gentle breeze, awash with the sound of bees, birds, and grasshoppers, floated into the living room. The faint sound of Scarlett crying echoed from next door and Elsie's heart went out to Gemma and Orla. Scarlett's teething had worsened again and as she was as stubborn as Gemma, her nightly battles to avoid sleep were often protracted until exhaustion finally took over. A faint rumbling sounded in the distance. A tractor maybe? Elsie ignored it.

Elsie stared at the books lining the shelves in the alcoves of the room. She had so many that they filled every space, not to mention the ones piled in her bedroom. She went to the one nearest the window and pulled a Brontë from the shelf. The farthest she'd ever been was Yorkshire. Haworth to be precise. To visit the Brontë parsonage and walk the moors as they had done. She'd also been to Bath to visit the Jane Austen Museum but never abroad. She quite fancied seeing Hemmingway's house in Key West or Emily Dickinson's home in Massachusetts. It would mean getting on a flight, but she'd already proved to herself that she could jump headlong out of her comfort zone when she wanted to. Could she jump far enough to get on a plane? The thought of jumping and planes implied crashing and parachutes so she turned her mind back to saving the library.

A faint sound of rumbling grew louder until the tranquillity of the countryside was destroyed by angry engines and the rat-a-tat-tat of heavy machinery. Elsie went to the window, casting it wide and peering out. A convoy of muddy yellow bulldozers and diggers rolled past. All around the green, people had come out of their cottages or were hanging out of upstairs windows to see the new arrivals. From the end of the lane, Jacob watched on with Leah at his elbow. Elsie was surprised people weren't hissing and booing or throwing rotten vegetables at him. Their eyes met for a second and Elsie yanked the window closed.

Moving back to the sofa, she held her wine glass in tense fingers. As devastated as she was, the bulldozers and diggers had rekindled the feeling of righteousness that burned within her. But what to do now? What other action could they take? The plan had been to step up the revolt and that was exactly what she intended to do.

Grabbing a piece of paper and a pen she began brainstorming ideas as to what her possible next steps might be. There were only two weeks until the library closed for good and, no doubt, its tearing down would begin immediately after, especially as the machinery had now arrived to dig up the fields. A knock at the door lifted her attention from the blank page and Elsie knew immediately who it was. Gemma stalked in as soon as she opened the door with baby Scarlett in her arms.

'Did you see that? Did you see all those trucks and things going past? I'm sorry, I know you wanted to be alone, but I'm so angry I could scream. I mean, not only are we annoyed about the library, but we'd literally just got Scarlett to sleep and then – wham! – that lot come through. Now she's wide awake.'

'Do you want me to take her?' Elsie held her arms out and Gemma gratefully handed her over.

'Yes, please. She's driving us potty tonight. I brought her with me to give Orla a break. I thought Orla was going to cry when those diggers startled Scarlett. Look at her now.' Gemma pointed at Scarlett, who was smiling and gurgling at Elsie. 'She does love her Auntie Elsie, and at least she's smiling and not whingeing for a change.'

Scarlett gazed around with her balled fists in her mouth. 'Are those horrid toothy-pegs bothering you tonight?' Elsie asked. Scarlett grinned and gurgled. 'Come on, let's give Mummy a rest and get you to sleep.'

Lying her down in her arms, she cradled her and rocked gently from side to side. Though Scarlett was not inclined to rest, she did at least lie happily gazing up at the ceiling and Gemma flopped onto the sofa. Elsie sat down too and pulled out a book she'd loaned from the library and planned to show to Scarlett tomorrow. She might as well do it now as she wasn't going to sleep and Scarlett was beginning to love books.

'How's Orla?'

Gemma sighed and ran her hand over the fabric of the seat. 'She's so up and down I don't know what's going on. She just won't talk to me.'

'Do you still think it's to do with the village and everyone being at odds?'

'That's all I can think it is. I mean, that's when it started, but then—' She paused, and Elsie mentally urged her to continue. 'Something weird happened last night.'

'What?'

'When I got home, she was reading a piece of paper and when she saw me, she quickly shoved it into her pocket. I asked her what it was, and she said a shopping list, but then she was really careful with it. It was like she didn't want me to see it.'

'Have you looked at it?' Gemma didn't respond. 'Gemma?'

'I was so tempted, Elsie, but no, I didn't.' Elsie's shoulders fell with relief. Gemma could be quite impetuous and as trust was the basis for every good relationship, she didn't want Gemma to risk ruining theirs. 'Orla fell asleep before me last night and I nearly got up and took it from her jeans. They were dumped on the floor by the bed and so many things were running through my head. That it was a love letter from someone—'

'I don't think people write love letters anymore.'

'Or that it was a letter telling me she's leaving me. We've never sniped at each other like we have lately. I know I should hold my tongue, but you know what I'm like. Sometimes it's out of my mouth before I can help it.'

'I'm sure if she says it was a shopping list then it was.'

'I hope you're right. As hard as it is, I don't want to break her trust by looking.'

'Good. Do you want me to talk to her?' Elsie lowered her voice as Scarlett's eyes began to droop. 'I don't mind having a chat if you think it might help, but I don't want her to think I'm prying.'

'Or that I set you up to it?' Elsie nodded. 'You're as much her friend as mine. If you don't mind, it'd really help to know there's nothing else bothering her. I'm really worried and my mind keeps going off on all sorts of horrible tangents.'

'I'll do it tomorrow. I'll stop in for a cake after I've been to the library and told everyone what's happened. A cake will be my reward for getting through it.'

'Is going to the library a good idea?' Gemma asked, scrunching up her eyes. 'Won't it be like rubbing salt into the wound?'

'Maybe.' Elsie shrugged as well as she could with a sleeping baby in her arms. 'But I feel I owe it to Winston and Bernard to let them know personally. Patricia will be there too so at least I can tell them all together. Rees-Hale hasn't banned me from the place so he can't stop me seeing my friends,' she added defiantly.

'Why, Miss Martin, you little tearaway!'

Elsie smiled and handed Scarlett back to Gemma. 'Here you go.

You can pay me for getting her to sleep later. Right now though, I've got some planning to do.'

'Phase two? What about Jane Austen?'

'After seeing those diggers I need to do something and I think better alone. You always get really shouty when you get carried away and then you'd wake Scarlett up.'

'Me? Shouty?'

'Yes.' Elsie chuckled. 'You.'

'Fair enough.' Gemma popped a kiss on Elsie's cheek and Elsie opened the front door for her.

Once she was alone in the cottage, she topped up her wine and sat back down, ready to begin her plan. There must be a hundred and one more things she could do to stop the library from closing. She needed to get creative. If this was one of the books she loved, maybe one of Liam's stories, she'd want to see the protagonist putting herself out there and shouting from the rooftops and that's exactly what she was going to do.

Thinking of Liam, she glanced at her phone. After he'd kissed her on Friday night, he'd said he'd call but hadn't yet and she was too nervous to make the first move. It had only been three days, but still she worried that perhaps the kiss hadn't been as nice for him as it had been for her. She willed her phone to ping with a message to reassure her, but nothing came so she turned her attention back to her list.

Taking up her pen, she listed the actions they'd already decided on with picketing at the top. That would be sure to get the villagers out in support. She could already see them on board with the idea. The trouble was, they needed more than just the village's support. Elsie was positive that publicly embarrassing the Yardleys was the best way to get what she wanted. She couldn't make a case that it wouldn't be profitable, she had no idea about that, and she couldn't suddenly pipe up that there were protected species living in those fields. That would be an out and out lie and if pressed on it, she'd soon come undone. Could she say the land was at risk of flooding? Not likely. Meadowbank River hadn't flooded in over two hundred years, according to Mr Hoffelmeyer. No, public humiliation was definitely the way to go, but she had to ensure there wasn't a repeat of last time. The sole focus had to be on saving the library and all that would be lost if it was knocked down.

She couldn't control what the press wrote, but she could do her best to get them focusing on the message she wanted them to hear. The message that tearing down the library would take the heart out of Meadowbank. For that she needed Jennifer Motley again. Even if she couldn't write an article herself, she'd be able to give Elsie some advice. Tomorrow, after she'd spoken to Winston, Bernard, and Patricia, she'd give her a call. That would also help distract her from the pain that was inevitably going to follow such a meeting.

But what else could they do? They could have a 'save our library' fête and maybe raise some money to buy tablets or laptops for those families who couldn't afford their own. But what if they could buy only a few? Who would they choose and how? That could be even more divisive for the village.

What else? Elsie tapped the pen against her chin. Keats jumped onto the sofa and curled up beside her and she stroked his fur, relaxing her shoulders down.

Disrupting their building and costing them enough money until they stopped was an option, but was it a likely one? And what was she going to do? Chain herself to the library door? She didn't really fancy getting arrested, but it was an idea and her piece of paper remained unnervingly blank. That would most definitely have to be phase three or possibly four or five if she couldn't come up with something else, which she really hoped she could.

A sit-in? If the picketing didn't work, they could sit in the library and refuse to move. That would also mean Elsie wasn't on her own, and it wouldn't involve a trip to the hardware store to buy chains and padlocks. She could get lots of people to join her and they could all sit in the library and refuse to move. In her mind's eye, Elsie pictured the library full of members of the mother and baby group, the book club, Winston and Bernard, and everyone else all sat in harmony. To make that as impactful as possible, it would need to be on the last day the library was open, and again, she'd need media coverage, keeping up the pressure.

The idea of a propaganda campaign floated through her mind, but who would care outside of the village? Not only that, she didn't have the facilities to print up lots of leaflets and deliver them. Elsie shook her head. It would take too long and give little results for the amount of effort needed. Of course, if she were to channel the suffragettes, she could do things like go on hunger strike but, given her love of cake, that would have to be even further down the list than chaining herself to the library. Some might even say it was a step too far.

Elsie's phone vibrated with a message, and she looked down to see Liam's number. Her fingers tingled with excitement as she picked it up. He was asking her out for dinner on Friday and had suggested a rather fancy restaurant in Witchbury because his agent was so happy at the response from the press and the book launch.

Elsie hesitated, her hand lingering over the screen. For some reason she had pictured them in a cosy pub, something much more relaxed. Maybe he was trying to impress her. Jacob defending her to Rees-Hale tumbled into her brain and she quickly threw him out. After all, he was still pressing ahead with his plans. Though she hadn't felt the same thrill when she met Liam, he was a nice, kind man who clearly loved the same things she did and before she could change her mind, Elsie typed back that the restaurant in Witchbury was fine and that she was looking forward to it.

With that settled, Elsie looked again at her list, but out of ideas, she searched online and the results that came up were rather disconcerting.

'Jesus wept,' she exclaimed, taking another sip of her wine for fortification. As much as she loved the library, there was no way she was going to set anything on fire, glue herself to something, sabotage the machinery (would she even know how?), or stage any kind of protest that meant she couldn't actually *go* to the toilet.

A picket it was to be. And she knew exactly when to hold it. All she needed now was a slogan.

Chapter 21

Elsie paused before she entered the library, taking a deep breath to steady her nerves and dry the tears that were already misting her vision. Removing her glasses, she widened her eyes and cleaned the lenses, anything to put off this moment for a little bit longer. As it was already ten o'clock, she had a feeling some of them might have guessed what had happened from her absence.

After replacing her glasses, she put one foot in front of the other and stepped inside. The familiar, reassuring smell of books produced a feeling of loss and nostalgia that hit her in a giant wave.

'Elsie,' Winston called from his usual chair. 'Where've you been? I asked Karen but she muttered something about books to put away and scuttled off to the back of the library.'

Books to put away? That didn't sound like her. Elsie glanced over to the desk where a woman she'd never seen before sat glaring at them. She wore a dark, old-fashioned power suit and had an expression that Mrs Dalloway would have described as a bulldog sucking a wasp. Her replacement. Karen appeared from behind a shelf of books and skirted over, glancing at the fierce woman behind the desk.

'Elsie, what are you doing here?'

'I came to say goodbye to everyone.'

'But you'll see them around the village. You shouldn't be here.'

'I am still allowed in the library, Karen. Rees-Hale didn't ban me from the building.'

'Yes, but she—' She pointed to Bookzilla behind the counter. 'Is here to make sure you don't cause any more trouble.'

'How do you know that?'

Karen stared like she was mad. 'Look at her! She's clearly not used to actually talking to customers. She's got a face like a smacked arse.' Rich coming from Karen, Elsie thought, but even though she was fired chose not to say so. 'She's taken over my office and has started going through things.'

'What things?'

'The stocklist, all my papers … everything. She's clearly here to start preparing the place for closing. I had to run in ahead of her this morning and hide all my magazines.'

'It was bound to happen sooner or later,' Elsie conceded, though it hurt to say so.

'Oh, and watch out, Jacob Yardley's here too.'

'Where?' She looked around.

'In the office, which is why misery guts over there is on the desk. He kicked her out, but I thought you'd want to know to avoid him.'

The idea crossed her mind, then Elsie straightened. She wouldn't be intimidated. She had every right to be here to say goodbye to her friends. Yes, she'd see them around the village, but it wouldn't be the same as being their daily companion here. Before the melancholy could take hold again, she thought of her plan and brightened. 'It doesn't matter. I've come to see Winston and everyone else.'

With a quick smile at Karen, Elsie went to the computers and newspaper corner, where Winston and Bernard were sitting. Through the window, the diggers were seen beginning to work within the field, churning up the mud, cutting deep rivets in the land. How long before they were cutting the earth where the library once stood? No. She wouldn't think like that. She wasn't done yet.

'Did you have the dentist?' Winston asked, but Elsie could tell that deep down he suspected the truth.

'No, I didn't, Winston. I was sacked yesterday.'

Bernard turned around from his computer. Elsie saw the headline as he spun: *Movie star Chris Hemsworth spotted in Beaconsfield McDonald's.* These celebrities really enjoyed rather mundane locations and there was no way she could imagine the well-toned Mr Hemsworth chowing down on a burger. 'That's appalling,' he barked. 'Who do I write to, to complain?'

'I'm not sure that'll do much good, Bernard.'

'We can try though,' Winston added. 'There must be something we can do?'

'Not about me, I'm afraid. But don't worry—' Winston was devastated for her, and she shot a hand out to comfort him. 'I've got plans for another protest. We've done the petition, we tried getting attention with Liam Chapstone but that didn't go so well, so I've got another plan.'

The two old men looked at each other, their pale, watery eyes sparkling. 'We're all ears,' Winston said.

'How do you feel about picketing outside the library on Saturday?'

'I'd say we're in,' Bernard replied, sitting back, his bushy beard rustling as he smiled.

'Good. I'll supply the pickets and Gemma will keep us stocked with treats to keep our energy up.'

'But, Elsie?' Winston asked. He reached out and took her hand. 'Are *you* okay?'

'Yes, I'm fine,' she replied with a firm nod. Could they tell it was more to convince herself than them? 'Now, I must go and talk to Patricia too.'

Elsie had seen her arrive in a swirl of magenta, but she'd stayed away, clearly sensing the secret nature of their conversation.

'What will you do?' Winston asked as she stood up. 'For a job, I mean?'

'I don't really know yet.' Fear shot up her back, sending a chill through her body. 'I'm sure I'll find something.'

Though what that something was she had no idea, but that was a problem for tomorrow. Her priority for today was getting people signed up to picket with her on Saturday.

'Oh, darling! It's rubbish!' said Patricia, her forehead wrinkling with worry as she finally approached. Had the news travelled round already, or could she tell from Elsie's body language? Patricia had always been very astute at reading people's moods. 'Tell me everything.'

Elsie went through the same conversation she'd had with Bernard and Winston, adding in some more detail about the disciplinary hearing and what was said. When she'd finished, Patricia hugged her closely.

'Oh, darling. I'm so sorry, but yes, I am ready and willing to picket. I've got absolutely nothing to lose. To think this is my last Baby and Toddler Toe Taps breaks my heart.'

'What?' Elsie gasped. 'When did they decide that?'

'This morning. That ferocious creature behind the desk told me as soon as I walked in. Now I'll never get to share this with my grandson.'

Elsie began to rub Patricia's back as she sniffled. 'Still no luck with your daughter?'

'No. She hasn't responded but her husband did, saying I was to stop bothering them.'

'What actually happened? If you don't mind me asking. All you've ever said is that you criticised him and he didn't like it.'

Patricia sighed. 'Blake wouldn't have been my first choice for my daughter. He's got some views I don't agree with and I'm surprised Aimee does too. We were having dinner one night and he said some horrible things about immigrants, and I couldn't keep my mouth shut. I've always bitten my tongue before, but this time I told him he was being obnoxious and that was that. He exploded and told me to leave and since then, Aimee's ignored me. I worry about her, you know. I don't think he'd ever hit her or anything, but Blake's clearly telling her what to do. I don't think she'd have cut me off on her own.'

'All you can do is keep trying, Patricia. I'm sure one day it'll happen. Even if the library isn't here anymore, it doesn't mean you won't get the chance to make up. It's strange how we attach meaning to things, isn't it? I've always thought this place was everything I could have wanted but since I've been stretching my wings a bit, I've realised how much I'd like to travel.'

'Maybe that's what you can do now. Take some time out and enjoy life.'

Elsie pictured herself walking through sunny Key West and seeing Hemmingway's writing desk, perhaps stroking one of the famous cats that live there. 'I might just do that. I'd better go though—'

'No, hang on. I umm—' Patricia checked her watch as if waiting for something.

'What?'

'Just umm … tell me more about what you might do after this is all over.' Patricia grabbed her arm and led her further away from the door. 'Or why don't you help me set up the last ever Toddler Toe Taps.'

'I'd better not. Bookzilla might turf me out if I actually touch anything. Apparently, she's been sent by Rees-Hale to make sure I don't cause any more trouble.'

'Well, I'm glad you've ignored her and planned something else, but I understand. Just—' She checked her watch again. 'Hang on for a tick, okay? Oh, I spoke to Maria, and I think you're right, I think she's been feeling a bit isolated lately. I've given her my number and we're going to meet up.'

'That's great.'

Patricia checked her watch again and Elsie wondered what was going on when Gemma appeared with the usual tray of cakes. Perhaps Patricia wanted to have one last piece together before she left. When Gemma lowered the cake tray a little more, Elsie saw the enormous cake upon it – in the shape of a book, of course – and her hand shot to her mouth.

'What's all this?' Elsie asked, trying to keep her emotions in check.

'I knew everyone would want to say thank you for being the best librarian – and friend – in the whole wide world, so I made you a cake. We couldn't let this moment go without commemorating it somehow.'

Winston and Bernard ambled over, as did Karen and some of the others who were in the library.

'You helped me find the only book my son has ever wanted to read,' joked one mum who'd arrived for Toddler Toe Taps.

'You've always been there for me with my problems,' Patricia said, eager not to say too much in front of the others.

'You always help me get logged on,' Bernard joked. 'But you know I've always appreciated our conversations, Elsie. My kids don't have a lot of time to talk to me about the things I like.'

'You helped me get through life when my Lillian died,' Winston added, his words chock-full of emotion. He pulled a handkerchief from his pocket and wiped his nose. 'It's probably a good thing the place is going because it wouldn't be the same without you.'

Everyone stared at her for a moment and for once she was too surprised to turn red with embarrassment. All she could feel around her was love and affection. 'Th-thank you all, so much. I really don't know what to say.'

Everyone squeezed in towards her to pat her arm, squeeze her hand, or give her an enormous hug.

Gemma yelped, 'Mind the cake!' and lifted the tray high above their heads before moving to the counter.

'You can't eat that in here,' Bookzilla grumbled.

Gemma ignored her and lowered the tray down. 'Yes, we can. We always do and even if we can't, this is a special occasion.' She began cutting the cake, disregarding the woman's baleful exclamations.

'Well, I never—'

'There's no harm in a bit of cake, is there, Maureen? I'm sure they won't make a mess.' Jacob's voice, loud and clear, carried over the din.

Elsie moved towards the counter. She hoped he wouldn't talk to her like he had yesterday. She was feeling decidedly tender after all the lovely things people had said. She reached for a slice of cake. Gemma had made her favourite: a rich chocolate sponge with delicious chocolate buttercream icing and white chocolate drizzle. So far, there hadn't been any problem this cake couldn't solve. She cupped her hand underneath to catch the crumbs, but it didn't stop Bookzilla from tutting.

'I know I've said this before, Elsie, but—' He stepped closer to her – so close she became hyperaware of every movement she made – as everyone pretended not to listen, but Elsie knew full well they were. 'I really am sorry things have turned out this way. I never wanted that to happen.'

Once she'd taken a bite, she responded but kept her voice cool. 'Knocking down my place of work was always going to result in that.'

'Not necessarily. I know there were other options. And I never wanted you to get told off for speaking your mind.'

Told off? Told off? All the pain of the meeting and the responses of her friends flooded her. The grown-up thing to do would have been to be polite, or ignore him altogether, but the subject always fired something inside her and she spoke the words that flew into her brain. '*Told off?* Is that what you tell yourself so you can sleep at night? Oh, that's right, you've stopped sleeping so well, haven't you? Maybe you should ask yourself why.'

'Look, whatever you think of me, I am truly sorry. Rees-Hale is …' He searched for some words but struggled to find them. 'Well, he's—'

Was he going to try and pin this all on Rees-Hale? Yes, the man was pure evil, there was no doubt about that, but if Jacob thought he could place all the blame on him, rather than take his share, he had another think coming.

'Rees-Hale's no better or worse than you are.'

The room went silent. Jacob said nothing but fastened the button on his well-fitting suit jacket, his cheeks flooding with colour. 'I'm sorry you feel that way,' he replied coolly.

'Is it any surprise? If it is then maybe you're not cut out for this. Anyone could have told you the chances of me losing my job were high.'

'I did try to—'

'Yes, I heard. Clearly, it didn't do any good.'

For the first time in her life, she wasn't the one stood there blushing. Jacob's cheeks were bright pink but sadly it made him even more attractive.

'I-I don't know what more I can say. I'm sorry,' he mumbled again and with a glance around, walked away. Had she been justified in her reaction? Her broken heart told her she had, but seeing how unhappy he seemed, it made her feel guilty.

'You're not supposed to eat inside a library,' Bookzilla mumbled.

'Well, you're not supposed to knock them down either,' Elsie replied with a glower. And with that triumphant parting remark she took a large satisfying bite, not caring where the crumbs flew.

Chapter 22

On her way to the bakery to see Orla, Elsie stopped at the bench by the duck pond. It felt so alien to be doing whatever she wanted at ten o'clock in the morning. Normally by now she'd have made a to-do list and would be happily working her way through it.

The ducks were oblivious to the time and had no idea how strange it was for Elsie as they swam about thoroughly enjoying themselves, but a disquiet settled on her shoulders, pulling the muscles taut. An endless stream of time stretched out before her with no purpose and nothing to fill it with. She felt lost. Like a boat cast adrift.

For a while she watched the ducks paddling and the water of the pond trickling down to the river, when angry voices grew loud. Beyond her, two women from the village were shouting at each other, shuffling on the spot as if their handbags were about to be used as weapons. Considering Bonnie's bag was enormous, Elsie didn't fancy the more petite woman's chances.

'You signed that petition?' Bonnie exclaimed. 'But you know how Davey and I feel about our Ian. We never see him now he's moved to Witchbury. How could you, Wendy? I thought you were my friend.'

'I am your friend, Bonnie. Surely there's enough room on that plot for houses without getting rid of the library.'

'I can't believe you. After all the times I've cried on your shoulder about missing my boy.'

'Bonnie—'

'Nope. I'm not interested. I'm just glad that petition did bugger all. And don't come to me next time you need someone to look after your cats, because I am not interested.'

Bonnie marched away leaving Wendy crestfallen. Elsie hunched down hoping to hide behind the large rushes of the duck pond. She didn't want them to spot her and be next in the firing line. Guilt roiled her stomach as if the cake she'd just been enjoying had been poisoned.

Had she done this to the village or had Jacob Yardley? She wanted to say it was him, but the fact was she was the one who couldn't accept that her cherished library was going to close. Would there be this amount of acrimony if she hadn't fought against his plans? The village would have been united in sadness, but would there now be these distinct factions?

Swallowing down the fear that she was the one pulling the village apart, she made her way to the bakery. Her stomach had settled a little by the time she got there, but she wasn't quite ready for another cake just yet. As she'd agreed with Gemma, Gemma had gone back to the bakery and picked up Scarlett, taking her out for a walk, so Elsie could talk to Orla alone.

Walking in, Elsie picked up the smell of freshly baked bread and her favourite szarlotka scenting the air. The aroma of apples and cinnamon and that hint of lemon that made the other flavours all the more delicious instantly caused her mouth to water. Perhaps she would have enough room for one of Orla's cakes after all.

'Elsie, how are you feeling today? Did you like your cake?' Orla welcomed her with a cheery smile.

'I did. It was delicious, thank you.'

'Good.' Her blonde hair was tied back in a ponytail and her bare face showed signs of tiredness. Normally smiling, Orla's mouth was now turned down and the delicate skin under her eyes looked bruised. 'It was Gemma's idea. She knew we had to mark the occasion even though it isn't the most pleasant of ones. But if we did nothing, it would have been even worse.'

Orla was such a caring person, she always worried she was offending someone and Elsie was quick to reassure her.

'It was a lovely idea and I really appreciated it. And you're quite right. If I'd have slunk away like a naughty child I would have looked back and wished I'd held my head high.'

'You did all the right things.'

'I hope you're right.'

Mrs Bostock, who had taught for years at the primary school, came in and Elsie paused her conversation. She didn't know how Mrs Bostock felt about the housing development and she didn't want to risk a telling-off by mentioning it. Instead, she made small talk about the weather and the naughty ducks that were edging closer to the bakery door hoping for crumbs. Mrs Bostock purchased her fresh loaf and a cream horn before heading back out again.

'Are you worried you made a mistake?' Orla asked as if sensing Elsie's unease.

'Sort of.' She sat down and when she'd finished cleaning the counter, Orla joined her. 'I've just seen Bonnie and Wendy at each other's throats, and I can't help but feel responsible. I feel like I'm the one tearing the village apart, not Jacob. And I heard from Rees-Hale that he actually tried to stop me facing a disciplinary for speaking at the public meeting.'

'He did?' Elsie nodded and Orla considered for a moment. 'But I'm not really that surprised.'

'No? I was.'

'Why? Because you've decided he's not a nice man because he believes something different to you? That's quite prejudiced, Elsie.' Elsie lowered her head. She'd been so busy standing up for what she believed in she hadn't thought of it in that way. 'Not everything is black and white. He could be annoyed that you faced something like that just for having an opinion and still want to build houses. It doesn't always have to be one thing or another.'

'That's true,' Elsie conceded.

'We can only do what we feel is right. Each of us must make that choice.' Orla's gaze became suddenly distant and Elsie paused.

'Is it getting to you, Orla? The arguments in the village?'

'A bit,' she said with a thin smile. 'This place has always been so peaceful and welcoming, especially to me, an outsider. It's hard to see so many people fighting.'

Elsie waited for her to say more but Orla stood and began wiping the two small tables before moving back behind the counter, tidying and sorting. 'Orla, Gemma's worried about you and I am too. Is everything okay?'

'Of course. Why would it not be?'

'You're just not yourself.'

'I'm fine, Elsie. Don't worry about me. Are you excited for your date with Liam?'

That was a diversionary tactic if ever she'd seen one but what could she do? She couldn't grab Orla by the lapels, shine a light in her face, and make her talk. Not just because she didn't have any lapels, but the overhead light wasn't adjustable either. Elsie decided to answer and see if she could bring the conversation around to the note Gemma had seen later.

'Yes, I am. He was so nice at the book launch—'

'And he's a good kisser?'

He was a very good kisser and Elsie smiled at the memory. 'We have so much in common it should be a really lovely evening.'

'I'm sure it will be.'

How could she bring up the subject of the note now? Off the top of her head, she couldn't think of any way of doing so without making it clear what Gemma feared. Looking at Orla and knowing how in love they'd been only weeks ago, she couldn't imagine it was anything as bad as that, but love made us all crazy at times. She was certainly getting crazy nervous over her date with Liam.

She ignored the image of Jacob's warm smile when he'd kicked the ball back to the little boy.

To find out if the note was a shopping list or not, she could only think to say, 'Would it help if I did your shopping or helped out a bit more? Apart from making some more pickets, I haven't got much else to do.'

Orla's hand didn't go to her jeans, but the mention of shopping had brought a slight flinch to her brows. 'No, that's fine. We've got pretty much everything we need for the week.'

'You'll ask me if you need anything though? Promise? And promise me you're okay?'

'I promise,' Orla replied. 'I'm just tired. I only have to make it till Sunday when I'll get a day off.'

Though Elsie didn't quite believe her, it did seem the most likely reason given that she and Gemma ran a bakery that involved early starts and Scarlett often gave them late nights. 'Perhaps I could take Scarlett for a while on Sunday and give you both some time to pamper yourselves? Spend some time together just the two of you.'

'That might be nice. But let's see how your picketing goes on Saturday. There is every chance you could be in a police cell come Sunday.'

Elsie's eyes widened, but for once Orla didn't laugh to show she was joking. Her stomach turned over and her need for cake evaporated. A criminal record wasn't going to help her career prospects at all.

Chapter 23

'Mr Yardley? Mr Yardley?'

The high-pitched voice called out to him as his pace slowed from a jog to a walk. Turning, he saw it was the young woman who had spoken out at the public meeting in defence of the baby group. He readied himself for another attack, finding it harder and harder to deal with the comments and hostility of some of the villagers. The only conclusion he'd begrudgingly come to was that his heart wasn't as in it as he'd hoped. The affordable housing development had been the only thing aligned with his values that he'd worked on, but it still wasn't enough.

'Mr Yardley, can I have a word with you, please?' She pushed the buggy along the lane, and he matched his speed to hers. The little girl inside it was fast asleep.

'Of course. What can I help you with?' Though he already knew the answer.

'I—' She stopped and took a breath as if reminding herself of what she'd planned to say. 'I wanted to beg you to reconsider about the library.'

Beg? The word sent an icy blast over him. Had he reduced her to this state? He felt sick and knowing he was going to have to say no (because what other answer could he give without ruining his relationship with his father) made him feel even more guilty.

'I'm sorry, Mrs …?'

'Maria's fine.'

'Maria, I'm sorry but I understand that Mr Rees-Hale is ensuring—'

'No, you don't understand,' she said quietly, tears forming in her eyes. She hastily looked around before continuing. The village was unusually quiet, or perhaps everyone was at home having their dinner. He wondered why she was out. Had it been just to speak to him? 'You have no idea how isolating it is being a mum and the only thing that's stopped me feeling so alone is the baby group.' She flicked her eyes around again. 'Most people don't know this, but I've really struggled since having Daisy. My husband works in Witchbury so he's out all the time. Coping on my own is difficult. Everyone thinks I've got everything together, but …'

He listened intently, guilt growing inside him again. Elsie had been right. The library was so much more to everyone here than just a place to find books, and Winston wasn't the only one who needed it.

'You don't understand how hard it is and we only have one car, so I can't just go to another group somewhere else. It's been hard enough to try and make friends here. I've lived here all my life but finding friends who understand how utterly terrifying it is having a child and taking them out somewhere is difficult. My old friends don't have children yet.'

'I'm sure you've more friends than you realise,' Jacob said, soothingly.

She gave him a sad smile and reached out to caress her daughter's chubby foot. 'I've got Elsie and Patricia, but even then, I-I find it hard to let people see the real me. I used to have everything together, but life gets messier when you have a baby. It's hard to let people know you're struggling. That's why you have to keep the library safe. You have no idea what a lifeline it is for people.'

'Maria—'

'I'm sure I'm not the only one who feels this way. If there's any way you'd think about changing your mind, please, please do so. You don't know what difference it would make to people.'

As Jacob searched for something to say, a car pulled out of a side road, driven by Elsie's dark-haired friend. She had someone in the car with her, and Jacob's eyes narrowed as he studied the familiar profile before they widened in surprise. It was Elsie. Her curls had been tamed by a long plait that hung over one shoulder. From her position in the car, he could see an expanse of pale flesh from her neck to her shoulders and the hint of cleavage. She looked as beautiful as usual but slightly more … confident. He wondered where she was going. She wasn't trying to blend into the background tonight. Were they out for a girls' night? He knew that the dark-haired friend owned the bakery with her partner, and they had a young daughter. Somehow, he couldn't imagine them leaving the other woman out.

It could only mean one thing. That Elsie Martin had a date and he bet he could hazard a guess at who with. That bloody author Liam Chapstone, who'd stood there spouting on about how his heart broke a little every time a library closed. Suddenly, his breath, that he had only just regained, vanished again.

'Mr Yardley?' Maria asked, bringing his attention back to the awkward conversation.

Seeing the genuine distress in her eyes, as he'd seen in Winston's, he balked. How he wished he was in a different job, helping people instead of hurting them. But what could he say to her? There was no way he could change the plans. Even thinking about having that conversation with his father made him queasy.

'Maria, I'm sorry. I really wish there was more I could do but the plans are set.'

Her face hardened. 'Then I'm sorry to have bothered you.' She wheeled the buggy around and marched back off in the opposite direction.

He felt like scum. Like the lowest of the low. The only feeling stronger than that was the jealousy pounding through his system as he thought of Elsie laughing and joking with Liam Chapstone.

Could he suggest to his father that they keep the library? There was no reason to, other than to make the villagers happy. There was nothing wrong with the sale or the land and without a tangible reason that involved profits or costs, his father would never listen. He tried to call to mind the images they'd created of the new houses but they no longer seemed to fit where the library stood. So much of Meadowbank was perfect as it already was. He was beginning to love the quiet of the green, the wandering, belligerent ducks, and the small, artisanal shops.

He stared after the car again, but it had already moved out of view. He'd never be able to admit his feelings for Elsie because she'd never even consider going out with him now, and he could never tell his father that he was beginning to change his mind without losing what little respect he'd been able to gather. The situation was hopeless and the sooner he was out of Meadowbank the better.

* * *

'Be good then,' Gemma said with a smile as she dropped Elsie off down the road from the restaurant. She'd offered a lift so that Elsie could have a drink, knowing how nervous she got. Elsie kept the car window open all the way there to try and keep her cheeks cool, but they were warming already. 'And if you can't be good, be careful.'

'I'll be both good and careful.'

'Ring me if you need a lift home.'

'Don't be silly. I'll get a taxi.'

'Okay, well, not that it will be, but if it turns out to be the worst date of your life you can always ring me to come and save you.'

'I'm pretty sure it's going to be the best date of my life.' Elsie's nerves fizzed once more as she listed all the things they could talk about.

'So am I.' Gemma flashed her eyes as she put the car into gear. 'See you later.'

After smoothing her dress, Elsie adjusted her glasses and made her way down the street to the restaurant. As she passed the large windows looking out over the busy road, she spotted Liam already at the table, staring at his phone. She took a deep breath. Dates had been few and far between and she didn't really know how to act, but with a roll of her shoulders, she decided she'd just be herself. If Liam did the same, they were bound to have a wonderful time.

Liam saw her as soon as she walked towards the table and his surprise at her fancy dress and plaited hair made her smile. His eyes roved over her, and it was clear he liked what he saw.

'Hi.' Liam leaned forwards and placed a kiss on her cheek.

Remembering the kiss they'd had before, she'd hoped for something as all-encompassing, but this time it wasn't as powerful. She'd noticed Jacob as she was leaving Meadowbank and the expression on his face had shaken her, but she wasn't going to let him ruin her date.

'You look amazing. You're so beautiful.'

'Thanks. I wish I thought so too. Sometimes I think I'm okay if you squint and tilt your head to the side so you're only looking out of the corner of your eye.' She'd hoped he'd laugh but he stared at her a little confused. She must have been blathering.

'Sit, sit!' he said, pulling out a chair for her.

As Elsie sat, her leg pressed against his. She wondered if she should pull it away and waited for a rush of heat to spread through her as it had when her fingers had touched Jacob's as she handed over the petition. Why wasn't her body reacting to Liam how she wanted it to? 'How's the writing going?'

'Great. I've started on my debut thriller. I thrashed out the plot with my agent the other week. She said this could be the thing that makes me.'

'But I thought you already had "made it" because of your romances?'

'Not really.' He grabbed a breadstick and began chewing the end. 'Romance isn't really valued in the literary world. This thriller is going to make my mark.' He tapped his finger against the table as he spoke and that was when she noticed the empty pint glass next to him. She hadn't expected him to sit there with water while he waited for her, but she hadn't been late and wondered how quickly he'd necked that before she arrived. 'Thrillers are the way to get noticed. That's what my agent said. I'm including an FBI element too.' He leaned in, all excitement. 'The Americans love an FBI element.'

'Right.' It was a shame he was so eager to cast off his romance-writing reputation, but maybe it was just ambition. She'd never been particularly ambitious so couldn't understand that push for more.

Elsie picked up the menu and began to read through. It didn't normally take her long to decide what she wanted, but this one was quite extensive. The waiter appeared and without even asking if she was ready to order, Liam reeled off what he wanted and asked for another beer before looking at her expectantly. Quickly, Elsie decided on something for each course and ordered a glass of wine. When it was delivered, she took a sip wondering why the evening wasn't getting off to as good a start as she'd hoped. Perhaps she was so out of practice her expectations were off.

'So,' Liam continued. 'My agent said—'

He really liked saying 'my agent'. 'Does your agent have a name?'

'A name? Yeah, of course she does.' He laughed. 'You are funny, Elsie. Anyway, she said the FBI thing will really appeal. I don't know if I'll write the screenplay myself or if we'll get someone else in, we'll have to wait and see.'

Wasn't that a little presumptuous? Elsie opened her mouth to speak – not to say so, that wouldn't go down well at all – but Liam jumped in, full of the things he was researching for his thriller. She smiled and maintained as much enthusiasm as she could, but after half an hour, and growing increasingly hungry, it was wearing a bit thin. She took another sip of her wine and as soon as he paused for breath, said, 'We're starting the next stage of the campaign tomorrow. We're going to be picketing outside the library.'

'Picketing? Wow. You're a little firecracker, aren't you?'

'Do you want to come?' She'd planned on asking him since the date was set, partly so she could see him again and partly to help their campaign.

'Me? Oh, I-I can't this weekend, sorry. I've got an important meeting with my agent.'

'On a Saturday?'

'Yeah. We've got some other things to discuss. She messaged me actually. Do you remember I said I should put you in a book? The perfect feisty heroine?'

Warmth grew in her chest as she remembered his words and the kiss that had followed, though this man appeared different to the one she'd met the other week. Arrogant or not, she did quite like the idea of one of his romances featuring a plucky librarian.

'I'm thinking one of the FBI agents could be like you.'

'In one of your thrillers?' That hadn't been quite what she had in mind. A gun-carrying, clompy-shoed agent of the law would be nothing like her. She bet they'd have smooth hair as well.

'Yeah. Wouldn't you like that? Though Elsie's a lovely name, we'll need something more … up to date.'

'Right.' She tried to muster some enthusiasm and attempted again to talk about something else. It wasn't that she wasn't interested in his work or that she begrudged him his excitement, but it had dominated the conversation since she arrived. She had hoped he'd ask how she was or what was happening with the library, but so far, he hadn't. She hadn't even had the chance to tell him that she'd lost her job.

As their starters were finally delivered, Elsie tucked in, her stomach feeling empty.

'I have to thank you though, Elsie.' Liam placed his fork down and reached out for her hand. His expression was serious, and she wondered if things were about to take a turn for the better. Would this date continue how she'd hoped it would? 'If it wasn't for you and all the media attention, I wouldn't be in this position now. There's no way my agent would be so fired up if we hadn't made such a splash revealing my identity.'

And what of the library? He hadn't even asked about it and as soon she'd mentioned it, the conversation had quickly returned to him.

'I really can't wait to leave the world of romance behind.'

This time, Elsie couldn't stop herself. 'Why? I thought you loved writing about happy-ever-afters and people falling in love.'

In a way, she was relieved. She'd begun to think only Jacob had the effect of making her speak without thinking.

Liam chuckled in a way that made him far less attractive, and his tone was less than convincing. 'I do. I'm just looking forward to a change. I'd like to write something that makes the critics really sit up and listen.'

Elsie tried to rein in her galloping thoughts. Was the man in front of her really that different to the one she'd met previously? Maybe he was justifiably excited about his future and she wasn't because hers looked so bleak, but that argument didn't sit well. Regardless of his feelings on his latest writing project, she couldn't pretend he was showing so little interest in the library. She'd thought they'd connected over it, but she was wrong.

The rest of the meal continued in exactly the same vein. Every time Elsie tried to talk about the things that were important to her – the library, her friends, Keats the cat – he showed a passing interest and then as soon as humanly possible drew attention back to himself.

When it came time to leave, Elsie couldn't get out of there quick enough. As she stood on the pavement waiting for her taxi to arrive, Liam tried to kiss her again and she turned her cheek to him so he couldn't reach her mouth. It had become clear that she'd got him totally wrong. He wasn't the romantic soul she'd thought him, and she wasn't even sure now that he had cared about the library. It was more that he'd seen it as a publicity stunt, and it wouldn't have killed him to ask about her and what she was up to.

'When shall we see each other again?' he asked, pushing his hands into the pockets of his jeans.

'Oh, look, my taxi's here.' She dived in, and through the window she saw Liam make the telephone sign with his fingers. She didn't know how she was going to let him down. She never normally got that far. If Liam Chapstone was the best the world had to offer, perhaps she was better being single. A man walked down the street looking vaguely like Jacob and she cursed herself for letting him into her thoughts. She'd have enough to say to him tomorrow.

So much for the best date of her life. She didn't have much experience in that department, but it was safe to say it had definitely been the worst by a good country mile.

Chapter 24

On Saturday morning, Jacob was awoken from a rather nice dream – where he was lying on a yacht in the middle of the Mediterranean Sea eating olives and drinking beer – by someone shouting his name like the house was on fire. Was the house on fire? *Shit! The house was on fire!* He sat bolt upright and jumped out of bed. Though he couldn't smell smoke, or see any billowing up past his window, he made for the door towards Leah's shouts.

'Jacob? Jacob!' Her voice grew sterner, sounding more like an angry mother than someone afraid they were about to burn to death, which he supposed was a good sign. Of sorts.

He pulled open the door and called down the stairs, 'What is it?'

'You'd better get dressed quickly.'

'Why? What's going on?'

'Just get dressed and come with me,' she snapped.

Jacob didn't particularly enjoy being ordered around. He had enough of that from his father. What did Leah want him to see? After slinging on his jeans and a pale lemon short-sleeved shirt, he made his way down to where Leah awaited at the foot of the stairs.

'What's the matter?'

'You need to come with me. Now.'

'I haven't even brushed my teeth yet,' he replied. 'What's wrong? You look like you've seen a ghost.'

'Huh, that'd be nothing compared to this.' She rubbed her temples. 'Just go and brush your teeth then we need to leave straight away.' She checked her watch before crossing her arms over her chest.

Jacob dashed back upstairs feeling more than a little put out. Had his father called? Had something happened at the site? No, it couldn't be that. They'd have called *him*, not Leah. Grabbing his phone while still brushing, he double-checked the screen. There were no missed calls, no messages. Leaving the bathroom, he slipped his feet into his trainers and met her at the open front door. She banged it loudly behind him and stalked off towards the site.

The village was busy, but that wasn't surprising as it was a Saturday. People darted about full of excited chatter and he wondered if he'd missed news of a fête or some special event. He could imagine Meadowbank was wonderful on summer fête days or Christmas parades. It wasn't until he reached the end of the lane and saw the villagers gathering in front of the library that his stomach shot to the floor before ricocheting up and hitting the bottom of his throat. He felt sick. Christ, if his father saw this, he'd be a dead man. There'd be no reprieve. No second chances. Fifty or more people were walking around outside the library with large placards, chanting, 'Save our library!'

'When did this lot happen?'

'I saw more people than usual going past the cottage about half an hour ago.' Though she didn't smile, there was a strange tone to her voice. Was she enjoying this? He glanced at his watch. It was only ten o'clock and yet there were so many people with more joining the throng all the time. 'I nipped to the end of the lane and that's when I saw them all here. I've already called Conrad. He's on his way down.'

'What?' Jacob halted, spinning to look at her. 'Why did you do that? I could have handled this.'

222

'Clearly you can't. Did you have any idea they were planning this?'

'No. Did you?' It was a childish reply, but it unnerved him that she was suddenly distancing herself and putting all the blame firmly on his shoulders, even if that was ultimately where the blame sat.

She pushed her hair back from her face. 'No, but then I'm not in charge of the project. If I were you, I'd get in there and try and get them to disperse before your father arrives, which should be in about half an hour knowing the speed he drives.'

Jacob wasn't quite sure why she was enjoying this so much. Perhaps she saw no way out of this monumental fuck-up and was bailing while she still had a chance to come out of it looking good.

His eyes scanned the large crowd. They even had a table set up for drinks. A huge tea urn sat atop a red gingham tablecloth and an old dear behind it was handing out proper cups and saucers. If only it was some kind of village celebration. He liked being in the countryside and there was something special about Meadowbank that he was beginning to prefer over his own hometown and definitely over London. But it was surreal to watch someone lean their placard up against the table while they sipped from china cups and nattered like it was a church bazaar. Another table next to it held cakes and was where Elsie's dark-haired friend stood with a baby in a highchair beside her. Everyone was cooing over the baby while she cut and distributed cake and biscuits to the waiting line. He thinly hoped that most of them were there for free cake and would leave as soon as they'd got some, but he wasn't convinced.

Jacob's gaze penetrated the crowd and there, in the middle, sitting on a camping chair with a circle of elderly people in deck-chairs around her was Elsie Martin. She looked slightly terrified by the whole affair, but there was also glee in her eyes. Glee at her success, but she had no idea how much she had cost him.

Knowing he had to be authoritative and stamp his control

223

on the situation, he marched into the centre, ignoring the picket signs that almost smacked him in the face. One cheeky man he recognised from the public meeting tried to hit him on purpose, but he dodged just in time. 'What's happening here?'

'What do you think's happening?' shouted Winston from his red-striped deckchair. 'We're protesting! I haven't done this since the Sixties,' he said to Elsie, thoroughly enjoying himself.

Elsie glared at Jacob, and he placed his hands on his hips. 'I can see what you're doing but why are you doing it? There's nothing to be done. The sale's gone through, the land's ours. It's over, Elsie.'

'Oh, is it?' Elsie shot out of her chair and was right in front of him, looking him squarely in the eye. He shouldn't have felt a thrill at her presence, but he couldn't help it. Her clear skin was luminescent in the sunlight and though her hair had been scraped back in a ponytail, the waves couldn't be tamed, and a few strands broke free of the band. Her brown eyes shone like new chestnuts behind the lenses of her glasses. 'Can't you see that the people who live here, the people you claim to be helping with your new development, want the library to stay?'

'Exactly,' her dark-haired friend shouted from the cake stand, and a supportive jeer followed.

Stunned into silence, Jacob blinked.

Someone bustled forwards from behind, shoving him side-ways, and he instinctively took hold of Elsie, protecting her from whoever it was. The firm pressure of her hands on his chest sent a ripple of longing through every muscle. Elsie, though, didn't seem to feel anything as she stared at him aghast then wriggled herself free. The person who'd shoved their way through, stopped with their hands on their hips. It was a formidable-looking old woman whose mouth had pursed.

'Elsie Martin, I'm ashamed of you.'

'Me?' She reached a hand up to point at herself.

'Yes, you. You should know better than cause such a kerfuffle. What would your parents say? Your mother would be furious.'

'Mrs Edwards, I—'

'Don't you "Mrs Edwards" me! Now, I know you don't want to let the library go but what about looking forward, hey? What about thinking of future generations?'

Some people called out in agreement with the old woman and a stab of empathy shot into Jacob as he watched Elsie curl with embarrassment. Her cheeks grew pinker, but the firm set of her jaw showed this woman was not going to intimidate her. It was amazing really. He was fairly intimidated already, and she wasn't even shouting at him.

'Mrs Edwards, you might not agree with me, but you of all people know how important it is we stand up for what we believe in. I'm sure you taught me something similar when I was at school.'

'That's as may be' was all she said before Winston stood up and began telling Mrs Edwards off.

Within seconds, the voices had grown so loud, none of them heard the arrival of the cars bearing camera crews and reporters, who were jumping out and setting up ready to record. When Jacob turned, he watched in horror as one such reporter straightened his shirt and tie and held a microphone under his nose.

'Jacob,' Leah hissed, grabbing his arm and pulling him out of the fray. 'You've got to get a handle on this. Your father will be here any minute. If he sees this lot, he'll go mad.'

'Mad' was an understatement, but ultimately Leah was right. He glanced at her, then at the group now toe to toe and nose to nose, and dived back in. Everyone was listening to Elsie. If he could persuade her to call all this off and to send everyone home, he was sure they'd do it.

'Elsie?' He found her in the middle calming a group of angry mothers who were arguing for the baby and toddler group. Either she was ignoring him, or she couldn't hear over the insane amount of noise that made his ears ring. 'Elsie?'

'What do you want?' She crossed her arms over her chest.

'Can we talk?' He motioned to the side of the library, away from everyone, and after a quick glance around, she followed. 'Why are you doing this?'

It was a stupid question, but he didn't know how else to start the conversation. His father had always told him starting conversations in this way was a sign of weakness, but his father's advice wasn't getting him very far at the moment.

'You know why.'

'I can't give you what you want, Elsie, and it isn't just me and my choice. It's my father's too. He's made the decision and I don't have the power to change it. Even if I changed my mind, it wouldn't make a difference.' Even to his own ears he sounded pathetic blaming his father, but it was true. 'This really is a waste of everyone's time. I understand why you're doing it but it's upsetting your friends and everyone in the village.' He saw this remark hit home and though his father would have pressed the advantage, he couldn't bring himself to. The pain in her eyes closed his mouth for him. 'If you tell everyone to go home, then this will all blow over quicker. The houses will go up with minimum fuss and I'm sure you'd like them if you saw them.'

'You could build a Jane Austen theme park and I wouldn't like it if it was in place of the library. God, you just don't get it, do you?' She pushed her glasses up firmly. 'Like I said in the meeting. This isn't about books and bricks and mortar. This is about people and belonging and support and care. The library is so much more than books. Why can't you see that?'

The trouble was, he *was* beginning to see that and the conflict it caused him was physically hurting, but he couldn't promise her something he didn't have the power to give. His father would never agree to a change of plans. He took a breath. 'What do you want from me, Elsie? I can't give you what you want.'

'Maybe your father can.' Her words were like a punch to the jaw. 'I want you to keep the library.'

'You know I can't.'

'Then we have nothing more to say to each other.'

She walked away from him, only pausing to pick up the placard she'd rested against a table. He followed, and she began pacing around with her friends, chanting 'Save our library!' over and over again. A reporter shoved a microphone in her face and drew her aside for an interview while all Jacob could do was try not to get hit as he made his way back to Leah.

A shiny black Lexus drew up beside him and his heart plummeted as his father climbed out. He must have been overtaken by rage to have driven himself rather than organise a driver. He loved the distinction a driver gave him. The crimson cheeks and steely gaze did nothing to reassure Jacob he'd come out of this looking good. He might as well book himself a spot in the graveyard by the sweet little church because if the protesters didn't get him, there was every chance his father would.

'Jacob? What the fu—' He pulled himself back in time. 'What's going on here?' he whispered as he came over. 'I couldn't believe it when Leah called and said something about a picket line. How can you be picketed by these old duffers?'

His father never intended his voice to carry but as he'd grown angrier, his words resounded around them, and the outraged response did nothing to calm the situation.

'Who are you calling an old duffer?' Winston responded. 'I can see where your son gets his charm from.'

Ouch! That one hurt. If there was one person in the world Jacob hated being compared to …

Conrad leaned in and lowered his voice. 'How are you being bullied by a bunch of old fogies? This is preposterous!'

'They're not all old folks,' Leah offered, suddenly joining the conversation. They must have looked utterly ridiculous, all three of them huddling with their heads together. Leah pointed to Elsie. 'She's the ringleader.'

'Her?' Conrad straightened up and stared straight at Elsie. With her shyness, Jacob had expected her to be cowed by his father, but he should have known better. She inhaled a deep breath that made her chest lift and Jacob forced his eyes away. 'She looks like a librarian.'

'She *is* a librarian,' he replied. 'That's why she's so angry. That's Elsie Martin.'

'How have you let it come to this?' Conrad asked, waving his hands around. Jacob felt himself colouring as everyone watched him being berated by his father like a naughty schoolboy. He gritted his teeth. 'This is an absolute PR nightmare. Have you seen the camera crews?'

'Yes, but—'

'And look, there's Jennifer Motley. Damn it!' Jacob felt heat rising up his back and he placed a hand on his neck to quell it. 'She's talking to your librarian. If she runs another story, there's every chance this whole shitshow will be featured in a national paper and I don't mean a passing comment in a Sunday supplement. I mean a full-blown article on the front page. Christ, boy, you've made a complete mess of this.' Conrad glanced around at the other reporters. 'Tell me you haven't given any interviews?'

'No, not—'

'Good. That should help me contain this mess a bit.' Conrad turned around and marched into the crowd. 'Right, everyone, thank you all for making your voices heard this morning. We appreciate and take into consideration all possible feeling when we come up with our plans.' He turned to face the reporters. 'My son, Jacob, will be meeting with Miss Martin who's been organising these … objections to discuss a possible compromise. If there is one, we'll find it. Like I said, at Conrad Yardley Construction, we listen when people have something to say. Once they've met, we'll update you all. Including you, Gavin,' he said, pointing to one of the reporters. 'I should have known you'd be here. Until then, everyone, it really would be better if you went home. It's a hot day. You don't want to get sunburnt.'

Somehow, his father had managed to take the wind out of the

picketers' sails. The arguing died down as hordes of people shuffled away. Seeing as there wasn't going to be any more drama today, the reporters upped and left, and once the crowd had seen them go, they too headed off home, leaving the cake stall decimated. The only few who remained were Winston, Elsie's dark-haired friend, the lady who always wore purple, and of course, Elsie.

His father came over to him. 'That's how you sort these things out. It's all about power and control. You have to show people you're the one in charge and they'll fall in line.' He looked over his shoulder at Elsie and shook his head. 'I can't believe you've been bullied by that.' Jacob felt himself stiffen. 'Sort her out and get her onside.'

'And how am I supposed to do that? She has a backbone of iron. I don't think anything except leaving the library standing is going to satisfy her.' He summoned some courage from deep inside. 'If this is the strength of feeling, Father, maybe we should consider—'

'Don't even think it,' he snarled. 'I'm warning you. All you have to do is keep her thinking it might not happen until the day we knock it down. Take her for dinner. Wine and dine her and tell her exactly what she wants to hear until the day it gets demolished. Hell, then you can even blame me. We're still on schedule for that to happen in three weeks, right?'

'Definitely,' Leah piped up, keen to show some things were going right with the project and that those things were with her.

'Good. But whatever you say to her, Jacob, make sure you've got plausible deniability. I don't give a monkey's about some four-eyed girl, and I'm surprised that you do. She's got nothing on Allegra, that's for sure.' He stalked back to his car and over the roof, shouted, 'I don't expect to have to come down here again', before getting in and driving away at breakneck speed.

Ignoring Leah's rather smug smile, Jacob walked over to Elsie. 'We need to talk about this like civil, grown-up human beings before anything else gets out of hand. You're not planning on chaining yourself to the library door, are you?' He'd asked it as a joke but the way she dropped her eyes worried him. 'Why don't you have dinner with me tomorrow and we can discuss everything?'

She must have thought she'd won from the genuine smile that pulled at her lips. Seeing it crushed his soul. He was an awful human being. Was he really going to string her along like his father had suggested? The thought made his throat close over and the queasiness surge again. Perhaps there was a compromise that he hadn't seen yet? Some way to ensure the library continued in another form. He'd give it some thought and try to come up with something that would appease her, otherwise he might as well sell his soul to the devil right now.

'Okay,' she agreed. 'Where?'

'At the pub?'

It was as good a place as any and he had as much chance of being accosted there as anywhere else in Meadowbank.

'Fine. But I warn you. I'm not backing down.'

Jacob nodded, unable to form any words through the disgusting taste in his mouth. When he'd first met her, the prospect of getting to know her and asking her to dinner had played in his mind as an enticing thought, but the date his father had planned for them was not what he wanted at all.

Chapter 25

Elsie paced around her living room, brushing her hands down her hips, smoothing out her jeans. She'd chosen to wear a normal outfit of jeans and a nice top and hadn't bothered with a dress. She thought of the dress she'd worn on her date with Liam and embarrassment at having read him so wrong warmed her neck. Though thinking of the things Gemma had called him when she'd relayed the night's events did make her smile, she didn't want the reminder. The only thing she wanted from her outfit was to give her the confidence to match Jacob's. He always seemed so self-assured. So together. When she'd spoken to him yesterday, her stomach had fluttered uncontrollably, especially when she pressed against him, and she needed to feel in charge if she was to negotiate a compromise that would save the library.

This was a big step. An important meeting. Something she'd hoped, but never really allowed herself to believe could happen. Now her efforts might actually come to something. Saturday's picketing had been surprisingly fun. She'd enjoyed the action, the sense of momentum the day had. Life seemed to have stepped up a gear for her and instead of dreading it, as she'd always imagined she would, she was loving it. Craving it.

Conrad Yardley had clearly been embarrassed enough by the

camera crews turning up to force his son to meet with her. A twinge of guilt hit as she recalled the way he'd spoken to Jacob. He treated him like a child – one he didn't particularly like – and there was a tone in his voice like he was ashamed of Jacob, as though he'd never quite come up to par. It was terribly sad, but she couldn't afford to be weak as far as Jacob was concerned. Not tonight.

Would his horrible colleague be there? She hoped not. She was constantly being rude to Gemma, and Meredith in the shop, and yesterday, she'd had an almost smug look on her face when Jacob was taking a verbal battering from his father. She was clearly happy he was taking all the blame. They couldn't be sleeping together. Jacob treated her as a colleague, nothing more, and Elsie wished it didn't relieve her as much as it did.

They were meeting at the pub at seven, and Elsie had rehearsed a few of the things she wanted to say. She hadn't prepared any other notes because she only had one demand and was determined not to back down. She clearly had the upper hand and no matter how charming he was, she had to press her advantage. Gemma had reminded her of how smooth he could be, how amiable, and told her not to take any flimflam. She wasn't intending to.

It was five minutes to and time to walk over.

'Wish me luck, Keats,' she said as she stroked his soft fur before grabbing her keys and closing the door behind her.

The evening sun was lowering in the sky, casting a deep golden light over the ground. Sleep had been absent since she'd been sacked, but at least without having to get up every morning, she'd been able to lie in. She was trying to keep a normal routine, but the extra hour helped a little. Still her eyes burned with lack of sleep.

The door of the Drunken Duck stood open, and Elsie walked in to see Jacob leaning against the bar. He was hunched over, as if the weight of the world pressed on his shoulders, and Elsie worried her lip, guilty for adding to it, but what else could she do?

'Hi,' she said tentatively, and he turned to look at her.

He was wearing a T-shirt that hugged his biceps as he proffered his hand for her to shake. The only other times she'd seen him dressed so casually was when he was running, and she found the way the shirt wrapped around his frame incredibly attractive. 'Thanks for meeting me. Would you like a drink?'

'I'll have a white wine, please.' He turned and ordered from Dean, the landlord, and she noticed that unlike Liam, he hadn't had anything to drink before her arrival. 'Is your colleague not with you?'

'Leah? No. She wanted to come.'

I'll bet she did.

'But I thought it best it was just the two of us.'

She swallowed. If only it was the two of them – under much nicer circumstances. She'd actually have quite enjoyed being wined and dined by him if he wasn't trying to destroy everything she held dear. His manner was so easy, even in this situation, yet she could feel the stress in her shoulders, stiffening her body.

Jacob's thin, watery smile didn't meet his eyes, dulling the brilliance of the bright blue. He wasn't enjoying this either and seemed more vulnerable than he had been before, but she would not soften. She couldn't afford to. 'Shall we find somewhere to sit?'

'I've reserved you a table,' Dean replied. 'Over in the corner there.' He pointed to the back of the pub. 'Thought you might like some privacy for your discussion, otherwise everyone'll be earwigging.'

A few tuts met him from further down the bar – they clearly didn't want to miss out – but Dean ignored them. Elsie smiled. Dean's thoughtfulness was so typical of the village and she hoped Jacob realised that.

'Thanks, Dean,' Elsie said, and Jacob politely echoed her.

Once they were seated in a quiet corner, she waited for him to speak. The silence drew out, long and uncomfortable, but she was determined not to be the one to break it. She could well imagine Jacob, and especially his father, seeing it as a sign of weakness.

'Thanks again for meeting me,' Jacob said, sipping his gin and tonic. 'I appreciate that this has been a difficult time for you.'

He looked at her for a response, but she kept her gaze pinned on his collar bone, unable to look at him directly but too proud to drop her eyes.

'I want to start by saying how sorry I am.' She kept her mouth closed, pressing down the urge to reply. His genuine upset for her was unnerving. His whole demeanour was awash with honesty as he traced his finger around the top of his glass. 'I wasn't sure if you'd believe I am sorry, but truly I am. I'm sorry that you lost your job, and I won't give you pathetic and contrite comments like "something better will come along" or "this is all fate". I won't insult your intelligence.'

This time, she was convinced he was genuine, yet couldn't help but feel annoyed. 'Would you be sorry if I hadn't kicked up a fuss? I mean, are you saying this to Karen?'

A tinge of pink came into his cheeks. 'I have spoken to Karen, yes, and I said something similar, but I don't think she's as much of a bibliophile as you.'

So he did know that word. The hairs on her arms stood on end and she pulled her wine glass closer. Why couldn't her body have reacted this way to Liam? It would have made life a whole lot simpler. She really had to stop finding Jacob so attractive. It was very distracting, and he was, of course, evil. Totally evil. She had to get things back on track. 'No, she's not. She was quite looking forward to working somewhere with air-conditioning and a canteen. I don't know whether to feel happy or sad now you've agreed to change your mind about the library. It almost hurts more to know it'll be there and I won't be working in it.' She saw Jacob's throat move as he swallowed. 'What made you change your mind?'

'Well, you see … I—' he stuttered. 'About that, I wondered if there's any way we can find a compromise?'

The word 'compromise' hit her, and the thought that she'd

misread the situation chilled her. 'What sort of compromise? One that still involves knocking down the library?'

'Let's just say we did stick with the original plans—'

'No! Let's not say that. That is not what your father said.' It took everything she had not to rise out of her chair as if someone had hit an ejector button.

'Just hypothetically.' He held his hands out in surrender. 'I was thinking we could work with the council to ensure they were doing outreach work in Meadowbank.'

'Outreach work?'

'Yes, for those who are lonely or isolated.'

'Do you know how outreach actually works?' That was so typical of people like him – developers who came in making sweeping changes but had no idea what the implications actually were. It was like a child using words they didn't understand.

'Well, no, but—'

'Outreach works by people organising events and activities in places like libraries and community centres to reach those who need it. They don't go into people's homes. Without our library it would still mean them travelling somewhere.'

'Right.' He deflated a little. 'I could speak to Rees-Hale to make sure the mobile library that serves the other villages could stop by here. I'm sure that's his intention anyway.'

She scoffed. 'I've heard that the mobile library will be going soon to save money.'

'Oh. I wasn't aware of that.'

'Have you actually thought any of these ideas through?' Elsie asked. The slight pinkness of his cheeks deepened. 'And if you're thinking of something like care staff, Winston and Bernard won't take kindly to random strangers coming into their homes. They've already made their cases for not travelling for miles. You saw what happened to Winston when he tried to ride his bike the other day. Imagine if he tried to ride to Witchbury. All those main roads would kill him.'

'I'm sorry.'

Seeing Jacob's eyes drop, she softened a little. At least he was thinking about ways to help. It wasn't what she wanted, and she would press him for a promise about the library, but she didn't need to be quite so rude. He obviously got enough of that from his dad. 'And the mums don't want to travel all that way. They've made friends here in the village. Being a new mum is hard enough and it's the sense of community they need. They feel so isolated otherwise. The library provides a respite to that.'

'That's what someone said to me the other day.'

Had they? 'Who?'

'She said her name was Maria. She had a little girl in a pushchair.'

'Did she look immaculate? And the baby too?'

'Yes.' His brow furrowed in concern and the ice-blue of his irises deepened to a warmer hue. 'It took me by surprise when she spoke to me. Is she okay?'

Elsie couldn't match this man in front of her with his genuine concern, to the one who was leading the development and had spoken at the public meeting. 'I don't know,' she replied. 'Did she really say she'd been struggling?'

'Yes, and she spoke about isolation.'

'And that didn't change your mind?' The words were out of her mouth before she could stop them. Hurt flashed across his eyes and Elsie wondered who this person was speaking in her head. She needed to rein in the confident version that had emerged lately before she went too far. She'd have to go and see Maria. She clearly needed some extra support right now. 'The library helps people in so many different ways, Jacob. Have you ever felt isolated? It's horrible. I said all this to Jennifer Motley yesterday.'

'Mrs Motley?' Jacob's head shot up, fear ringing in his voice. He'd clearly heard of her reputation as a journalist. The local news was all well and good, but Jennifer was sure she could secure them national coverage as the saga had continued.

236

'Yes. We were chatting just as your father arrived and I've got another call with her tomorrow.'

'Tomorrow?' He was spooked and she was both relieved and saddened. 'I do understand why the library is important to you and other people,' he said quietly. 'And I understand about isolation.'

The only time she'd ever felt isolated was at school before she and Gemma made friends. She'd always been teased for being a bookworm and some of the cooler girls who wore eyeshadow would stare at her through the library window and tease her. It was there she'd met Gemma, a fellow book lover, only one who was a bit more vocal than she was. As soon as they'd become friends, the other girls left her alone. Isolation like that was hard enough, but the isolation Bernard and Winston felt, even Patricia, was harder.

He drank the last of his gin and tonic as if he needed the courage to speak. 'Would you like another drink?' She shook her head, having barely touched hers. 'Do you mind if I do?'

'No, go ahead.' It was sweet of him to ask. *No, it wasn't!* she thought quickly, before her brain had time to believe it.

When he came back with two menus as well, he said, 'I grabbed some menus in case you were hungry.' Where was this genuine thoughtfulness coming from? It was as he'd been at their first meeting, but which was the real Jacob? She surreptitiously looked at his face from the corner of her eye, checking for any signs that he was trying to charm her onside.

She took a sip of her wine, determined to keep things focused. 'I'm okay right now. We were talking about being isolated.'

He shifted in his seat and then let out a sigh. 'Do you remember at the public meeting I talked about people leaving villages? I know it may seem like tosh to you, but I do really believe that these small villages need some affordable housing so people don't have to move away. When I grew up, I was lucky enough that my dad had lots of properties I could live in. He gave me a cottage in our hometown. It's not dissimilar to Meadowbank really. I was 20 and had just finished university. My friends in the village lived with their parents or stayed at mine as much as they could but, it wasn't sustainable in the long term. One by one they started moving away until I was the only one left. They wanted to stay there but couldn't. There weren't any jobs in the area, and they couldn't afford any of the houses. The trouble with these gorgeous cottages is that the period features drive the prices through the roof and the only time things do come up, they're so run-down they're virtually uninhabitable and need a fortune spent on them.' He shook his head sadly. 'I moved to the city to work in the firm but ...' He let the sentence trail off.

Though she hated to admit it, it was true. 'I do understand what you're saying.'

'You do?' He looked at her hopefully, but she couldn't back down.

'Yes, but I still don't see why you have to knock down the library. You could easily save it. You're just choosing not to.'

'The fact of the matter is—' He leaned in closer, cupping his hands around his glass, and she noticed for the first time how long his fingers were. They'd wrap around her hand perfectly.

Stop it, she told herself firmly.

'I do understand that Meadowbank may be different to other places—'

'You do?'

'Yes.' She had the feeling he wasn't sure he should have said that out loud. 'But developments are about profits and to get the most profit we need all that land including the library space.' He scrubbed a hand through his hair. 'I hate talking about profit and loss.'

'You might have picked the wrong line of work then.'

He laughed and it sent her heart pounding. She wasn't imagining this connection between them, was she? 'I think I did. You've met my father; I didn't exactly have much choice.'

'Why not?'

He paused. 'Expectations.' It was only one word, but it seemed there was a lot more baggage behind it.

'So you didn't want to go into developing?'

'No, I didn't. But I shouldn't really be telling you any of this.' Their eyes met again for a second and the atmosphere in the pub changed around them. 'If my father were here, I'd be hung, drawn, and quartered for not toeing the party line.'

A small smile crept over her lips. 'What would you do if you didn't work for your dad?' she asked before she could help herself. *Oh, Elsie!* her brain cried. *Who cares what he wants to do?* She had to control this horrible niggling to know more about him. Knowing more about him wasn't going to change anything. She was not going to let her library friends down by focusing on his biceps or his eyes, or the way his tongue occasionally sat behind his teeth.

'I'd actually love to work for a charity, but that's not on the cards for me yet. Maybe one day when I've run my father's company into the ground, which he's sure will happen if he leaves it to me based on my current work experience. This project was my first solo one to show I'm capable of taking on more responsibility.'

And she was messing it up for him. 'That sounds belittling.'

'Ha! You nailed it. But …' He didn't finish the sentence.

'I'm causing you quite a lot of trouble, aren't I?'

'You are.' Something sparked in the air between them as he looked at her. 'When I first met you, I thought about asking you to dinner, but I didn't think it would be like this.'

He'd thought about asking her to dinner? She could barely believe it and as he blushed, she took a sip of her drink, trying to think of something to say. It was only then she noticed that up until that point, she hadn't been blushing while he had. Even when she'd thought about his biceps and his gorgeous blue eyes. She had no idea what that meant. Probably only that she was focused on her task rather than anything else, but she did feel strangely comfortable around him when they weren't talking about the library.

Unable to stifle it, Elsie let out a huge yawn, and she clamped her hands over her mouth. 'I'm so sorry.'

Jacob sat back, chuckling. 'No, I'm sorry. I'm not very interesting. Since working for my father my conversations only seem to cover developments and profits.'

'It's not that.'

'Are you still not sleeping well?'

'Not really. You'd think my body would be used to it by now, but it never gets easier.'

'And you've found nothing that helps?'

Elsie shook her head. 'Nothing at all. Sometimes reading, or audiobooks help. I love poetry and I've got a couple that are my favourites. Otherwise, I just have to live with it, which is easier said than done some days.' The easy atmosphere was so different to the one on her date with Liam, she wanted to shout at the world, asking what it was playing at.

'Which poets are your favourites?'

'Oh, umm … I love Christina Rossetti and Keats.' Another yawn forced its way up.

'Perhaps something to eat would help?'

Her stomach did feel empty. Would eating with him, in front of the rest of the pub, cause any problems? Surely people would think she was continuing to talk about the library, which they would be, of course. She hadn't yet had that concrete promise she wanted, and she wasn't leaving until she got it. She might as well eat while she was waiting for it, and there were worse things to look at while she ate.

After making their choices, Jacob went to the bar to order and came back with another wine she hadn't asked for.

'I hope you don't mind but I saw yours was nearly empty.'

'Oh, thank you.' Could he really be this considerate?

'So which poems? I remember Rossetti's famous poem—'

'"Remember me when I am gone away"?' she asked, quoting the first line, surprised that he knew it. She should have known from his posh accent he'd have had one of those educations that meant he could answer all the questions on *University Challenge*. The poem was one of her favourites and she tried to ignore the feeling of connection it had spurred between them. There weren't many people who knew and liked poetry these days.

'You know I said I found a book of poetry in the cottage? It's funny how we bring our life experiences to every line we read. Don't we?'

'Yes,' she said quietly. It was exactly what she thought herself.

Their food was delivered by Lynne Noble, who, after placing Elsie's plate down gently, clattered Jacob's onto the table with such force even Dean tutted.

To Jacob's credit, he smiled and thanked her, embarrassment etched on his features.

'The food's really good,' she said, trying to ease the situation. It was much more delicious than what she had at the fancy restaurant in Witchbury that Liam had taken her to. Tonight, she'd refused a starter, not wanting the dinner to feel too much like a date, but now a part of her wished it was. As they ate, the conversation turned to topics she had never expected to discuss with him. They'd return to the library soon though. No matter how charming he was.

'Do you read other things apart from poetry? I'm assuming you do, being such a bibliophile.'

That word again. The hairs on her arms lifted once more. 'I read all sorts of novels. It's my job – or was – to know about good upcoming books, new releases, and trends in the publishing industry.'

'Have you visited the Bodleian Library? It's absolutely beautiful. One of the most beautiful libraries in the world.'

'I went a few years ago. It's wonderful.'

'Sainte-Geneviève Library in Paris is incredible too. Have you ever been there?'

Elsie began to feel uncomfortable. There was every possibility that if she admitted to never having left England, he'd laugh at her. She couldn't lie though. 'No. I'm not a huge one to travel outside the UK, especially if it means getting on a plane.'

'Not keen on flying?'

'Pathologically terrified.'

'What scares you about it?'

Why did he care? She took a mouthful of her food and thought about how to answer. 'I don't know exactly. Just the idea of being that far up in the air in a tin can that could fall out of the sky at any moment. It's terrifying and to be honest, I think it's insane more people aren't petrified at the idea.'

He laughed and she felt ridiculously happy she'd been the one to make him. 'You're not wrong, but do you know each plane is tested for around seventy man-hours to make sure it's fit to fly? Checks are made after every flight as well. You probably know all this already.'

'I'm sure it seems silly to someone like you.'

'Not at all, but … someone like me?' He frowned, his expression quizzical rather than accusatory.

'Yes, someone who travels a lot.'

'I'm no different to anyone else. I've been on a few holidays, but I'm not jetting off here, there, and everywhere. Was it my wind-swept and interesting good looks that made you think that?'

'Partly,' she replied, aware that the tone had lightened. Was he flirting? And had she just admitted she found him handsome? If he'd noticed, he hadn't responded.

'Would it help if I admitted to being terrified of flying too? At least, I was when I first started travelling.'

'Really?' She hadn't imagined Jacob being afraid of anything. If he could get over his fear, maybe she could too.

He nodded. 'At first, I'd do anything to get out of taking a plane. Honestly, I'd travel for sixteen hours by bus and train and car, rather than get on a two-hour flight. It was ridiculous.'

'How did you get around it?'

'I learned about all the different checks that airplanes have to go through before they're even allowed on their first flight. Then I learned about all the things pilots had to learn. I could probably have become one with all the time I spent looking into this. If I had the nerve that is, and I really don't.'

'They do say knowledge is power.'

Lynne came to retrieve their plates and Jacob thanked her, though she stared at him like she'd shank him with a dinner knife if he wasn't careful. When she delivered their desserts, Jacob praised how delicious they looked. 'Wait till you taste it,' Lynne replied. 'But don't worry, I didn't poison it, even though we don't like you being here.'

Elsie felt a rush of pity for Jacob, who shrank into his chair. 'Umm, thanks.'

Lynne bustled off and Elsie wondered how to re-start the conversation. She'd been enjoying it far more than she had her conversations with Liam, even with Lynne threatening physical violence.

'So where would you go?' Jacob asked. 'If you could go anywhere and be excited about every aspect of it, what would be the first place on your list?'

'I've always wanted to see the Main Reading Room at the Library of Congress in Washington. I've heard it's phenomenal.'

'It is.'

'You've been?'

He nodded, grinning. 'Yep. I've always been interested in American history. When I got the chance to go to DC, I had to visit.'

'Have you been to Emily Dickinson's house in Massachusetts?' She felt a slight warmth at the enthusiasm in her voice. 'I've always wanted to go there too.'

'No, I haven't. To be honest, I never even knew it existed, but it sounds fascinating. I don't think I know any Emily Dickinson poetry.'

'You know she was a poet, which a lot of people don't. Most people in the UK haven't heard of her.'

'Is she another favourite?'

They fell into a new conversation, all thoughts of the library forgotten a while ago, and it dawned on her that once she'd sheathed her dagger, she'd had one of the most enjoyable evenings of her life. In some respects, Elsie felt like a traitor. Jacob had a depth of soul she hadn't realised, but she'd intended to sit with knives drawn for the entirety of the evening and she hadn't. And she still hadn't heard the assurance she needed.

As some regulars left with a wave, leaving them and only a handful of others in the pub, the evening sky had turned dusky and hints of star-lit blue appeared through the window.

'So, Jacob, can you promise me you're going to change your plans and save the library?'

'Elsie, I—' His phone beeped and he quickly checked it, his brow creasing as he did so.

A surge of worry constricted her muscles. Had the message upset him or was he stalling? 'Jacob?'

'Elsie, honestly, my father said—'

'I want you to promise me that the library won't be knocked down. Your father said so.'

'Well, he said—'Another message appeared on his phone, and he looked at her apologetically before dipping his eyes to read it. Whatever it was it concerned him. As his frown deepened, two small lines appeared at the top of his nose, but she was growing too angry to care. If he thought she'd be easily brushed aside, he clearly still had no idea whom he was dealing with. She wasn't the shy, retiring creature he'd first met. She was more than that now. Conrad had said they were meeting to discuss a compromise and as she'd said no to the outreach idea, there was only one other settlement: the library stayed. Though their conversation had included other things, Jacob must have known she'd want a guarantee.

'Jacob?' she asked again. She met his gaze, and something passed over his eyes that she couldn't read.

'Elsie—' He hesitated, glanced at his phone one more time as yet another message pinged into existence, then stuffed it in his pocket. He sighed. His eyes lifted to hers, heavy and dimmed but with what? Sadness? 'I-I'm sure there's something we can do.' He began tugging notes from his wallet and dropping them onto the table. 'I'd better go.'

She let out a breath. 'Thank goodness. I'm glad we were able to sort things out. I take it there'll be another public meeting to announce the change?' As she glanced at his fingers, she noticed a slight tremble. 'Here,' she replied, searching in her bag for her purse. 'I'll pay my half.'

'No, no. It's fine. I insist.' Why was he hurrying so much? He only had a thirty-second walk back to his cottage and it's not like he'd have a meeting at this time of night. 'Good night, Elsie.'

She was still gathering up her bag when, without making eye contact, he headed out of the door, leaving her standing alone in the pub.

From the way he'd acted this evening he could be quite a gentleman when he wanted to be. She could imagine him taking her out on a date and treating her wonderfully, pulling chairs out for her, holding doors open, bringing flowers and chocolates, and showering her in compliments, but that ending had been strange to say the least.

'Has he gone?' asked Dean, coming over to clear the dessert plates – clearly Lynne wasn't allowed near them anymore.

'Yes, he has,' Elsie replied, unable to stop herself staring after him.

'That was quick, wasn't it? You must have scared him off, Elsie. Good on you. You've done a brilliant thing saving our library. I think next to my pub it's the most popular place in Meadowbank.'

She hoped the cool evening air might blow away the strange feeling in her stomach. She should have felt relieved – she'd won – but a sense of unease settled in her chest. Something was off and she couldn't quite figure out what it was. She didn't like how rattled he'd been with all those messages coming in and wondered if he was okay. Was his father bullying him again? She shouldn't concern herself with that. The only thing that mattered was that he'd agreed to do something. She had his word and she had to trust it.

He'd even told her about his father and not wanting to work in the family business. They were all things she could use against him if she wanted to, but he'd trusted her with that sensitive information. Whatever messages had spooked him, forcing him to leave, at least in the next few days revised plans and a press release would come out from Conrad Yardley Construction telling everyone the news she'd been longing to hear since this whole thing began.

So why wasn't she smiling?

Chapter 26

Rain battered the window as Elsie looked out into the street from the living room of her cottage. It had been raining solidly for three days now. The day after she saw Jacob, the sunshine had vanished, replaced by thick, dark grey clouds and gloom, and what had started as a light drizzle and a short, sharp storm had turned into the torrential rain she normally associated with deepest winter.

Elsie's eyes traced the drops as they raced down the window. As soon as one hit the bottom another was already halfway down, and she wondered with a sigh when it would ease. She'd seen her friends head to the library at all their usual times and though some had stopped by, the majority of the last few days had been spent alone, obsessively checking her phone for the official announcement from Jacob.

Every time she searched his company's website, or the council's, or heard a knock at the door, she expected it to be him, telling her that the plans had now been changed. After that, she'd imagined a fresh start for them and the possibility of … something, unable to deny the attraction she felt. With each passing moment, a feeling of dread, of being duped and fooled, rose up. Elsie sighed and went back to her sofa and the cup of tea waiting for her.

At the start of their dinner, she'd expected him to try and bring her round with all the skills of a con man, but as the evening had worn on and conversation had drifted into other areas, she'd been surprised at the man under the well-cut suit.

Had she read him wrong?

It was entirely possible. She'd never had to negotiate anything before and as far as Jacob Yardley was concerned, it was getting harder and harder to trust her own instincts. They were so confused by the attraction, her brain couldn't resist, and the way they had connected … But surely, he wouldn't have looked her in the eye if he'd been lying?

She'd finally slept well having received his word that the library was staying. The nights of insomnia had been taking their toll, but as each day passed with an absence of news, her sleep had diminished, and she had no hopes at all for tonight. Maybe it was time to go and see him instead of waiting.

Glancing once more at the window, she pulled her shoulders back and stormed towards the door only to be stopped by the ringing of her phone. It was Jennifer Motley and Elsie accepted the call as quickly as possible.

'Hi, Jennifer.'

'Elsie, oh, Elsie, I'm so sorry.'

'What? What is it?' The heavy feeling in her stomach pulled her down to the ground, sticking her feet to the floor.

'I know you said Jacob Yardley had promised, but – I'm sorry – I think he might have been lying to you. I've been checking with Yardley Construction and the council and nothing new has been put forward. All the plans are exactly the same as the ones they submitted before and a contact of mine in the council has said that there are absolutely no plans to change anything as far as they're concerned. I'm trying to get in touch with someone at Yardley Construction to verify it because out and out lying is a big deal, but I thought I should let you know. I really am sorry.'

Elsie's heart sank and she took a breath before pushing the

words out. 'Thanks, Jennifer. I probably shouldn't have believed him.'

'Don't blame yourself, Elsie.'

But she did. She did blame herself because there was no one else to blame. She hung up, her hands shaking as she dropped her phone onto the sofa. A deep hurt solidified, but also a fury like nothing she'd ever felt before, and she threw her hands into her hair, pulling her head back. The tightness in her throat eased for a second as her eyes stared at the ceiling then she let her head dip back down. Muscles tensed, she wanted to punch something, to scream and shout, to kick her legs to ease the energy pulsing through her. After grabbing her phone, she marched to the door and shoved her feet into her trainers before pulling her denim jacket from its hook. She didn't have time to go searching for her winter coat, which up until now, she hadn't needed for months.

Without knowing what she was going to do or say, she slammed the door behind her and made her way to Jacob's cottage. Elsie considered going to the site but already knew from Winston that there'd been no action there since the rain began. She'd stupidly wondered if it had something to do with the promise Jacob had made. More fool her.

The pounding of the rain on the lane was matched by the blood rushing in her ears. She barely registered the puddles she stepped in or the rain soaking through her trainers, wetting her socks and chilling her toes. The only thing that caught her attention at all was the level of the river. She'd never seen it so high, or heard it rush so fiercely. If they had any more rain it would be as near to the top as she'd ever seen it.

Opening the gate to Jacob's cottage, she could already feel eyes on her from the neighbouring properties, but regardless of the exhibition she was making of herself, Elsie brought her fist down hard on the front door.

'All right, all right. I'm coming.' The door opened and Leah's face peered out. Her sleek ponytail only annoyed Elsie more as she knew her own hair was a mixture of wet rat tails and frizzy waves. 'Oh, it's you. What can we do for you, Miss Martin?'

'I'd like to speak to Jacob.'

Leah glanced behind her, careful to pull the door closed as she did so. 'I'm afraid he's unavailable.'

'I'm not stupid.' *Well, not completely stupid*, she thought. 'I know he's not at the site on a day like this. If he doesn't come to the door and speak to me right now, I'm going to go back to your diggers and bulldozers and really start making a nuisance of myself.'

Elsie hoped that vague threat would work because the words had come out of her mouth before she could stop them, and she didn't really know what she'd do to the bulldozers and diggers even if she was capable of scaling the huge metal fence. She crossed her arms and tried to look threatening, wondering where this strength and power had come from. 'Failing that,' she added. 'I'll stand here constantly knocking on the door until he comes out.'

Now *that* she was entirely prepared to do. She was already soaked through to the skin and couldn't get any wetter. She was pretty sure even her bones were waterlogged.

After a second, Leah decided she wasn't kidding before glancing over her shoulder. In the background Elsie could hear Jacob's mumbled voice. 'Fine. Hang on.' After more mumbled conversation, he came to the door with an expression that could only be described as fearful. 'Elsie.'

'Got anything to tell me, Jacob? Maybe something about Yardley Construction's plans not changing at all and that despite you telling me in the pub the library was staying, you're actually going to knock it down anyway. Anything along those lines?'

'I – uh—' He reached to the back of his head. His arm didn't move up or down, but simply grabbed a handful of hair and held it. 'Elsie, the thing is that …'

The sentence trailed away.

'Yes?'

'Well, you see, the other night—'

'You lied to me. You lied straight to my face, and I was stupid enough to believe you. God!' She rolled her eyes at her own ignorance. 'I am so ridiculous. I can't believe I honestly thought that just because I had a nice time with you and you looked me in the eye, you were telling me the truth.'

'I did tell you the truth about—'

'No, you didn't. You conned me into thinking you'd change the plans. You said there must be something you could do, but you knew there wasn't, didn't you? You and your father never intended to save the library, did you? You're such a liar.'

'No, Elsie, listen—' He reached out to make her wait. 'Everything I said about isolation and flying and poetry, that was all true and I've been trying to—'

'Ah, that's okay then. You only lied about the library part.'

'I didn't mean to lie. I was trying to—'

'How can you not mean to lie? You literally told me a lie straight to my face.' She pointed at her face for emphasis then felt a bit silly. Her glasses were blurred with raindrops so he couldn't see the hot tears welling in her eyes.

'Elsie, I'm sorry. It's not that I don't see your point of view. I do now after being here for a while, but my father—'

'Don't blame your father, you gutless windbag.' Jacob's head shot back like she'd slapped him. 'I don't care what your father told you to do, you're the one who decided to go along with it. You're the one who knew there was never any hope for the library but strung me along anyway. This is all on you, Jacob. I can't believe I actually fancied you when you nearly knocked me over in the street. I actually thought we could be …'

Her words faded as anger gave way to pain. She was so busy ranting, she couldn't control the thoughts tumbling from her mouth with such speed and passion.

'We could what?' he asked, his eyes wide and focused on her.

'I don't know,' she shouted, too angry to be embarrassed. 'Be *something* I suppose.'

251

His jaw dropped slightly, then he gathered himself. 'Elsie, please. I've spent the last two days trying to sort something out. Get promises from Rees-Hale that the mobile library won't be sold and trying to find somewhere else for the outreach work. I've been trying to make it better.'

'I don't believe you. And even if I did, it doesn't change the fact that on Sunday night, you lied to me. I should never have trusted you.'

Elsie turned on her heel and marched back down the path, leaving Jacob stood in the doorway. Pain twisted his features, but it was only because he'd been caught out. He'd strung her along.

A shiver racked her body, her teeth chattering. Could she rally again and counterattack one more time? Right now she didn't have the energy for anything more than a change of clothes and a cup of tea. She felt utterly and completely defeated, but worse than that, she also felt heartbroken. The second chance she'd thought they had, had been cruelly taken away. Cursing his name, she admonished herself for expecting anything else.

Chapter 27

Jacob watched Elsie march off down the street, puddles splashing in her wake. She must be freezing cold. His chest was frozen as the rain battered against his T-shirt but however uncomfortable his clothes were, it was nothing compared to what a slug he felt on the inside. No matter how he tried to excuse himself, he hadn't been honest with her. He'd caused her more pain by saying there must be something he could do when he knew the chance was slim. Even studying the plans and running over every possibility over the last few days hadn't helped. He was the lowest of the low. His father might not have had any scruples about doing things like this, but he had. Or at least, he'd had them before. They'd been slowly whittled away by working for his father. The barrage of text messages he'd received during their meeting in the pub hadn't helped either.

He hadn't enjoyed anyone's company as much as Elsie's for a long, long time. Allegra had been sweet, but as he looked back on their conversations, so much of their time had felt uncomfortable and forced. Yes, the evening with Elsie had started off difficult and awkward, but as the discussion had turned to other things, the natural connection between them that had been clear from their very first meeting had come back even stronger. Conversation had flowed and he'd loved every second of it. It had been clear to him then that if they could only get past this, there could be something between them. Something … special.

Then, at the end of the night, everything had come together in a perfect storm. She'd been pressing him for an answer, and text messages had flooded in from Leah and his father asking if he'd got her onside. What had he said? Had he pacified her? When would he be giving an update? Make sure he didn't say this or do that. It had all got too much. The pressure had mounted, and feeling like a caged animal, seeing his father's face peering through the bars at him, he let the words slip from his mouth. As soon as he'd said them, he'd regretted it. His heart had turned to stone and sunk down into the depths of his stomach. After that, he couldn't look her in the eye and had left as soon as humanly possible.

'You're going to have to call him back,' Leah said, pointing at his mobile phone still resting on the coffee table where he'd dropped it. 'He isn't going to be happy till he's got it all out of his system. You know what he's like.'

When Elsie had arrived, he'd been on the phone to his father and had cut him off abruptly so he could speak to her. 'I know. Thanks for taking over with him while I spoke to Elsie.'

'*Elsie?* I wouldn't let your father hear you talking like that. First-name terms? He won't like that at all.'

She was right. His father would have ignored her and not come to the door, but Jacob had felt the need to see her: the need to explain. He'd been planning to visit her cottage, but his father had called and stopped him. Rees-Hale had been in touch after finding out Jennifer Motley had been sniffing around and his father's sole purpose had been to order Jacob not to speak to Elsie again. He couldn't have been any more pissed off. The bad weather was delaying the project considerably and Jacob still hadn't got Elsie 'under control' as his father put it. Jacob had almost bitten the inside of his cheek he was chewing it so hard to keep his temper. Conrad was even threatening to come down again, but what could he do? Nothing, except shout at Jacob until the weather turned. Once it had, things would be full steam ahead. The library was due to close in less than a week, though they wouldn't be emptying it until this had all died down. The bitter sting of regret shot through him.

He was about to dial his father's number when it began to ring. Clearly, his father's patience was running low, more than usual. 'Yes, Father?'

'What are you going to do?' Conrad asked, or rather, shouted down the phone. 'If Jennifer Motley lands a national piece, we're toast. Our reputation will be dragged across the broadsheets. Anything more than a local rag classes as a major fuck-up in my book. Did I hear Leah say that troublemaker was at the door? What did she want?'

He glanced at Leah, but she busied herself with her laptop. Jacob took a deep breath. In their previous conversation, when his father had asked how the dinner had gone and what exactly had been said, Jacob had stumbled, knowing that he hadn't followed his father's advice about plausible deniability. Coming clean now wasn't going to be fun, but for some reason Jacob felt he needed to do it for his conscience. To regain a piece of the man he'd always wanted to be.

'Hang on a second, Father.' He held the phone away from his ear and turned to Leah. 'Leah, could you give me a minute, please?' She huffily grabbed her things and went upstairs. When she'd gone, he inhaled deeply and braced himself for the inevitable derision and denouncement. 'The thing is, Father, when I was speaking to Elsie at dinner, I said there must be something we could do—'

'You what?' The explosion of noise almost burst his eardrum and he winced. 'I thought I told you plausible deniability. Plausible. Deniability. It means saying things you can deny, or claim were misunderstood. I thought we'd been through that before I sent you down there?'

255

'We did, but—'

'But what? You forgot? You didn't bother to listen the first time? By saying there must be something we can do, you're basically promising some sort of change.' Jacob felt about 5 years old and resisted the urge to drop his head and scuff his shoes like he would have done at boarding school.

'Father, I—'

'I can't believe you couldn't even handle an unhappy librarian. It sounds like the punchline to a bad joke, only there's nothing funny about this situation.'

Jacob didn't add that it was his father's barrage of text messages that had forced him into lying to the one woman he'd cared about in years because, however hopeless it was, he really did care about Elsie and wanted to be with her. Not that she'd ever take him now.

'There's nothing for it, you'll have to pretend she misheard you, or that you said something else.'

'Out and out lie?' He didn't know why this was such a shock. His father had done it a million times, but Jacob never had, clinging to one last principle like it was a life raft. Regardless of the consequences with his father, no decision he'd ever made had settled so badly on his shoulders and he wasn't going to do it. Elsie had got under his skin. The fact she was now stomping through the village hating him more than she ever had before made him feel sick.

'*Out and out lie?*' his father mimicked. 'Yes. There's nothing else to do but lie. Either say you didn't say it or that you said there's nothing you can do. Say that you looked at other possibilities and there aren't any. It's tough toenails. Nothing doing.'

Jacob tried to think about what his father was saying but all he could see in his mind was how wide Elsie's eyes had become when they talked about flying and how the corners of her mouth had picked up when she'd listed the places she wanted to visit. In another life he could have gone with her and stood beside her when she finally saw Emily Dickinson's house. He'd seen the real Elsie, the one behind the anger he'd forced out of her. And, now he came to think about it, he'd seen glimpses of the real her every time she'd been kind and caring towards someone, even to him when they met at the deli. She was truly special, and even if a chance had existed for them, which it didn't now, he wouldn't have deserved her. Not with the way he was behaving. The man he was becoming.

'Jacob? Are you listening? No doubt Jennifer Motley has been talking to her and if she hasn't, she will be soon – they live in the same village after all – and then we'll have a big, big problem. If Elsie tells her you gave a categoric yes and you've gone back on it ... Jesus!' The vehemence of the exclamation shocked even Jacob, who had heard his father's tirades a million times before. 'Why couldn't you have said, "We'll have a look"? That's slightly better. But "There must be something we can do"? Christ. I can't believe we've dealt with more high-profile stuff than this with no worries, but a tiny village in the middle of nowhere and a fucking librarian are giving me bigger problems than all of them put together. Oh, and you, of course. This wouldn't be happening if you'd handled this project properly and stayed on top of things.' Jacob felt his shoulders crumple under the weight of disappointment. 'Maybe we need to get to Jennifer Motley and try and get her onside. Try and show them the good we'll be doing.'

Jacob paused. He knew it wasn't a good idea to say the things simmering in his head, but a small piece of him was fighting back, pushing its way through the weight of disappointment. Knowing how much he'd already let his father down was oddly freeing; it didn't seem he had much more to lose. 'We could always think about actually saving the library and building around it.'

'I hope that's a joke, Jacob.' Conrad's tone was stone cold. A heavy silence came down the line, freezing him, but Jacob steeled himself and continued.

He owed this to Elsie and to himself because he'd come to realise how right she was about the library: how it was so much more to Meadowbank. So central to the life of the village. 'The strength of feeling in the village is huge and Rees-Hale's words about provision are hollow. The people here will be left with nothing if we knock it down. We can build around it. Incorporate it into the designs and rejig the plots. I could speak to Dom and Francis about—'

'You'll do no such thing.' In an unusually calm voice, Conrad said, 'I'll be deciding our next steps so don't do anything. You're no longer in charge. Just keep the site safe and get started on the groundwork as soon as the foreman says you can. I don't want you going near Elsie Martin or that library. If anything else happens, I want to know about it straight away before you open your trap. Got it? Keep me informed.' He hung up.

Briefly, Jacob considered how much damage he'd done by following his heart and suggesting it. A terminal amount it seemed, but did it matter? Was he really going to do this for the rest of his life? For the first time Jacob realised just how much the future before him was unpalatable. He couldn't face doing this for the next fifty years and the longer he stayed, the harder it would be to leave. His plan to one day set up a charitable wing was ludicrous. His father would never agree. If he wanted to do something to help others, he was going to have to get out from under his father's firm grip and face the consequences. A sense of freedom he'd never experienced before lifted some of the weight from his shoulders. He couldn't sink any lower in his father's expectations, which meant he had nothing more to lose.

Jacob stared at the ceiling. Then he moved to the sofa and flopped down. Whatever his father said, he'd continue looking at the plans, seeing if there was some way to save the library. He'd speak to Rees-Hale again too and try to ensure some further provision for Meadowbank. Then when this was all over, he'd quit. He'd finally do it. He couldn't go on being this unhappy. His father may never speak to him again, but wasn't that better than spending his days hurting people?

His father was right that he'd messed this whole thing up and let him down, but the thing that hurt most – because he knew he'd lowered himself even further in her eyes – was that he'd hurt Elsie too and even once he'd left Meadowbank, the little town he was actually coming to love with its crazy ducks and eccentric community, that feeling would haunt him for the rest of his life.

Chapter 28

In the days that followed, with all hope lost, Elsie scoured the papers and job sites but there was nothing that suited her. There were a decent number of roles in Arts and Culture, but none that involved librarianship of the kind she was used to. She'd found one job at the university library in Witchbury, and though it might be her only hope, she couldn't muster the enthusiasm to apply. University libraries had a different feel to community ones. They had none of the charm of her little place. There were no equivalents to Baby and Toddler Toe Taps or book clubs, and if there were book clubs, all she could imagine were groups of students sat around talking about the heavy literature they were reading for their courses, not the commercial fiction she loved to read and talk about herself.

With a sigh, Elsie placed her fork down on the side of her plate.

'Do you want some more bigos?' Gemma asked.

'No, thank you. I'm not very hungry.'

'You must eat,' Orla said, ignoring Elsie's refusal and serving another spoonful of the delicious Polish stew. 'You have lost weight this week.'

Had she? She was pretty sure that wasn't true. She may not have been eating three solid meals a day, but she had been snacking for England and been forced to make several trips to the deli for some of their delicious biscuits because she'd run out. Again.

'If I see Jacob Yardley,' Gemma said, 'I'm going to punch him in the face.'

Elsie grinned. 'Only after I've punched him.'

Orla smiled as Elsie forked the last of the stew into her mouth. 'And me too. He should be ashamed of himself, lying to your face like that. Pretending there was something they could do. What will you do now?'

'Continue looking for a job, I suppose. What else can I do? Are people still arguing in the village?'

'Afraid so,' Gemma replied after sipping her wine. 'We had Mr Fisher and Mr Bateman arguing today. Mr Fisher said he was sad the rain had come and stopped the work and Mr Bateman called him an ignoramus and told him he was short-sighted and petty.'

'Gosh. I don't think I've ever heard Mr Bateman say more than three words together. That must have been quite a feat for him.'

'It was. I don't know if it was that or what he actually said that shocked Mr Fisher most.'

Without thinking Elsie gave a heavy sigh and let the words in her brain escape from her mouth. 'I just wish Jacob wasn't on the wrong side of all of this.'

'What do you mean?'

'When I first met him, I thought that he was nice and even with everything, that impression has been kind of difficult to shake off. Just the way my heart reacted to him …' She let the sentence evaporate.

'I have a reaction to Marmite,' Gemma said, 'but some things it's better just to steer clear of.'

Orla tutted playfully at Gemma's teasing then turned to Elsie. 'I think you think he's more than just nice. Something happens when you see him or talk about him. Something changes inside you. We can see it. Doesn't he make your stomach tighten and flutter? Do you long to see him?'

'Yes to the fluttering. I haven't always longed to see him because of everything else that's happened, but every time I'm near him, I can't help but speak to him. Not always very nicely, I'll admit, but at dinner the other night ...' She didn't know how to finish the sentence.

'Come to think of it,' Gemma said, tilting her head as she thought. 'You do come out of your shell around him.'

'Sometimes I don't even blush.'

'What?' Gemma and Orla cried in unison and Elsie smiled.

'I know. But apart from the ... umm ... physical reaction I had to him, when we had dinner the other night, I just thought that maybe he wasn't such a bad guy after all. I know I was wrong,' she added, as Gemma took her hand. 'But I haven't ever felt like that about anyone before. Why couldn't I feel that with Liam and not him?'

'Has Liam called you again?' Orla asked.

'He's rung me three times today. I know I can't keep putting it off. I'm going to have to tell him he's a douchebag at some point, but I'd rather do it when I feel like I can say it without being cruel. Right now, I'm a mess.'

The video monitor came to life as Scarlett wiggled and began to cry in her cot. Orla stood. 'I'll go.'

'No, I'll go.' Gemma moved to the door. 'You have a sit-down. You were up early baking.'

Elsie smiled at the kind gesture, but Orla's face darkened. 'I'm perfectly capable. I'm not an old lady.'

'I know, I just thought you deserved to put your feet up.'

'You treat me like I am a hundred years old.' Orla gave a slight chuckle, but it was clear she wasn't finding it very funny.

'No, I don't.' Scarlett cried again and Elsie could see Gemma was torn between going to her daughter and resolving this strange and unexpected response from Orla. 'I'm trying to look after you.'

'Okay, but I'm not some ancient granny.' Orla's tone was tense and edged with irritation.

Gemma took a step away, then turned back. 'What's the matter? Every time I try and do something nice for you, you get annoyed at me. I can't do anything right at the moment. You'd think I'd be better ignoring you.'

'Yes, please. Ignore me.' Orla waved her hands around as she spoke. 'It would be better than all this fussing. I'm going for a walk.' She marched to the front door and grabbed her jacket and an umbrella before heading out.

'I have to see to Scarlett,' Gemma said apologetically to Elsie, before racing upstairs.

Elsie stared around at the empty space she now found herself in. 'I guess I'll wash up.' The last thing she wanted was for them to calm down and have to face the fallout from dinner.

Orla's behaviour was more than a little disconcerting. She'd assured her the library wasn't causing her unhappiness, though it couldn't be denied that her mood had changed since the housing announcement was made, but if the constant arguments in the bakery were getting her down, why wouldn't she mention it to Gemma?

Elsie began stacking plates into the dishwasher and putting a few bits in the sink to soak. On the monitor, she could hear the sound of Gemma hushing Scarlett and the crying dying down to a whimper. Elsie was about to smile at the comfort only a mother could give when she heard something else through the monitor that made her pause. Gemma was sniffing and Elsie peered at the tiny video screen. She was crying. Gemma never cried. Something was seriously wrong if Orla was shouting, and Gemma was crying. Could she speak to Orla again and encourage her to confide in her? Though she didn't want to be nosey, she glanced around the kitchen for any sign of the note Gemma had mentioned but there was nothing.

A few minutes later, Gemma came back down and flopped onto the sofa. Elsie wiped the last dish and put it away before joining her.

'Do you think this is the end for us?' asked Gemma, tears welling in her eyes again.

Elsie leapt towards her friend, wrapping her arms around her. 'No! God, no! You're just going through a rough patch. It happens to everyone.'

'Well, I wish I could work out why. She swears it's not the arguments in the bakery, or that she's seeing someone else.'

'You've asked her?'

Gemma nodded. 'She's never been like this before and I didn't know what to think. When she said it wasn't, I thought maybe she was working too hard and if I started looking after her more, appreciating her more, she'd feel better but as you can see, that hasn't worked well either.'

'I'm sure we'll figure it out or Orla will tell you when she's ready. Hang in there, okay. Do you want me to go out and look for her?'

'No, you better leave her be. She clearly wants some space. Thanks for doing the washing-up. You didn't have to.'

'I know.'

They descended into silence and after a while, it was clear Gemma needed to be alone. After having received so many hugs from her best friend over the past few weeks Elsie returned the favour, letting her friend know she was there for her, before saying goodnight. The unsettled feeling grew in Elsie's stomach and she knew she was in for another long and wakeful night, but this time she had more to think about than Meadowbank Library or Jacob. So much more now seemed to be hanging in the balance than just her own future.

Chapter 29

As the pale light crept in through her bedroom window, Elsie pressed her face into the cool softness of the pillow. Keats had curled into a ball and pressed into her feet, his furry body as comforting as always.

'Are you awake, Keats?' He didn't move, but Elsie needed to talk to someone – even the cat – and she shifted position, knowing it would disturb him. He sleepily raised his head. 'Oh, you are awake. Good.' She didn't think cats could scowl but was sure Keats did.

As expected, sleep had neither arrived nor shown any sign of appearing and through the long hours of the night Elsie had tossed and turned and tried all the tricks she'd told Jacob about that night on the library bench.

'Why did he have to lie to me, Keats? And why couldn't he have gone to a different village?'

It had become clear now they were never destined to be friends or anything more and the sooner he was out of her life the better. With no new plans submitted it wouldn't be long until that was the case. Once the rains stopped the library would be gone, and Elsie was sure there was nothing they could do about it now. Jennifer Motley was finishing her article, but Elsie wasn't sure this last stand would be enough. The way the village was falling apart, with neighbour turning against neighbour, it hardly seemed worth it. Ironically, the destruction of the library was the only thing that would bring harmony back to Meadowbank.

As the birds began to sing their tentative early morning chorus, Elsie huffed. Normally, she loved the sound of the birds and would often sit on the library bench, close her eyes, and listen, but when insomnia held her firmly in its grip and her cheer failed, there were times when the chirruping felt more like an omen of doom. The last possibility of sleep was slipping away and with it, any chance of rest. Working in the library had helped her to get up and seize the day, but without it, she couldn't muster any enthusiasm.

Feeling tears of frustration sting the back of her eyes, Elsie climbed out of bed and dressed. The rain that had battered against the windowpanes the previous week and all through the night had ceased and she looked forward to breathing the fresh, clean air. The older residents of the village had all commented they'd never seen anything like it. This recent bout of rain had been so incessant there were no actual words to describe it.

After brushing her teeth (she might as well, as the day was starting whether she wanted it to or not), she closed the front door behind her and headed towards the green. Her feet splashed in the deep puddles filling the potholes as the darkness of night receded. None of the villagers were awake but why should they be? It was still early in the morning. The old-fashioned streetlights that lit Meadowbank's tree-lined lanes were beginning to flick off as she passed and the sky grew to a pale lemon brightness on the horizon. Remnants of blue-grey clouds drifted in it, warning her that more rain was possible if she stayed outside too long.

Was she mad to be out at this time? Insomnia made you feel slightly mad if you didn't keep a hold on it. It forced you to question your decisions and kept you scared that every day would be torture unless you concentrated on what was real and what were merely your fears coming to the fore. Sometimes people didn't understand that. They hadn't at uni, and her midnight walks had singled her out as the weird girl, yet here at Meadowbank, they had been accepted. No one reported her to the police for wandering around at night and if anyone did notice, it was with gentle concern they asked if she was okay. Community was what made Meadowbank special, and Elsie promised herself that even with the library gone, she would do everything she could to ensure all her friends still felt that sense of support, even if she had to turn her own little cottage into a library to do it.

As the village green came into view, Elsie paused. The grass had disappeared under a vast body of water. She knew where she was and where exactly it should be, but it wasn't there. Instead, the ducks were merrily swimming about as if they'd just been moved to a nicer, more extensive property.

She slowed as she drew near, tentatively dipping her booted toe in to see how far below the water the grass was. The duck pond had never burst its banks before. The water hadn't yet reached the houses and shops that lined the other side of the green, but it wasn't far off. They'd need some sandbags, but where would they get them? As Mr Hoffelmeyer had said, Meadowbank River hadn't flooded in over two hundred years.

Though Elsie knew it had been only a few minutes since she'd checked the time, she did so again, reassuring herself she couldn't go waking people up at such an ungodly hour. Their houses weren't in immediate danger, but she'd definitely call in to her neighbours as soon as it was respectable to do so.

The uneasy feeling welling inside erupted as the sound of rushing water hit her ears. The brightening sun reflected in the expanded waters of what had once been a gently babbling brook but was now a fast-moving river. It rapidly sprang away from the green and the centre of the village, on towards the library. She picked up her pace, her uneasiness changed to out and out worry. The houses by the green might be safe, but the library was much nearer the riverbank. If the water had overflowed here, there was even more chance it had done so there. Elsie began to run, only stopping when her deepest fears were confirmed.

The library bench on the bank of the river appeared to be floating and the cherry trees that had remained in bloom for so long were bare. Tiny pink blossoms were pushed and shoved by the swells of water that swept forwards and hit the building. How much water had got inside? Elsie splashed her way to the nearest window and peered in. The floor of the library was covered and though she hadn't seen the roof from outside, some roof tiles must have loosened in the wind or from the force of the rain as water was dripping down from the ceiling in several spots.

'My books!' Elsie yelped, stepping backwards and nearly losing her footing from the weight of water pushing against her legs. She moved to another window, trying to see into the children's section. When she found a good view, she gasped. As was usual in libraries, the bookcases were lower in the children's section and the pretty, brightly coloured rugs that had covered the floor, as well some of the wonderful children's books they treasured, floated on the surface of the water. 'Oh no.'

'Elsie?'

She spun round at the sound of the voice coming towards her. 'Jacob?'

If he was going to ask her to go, he could jog on. There was no way she was leaving the books to fend for themselves. Not to mention all the local historical information in the reference section or the archaeological finds in the display case. There were drawers full of microfiche containing centuries of census records to rescue. They were important to the history of the village and everyone who lived here. There was so much to salvage and by the looks of the grey-blue clouds amassing in the sky again, there wasn't going to be much time to do it in.

'I woke early,' he said, tucking his hands into the pockets of his thin waterproof jacket. 'And when I saw the green was flooded, I thought I'd better come and check the site.'

'The site?' she exclaimed. 'It's still a library for another week or so.'

From the way he shivered he was feeling the cold bite. 'You're right, of course.'

She turned back to the window. 'I wish I still had my keys, then I could get in there and start saving some of the books.'

Jacob joined her at the window, peering over her shoulder. He smelled of fresh lemons and his eyes were filled with worry. She had no idea why. Surely this made life easier for him. It meant he could strip the place and knock it down quicker.

'I've got keys,' he replied, digging into his coat pocket. 'As we've been using Karen's office, they let me have a set. Here.' He held them out to her, and she hesitated, examining them as though this was a trick. 'Please, I want to help and don't worry, I'll take the flak from Rees-Hale if he turns up.'

'Flack?' She gave an incredulous half-laugh. 'It's not like I could get into more trouble. Though I suppose he could have me arrested for breaking and entering.'

'I'm not sure you can be arrested if someone has given you permission … and keys.' The water swilled around his feet, soaking his shoes and reaching up his jeans. She raised her eyes and met his gaze for a second. There was that genuine look about him again and a part of her longed once more to trust him. 'Come on, we better hurry. We've got some books to save, and I think it's going to start raining again any second.'

'Why are you helping me?'

'Because I'm sorry for lying to you and ashamed of myself for doing it. This version of me isn't who I really am, Elsie. Please believe me. Believe it or not, I don't want to see these books drown. I'm so sorry for lying to you.'

His apology took the wind from her sails, but was this another of his father's tactics? Had Conrad been on his back again? She could well believe it from the way he'd treated him before. She couldn't imagine a parent treating their child with such disdain.

From what Jacob had said in the pub, Conrad was a bully and no doubt Jacob was getting one hundred per cent of the blame for the trouble she was making. Not that she regretted trying to save the library, but she could see the emotional fallout had been as heavy for him as it had been for her. The intensity of his stare held her spellbound. 'You-you are? Sorry, I mean.'

'I am. Elsie, I should have been straight with you.' He took her hand, placing the keys into her palm, but then failed to let go. His hands were warm against the cold of her skin. She didn't pull away. 'My father did tell me to keep you onside. I was told to maintain plausible deniability. It's my father's favourite term. He told me yesterday I should lie if you said anything and make out you'd misunderstood me.' He must have feared an assault on seeing her expression, and he hurried on. 'But I'm not going to do that. That's not who I am.'

'I don't know who you are or what I'm supposed to believe. People like you lie all the time.' She didn't quite believe the last part even if the words had come from her.

'People like me? You saw the real me when we had dinner. When I made you laugh about overcoming my fear of flying. When we talked about all the places you'd like to visit.'

'That was one fleeting moment,' she said, regretfully, unable to keep the pain from her voice. She remembered their meeting when Winston fell – his kindness. She remembered their conversation at the deli and the way he'd kicked the ball back to the little boy. She'd felt then that was the real him. If things had been different, they could have been more, but she couldn't see a way forward for them now. How could anything good come from this beginning? 'I know what you'll do now. You'll take the chance to strip the library and knock it down even sooner.'

'Since our dinner I've been trying to—' He stopped himself and she wondered what he'd been trying to do. 'All I want to do right now is save as much of the contents as we can. Whatever you think of me, I'd like to help.'

It suddenly hit her that Patricia's story things were in danger. 'I've got to save the story mat. Patricia will be devastated if that gets damaged or the puppets she's made.' She spun back to the window.

'Then we'd better get in there and save them.'

He motioned for her to lead the way to the door. The water was rushing against their ankles, making movement slow and leaden. Elsie's fingers were icy as she fumbled to find the right key and unlock. Even when she'd managed it, pulling the door against the current of the water proved too hard. She tugged again, but it didn't move. Jacob stepped behind her and reached forwards, grabbing the handle. She felt the warmth of his body through his damp jacket and something inside jolted.

'One, two, three.'

With a huge effort they managed to pull open the door, heaving it against the rushing water. After stumbling in, Elsie gazed around in shock. She dashed to the hidden cupboard and pulled out the story mat and bag of toys. They were slightly damp but salvageable and Elsie let out a sigh as she waded over to the counter. She opened the bag and though she didn't particularly care about Barbie and Ken, who would be perfectly fine with their weirdly shaped plastic bodies, the crochet figures were too precious to lose. Elsie pulled them out one by one and laid them on the counter as tears welled in her eyes. There was Patricia in her purple dress, Winston in his suit, Bernard with his large bushy beard, and then her in her glasses. She'd take them home and give them back to Patricia when she next saw her. She'd put in so much effort to make them that it didn't seem right for them to be lost with the library.

Despite what Jacob said, she was sure his father and Rees-Hale would use this flood as a chance to move everything on quicker. The most she could hope for was saving the things she loved most.

'What should we save first?' Jacob asked.

'We need to get all the family history stuff. We've got old

electoral registers from 1901 here; they're not exactly priceless but as near to it as emotionally possible. When someone finds their house and sees who lived there before them—' She faltered. 'Those things are impossible to replicate. I'm going to start getting this lot safe.'

Elsie went to move, and Jacob pulled her back. 'Wait, I didn't even think about the electricity.' He pulled out his phone and dialled. 'Dominic, it's Jacob. Yeah, sorry. I know it's early. Listen, the library's flooded and I need you to call the supplier and make sure the electricity is switched off. We've got some books to save. And we need sandbags too. Lots of sandbags. Bring enough for the village.'

The village? Elsie edged away quietly so she could listen in and opened the cupboard door containing the microfiche.

'Yes, I know he won't like it, but this is on me. When I walked over here, I saw some of the houses were in danger. If the pond keeps overflowing, it'll eventually reach the other side of the green and there are homes and businesses all along there. Okay, okay, I promise I'll be out of here in a minute.' From where she was, she could hear Dominic's voice rising. He was clearly telling Jacob to get out as soon as possible. Jacob replied with appeasing responses. When he'd hung up, he said, 'Elsie, perhaps we should leave the building until Dominic tells me everything is safe.'

'No! Once I've got the reference section sorted, I need to start saving the books on the lower shelves. All of them.'

'Elsie' – he came to her and placed his hands on her shoulders – 'books are important but so are you.'

She was?

'Please, come outside with me until we know the place is safe.' He held his hand out to her but she stayed put, deciding whether to take it or not. It felt like she was yielding more than this one thing, but the sensible side of her won out. She hadn't fancied setting anything on fire to save the library and getting electrocuted now wasn't the best option either.

'Hang on!' Just as their fingers touched, she pulled away and waded to the desk grabbing the story bag and mat. Jacob's hand was still out and she slipped hers into it. It felt natural, safe, and an image of all the walks they could have taken hand in hand flittered across her brain.

Once outside, he kept hold of her, guiding her back towards the village green and the dry land on the other side of it. When they came to a stop, he showed no intention of letting go. Then Leah came hurtling towards them under a giant umbrella, followed by Gemma, and Orla, who was carrying Scarlett. On seeing her friend, Elsie let her hand drop and felt Jacob stiffen as she did so. Embarrassment and confusion inched up her spine.

'Jacob?' Leah shouted, coming closer. Her umbrella was so large that when she stood beside them, all three were sheltered from the drizzling rain. 'What the hell's going on?'

'The library's flooded,' he answered, coolly.

'Right. We need to get this under control. Quickly.' She glanced at Elsie from the corner of her eye before lowering her voice as she spoke to Jacob. 'Have you asked Dom to—'

'I've already spoken to Dominic. He's turning off the electricity and getting sandbags.'

She seemed surprised he'd acted so quickly. 'What does your father say?'

'I haven't spoken to him yet, but I've got the boys coming to secure the houses.'

Her face registered more surprise and then something else she couldn't name, but Elsie could tell she wanted no part in any decision his father might not like. 'This is an emergency situation, Jacob. We need to use what we have to secure the site.'

Jacob didn't say anything but glanced at Elsie, a knowing look in his eye. Was helping the village his way of making up for lying to her? Her heart rate quickened.

'Elsie,' Gemma said, moving to her friend, 'I was getting up for the early shift when I saw the green. Are you okay?'

273

'Cold and damp but otherwise fine.' Her teeth chattered as she tried to wiggle her freezing cold toes and bring them back to life. 'I rescued Patricia's story stuff.'

'She'd have been devastated to see it ruined.'

'You should come back with us and warm up,' Orla said. 'There's nothing more you can do.'

Elsie shook her head. 'I can't. I have to go back and save as much as possible. There's all the family history stuff, the local finds, the children's books … everything. And we don't know how much more rain will come.' Orla tried to move her umbrella over Elsie, but it wasn't big enough for them all. 'Keep you and Scarlett dry, Orla. I can't really get any wetter.' Orla's eyes were so full of concern she felt the need to reassure her further. 'Honestly, I'm fine. I promise.'

'She's calling my father,' Jacob said, nodding towards Leah, who had moved away from the group. Elsie turned to watch as Leah spoke into her phone, casting suspicious glances over her shoulder. 'He'll put a stop to the sandbags for the village.' Tugging his phone from his inside pocket he made a call. 'Dominic, where are you? Good. Brilliant. See you in a minute. I'll meet you at the green first, then onto the library, okay?'

'When will they get here?' Elsie asked.

Jacob's eyes darted over her head and then dropped down to her face as a fleet of trucks pulled into the village, creeping slowly through the mass of water. One of the trucks stopped next to Jacob and the man she presumed was Dominic leaned from the passenger window.

'The old man won't be happy about this,' he said with a wry smile.

'I know,' Jacob replied. 'But he can't be anymore pissed off with me than he is already. This is going to be my last solo project anyway. So …' He gave a resigned shrug.

'He'll calm down eventually,' Dominic said. 'It might take a decade or two, but he will.'

Jacob shook his head. It was clear he didn't believe what Dominic was saying. Then he rallied. 'Let's get these sandbags unloaded, lads, please. Start distributing them to the homes and businesses around the green most at risk of flooding and then we'll move on to the library.'

'I've brought a pump,' Dominic said, 'but there isn't much point until we've stemmed the flow at source.'

Though it was early, the activity had woken some of the village and as they opened their doors to see the devastation for themselves, lights flickered on in other houses and soon the street was filling with people. Gasps of shock grew louder as the small army of young men delivered sandbags to people's houses, waking those who hadn't already been disturbed by the rising tide of voices. As they did, Elsie could hear the responses of many grateful recipients.

A giant purple mac floated towards them. 'Oh, Elsie, I saw the green and I—' Her eyes dropped to Elsie's hands. 'You saved the story bag! Oh, thank you, darling. Thank you.' Ever loving, Patricia wrapped her in a hug despite Elsie being soaked through.

When Jacob moved away to speak to Dominic, Gemma whispered, 'Okay, what have you done to Yardley junior?'

Elsie's brows knitted together. 'Nothing. Why?'

'Because he's suddenly full of community spirit and helping everyone out. And I mean literally, everyone. Look around you, Elsie, look how happy everyone is. Do you think he's doing this out of the goodness of his heart or as a PR stunt?'

Before, she would definitely have said a PR stunt, a trick to win everyone over, but he didn't need to do this. He'd already won. And the flooding of the library had only sped up that victory. He had no reason to help them, especially as his father wouldn't approve of them using company resources.

'I think he's helping us because he wants to.' Gemma's eyes widened. 'The library's finished. There's no way it'll be saved now, but his father's going to kill him for helping the village and look at Leah stirring the pot. Jacob knows he'll be in for it when Conrad arrives, which I've no doubt he will soon. Jacob's done this because he wants to.'

'Then wonders will never cease. Or perhaps he's doing it for you.'

Could that be true? She had to admit, a tiny piece of her heart hoped so. Or was it more than just a tiny piece?

Chapter 30

'Right, that's everyone sorted here. Shall we go on to the library?' Jacob asked. He was the most alive she'd ever seen him and had a sparkle to his eyes. Not one that said he was enjoying himself at everyone else's misery, but a change had come over him, like he was passionate about something and in this case it was helping the village.

Elsie followed with Gemma as the trucks moved onwards. By now, Winston and Bernard had joined the throng, and they marched ahead like the rain had poured new life into them. Karen was conspicuous by her absence.

'He's very chipper,' Gemma said as they strode along behind, watching Jacob make Patricia laugh. Orla had taken Scarlett back home. As much as she wanted to help, this weather and the library were no place for a baby. 'You'd think knowing his father was about to arrive on the warpath he'd be a bit more worried.'

'Maybe he's not as bad as we thought.'

'He is trying to help us and that counts for something. Are you okay, though? If you think they'll use this as an excuse to knock the library down quicker, this really is the end of the road.'

Elsie took off her glasses and wiped at her eyes. The devastation was beginning to sink in and with it the hurt she'd been keeping at bay for so long. 'It hurts more than anything, Gem, but at least I can be proud we gave it all we could.'

'We certainly did that.'

Following behind them were ladies armed with flasks of tea and baskets of cakes they'd had lying around. It was another eccentric Meadowbank tradition to make cakes just in case you needed them for emergencies. Jacob too was surprised by the food being rolled out. He'd caught Elsie's eye several times on the short walk down the lane and each time she'd felt a fire burn inside her, but not the angry fury she'd known before, this was something much more heart-warming.

When they reached the library, everyone paused and stepped aside for her to enter first. She wasn't quite sure why, or how she felt about it, but the village had grown to see her as some kind of leader. She hadn't been a very good one. She'd lost, but no one was holding it against her. In fact, the village had come together this morning. She'd even spotted Mr Hawthorne, who allowed Jacob and Leah to stay in his property, helping Mrs Dalloway, who had thrown Leah out of hers.

'Where do we even start?' asked Winston, his eyes watery as he surveyed the devastation.

'I think we should split into teams,' Elsie said, turning to everyone. 'Winston, can you find some help and work on the A to C shelves then just keep going?' He nodded. 'Patricia, can you work on the children's section?' Patricia smiled, instantly finding people ready and willing to assist.

That left the reference section and their all-important historical records. Elsie was happy to lead that team herself, but when she saw Amelia Williams had arrived, and knowing how much she too loved family history after her recent discoveries, Elsie asked for her assistance.

'Where are we going to put everything?' Mr Dobbs asked.

The drizzle had eased off again and the sun came out from behind the clouds, shining down on their efforts.

'I guess we'll have to put anything we can save in my cottage,' Elsie replied. There didn't seem to be anywhere else. 'Anyone else got any ideas?'

The sea of heads shook in response.

'Let's use the trucks,' Jacob shouted from near the back. 'I'll get the lads to sweep them out and put some plastic down. We can then move things in bulk.'

He held Elsie's surprised gaze and his eyes shone brighter than ever across the crowd between them. Leah scowled like he'd betrayed her, but it was an excellent idea and with Conrad due to arrive any moment, they had to do as much as they could now. He'd probably pull the plug on any type of assistance as soon as he stepped out of his car.

'Okay. Good idea. Gemma, could you supervise from my cottage? Keats will probably hide upstairs.'

Gemma agreed and headed off. There was no one she trusted more to look after Keats and her stuff while her cottage was open to all and sundry.

'Anything we can't save we'll have to leave where it is, or if it's going to be in the way, move it to the corner over there.' She felt a kind of grief for the books that wouldn't make it and reminded herself they were replaceable.

The sound of cars and vans could be heard moving through the village and before long they were parked at the library, but it wasn't just the lads from Yardley Construction who were here. The media had arrived again and were setting up cameras. Jacob's face paled. There was no doubt about it, Conrad would do his absolute nut if he saw this lot. They were beginning to call Jacob's name and ask him questions. Jacob went back to the door and ushered the last few villagers inside and away from them.

'Please stay outside and let us work,' he said calmly. 'We've a lot to do.'

Winston slid his old, wrinkled hand into Elsie's own. 'I'm so proud of you, Elsie, the change that's come over you.'

She was proud of herself. Though she hadn't saved the library she'd grown in confidence, and in many ways she was almost unrecognisable to herself. Yet, it felt right. Like she'd finally cast off a heavy coat and was embracing life. She gave him a kiss on the cheek. 'Thank you, Winston.'

They all set to work, and Elsie began stacking up the rolls of microfiche in their small boxes and moving them upwards into the top cupboards. She and Amelia had decided this was the best approach: get the books and records out of harm's way and then clear the huge wooden cabinets completely. If they spent all their time taking things out and moving backwards and forwards to the trucks, items left in the wet would sustain more damage. Without knowing how much higher the water would rise, they wanted to empty every cabinet before the end of the day. The water was up to her shins now and so much would be lost if they didn't act quickly.

They were just starting when Mr Hoffelmeyer turned up in a full set of waders and waterproof jacket that were about three sizes too big for him. He looked like he was going on some ancient diving expedition. 'Oh, Elsie! The records. All our lovely records.'

'Never fear, Mr Hoffelmeyer, I'm on the case. As is Amelia.'

He gave them both a rather sappy smile. 'Then I shall join you.'

With an enormous amount of rustling, he bent down to begin clearing a cupboard, muttering oh dears to himself as he did so.

'Who's Keats?' asked Jacob, appearing behind her. He crouched down and began moving handfuls of small hardback books containing the electoral registers.

'He's my cat. A giant tortoiseshell furball with the grumpiest face known to man, but really he just loves cuddles and treats.'

Jacob smiled. 'I like cats. My father's more of a dog person. When he bought his first big house, he thought we should get either giant hounds or King Charles spaniels like old royals.'

'What did you end up with?'

'Father got an Afghan hound that's almost as tall as he is and he's been absolutely terrified of it since it thought his moustache

280

was a mouse and tried to bite it off his face.' Despite herself, Elsie laughed. 'You have a very sweet laugh, you know?'

Her heart stirred violently. 'Why are you here getting wet and helping us to save these books when you've won?'

'I never saw this as winning or losing. And I've come to understand I was wrong, especially about this place. I couldn't go back to my cottage and leave you all to deal with this. I like books.' He took a breath. 'The truth is that helping with the sandbags, helping people save their homes, it makes me feel ...' He searched for the words, embarrassed. 'Good. Really good. Like I am doing something worthwhile. Do you remember when I told you in the pub that I wanted to work for a charity? Well, today feels like the closest I've ever come to that dream.'

She met his gaze. 'You could always tell your father you don't want to work for him and do something else.'

'Honestly, I never thought it was an option before,' he replied, bowing his head.

Before? Did he think he'd get sacked too? Elsie was about to ask what had changed when Rees-Hale pushed his way through the throng. He had a pair of wellington boots over his suit trousers and an open umbrella. He raised his head and watched the trickles of water escaping through the ceiling. 'Mr Yardley? Thank you for your help. Oh – Miss Martin. I suppose I should have known you'd be here.'

She stood, straightening her shoulders. 'I know I probably shouldn't be, but I couldn't let these records be destroyed when there was something I could do to help.'

Jacob stepped in. 'Elsie was the first on the scene. She discovered what had happened, so I opened the place and we set to work once everything was safe. I apologise for not calling you, I thought it best to get started.'

He nodded. 'Admirable, Miss Martin. Thank you for your help and quick thinking. I saw a truck outside; where is everything being taken?'

'To my cottage,' Elsie answered, and Rees-Hale's eye twitched. 'There wasn't really anywhere else.'

'Fine. We'll carry on like for that for now and I'll arrange a storage facility.'

'Thank you.'

He didn't say anything more and left.

'I think he likes you,' Jacob said, grinning.

'I keep turning up where he doesn't want me.'

'But if it wasn't for you, all of this would be lost. And there wouldn't have been as many volunteers if he or I had asked the village to help. They're here because of you, and he knows that.'

The thought sent a tingle through her cold body.

No sooner had Rees-Hale left than Conrad arrived, marching in in luminous yellow waterproof trousers and an equally bright hard hat. He looked like a dressed-up Mr Potato Head.

'I don't think the library has ever had this many visitors before,' she said, making Jacob smile.

'Jacob?' Conrad shouted, his face an angry puce colour. 'Jacob? Why the bloody hell are you smiling?' Jacob turned to face him, and Elsie felt her breath catch as the two men stared at each other, but for the first time there was a steely glint in Jacob's eye and he refused to be cowed. 'Find this funny, do you?' Outrage rose inside Elsie at his disrespectful tone. Had he spoken to Jacob like this his whole life? 'Because as far as I can see, there isn't anything to be laughing at.'

'We were simply sharing a joke,' Elsie said, aware that she would probably receive a barrage of abuse in return.

'Bah! The librarian. I should have known you'd be here.'

'Well, it is a library, Mr Yardley,' Elsie replied. 'That's generally where librarians hang out.'

Jacob's mouth fell open.

'Thought you were sacked though. Shouldn't you be off somewhere else?'

Ignoring his rudeness and unable to be intimidated by such

a comical-looking man, she smiled. 'You might want to step outside, Mr Yardley. We've been told the ceiling might come down at any moment.'

He glanced up in mild panic and Elsie shared a mischievous glance with Jacob before walking off.

'Outside,' Conrad shouted at Jacob, striding to the door. 'Now.'

As Jacob reached the door, he glanced over his shoulder at Elsie and her heart beat hard against her chest. She followed their progress down the side of the library, away from the reporters milling about outside. A moment later, their voices carried in through one of the side windows. Unsurprisingly, Conrad's was loudest even though he was trying to keep it down.

'And who's going to pay for all these sandbags, hey? Who's going to foot the bill for all this "help" you're giving?'

'I will.'

'You?'

'Yes. I've got money and God knows I've got nothing to spend it on. I'll pay for everything.'

'Bah!' There was a silence and Elsie noted everyone in the library was listening avidly. 'The pressure has got to you, hasn't it? Having to run the show on your own. It's been too much. I guess it's my fault really. I should have known after the first blunder you weren't ready.'

'It's not that I'm not ready, Father, it's—'

'Of course it is. And I suppose I need to take my share of the blame, though I don't see what I could have done differently.'

I'm sure you don't, Elsie thought. He was the type of man who could never blame himself for anything. It couldn't have been easy for Jacob with a father like that. Any girlfriend of his would have a lot to put up with. The thought of being his girlfriend sent a shiver down her spine.

'Well,' Conrad continued, 'you *can* foot the bill, as you've used my resources, and you might as well keep clearing this place. It'll all need to come out eventually, but don't think about putting any of this in storage on the company account. I'm instructing Leah to block any payments.'

'We've got it covered, Father. And—'

'Right now, we need to think about the plans. If this river's prone to flooding, we might need to tinker. Though it could be a one-off. Some batty old man in a cravat was telling me this river hasn't flooded in two hundred years, so we might be all right.'

Jacob's voice went quiet, and Elsie wondered what he was thinking. A moment later, he said something she couldn't make out and he and his father left, their voices growing fainter. She went to the window and watched them go. She had no idea after that if he would come back and confusion knitted her brows together.

Orla arrived with the welcome sight of a tray laden with cake. Even a flood didn't stop elevenses in Meadowbank. Scarlett dangled from a sling tied around her chest, one chubby fist plunged into her mouth. Orla placed the tray on the desk, and everyone gathered around for a snack.

Elsie gazed around in wonder. You'd have thought it was a normal day at the library, not that everyone was stood shin-deep in cold, dirty water. Her tiny village really was an amazing place. All those who had been arguing had come together to save the library's contents, though they couldn't agree to save the library itself. Sadness filled Elsie once more that this would be the last time she worked there.

'You should go home and change into some dry clothes,' Orla chided. 'You'll catch a cold.'

'I know I should, and I will, as soon as I get the reference section sorted out.'

Scarlett wriggled and kicked, trying to twist to see her mum. As she did so, something fell from Orla's coat pocket. Hastily, she bent to pick it up, but it was difficult with Scarlett wiggling like a worm and Orla's fingers brushed the water, pushing it forward. Elsie grabbed it before the paper got too wet.

'No!' Orla cried.

'It's okay, it's not too damaged.'

'Can I have it please?'

The severe and nervous look on her face made Elsie pause. Was this the letter Gemma had mentioned? The one Orla had been hiding but had assured her was only a shopping list. For Gemma's sake, should she look to see what it was? It went against everything she believed in, but she desperately wanted them to stop fighting.

'Please, Elsie?'

'Orla, I really want to give this to you. You're my friend, but so is Gemma. Is this the reason you and Gemma have been fighting so much? She mentioned she saw you hiding a note. Is this it?' Orla's usually kind expression changed to fear. 'Is there someone else, Orla? Have you fallen out of love with Gemma?'

'What? No!' The vehemence in her voice convinced Elsie straight away.

'Then what is it?'

With a sigh, and a stroke of Scarlett's fine blonde hair, she said, 'It is a letter from my parents. You remember how they were angry I'd moved away with Gemma? They've been back in touch and want to come over.'

'Why didn't you tell Gemma?'

'I didn't know if she could forgive them. I can. They're my parents and I love them. They're genuinely sorry for what they did, I can tell from Mum's letter. And I miss them.'

Tears welled in Orla's eyes and she closed them, dipping to kiss Scarlett's head. It must have been so hard for her moving away from her family and leaving on an argument. Elsie immediately embraced her.

'You need to tell Gemma, Orla. Especially if you'd like them to come over and visit. Or would you go over there?'

'I don't know. I don't know if Gemma would come with me.'

'Orla, I know Gemma can be a bit feisty sometimes, but she

loves you. She'll do anything she can to make you happy. She's been worried that you've found someone else. That you don't love her anymore. You have to go and tell her.'

'I will,' she replied with a relieved smile. 'It's good to have told someone about this.' She looked at the letter. 'I'll go now. I never meant to hurt her. I just wanted to make my decision before I showed her the letter.'

'I understand, but today seems to be a day for forgetting our disagreements.' She pointed to Mr Fisher and Mr Bateman who were working together in the F section. 'Why don't you head to my cottage now?'

Orla nodded, leaving the tray of cakes. 'I suppose it has been going on long enough.'

'I promise, Orla, Gemma will understand, and she'll support whatever decision you make.'

After Elsie placed another kiss on Scarlett's head, they left and she resumed her work. Jacob still hadn't returned, but instead of thinking he'd got bored and gone off to tear down another building, she began to worry about him. Conrad had been furious when he'd arrived, she couldn't imagine Jacob was going to come away with anything less than a sore ear, but what derogatory, harsh things would he say before he'd finished?

Would Conrad take the project away entirely so she'd never see Jacob again? She'd seen a different side of him today: a side that previously she'd only glimpsed. The side she wanted to know better. Now more than ever she believed that there was more to him than she'd first thought. He was the Jacob she'd seen at their first meeting, the one she realised now that she'd harboured hopes of falling in love with.

Chapter 31

A few hours later, Jacob rounded the door to the library, and pulled the smile from his face, not wanting Elsie to misconstrue it. He didn't want her to think that in the time he'd been missing, he and his father had been out celebrating the library's destruction. He couldn't believe he'd thought of a possible solution or that his father, however begrudgingly, had actually listened. All he could do now though was cross his fingers and wait. He made his way to Elsie. The water had receded a little thanks to the sandbags on the bank, but not by much. She was coming to the end of clearing the reference section and the heavy, dark-wooden cabinets with their large panes of glass revealed empty shelves.

'Wow, you've made amazing progress. Sorry I got waylaid. My father likes to make his point, then make it again. Then make it again. And again.'

'I'll bet he does.' She smiled warmly. Was she happy to see him? No, it was hoping too much.

'I did try and get away to come and help,' he added. It was important she understood that.

Elsie stood up, stretching her neck from side to side. 'I believe you.'

'So what shall I do now?'

She looked around, surveying the work completed so far. 'A to E is clear. F to K is going quite well. I think Patricia could use a hand in the children's section.'

'Right you are, boss. Have you had a break?'

'Not for a while.'

He noticed a single small piece of cake left on the desk and grabbed the plate, bringing it over to her. 'Here.'

'Don't you want it?' He shook his head and proffered the plate once more. 'These are my favourites. They're called szarlotka and Orla makes them. They're delicious.'

'Then as it's your favourite you should definitely have it. You deserve it after sorting out all this lot.'

They fell into a strangely loaded silence. The way Elsie was looking at him – with a warmth to her expression – unnerved him. Had she stopped hating him just a little bit? Could he ask her to dinner again? Surely she wouldn't want to cook after a long day standing in freezing cold water, but that didn't mean she'd want to eat with him either. How he wished he had the courage to ask, but he couldn't summon the words to his mouth.

'I think we're going to have to finish soon,' she said, breaking the tension between them. 'We've cleared as many of the lower shelves as we can, but I can't ask people to stay any longer. They've been here for hours, literally since the crack of dawn and it's now—' She checked her watch. 'Gosh, it's gone four o'clock. Everyone must be exhausted.'

'Are you?'

She thought for a moment as if the adrenalin had been pumping so hard she'd hardly thought about it. There were dark shadows under her eyes. Her insomnia must have been keeping her awake for days. 'Do you know, I think I am. I might actually sleep tonight. Or at least fall asleep for a bit. I'll probably be awake at three o'clock worrying about all the books we didn't manage to save.'

'I'm sure the books above the water line will be safe tonight.

It's stopped raining again and Dominic and the lads have spent the day sandbagging the riverbank so there shouldn't be any more water coming in. They've done an amazing job. We can start to drain some of this out tomorrow hopefully.'

As he finished the sentence, Elsie's face froze. Though this was good news to him, and there was the prospect of more good news to come, it wasn't to Elsie. She didn't know about the discussion he'd had with his father. About the possibility that— He didn't finish the thought, worried that if he did, he might jinx it. Dominic was on board and he held more sway with his father. If anyone could convince him, Dominic could. It was going to be a long night as he waited for the decision, but his father had promised it by nine o'clock tomorrow morning. It wasn't until Elsie called out that he realised what had taken her attention.

'Liam!'

He was talking to the camera crews in the doorway and had virtually invited them inside. Jacob's jaw tightened. Liam waved at Elsie but didn't break his conversation with the reporter. Eventually, he came over.

'Elsie.' Liam's voice was loaded with a fake sympathy that set Jacob's teeth on edge.

'What are you doing here?'

'I saw what had happened on the news this morning and thought I'd come and help.'

She looked at her watch. 'It's four o'clock.'

'Yes, sorry. I was busy writing.'

'But we're just finishing.'

'Are you? Oh, what a shame.'

Though he might have misread her reaction, Jacob was sure Elsie was biting her tongue.

Liam edged closer to Elsie. 'Shall I take you to dinner? I've been hoping to since our last date.'

So he'd been right, Elsie had gone on a date with Liam. Pain sprang up inside. Liam was far more suited to her than he was.

She hadn't hated him for a start. If only she knew about the conversation he'd just had, but he couldn't tell her. Not yet. As much as he wanted to, he couldn't get her hopes up until he knew for sure.

Since his arrival, Meadowbank had opened his eyes to what community really meant and Elsie's arguments that they could build next to the library while still saving it was a perfect solution, but he'd been too intent on winning his father's approval to see it. He still felt that affordable housing was necessary and important in small villages like this, but he'd come to realise that libraries were hubs where people connected with one another.

The flood had been unwittingly helpful. Before, he'd never seen any way he could convince his father to change his mind. Conrad saw change as weak unless he was the one making it. He'd say that Elsie had got to him. That he'd been swayed by a pretty face, but that wasn't Jacob's only reason. The realisation had been dawning for some time now, though he hadn't wanted to admit it.

'So, dinner?' Liam asked Elsie again.

'Umm, thanks for the offer but no.'

Jacob's head shot up in hope as Elsie took Liam's arm and led him to the side of the room. He couldn't hear the conversation, her voice was low and calm. He hoped she was brushing him off, but they could still have been making plans. A moment later, after giving her an incredulous shake of the head, Liam walked out.

When Elsie came back, her expression carried such sadness his heart almost burst. Had it been caused by her exchange with Liam or by the state of the library?

'I suppose I'd better give you back your keys.' Elsie held them out to him, her hands pink and trembling with cold. He took them hesitantly as more volunteers bid them goodbye and Elsie thanked them for their time.

'Shall we close up, then?' he asked gently. 'I think we could all do with a hot meal to warm us up.' He wanted to ask more about Liam and the conversation but knew he had no right.

'After how hot it's been it seems mad to be craving food I normally only want in winter. I wonder if the fish and chip van is visiting from Puckleton.'

'Are you not eating with Liam?' He hoped his voice sounded casual though his heart was racing.

'No,' she replied with a slight chuckle. 'Liam's a nice guy but very busy with his new career.'

'I heard him mentioning it to the reporter earlier.'

'I'm not surprised. I think he was only here for the publicity. No one else turned up as the work was finishing for the day.'

The hope that she'd gone off him sent Jacob's cheeks lifting into a smile. Perhaps there was the slimmest chance for them after all.

'Where does the fish and chip van normally pitch up?'

'Near the green. I'm hoping they haven't cancelled knowing their parking space is currently occupied by ducks.'

He hesitated before saying, 'Do you mind if I come with you? I don't really fancy cooking tonight.'

She cast a shy glance at him. 'Umm ... sure.'

Locking the library doors behind them, they headed back towards the green and were pleased to see the fish and chip van parked opposite its usual spot. Clearly, many of the villagers had felt the same way as a long queue weaved its way around, avoiding the enormous puddle.

'Wow,' Jacob said as they joined it. 'It's busier than I thought. Are the fish and chips that good?'

'I can safely promise you've never tasted fish and chips like it.'

As villagers he'd previously seen arguing embraced each other in the queue in front of him, he said, 'This village really is extraordinary.'

'This community is extraordinary,' she corrected. Though from the smile on her lips he could see she was teasing rather than chastising.

'You're right.'

'I am?'

'Yes. I've talked about community and making sure people can stay in their villages, but I've never seen a community as close as this before. I think there's something incredibly unique about Meadowbank.'

Elsie didn't answer and conversation fell to the usual and mundane as they edged along the queue. Jacob's arm brushed hers and he realised nothing about Elsie Martin was mundane, and every word that passed between them absorbed his attention. The time would come soon when they would be served, and he'd have to go back to his cottage, and Leah. He wondered where she'd gone today. As soon as she'd seen him and his father talking, she'd joined them and had disagreed vehemently with his suggestion to change the plans. That was until his father started to change his opinion as Jacob mentioned flood plains, then she'd seen the benefits.

The serving of haddock and chips that was delivered to him was so large he could hardly believe his eyes. 'We could have shared this,' he said without thinking and the blush that up until recently had reddened Elsie's cheeks whenever they'd spoken, returned once more. It was almost as if she'd been so focused, she'd forgotten all about being embarrassed until now. Would she have liked to share his supper with him? The thought sent a flare of hope.

When Elsie took her portion in a large, wrapped paper parcel, they made their way towards her cottage. Through the front-room window, he could see the enormous piles of books transferred from the library.

'Is there going to be enough room for you in there?'

'I'll be fine. I don't need much space. To be honest, I might break my own rules and have an early night.'

'Well, my head's spinning and I don't imagine I'll sleep much tonight.' Could he say it? Should he? He swallowed his nerves. 'If you're awake at 3 a.m. you could always text me, we can have a chat about the plan for tomorrow. Here—' He pulled a business card from his wallet, his heart pounding in his chest. 'Here's my mobile number. If you think of anything, feel free to call or text or—' Her wide eyes behind the lenses of her glasses stared at him in bewilderment and he stuttered. 'Or whatever. We can always just meet at the library at nine.'

'Oh … yes … okay.'

The door to her cottage opened and Gemma stood watching them. She had eyes like a hawk and Jacob had the feeling of being assessed and found wanting. Or perhaps that was how he was feeling about himself. Working with the village, the suggestion he'd made to his father, all these things had made him feel more like himself than he had in a long time. More his own man.

'I'll see you tomorrow then,' Elsie said, edging down the path to her front door.

'Goodnight.'

She gave a small wave and went inside.

Jacob smelled the fresh, clean air peppered with the aroma of fried fish and chips as he walked towards his cottage. He'd wait and see what his father's response was tomorrow and if it was everything he hoped for, as soon as the deal was done, he'd resign from Conrad Yardley Construction and find a new job. Something far more rewarding and who knows, maybe then, Elsie Martin might consider having dinner with him.

* * *

As Jacob expected, he hadn't been able to sleep a wink. His body felt heavy and his eyes tired, but his mind wouldn't stop working. A million thoughts ran through as to what could be possible in the future, and a sense of freedom filled him that he'd never felt before. He'd always been so busy trying to fill the mould his father had made for him, but he'd always been a square peg trying to fit into a round hole. How had it taken him so long to realise and gain enough courage to tell him?

He looked at his mobile phone, it was two-thirty. Would Elsie be awake? He went to his window and stared out. The water was receding slowly, but the rains had brought a freshness to the night air and feeling the hairs on his arms stand on end, he climbed back into bed and glanced at his phone once more.

The book of poetry sat on his bedside, and he remembered Elsie talking of her wish to visit Emily Dickinson's house. He opened the book and searched for her. There was one called '"Hope" is the thing with feathers'. Fitting, given his current situation and the answer he was hoping for tomorrow.

He read it through once, savouring each word. Glancing at his phone again, he banished thoughts of Elsie from his mind. He couldn't message her at this time of night. He wasn't even sure she'd want to hear from him. At times during their conversations today he'd thought so, but he still wasn't one hundred per cent sure. He read the poem again. It was beautiful. He'd never really read any Emily Dickinson. He'd always focused on English poets rather than American ones and he was sure Elsie would like this one. She probably knew it by heart.

Just as he was about to turn off his light and try again to sleep, a message arrived on his phone. Normally the only messages he received at this time of night were from his father and he almost ignored it. It was only when he saw a number rather than a name at the top of the screen that he took notice. The message was short and sweet, but the words sang in his ears.

I can't sleep.

It had been a day for changes, and taking courage from that thought, he swallowed and rang the number.

The few rings it took her to answer filled him with dread. Had he misunderstood the message? Had he presumed too much? Had she fallen asleep in the short time between sending it and him calling? When she answered, and her soft voice drifted into his ears, he smiled in relief.

'Jacob?'

Taking a breath to steady his nerves, he lifted the book and began reading the poem. His voice wavered as he tried to keep it calm and even, and there was a slight gasp as he made it to the end of the first verse. It was only a short poem and when he finished, a wave of cold panic hit him. Did he hang up now? Should he make small talk about the weather or plans for tomorrow? What if she thought he was a weirdo? Was she going to report him to the police?

Her soft voice sounded sleepy as she said, 'Can you read another one?'

Placing his phone on the pillow beside him, he rolled over and began reading the next poem to her. He carried on like that until the only reply he received was her gentle, rhythmic breathing and instinctively, he knew she was asleep. Hanging up the phone and placing it back on his bedside, he turned out the light and closed his eyes. It wasn't long before he too fell into a deep, restorative sleep, a smile still playing on his lips.

Chapter 32

When Elsie awoke, her eyes sprang open, and she couldn't believe how rested she felt. It had taken all her courage to text Jacob, and yet, it had felt right. The nerves that had bubbled in her stomach as she typed the message instead of throwing on her clothes and going out for a walk had almost stopped her, but somehow, she had known that Jacob wouldn't laugh or dismiss her.

She hadn't, however, expected him to recite poetry. As she'd noticed on the first day she'd met him, his soft, velvety voice lent itself to the form. When most people recited poetry, they didn't really know how to do it and the result was always stilted and uneasy. Jacob read with soul and expression, and she'd been absorbed first by the words, and then, as sleep took over, by the sound.

After the public meeting and being so at odds, Elsie had never thought she'd say that she was looking forward to seeing him, but this morning, she couldn't wait to get to the library, even though the state of the place was heart-breaking. She was still conflicted: not wanting to let it go but knowing that fighting for it now was pointless and it made her even more confused over Jacob. He'd wanted to help yesterday. Wanted to save the books and records, and he'd even said how much he realised she was right, but the plans of Conrad Yardley Construction hadn't changed.

However she felt, Elsie knew she couldn't stay in bed any longer and while the birds sang and the sun poured in through the window, she dodged the stacks of books that were everywhere around her, dressed, and hurried outside. As she closed the front door, she glanced at Gemma's cottage. Had Orla spoken to Gemma yet? She hadn't when she arrived home last night. Elsie worried that Orla would continue to hide her secret and that she too would now be a part of it, but she had to trust Orla. Maybe she just needed a little more time.

As Elsie passed the village green, she was surprised at how much water had disappeared overnight. Sandbags still lined the river-bank and the water lapping gently against it was a fierce contrast to the gush that had cascaded over only yesterday morning. The river had eased back to the other side of the lane, but Elsie had no idea how much was still inside the library. She gazed at the sky, a pure slab of blue as far as the eye could see. How could twenty-four hours make such a difference? There were a few wispy white clouds bobbing gently in the breeze, but all around it was as if this last week of continual rain had never happened.

Waiting by the library door were a whole group of volunteers, some of whom had been there yesterday. Some were new but eager to do their bit. Winston, Bernard, and Patricia were at the front, ready to lead the way. Patricia was laughing again at something Jacob was saying and Elsie pushed up her glasses before heading over.

'Ready for round two?' Winston asked. He looked quite lively this morning. All this Dunkirk spirit had lifted him.

'Yep. What's that noise?' she asked as a humming sounded from the other side of the door.

'It's a pump,' Jacob said. 'Dominic set it up this morning to pump out any remaining water from the library, but we wanted to wait for you before we got started.'

'Really? That's brilliant. We should be able to work in a little more comfort today then. And no doubt Gemma or Orla will be along later with cake.' She was so focused, she hadn't even thought of being embarrassed about last night, until now.

'I hope so. Those szarlotka things looked amazing,' Jacob replied. 'Ready?'

She nodded, somehow keeping the blush from her cheeks. 'Let's see what we're faced with today.'

Jacob unlocked the doors and they stepped inside. He seemed happy to be there, though Elsie was conscious of him checking his watch in a slightly agitated manner. Had he changed his mind about helping? Did he have somewhere else to be? She shook the thought away as the smell of damp hit her nostrils. Most of the water had gone except for a thin, filmy layer on top of the carpet. Their shoes squelched and Elsie was glad she was wearing boots as the carpet was so waterlogged the water threatened to come up over her toes.

'We can still use the trucks,' Jacob said. 'And Rees-Hale called me this morning to tell me that he's sorted out the storage facility. He's sent me some directions.'

'Good, because I don't think I can fit anything else in my cottage.' Knowing she hadn't thanked him for his poetry reading last night filled her chest with warmth that then flooded through her body to the tips of her fingers. She was about to mention it when he checked his watch again and muttered to himself.

'Nine o'clock on the dot.'

'Is everything okay?'

'Yes, fine.' He pulled the sleeve of his jacket down. 'Where shall we start?'

The moment had gone and she carried on with the task at hand. 'I guess we crack on like we did yesterday. Patricia, are you okay to keep clearing the children's section?' She nodded. 'And Winston and Bernard—'

'We'll carry on going shelf by shelf through fiction.'

They all headed off in their different directions, ready to begin work. Elsie had no doubt that more volunteers would join them throughout the day.

'What about us?' asked Jacob.

She liked the sound of him saying 'us' far more than was healthy. 'We can probably start on non-fiction. I'd like to save as many audiobooks as we can. The older villagers love those, and I should probably have prioritised the large-print books too.' She reached a hand up to adjust her glasses, frustrated she hadn't thought of it yesterday.

Jacob's arm rested on her shoulder. 'You did a great job yesterday. We saved as much as we could and all the stuff that was in immediate danger. You were brilliant.'

Looking back on the whole ordeal, she marvelled at the inner confidence she'd found: a hidden well of it that had been inside her somewhere. She could have gone for that promotion here at the library and spent the last few years making it the best it could be, but instead she'd been too scared to try. Would its fate have been different if she'd been at the helm? When all this was over, she was getting on a plane to Massachusetts. She deserved a holiday and where better to start her love of travel than one of the places she'd always longed to go.

A short while later, Gemma arrived with supplies and Elsie was relieved to see she was smiling, happier than she'd seen her in weeks. Once everyone had taken a piece of cake and they were left alone, Gemma said, 'Has Orla spoken to you?'

Elsie shook her head. 'Not since yesterday.' She wondered whether to say more but thought it best to hear Gemma out first.

Gemma's smile grew even wider. 'It wasn't me at all. And it wasn't someone else. She was homesick and regretted the way she left her family.'

In among the quickly spoken words, Elsie made out that plans were now forming for Orla's parents to come over and for Scarlett to meet her grandparents.

'I'm so happy for you, Gemma. I'm glad you sorted things out.'

She gave Elsie a hug. 'Thank you for being there for me. As usual.'

'Ditto,' she replied, feeling tears sting her eyes. When they separated, Gemma was wiping her eyes too. 'Now go! We'll need more cake for this afternoon too. I think it's going to be a long day.'

Gemma left and Elsie smiled to herself. That was one thing off her mind at least, leaving only clearing the rest of the library and finding a new job. And she still wanted to find a way for Bernard and Winston to have more contact without having to travel to other libraries.

As Gemma left, a young woman arrived who Elsie didn't recognise. She hadn't seen her around the village before.

'Can I help you?'

'Yes, please. I was looking for Patricia Skinner. I was told she was here—'

'Aimee?' Patricia ran over to the young woman and embraced her tightly. For a second, the woman stared over Patricia's shoulder in shock, but then her arms returned the embrace.

'Hello, Mum.'

Elsie's hand pressed to her mouth. Patricia finally released her daughter, but only enough so she could hold her shoulders. It was as if now she'd returned, Patricia wasn't going to risk letting go. 'What are you doing here?'

'I saw the library on the news, and I know how much you've always loved it.'

'What about Blake?'

Aimee looked down at her hands. 'We've split up. After he banned me from having contact with you, things got worse. He started questioning me every time I went out and I put up with it for a long time not realising what was happening. It took a lot of courage, but I've left him.'

'Where are you staying?' Patricia asked, cupping her daughter's cheek.

'With a friend.'

She met her daughter's eye. 'Would you like to stay with us? Your dad and I have missed you terribly you know. And Vinnie.'

Aimee wiped at her eyes and Elsie noticed the tears falling from her lashes as she collapsed against her mum. 'Yes, please.'

Elsie backed away but, once they'd had a moment, said, 'Patricia, why don't you and Aimee go and get a coffee or something? We can manage here.'

'Are you sure?' Patricia asked and Elsie nodded. 'I'll be back later, I promise.'

'What was that?' Jacob asked as they set to work again.

'A reunion that's been a long time coming.'

They continued on in silence with Jacob often checking his watch. He was on edge today and Elsie worried something had changed for him, that the purpose he'd found yesterday had been swept away by his father's constant nagging. Or that he regretted reading to her last night and wanted to get away from her. She thought about saying something again, but still couldn't figure out what and busied herself with saving more books.

At ten o'clock, as they were discussing the latest bestseller, Jacob's smile faded and his father arrived, marching in and straight up to them both. Jacob stiffened as if he were the accused in the dock, waiting for a final verdict. Gemma, who had been to the bakery for a second lot of cakes for the numerous volunteers, followed close behind, but sensing something was about to happen, she silently deposited the tray on the desk and stood near Elsie.

'Jacob,' Conrad said sternly. He spoke to his son the way someone commanded a dog and Elsie felt herself bristle.

'Father.'

'I've made my decision. Are we talking in front of her?' He jabbed a finger at Elsie.

'Apparently so,' Elsie replied, crossing her arms over her chest. 'As you're standing right in front of me.'

Jacob bit back a smile. Allegra would never have spoken to his father like that.

'Hmm.' Conrad turned his attention back to Jacob. 'If you're prepared to pay for the refurbishment and the flood defences, then I agree.'

Jacob's face filled with a smile so wide, his cheeks could barely contain it. 'Good. I'm glad we could come to an arrangement.'

'But I'm putting someone else in charge. You've proven that this' – he cast his arm out in a circular motion – 'is all too much for you right now. Maybe someday.'

'Actually, Father. I was thinking that after this project, I'd leave the business and perhaps Dominic could take my place. He's got the knowledge and far more experience than I do. I think we have to agree that this isn't something I'm good at.'

'You should be, with me as a father.'

'Maybe, but can you honestly say you've enjoyed having me around in the business?'

'Not especially. But who will take over when I die?'

'Die?' Jacob chuckled. 'Father, I'm pretty sure that's some way off yet and whoever takes over can continue with the company name as Conrad Yardley. That doesn't have to change. I'm certain that having Dominic in charge would mean the firm carries on for far more years than if I were at the helm.'

'Is this really how you feel?' Conrad asked, assessing him with his wily eyes.

'It is. And I think we both know it's for the best.'

'This project has certainly shown you're not cut out for this sort of business.' He stood straighter. 'I'll talk to your mother and if she agrees, then fine. But if you leave the business, don't come running to me for money when the job you get pays a pittance.'

'I can assure you I won't. Do we have a deal?' Jacob held out his hand for his father to shake.

The size difference between the two really was quite comical. Jacob towered over his father, but Conrad's bearing made him the central figure of any room. 'We do.'

He shook his son's hand and then marched off, shouting for Dominic as soon as he reached the door.

'What was all that about?' Elsie asked.

'I've made an agreement with my father that the library stays.'

'What?' She could feel the tautness in her forehead as she frowned. 'How? What did you agree?'

Jacob took her hands. His strong fingers wrapped around hers and her heart beat hard, pummelling her chest. 'You were right about what libraries stand for. They've not been made obsolete by ebooks and mobile phones. I never realised before how they bring people together and stop them falling apart. The flooding of the library actually worked in our favour. I convinced my father that as this place has taken the brunt of the flooding, it might not be worth building houses here, and thanks to all the media attention you started, I convinced him that if we kept the library – and refurbished it – we'd come out of this looking like the saviours of the community, rather than those who tore it apart.'

'I was starting to feel like I was the one tearing it apart,' she said sadly.

'No.' He reached out a finger towards a hair on her face but hesitated and drew back. 'You were the one trying to save it and I completely underestimated how much the library meant to everyone. And you.' He paused for a moment and scratched the back of his head. 'I hope you don't mind, but I spoke to Rees-Hale too.'

'About what?'

'About you. I'm sure everyone here would agree that Meadowbank Library would be nothing without actual books and its favourite librarian.'

The assembled villagers nodded in agreement.

'But I got sacked.'

'Yes, but the library won't belong to the council anymore. It'll be a community library. There'll be a lot of work to do raising income and securing funding, but Yardley Construction will get it back on its feet physically.'

'You mean, *you* will? I heard your father say you were paying for everything. How can you, Jacob? It'll be too much money.' Her shock at Jacob's words was giving way to excitement as she thought of a library for and run by the community.

'Because I want to put my money to good use. I don't want to sit on it like a dragon hoarding its treasure. I want to make a difference. You've taught me so much, Elsie. You've taught me to be brave, to be myself, like you've always been, and not just go with the flow. I know this is the right thing to do. It's what my heart is telling me to do.' He pressed his hand to his heart like he had the first time they'd met, though she could see there was no falseness in the gesture. It was driven by pure instinct. 'The other thing my heart is telling me, is that …' He took a breath and reached out finally to brush her wild hair back from her face. 'I think you're the most amazing person I've ever met.'

She inhaled a short, sharp breath while her heart fluttered against her ribs.

'And I'm pretty sure I'm falling for you. If you wouldn't mind, I'd really like to take you out for dinner. On a date.'

'A date?' she repeated, stupidly. 'With me?'

'I was even hoping that one day, you might consider taking a trip to Massachusetts with me.'

Everyone around them, who were all watching on eagerly, muttered the word to each other. They clearly had no idea about Emily Dickinson's house and must have thought it the craziest, most unromantic location to visit, but Elsie didn't mind.

'I very much enjoyed reading Emily's poem to you.' A faint blush appeared on his cheeks while Elsie's remained pale and cool. 'And there aren't many women who'd stand up to my father like you did. That takes something special. I know we didn't exactly get off to the best start, but from the moment I met you, you've been in my head.'

Elsie felt as if some unknown force had lifted her up, spun her around, and deposited her on the ground upside down. Her mind whirred with a million and one thoughts, none of which made sense, and her body swelled with a mix of emotions. Despite the start they'd had, she did want to get to know him better. She wanted to do a lot more than that because though she'd never believed in love at first sight and their path hadn't run smooth, she was falling for Jacob too. Knowing she'd been standing there in silence and that most of the village were now waiting for her response, she forced herself to speak.

'I think I'm falling for you too. But—' Her courage wavered slightly, and everyone gasped. 'How do you feel about Paris first? At least we can go there by train.'

Jacob laughed and his shoulders relaxed. 'Agreed. If it's not too much to ask, do you think I could possibly kiss you?'

Several of the older ladies nigh on swooned and even Mrs Dalloway muttered, 'Oh my days.'

'I think that would be fine,' she stuttered.

Slowly, Jacob bent his head and she stood on tiptoe to reach him. When their lips met, a radiant joy filled her as if her soul was smiling. With the fluttering in her stomach, she felt like she was about to take off. Then Jacob's hand moved to gently caress her cheek and she released herself to him, because although they were only at the beginning of this journey, there was no doubt in her mind that she was about to fall hopelessly and completely in love.

Didn't that always happen to the best heroines?

Chapter 33

Six Months Later

October

Adam Noble, the local carpenter, wheeled in the last beautiful bookshelf he'd made from an old tree stump from Meadowbank Wood and once it was in position, Elsie placed the books of poetry onto the shining wood.

'I'm absolutely overjoyed to declare the new and improved Meadowbank Library open,' she shouted.

The assembled crowd laughed and clapped at the accomplishment. The exterior of the library was the same as it had been before. It was still single storey and looked more like a village hall, and the abundance of windows lit the room in a warm autumnal glow. Outside, where the benches lined the riverbank, the leaves on the trees had lost their vibrant brightness and were turning deep shades of russet and gold.

Inside, though, the place had been transformed. Gone were the standard issue strip-lights and in its place were locally hand-crafted giant glass baubles. They were huge and Elsie and Amelia

Williams, their resident designer, had lots of fun picking them out. They weren't quite sure how they were going to clean them, but with such an eager group of volunteers, they were sure they'd be able to manage it together.

The old MDF bookshelves had gone, and Adam had made all the new shelving using old scaffolding planks or bits he'd retrieved from Meadowbank Wood. The library was now even more spacious than ever as the walls were lined with shelves and in between were special pieces like the poetry bookcase. He'd even made a new glass display case for the fossils and archaeological finds they all treasured. The old dark-wood cabinets that had housed the reference section and family history resources had taken some flood damage but with some love and attention they were back in place. They had been there since Elsie had been a child, and it didn't seem right to get rid of them now.

Rees-Hale had allowed them to keep the stock as he didn't have anywhere to put it and Elsie was pleased to have her cottage back to herself. Though she loved books, falling over the piles that filled most of the rooms and bumping into them in the middle of the night had been rather testing at times.

The old desk had received too much water damage to be used and Elsie was now pleased to sit behind something with much more character. An old pine dining table, purchased when one of the villagers was selling it, had been upgraded with marvellous sculptures all over the front. Adam wasn't only a gifted carpenter but had an amazing artistic streak as well. The faces that poked out smiled and played with the children who came in every day.

Patricia still ran her story times, now with her grandson in attendance, and Maria had finally let her hair down and didn't keep holding herself up to the exacting standard she'd thought necessary before. Winston, who volunteered for an hour most days after he'd had time to read the paper, ran the book club with Mrs Dalloway, and Bernard was happy that he could continue his celeb-watching using the new computers Jacob had paid for as part of the refurbishment.

'Ready for your next adventure?' Jacob asked, smiling down at her.

Elsie nodded. 'My mind's already buzzing with plans for funding and events we can hold. And as Liam Chapstone has his new thriller coming out in a couple of months, he's agreed to hold his launch here. That should bring in some money. We'll offer discounted tickets to the villagers and everyone outside the area can pay a little more. Then there's—'

Jacob planted a kiss on her mouth. 'Just enjoy tonight before you race on to tomorrow.'

'I can't help it,' Elsie replied, her lips still tingling from the softness of his kiss. 'I'm so excited for everything. There's so many wonderful things to come, and look – everyone's so happy.'

Her eyes fell on Orla and Gemma, and Orla's parents, who were snuggling Scarlett closely. As far as Elsie could see, they hadn't put the child down since they arrived last week. Seeing Orla happier than ever made Elsie's heart sing as much for Gemma as for herself.

They'd catered for the grand reopening and the library tables were dotted with home-made drinks – Winston himself had made a rather fabulous sloe gin – and delicious foods from the bakery. Annie's Tearoom had supplied some savoury favourites like sausage rolls and enormous pork pies, and the deli had set out meats and cheeses from the Continent.

In the children's section, Bella, the primary school teacher, sat with her partner Nick and his son, Freddie, showing the kids the different books available. Some of them wandered over to join Patricia on the story mat, where she was making up a tale using the crocheted figures. Three new additions had been made recently: her daughter Aimee, her grandson Vinnie, and, of course, Jacob.

As Elsie surveyed everything before her, she couldn't have been happier at the outcome. The library was hers to run as she pleased. Every decision was for her to take. The sense of freedom was liberating, and her confidence had soared even more. Not least because of the man beside her.

Though their relationship may have started on unsteady ground, the path to true love had been smoother than ever. There was no doubt that after the affordable houses had been built next to the library, Jacob would be staying in Meadowbank with her. He already had ideas of different projects he could start with local charities and, despite his father's reservations, had supported the remainder of the project without problems. They saw very little of Conrad, though Elsie believed that he was warming to her. They'd had some interesting conversations about various subjects and though he was quite domineering, Elsie had the feeling he enjoyed their discussions. Jacob also called his mother at least once a week and though Georgia Yardley was soft-spoken and the opposite to her husband, she was certainly no pushover either. Elsie had liked her instantly.

With the library now officially open, all that remained was for her and Jacob to take their holiday together to Massachusetts, but as Elsie studied more and more holiday brochures, the list of places she wanted to visit was growing. There was still Paris and New York, Egypt, San Francisco, and Venice. Wherever they went Elsie knew that now they'd come together, there was no tearing her and Jacob apart.

Acknowledgements

Writing books is honestly the best job in the world and there are so many people to thank that I don't really know where to start!

I think the best place is with all you lovely readers, so thank you all so much for choosing to read one of my books. It means the absolute world to me and if it wasn't for you and all the amazing book bloggers, I wouldn't be here now.

I never take writing books for granted and would like to thank my publisher HQ Digital for all their support and for having belief in me and my stories. In particular, thank you to my lovely editor Sarah Goodey, who has been both a brilliant editor and an amazing friend while I've been writing and editing *The Little Library on Cherry Lane*. Thank you, Sarah, for being unbelievably lovely! Your support through some personally tough times has been incredible.

Then there's my agent, Kate Nash, and all at the Kate Nash Literary Agency who work behind the scenes. And I can't forget to say thank you to my family for their support.

Lastly, this book is dedicated to librarians everywhere and to those who use libraries. We need them, we love them, and we support them, so thank you for doing what you do and enabling us all to connect with others through books. Anyone who uses a library knows they're more than just about borrowing books and your hard work, dedication, and care are more appreciated than you know.

**Keep reading for an excerpt from *The Secrets of
Meadow Farmhouse* …**

Prologue

June 1959

The wedding dress hung in front of the wardrobe, elegant and beautiful. Premature, some might say as she wasn't even wearing a ring. But Vera couldn't help telling her mother about the engagement, and her mother couldn't help but fetch it for her.

Side by side, they appraised it together, her mother giggling like a schoolgirl, Vera giddy in her excitement. Arty had asked her to keep it quiet until he'd spoken to his parents, but Vera had never been that good at keeping secrets. She was an open book as far as her thoughts and feelings were concerned, wearing her heart on her sleeve. Her half-sister always told her she should toughen up, but Vera had never seen the need, and after the events of the afternoon, when Arty had paused in the middle of the coppice where the ground was lush with green and the tall trees formed a canopy over their heads, taking her hand in his and slowly going down on one knee, it didn't seem the right time to start now. How could she when there was little to no chance of containing her unbridled joy?

'Will you marry me?' he'd asked, with trembling hands and a slight shake to his voice.

As if there were any possibility she'd say no. She loved him more than anything else in the world. She'd never met anyone so kind, so funny or so handsome.

The sun had shone down on them, dappling through the leaves, causing shadows to dance on the ground. She'd replied instantly with a resounding yes that echoed around them and he'd picked her up in his strong arms and swung her about on the spot.

Replaying the moment over in her mind, she'd never felt a happiness like it. All he had to do was speak to his mother and father, which he'd do that very afternoon and who, he assured her, would approve. It didn't bother her that he'd asked before speaking to her father. He was a good man and only wanted her to be happy.

As soon as she'd returned to the farmhouse flushed with excitement, her mother had guessed and Vera admitted the truth without a thought. Even as a child, without hesitation she'd owned up to the things she'd done, having learned early on that lies were always writ large on her face. Her mother had been over the moon. Apparently they'd been expecting it any day now, and they had celebrated with cake. Even her stepfather had raised a glass of sherry to her good fortune. 'He's a fine man. And rich too,' he teased.

Vera giggled because they all knew that money meant nothing to her. It was him she loved. The shy, quiet boy she'd spotted in the fields as a young girl, then grown up with, becoming friends and now lovers. Soon they would become husband and wife, marrying at the small church in the village and picnicking on the green. Content in her plans, after the allowance of a small glass of sherry, Vera had tipsily gone to bed.

The night had been long and restless as her overactive mind refused to cease, unable to sleep for the joy and anticipation pulsing through her veins. She imagined herself in the dress, pictured herself dancing and dreamed of forever being Arty's wife. In the half-light, she stared at the wedding dress now airing

316

on her wardrobe door. It was, perhaps, a little old-fashioned, but she loved that it was her mother's, and her mother wanted her to wear it. The neck was too high and would need taking down; the sleeves, too, were long with frilled cuffs, but overall, she liked it. It would be her something borrowed, or perhaps something old.

A faint tapping at the window drew her attention to the day breaking outside. At first, she'd thought it was rain, but as she listened to its rhythmless nature and growing intensity she realised it was something else. With a thrill of excitement, Vera pulled back the covers and swung her legs out of bed. The cold spring morning penetrated the thin material of her nightdress and she pulled her dressing gown on before silently padding her way to the window.

As she pulled back the curtains, the emerging white light of the sun illuminated the slowly waking world, blinding her. The sky held patches of cloud here and there, harsh and dark, threatening rain. Her eyes dropped to the ground below her window. Arty. Arty had come to see her. A shiver ran down her spine at the romantic nature of this dawn visit, and as quietly as she could, she ran down the stairs, avoiding the patches of old wood that creaked and moaned underfoot, and unlatched the heavy back door.

Vera stayed in the doorway, propriety forcing her to hide. Though her mother had always told her not to worry too much about convention, there were some things that would not be tolerated, and meeting a beau in the early hours of the morning in nothing but your night clothes was one of them. Arty stood motionless in his shirtsleeves, his arms hanging limply by his sides. Goose bumps covered his skin from the chill morning air. 'Arty? What are you doing here?'

'I'm sorry, Vera,' he replied, his voice weak, almost inaudible. He'd been crying. His eyes puffy and red, bloodshot through lack of sleep and marked under with deep blue shadows. 'I'm so sorry. I can't marry you.'

Fear tensed her muscles and a burden of dread rested on her

chest. He hadn't said that. He couldn't have. 'What do you mean?' An incredulous laugh escaped her. 'What are you talking about?'

'I can't marry you, Vera. I'm so sorry.' Tears welled in his eyes once more and with a strong sniff he attempted to force them away.

'Why not?' A weight pressed down, tightening her ribs. 'You love me and I love you.'

'You know why—'

She shook her head. 'But you said you didn't care. You said—'

'I know what I said.'

Vera watched the rise and fall of his chest as he breathed heavily. Why was he hurting her like this?

'I have to think of others, not just myself.'

He was saying words that weren't his. He'd never have said anything like this before, when their relationship was purely friendship. It must have been his mother. She must have refused her consent. Vera felt the slow, steady tearing in her heart as it ripped so completely in two.

'You don't mean that,' she whispered, tears now falling down her face. Her heart ached, slowly breaking as his words sunk in. With white knuckles, she held tight to the doorframe, her body no longer able to stay upright. All her strength had disappeared.

'I'm sorry, Vera, but I do. I have to go.'

He turned and walked away, and as loudly as she could without waking the others, she called out to him, but apart from a slight turn of his head, he didn't stop, or acknowledge her anguish.

Vera's hands shook as she closed the door and leaned back against it as though it would stop her from disintegrating. Her legs gave way, unable to take the weight of her emotions. She slid down to the floor, curling her legs up and hiding her face behind them. Tears soaked through the fabric of her nightdress so it stuck to her skin. The grey clouds that had threatened only moments before let loose their burdens and as her life fell apart, the rains came.

Chapter 1

Paris

Present Day

The sights and smells of the Paris flea market were almost too much for Amelia's hungover senses to bear. Only her excitement at living in the city she adored, and a need to be out of her apartment, led her forwards.

Though the baking emanating from the nearby shops smelled delicious, the aromas changed with every step causing her stomach to roil and calm in equal measure. The strong scents of garlic and onion were overtaken by that of sweet pastries and butter. The crowds wove around her, all heading for the farmers' market at the bottom of the tiny street or returning up the hill with bags laden with fresh produce. In between, shopkeepers cast open their windows, displaying the eclectic range of goods they had to offer. Amelia's eyes darted between the numerous chandeliers that hung from the ceilings of one store, onto antique vases side by side on a small side table. Traditional French furniture lined the street outside along with stacks of paintings. On the other side of the street, smaller objects like perfume bottles, vintage jewellery and trinkets glittered as the sun hit the windows.

All around, the sound of chatter penetrated her ears, resonating through her sluggish brain. Fluent in French, Amelia could make out most of what was said, but when so many voices merged and the locals spoke so quickly, she struggled to keep up. Snippets of conversation met her, forming unusual and humorous sentences. She pushed her large round sunglasses further up her nose to shield her eyes from the sun's strong glare, and her stomach rumbled loudly.

Spring in Paris was a magical affair as flowers bloomed around the city, giving the air an overwhelmingly floral scent. She'd been there for eight years now, but the capital never failed to impress her. Each season affected the city differently, but whereas summer could sear the streets with a hazy heat, spring gave all the golden glow but with a much more temperate feel.

Pausing at her favourite café, with a mix of folding metal and wicker chairs tightly packed around small circular tables, she took a seat and ordered a café crème and a buttery, flaky croissant; the perfect thing to soak up the rest of the wine lingering in her system while she waited for Océanè to join her. She'd want to know all about her date with Bastien last night and by the time Amelia had something to eat and chatted to her friend, she'd feel well enough to look again for the perfect items to finish off the job she was working on. As an interior designer, Paris – with its chic fashions and varied shops – was ideal for her business. Could she have built this career in the tiny English village she'd grown up in? Probably not. Though regret at the way she'd left bubbled inside, causing her insides to roll again.

Twenty minutes later, Océanè arrived and ordered the same as Amelia. Amelia asked for another café crème before the waiter disappeared, knowing the questioning was soon to begin and a second caffeine hit would help her endure it. Her friend didn't exactly mince her words.

'So?' Océanè asked in her heavy French accent. 'How was your date last night? Was Bastien attentive? Did he buy you champagne? You have seen him, what? Five times now?'

'He bought me wine. And lots of it. Too much, in fact,' Amelia said, adjusting her sunglasses once more as the sun moved across the sky, climbing higher. The coffee was helping her headache, but she still felt a little fragile. This morning she had dived to the bathroom and hastily scraped her black hair into a chignon and swiped bold red lipstick over her lips, knowing it would give her pale complexion some colour. Over the years she had tried to absorb the Parisian style of dressing: classic, expensive pieces, simple lines, and most of the time she managed to pull it off, but there were times, like this morning, when fashion wasn't important. She'd thrown on old loose jeans and a jumper but it only took a moment with a real Parisian to make her feel sloppy and slobbish, and as Océanè cast her eyes over her outfit, she knew she didn't approve.

Océanè swiped her blonde hair over her shoulder. 'You do look a little, how do you say ...'

'Under the weather?'

'Pasty.'

'Thanks.' Amelia giggled.

'Did you not have a good time? He is very handsome, *non*?'

'We had a very nice time.' For once, Amelia was grateful that she looked so ill any blushing wasn't likely to show as thoughts of his intense and passionate kisses rang through her head. 'And yes, he is very handsome. He wined and dined me, paid me compliments, made me laugh, but I've left him to make his way home while I'm out.'

'You are avoiding him?' Her friend's tone was incredulous.

Bastien was almost perfect and she liked him well enough, but Amelia wasn't very good at the small talk made the next morning. It made her uncomfortable and embarrassed and to be honest, she hadn't had a lot of practice at it. An image of Adam flashed into her brain and she shook it away. Ever since she'd left him back home in the tiny village of Meadowbank, he'd pop up in her mind, most often when she was thinking about or trying to date someone else. No matter how much she tried, she couldn't shake him off.

'But you will see him again tomorrow?' Océanè asked. 'He is in love with you, I think.'

'I don't think he's in love with me. I know he likes me, but—' Amelia paused while the waiter delivered their drinks. She took a sip of coffee and saw the imprint of her red lipstick on the rim of the cup. 'I don't think it's love.' Sometimes, she found it hard to believe that someone would ever love her. Her life had been so destitute of it from such an early age. 'And to be honest, I'm not sure I'm in the market for that sort of thing at the moment. I like him, but …'

The words died on her lips. What could she say? He was another man who over the years hadn't made her feel the way Adam had? Océanè would laugh at her for thinking of a love that happened so long ago. An image of their goodbye at the train station floated before her, causing her throat to tighten. She dropped her eyes to her cup, focusing on the coffee inside it, hoping it would draw her mind and the pain away.

Océanè took a moment to understand the phrase, but realisation quickly dawned. 'You are mad. He has everything a woman could want: money, success, good looks.'

Bastien did have all those things and he was also kind and funny, which is how they'd made it to five dates rather than just one, but despite her best efforts, he still hadn't managed to break through to her heart.

'You are a cold woman. You care only for your work.'

Amelia raised her head at this remark. Was she cold? She didn't think so. She had friends and had been through some decent relationships, but they'd never felt strong enough to last. She wasn't cold, she was just focused on living her life to the full. She'd worked hard to become one of the foremost interior designers in Paris, and she wanted more than just a man who was perfect on paper. She wasn't prepared to invite a man into her life for the sake of it. She'd always done fine on her own and her life was far too busy for loneliness.

Océanè continued. 'I do not know how you can be so immune to his charms. Our men – French men – Parisian men – know how to win a woman's heart.'

'Your French men are pretty charming, but I'm far too busy with work to worry about love.'

'Don't your parents want you to get married? Mine do. They say that I should marry Émile and have children before they are too old to enjoy being with them. They say my eggs will die.'

'Your eggs?' Amelia almost spluttered her coffee.

'Eggs.' Océanè motioned towards her lap. 'Your parents do not worry about your eggs?'

A sharp pain shot into Amelia's chest and a hurt she'd convinced herself had been dealt with stabbed anew. 'My parents are dead. They died when I was a child.'

Océanè's hand paused as she tore off a piece of croissant. 'You have never told me that. We have been friends for years and yet you make no mention of this. Why not?'

Amelia shrugged one shoulder. 'It's never come up before.' That was a lie and she quickly changed the subject, unsure why she had suddenly admitted it. Perhaps she was more tired than she realised. Her temples started to pound again. She'd been out with friends every night this week, and last. Maybe a decent dinner cooked by herself – something hearty and wholesome rather than tiny, minuscule restaurant portions – and a quiet night in were in order. 'Once we're done here, I'd like to take another look around. I'm after some special pieces for an apartment I'm working on in Montmartre.'

'You will have to do that alone; I have to meet Émile. But you must think about Bastien. There are many women who would like to take your place in his bed.'

'He was in *my* bed, actually,' she replied, playfully eyeing Océanè over the rim of her cup.

'You know what I mean.' Océanè raised one perfectly shaped eyebrow. 'You can be too hard, Amélie. Too independent.' It always amused Amelia that Océanè called her by the French version of her name when she was being serious. 'One day, you will push a man too far away and he will not bother coming back.'

Not if he's the right man, Amelia thought, but didn't bother saying so. She hadn't planned on sleeping with Bastien last night and it had been a moment of weakness she was paying for this morning. She hoped that by spinelessly hiding out until he'd left, she'd avoid an embarrassing situation.

'You have a great business, yes?' Océanè said. 'You have a great apartment, yes? But you are never alone. Always you are with friends. A person cannot exist without love. Eventually, you will have to let someone into your heart. Why not Bastien?'

Feeling the prickle of embarrassment inch its way over her skin, Amelia pulled her compact from her handbag and topped up her red lipstick. She'd been without love all her life, since her parents' deaths but she couldn't face talking to Océanè about that now. 'I've done fine without a man so far,' she said light-heartedly, hoping that would be the end of the conversation.

After they had finished their coffees and talked about their plans for the rest of the weekend, Océanè left and Amelia took another walk around the flea market. Temptation sat on her shoulder and whispered into her ear as her eyes fell on different objects that would suit her already overflowing apartment. Some of her clients liked a minimalist style, but when Amelia saw something she wanted, it was almost impossible to resist. As a result, her small flat was now packed with possessions and her wardrobe overflowing with clothes.

Amelia haggled with a vendor to buy an ornate perfume bottle – a finishing touch for the Montmartre apartment – and a vintage copper milk jug for her own place. She'd find somewhere for it to go later. Maybe the bathroom? And made her way back to the Metro.

As she climbed the steps from the Metro station, the cold, fresh air blew through the elaborate dark-green metal bars and under the glass ceiling. The station design was so iconic she had a picture of one in the living room of her apartment. She'd bought it shortly after moving in all those years ago, and though it had been fairly inexpensive, it was still one of her most prized possessions.

Her apartment in Saint Germain was in a typical eighteenth-century block with white shutters and decorative ironwork across the windows. On hot summer days she would cast the windows open and let the light flood her apartment. As she stepped inside the communal hallway, she gathered her post and made her way upstairs. An envelope postmarked from England caught her eye and her lungs turned to stone. It had a company name she didn't recognise. Even worse, the town it came from was dangerously close to Meadowbank; the tiny village she'd grown up in with Great-Aunt Vera who had begrudgingly taken her in after her parents had died.

Curiosity almost forced her to open it there and then, but Amelia valued her privacy and continued upstairs. She pressed the key into the lock, hoping once more that Bastien had left by now. She really didn't fancy talking to him. He'd try to convince her to spend the rest of the day with him and all she wanted was to nap on the sofa as the soft breeze blew over her.

With a gentle push, the door opened and all was quiet inside. No sounds of snoring, no sounds of movement, and sighing with relief, Amelia advanced down the hall and into the open-plan living room and kitchen, anchoring the milk jug under her arm so she could see the envelope again. It nestled among bills, inviting Amelia to ignore everything else and tear it open without any further delay.

'Good morning, *ma chérie.*'

Glancing up, her eyes fell on Bastien, lying naked on her kitchen counter, one leg bent, the other outstretched and all of him on display. The copper milk jug fell from underneath her arm, landing on the floor with a deafening clatter. Bastien wobbled precariously and almost toppled forward onto the floor. His hand shot out, gripping the edge of the counter to steady himself. Amelia nearly dropped the pretty perfume bottle as well, but somehow managed to keep hold of it. She gazed around as if it might help her understand why he'd chosen the kitchen as the best location for his seduction.

'Bastien!' Her neck grew hot. 'What are you … umm—' So much for avoiding an embarrassing situation. Amelia decided the best thing was to pretend everything was perfectly normal, which was a bit of a stretch but doable if she kept her eyes only on his face. 'Wh – what are you still doing here?'

'I am waiting for you,' he replied, regaining his balance and lowering his voice to nothing more than a seductive grumble. In the current circumstances, it didn't really work. Bastien pinned her with his eyes, and his gaze never shifted. Of all the things she thought she might face if Bastien were still here this morning, she wasn't quite prepared for him to be naked and spread-eagled in her kitchen, and she found herself momentarily lost for words.

Amelia placed the perfume bottle on the counter, thanking the Lord it was still intact. Unsure what else to say, she stammered, 'I'm, umm, I'm a bit busy today, Bastien. Sorry.'

'Too busy for love?'

The sound of the L word twice in one day stiffened her shoulders as another image of Adam shot into her brain. Bastien gave her puppy-dog eyes and Amelia's headache intensified. How on earth was she supposed to remove him from her kitchen? It wasn't like she could grab a fish slice and prise him off the counter. 'Bastien, can you please put your pants on and maybe umm, get your bits off my worktop?'

He didn't move. 'Do I not tempt you? Come now.' He held out his hand to her but all Amelia could do was rub her forehead.

'Bastien, please, pants on.'

'Let us spend the day together.'

Amelia sighed and pressed her hand harder onto her head. This was exactly why relationships weren't a good idea. She should never have let her guard down and shared that second bottle of wine. 'Bastien, you're a very nice man and I had a great time last night, but I really can't see you today. Please, I really need you to go.'

'But—'

'No, Bastien.'

Sheepishly, he moved. She guessed the kitchen counter had been too cold to sit on for long because his pants were lying on the floor by her feet. He must have decided to forgo them only at the very last moment for full-on seduction. At least he was committed. Amelia picked them up using the tips of her fingers and handed them to him as Bastien's skin made a horrible squeaking sound as he pushed himself down from the counter. It looked like she'd be spending the afternoon disinfecting the kitchen before she cooked anything and seeing as his pants had been on the floor, she would have to wash that as well.

'You really want me to go?' Bastien tried one more time, attempting to impart some lust into his voice.

'Yes, please. I'm sorry, but I really have work to do.'

'But it is Saturday.'

The letter again caught her attention and curiosity built but as much as she wanted to know its contents, she couldn't open it with Bastien around. Frowning as she placed the letters on the counter, she turned away from him and went to grab a bottle of water from the fridge, hoping he'd get the hint that it was time to leave. Océanè's words that she was a cold woman echoed in her brain. She didn't mean to be cold with Bastien, but how else was she to get this naked Frenchman out of her apartment? Without turning, she was aware of him heading off into the bedroom and a few moments later, he placed a gentle kiss on her cheek and said goodbye.

The cold water slid down her throat and concern mixed with anticipation sent goose bumps over her skin. She didn't normally get letters from England and the company name sounded unnervingly formal. After spraying and wiping down the counter, she sat on a stool and opened the post, starting with the bright white envelope postmarked from England.

As soon as she pulled out the thick white paper, her eyes began to scan the words. An unexpected wave of emotion hit her, and her body shook in response. For a moment, her breathing became hard and erratic and she willed herself to calm down. Great-Aunt Vera was dead and had left her Meadow Farm: the draughty old farmhouse they'd co-existed in for ten unsentimental and lonely years, as well as the land around it. You couldn't even really call it living together because that implied a level of fondness that had never existed as far as her aunt was concerned.

Shaking her head at the memory, Amelia was glad she'd left for university and never returned. Vera hadn't wanted her and if it hadn't been for Adam, the only friend she had in the village, she'd have run away long before then. He'd talked her out of it so many times when Vera had told her off for doing nothing more than being a child. Vera had always made her feel so burdensome and ultimately forgettable.

A moment's respite from such intense emotions came as she thought of Adam again. The youthful face she remembered once more pushed its way into her brain and she swallowed hard. She'd missed him immensely over the years but had never been brave enough to contact him. He'd been her first love and she regretted that she'd left without saying a proper goodbye but there was no possible way she could have stayed in that place forever. He'd have got over it by now, Amelia reminded herself. He'd have forgotten her quickly. He'd probably been happy to be rid of her.

Swallowing down her feelings, Amelia reread the letter. As shock subsided to be replaced by grief and guilt, Amelia took another drink of water. She hadn't even known Vera was sick. Apart from exchanging Christmas and birthday cards, they didn't speak at all and her most recent Christmas card hadn't mentioned anything about declining health. Had it been sudden? The solicitor's letter didn't mention the cause of death.

Though she regretted how their relationship had ended up, unless someone knew Vera – knew how cold and hard she was, how unloving – people didn't understand. Some people were naturally private, and it was a behaviour Amelia herself had learned, but Vera took it to a whole new level, hating everyone. Amelia buried the turmoil threatening to rise and overtake her under the knowledge that she'd made something of herself. She took a breath in, counted to eight and let it out slowly, counting again as she did so.

Despite everything, Vera had left her Meadow Farmhouse and according to the letter, she'd made Amelia the sole heir. Amelia had always found the village hard to handle. The concern when she'd arrived and the constant reminders of why she'd ended up there had been overwhelming. Meadowbank was one of those places where everyone knew everyone else's business and, as she'd grown, she'd longed for somewhere impersonal where no one asked her questions or reminded her of the past.

Would Adam still be there? Would anyone even remember her?

After she'd left, Amelia had never planned on going back and yet now it seemed she had no choice. She had to return to Meadow Farmhouse.

Hello bookworms!

I hope you're all well!

Can you believe this is our last visit to Meadowbank?
What did you think of Elsie and Jacob's story? I really hope you enjoyed it.
If you did, can I ask a big favour? Please consider leaving a review because reviews really help us to find new readers. Just a couple of minutes to leave a rating or review can make a big difference.

Fancy a FREE short story too?
Just sign up to my monthly newsletter here: https://bit.ly/3gbqMS0 and you'll get one delivered straight to your inbox! I promise I won't bother you all the time, just once a month with a bookish update and occasionally when I have an offer or exclusive cover reveal to share.

I'm also a fan of social media (procrastinating? Me?!). And if you fancy a chat, you can catch me here:
www.keginger.com.
www.Facebook.com/KatieGAuthor
@KatieGAuthor.
https://www.instagram.com/katie_ginger_author/

Hopefully I'll see you again soon, and until then, happy reading, everyone!
Lots of love,
Katie
xxx